"Do you know why those men are after you?"

"I'm still not sure."

"We'll figure it out."

He clasped her to him, holding her in place, and she was content to lie on top of him, still marveling at the way they had traveled together to an undiscovered country.

"This is what we were meant for," he murmured, absolute conviction in his voice.

She understood what he was saying.

Always incomplete.

Until now.

"Why did it happen?" she asked.

"We have to find out," he said as he stroked her arm.

She gave a short laugh. "You're saying we can't just enjoy it."

"Is that what you want to do?"

She considered the question. "No. I want to understand. And of course, we still have to figure out why those men want to question me—then kill me."

'Do you know why those men are after you?'

'I'm still not sure.'

'Well, figure it out.'

He clasped her to him, holding her in place, and she was content to be on top of him, still warm from the way they had traveled together to another era or century.

'Maybe what we were meant for,' he murmured about her direction in the force.

She murmured what he was saying.

'I know, nonetheless—'

'And now—'

'My life is in danger?' she asked.

'We have to find out,' he said as he stroked her thigh.

She gave a short laugh. 'You're taking me, can't that stop it?'

'That's what you said now.'

She considered the question. 'No, I want to understand,' and she began to work how to figure out why those men would—suddenly are—then kill me.'

DIAGNOSIS: ATTRACTION

BY
REBECCA YORK

Published in Great Britain 2014
by Mills & Boon, an imprint of Harlequin (UK) Limited,
Eton House, 18-24 Paradise Road, Richmond, Surrey, TW9 1SR

© 2014 Ruth Glick

ISBN: 978 0 263 91356 9

46-0414

Harlequin (UK) Limited's policy is to use papers that are natural, renewable and recyclable products and made from wood grown in sustainable forests. The logging and manufacturing processes conform to the legal environmental regulations of the country of origin.

Printed and bound in Spain
by Blackprint CPI, Barcelona

Award-winning, *USA TODAY* bestselling novelist Ruth Glick, who writes as **Rebecca York**, is the author of more than one hundred books, including her popular 43 Light Street series for the Mills & Boon® Intrigue line. Ruth says she has the best job in the world. Not only does she get paid for telling stories, she's also an author of twelve cookbooks. Ruth and her husband, Norman, travel frequently, researching locales for her novels and searching out new dishes for her cookbooks.

Chapter One

Panic choked off Elizabeth Forester's breath as she turned the car onto Mulberry Street, the wheels screeching when she took the corner too fast. The maneuver didn't shake the car that was following her. She was pretty sure she had picked up the tail after she had left the motel where she'd been hiding out—using a car she thought nobody would recognize. She made a snorting sound. Apparently her precautions hadn't been enough.

For the past week, she'd been acting like she was in the middle of a TV cop show. But she'd decided the evasive action was necessary. Today it looked like she'd been absolutely right to try to cover her tracks.

It had gradually dawned on her that a dark-blue Camaro was appearing in her rearview mirror on a regular basis—following her during the day—and that the ever-present car must be connected to the case she was working on. Something too big for her to handle?

She hadn't started off understanding how big it really was. But a lot of little details had led her to the conclusion that she needed to protect herself by checking into the motel a few miles from her house and taking alternate routes to work.

She glanced again in the rearview mirror. The blue car was inching up, and she could see two tough-looking men in the front seat. She shuddered, imagining what they were going to do if they got their hands on her.

She'd almost decided to go to the police with what she

knew at this point, until she'd concluded that the plan was dangerous. It was terrible when you couldn't trust the authorities, but she had to assume that they were protecting the man who'd sent the thugs to intercept her.

As her work took her all over Baltimore, she had an excellent knowledge of the city. If she could get far enough ahead of the men tailing her, she could turn into the nest of alleys up ahead and disappear. And then what? For now the prime objective was to get away.

She made another quick turn into an alley, slowing her Honda in case a kid came darting out from one of the fenced-in backyards.

Glancing behind her, she breathed out a little sigh. She was in the clear. In the next moment, she realized her mistake as she saw the Camaro whip around the corner also. Damn.

Still on the lookout for pedestrians, she sped up again, turning onto the next street. To her horror, a delivery van had just pulled over to the curb. And a car coming in the other direction made it impossible to escape by crossing to that lane.

She swerved to avoid the van, thinking she could squeeze past on the sidewalk. But a woman and a little boy were coming straight toward her.

The fear on their faces as they saw the car bearing down on them made her gasp as she swerved again. If a lamppost hadn't suddenly materialized in front of her, she could have gotten away. But she plowed into it and came to a rocking stop.

The old Honda she was driving didn't have an air bag. The seat belt kept her from hitting the windshield, but she was stunned as she sat behind the wheel.

She knew she had to escape on foot, but she was moving slowly now. Before she could get out of the car, one of the men from the Camaro appeared at her window.

"Got ya, bitch."

Yanking open the car door, he dragged her out, hitting her

head on the car frame as he hurled her to the sidewalk. The blow stunned her, and then everything went black.

DR. MATTHEW DELANO's first stop on his morning rounds was the computer at the nurses' station, where he scanned for urgent cases and noted which patients had been discharged—or had passed away—since his last visit to the internal-medicine floor.

No deaths. He always counted that as a good sign. This morning most of the patients on the general-medicine floor were in for routine problems—except for one woman whom the cops had named Jane Doe because she didn't remember who she was.

As he read the notes from the E.R., he gathered that the whole situation with her was odd. For starters, she hadn't been carrying any identification. And she'd been driving an old car registered to a Susan Swinton.

But when a patrol officer had knocked on Swinton's door late in the afternoon yesterday, nobody had been home, and the neighbors had said the woman was on an extended trip out of the country. Which left the authorities with no clue as to the identity of the mystery woman in room twenty-two.

Matt noted the irony of the room number. As in *Catch-22*, the novel by Joseph Heller. The term had come to mean a paradoxical situation in which a person is trapped by conflicting circumstances beyond his control.

Dr. Delano skimmed the chart. The woman, who was apparently in her late twenties, had no physical injuries, except for a bump on the head. The MRI showed she'd had a mild concussion, but that was resolving itself. The main problem was her missing memory—leading to her unknown identity.

Her trouble intrigued him. But although he was curious to see what she looked like, he made his way methodically down the hall, checking on patients on a first-come-first-served basis. A woman with COPD. A man with a bladder infection he couldn't shake. Another man with advanced Parkinson's disease.

They were all routine cases for Dr. Delano since spending time in a dangerous African war zone a couple months ago and taking this interim job in Baltimore, where at least he could feel useful.

He hadn't really wanted to return to the States—he was more comfortable in a foreign country than at home. Here he had to do normal stuff when he wasn't working, and normal stuff was never his first choice.

He liked the rough-and-tumble life of doctoring in a war zone and the chance to help people in desperate need of medical attention. But now the rebels were systematically shooting any outsiders who were dumb enough to stay in their country and try to help the people. Since Matt wasn't suicidal, he was back in Baltimore, working at Memorial Hospital while he figured out the best way to serve humanity.

He made a soft snorting sound as he walked down the hall, thinking that was a lofty way to put it, especially for a man who felt disconnected from people. But he'd become an expert at faking it. In fact, he was often praised for his excellent bedside manner.

He stopped at the door to room twenty-two, feeling a sense of anticipation and at the same time reluctance. Shaking that off, he raised his hand and knocked.

"Come in," a feminine voice called.

When he stepped into the room, the woman in the bed zeroed in on him, her face anxious. He stopped short, studying her from where he stood eight feet away.

She wore no makeup and the standard hospital gown. Her short dark hair was tousled, and she had a nasty bruise on her forehead, but despite her disarray, he found her very appealing, from her large blue eyes to her well-shaped lips and the small, slightly upturned nose.

She looked to be in her late twenties as her chart had

estimated. About his own age, he judged. She sat forward, fixing her gaze on him with a kind of unnerving desperation.

"Hello," he said. "I'm Dr. Delano."

"I'd say pleased to meet you, if I knew how to introduce myself," she answered.

"I take it you're still having memory problems?"

"Unfortunately. I don't know who I am or what happened to me."

"It says in your chart that you were in a one-car accident."

"They told me that part. Apparently I hit a light pole. It's the rest of it that's a mystery." She gave her arm a little flap of exasperation. "I don't know why I didn't have a purse. The cops said there was a crowd around me, and a man had pulled me out of the car. The best I can figure is that he took the purse and disappeared." She dragged in a breath and let it out. "I don't even know if the man is somebody I know—or just a random thief taking advantage of a woman who had an accident. Either way, I don't like it. He left me in a heck of a fix."

"I understand," Matt answered, keying in on her fears. Some pretty scary things had happened to him in his overseas travels. In one African country, he'd been threatened with having his arms cut off—or worse—until he'd volunteered to remove some bullets from a bunch of rebels.

He'd been shot at too many times to count. And he'd been on a plane that had made an almost-crash landing on a dirt runway of a little airport out in the middle of nowhere. Taking all that into consideration, he still wouldn't like to be in this woman's shoes. She had no money. No memory. Nowhere to stay when she got out of the hospital.

She must have seen his reaction.

"Sorry to be such a bother."

"That's not what I was thinking."

"Then what?"

"I was feeling sorry for you, if you must know."

"Right. I'm trying to keep from having a panic attack."

He tipped his head to the side. "You know what that means—panic attack?"

"Yes. You get shaky. Your heart starts to pound." She laughed. "And you feel like you're going to die."

"You remember details like that but not who you are?"

"I guess that must be true."

"Have you ever had one?"

That stopped her. "Either I have or I've read about it."

"Is the picture of the syndrome vivid in your mind?"

"Yes."

"So it's probably more than just reading about the subject. Either you had one or you know someone who has."

Her gaze turned inward, and he knew she was trying to remember which it was.

"Your chart says you're doing okay physically. Let's have a look at you."

She sighed. "Okay."

"Does anything hurt?"

"The lump on my head is still painful—but tolerable."

"Good."

"And I'm kind of stiff—from the impact."

"Understandable. Let's check your pupillary reflexes."

She tipped her face up, and he looked into one eye and then the other with the flashlight, noting that the pupils were contracting normally.

"Okay, that's good. I'm going to check your heart and lungs." He pressed the stethoscope against her chest, listening to her steady heartbeat. "Good."

Up until then it had been a routine examination—or as routine as it could be when the patient had amnesia. When he put a hand on her arm, everything changed.

As he touched her, she gasped as though an electric current had shot through her, and perhaps he did too, because suddenly the room began to whirl around him, making it seem like the two of them were in the center of a private, invisible tornado. He knew the windows hadn't blown in or anything. The air in the room was perfectly still, as it had been moments before. The whirling was all in his mind. And hers because he was picking up on her confusion and sense of disorientation—as well as his own.

He should let go of her, but he felt as though he was riveted in place. With his hand on her arm, memories leaped toward him. Her memories—that she'd said were inaccessible to her. He was sure she hadn't been lying, but somehow recollections that had been unavailable to her were flooding into his consciousness.

The first thing he knew for sure was that her name wasn't Jane Doe. It was Elizabeth something. He clenched his teeth, struggling to catch the last name, but it seemed to be dangling just beyond his reach. Although he couldn't get it, he latched on to a whole series of scenes from her past.

Elizabeth as a little girl, at her first day of nursery school—shy, uncertain and then panicked, watching Mommy leave her alone in a roomful of children she didn't know. Elizabeth as a grade-schooler working math problems from a textbook. Elizabeth refusing to eat the beef tongue her mother had bought—to save grocery money.

Elizabeth alone in her room, reading a book about two lovers and wishing she could have the same feelings for someone. Elizabeth leaving the hockey field, distraught because she'd missed making a goal she thought should have been hers. And then in a college classroom—taking a social studies exam and sure she was going to get a perfect score.

The old memories faded and were replaced by something much more recent. From yesterday. She was worried about being followed. She was driving an old car she'd borrowed from a friend, glancing frequently in the rearview mirror— seeing a blue vehicle keeping pace with her.

She sped up, fleeing the pursuers, weaving down alleys

and onto the street again. She thought she was going to get away until a delivery van had blocked her escape. She plowed into a lamppost with a bone-jarring impact. While she was still stunned from the crash, a man rushed to her, yanking her from the car, hitting her head on the door frame as he pulled her onto the sidewalk, just as a crowd of onlookers gathered.

"Hey, what are you doing to her?" somebody had demanded.

That memory of the accident cut off abruptly with a flash of pain in her head and neck. She must have passed out, and one of the people who'd come running had called 9-1-1.

The recollections flowing from her mind to his were like pounding waves, but they weren't the only thing he experienced. As he made the physical connection with her, he felt an overwhelming sexual pull that urged him to do more than dip into her thoughts.

He was her doctor, which meant that ethically there could be nothing personal between the two of them; yet he couldn't stop himself from gathering her close. Somewhere in his own mind he couldn't squelch the notion that letting go of her would be like his own death.

And he knew from her thoughts that she felt the same powerful connection to him. It made her feel desperate. Aroused. More off-balance than either one of them had ever been in their lives.

He told himself he should pull away. But he was trapped where he was, because her arms came up to wrap around his waist. Well, not trapped. He wanted to be here, and she'd given him a reason not to break the connection.

She pressed herself against him, increasing the contact and the frustration and the sheer need. He breathed in her scent, picturing himself bending down so that he could lower his mouth to hers, imagining the taste of her and letting himself see what it would be like to kick off his shoes and climb into the hospital bed with her.

She made a small needy sound, and he knew that she was picturing the same thing as he was. Part of his mind was shocked and aghast at how far he was going with this fantasy. The other part ached to push her back onto the bed and roll on top of her so he could press his body to hers. Only first he needed to drag off his shirt and pants and get rid of her hospital gown.

That last frantic image was what finally made him come to his senses and pull away, breaking the physical contact and, at the same time, the mental connection.

He stood beside the bed, dragging in lungsful of air, feeling dizzy and disoriented and still achingly aroused.

And she was staring at him, looking like a woman who was ready for sex. When she reached out her hand toward him, he forced himself to step farther back.

He cursed under his breath, ordering himself not to think about making love with her, as he clawed his way toward rational behavior. For a few moments, he'd felt an overwhelming connection with Elizabeth—even though he was sure he'd never met her before. But he did know that she was a patient, and thinking about anything physical between them was completely out of bounds. It was morally wrong, and it could get him in big trouble, come to that.

Which left him trying to understand what had happened between the two of them in those seconds when they were touching. Both the flood of memories from her mind and the sudden intense sexual attraction that had threatened to wipe any reasonable thoughts from his mind.

He shook his head as he gazed down on her. She sat on the bed, looking stunned, her blue eyes wide, her breath coming in little gasps as she clenched and unclenched her fingers on the sheet.

"I'm sorry," he managed to say.

"Are you?"

"Of course. That was completely inappropriate."

"I think it took both of us by surprise," she said, making an excuse.

"You're a patient."

Ignoring the observation, she said, "What happened?"

"I don't know."

"Touching you made me recall things I couldn't remember for myself. And I got inside your mind, too. I didn't know a thing about you before we touched. Now I know you always went in for dangerous sports. Like mountain climbing. Spelunking. And ice camping."

"Yeah."

"Why?"

"They made me feel alive," he said, unaccountably admitting something to this woman that he had always kept to himself.

"And recently you were in Africa. In the middle of a nasty little war. They were shooting at you, and the guy next to you was killed. You stayed hidden, with him on top of you, soaking your clothes with his blood, until it got dark and you could sneak away."

He answered with a small wordless nod. It was something he'd tried to forget, and she'd pulled it from his memories.

"You went there to help people, and you saved a lot of lives. But you never knew quite how to connect with anyone." She gulped. "Just like me."

The admission jolted him. "What do you mean?"

She kept her gaze fixed on him. "You were in my head. You know I'm like you, with that feeling of not being able to…relate to people on the deep level you crave. Like everybody else has a secret handshake, only nobody ever taught it to you."

He'd never thought of it quite that way, but he nodded, because she had spoken the truth. All his adult life—all his life, really—he'd been searching for something he was sure he could not find. Something other people had, but he lacked.

Until now, with this woman. But that couldn't be possible—not after all the years of being alone.

"Why you?" he whispered.

"I don't know."

"Because you can't remember your past?"

"What would that have to do with it?"

He shrugged. "I don't know."

"But touching you brought back memories I couldn't reach a few minutes ago," she said again.

He nodded.

"Let's take it from the opposite angle. Why you?" she murmured.

"I have no idea."

Neither one of them seemed capable of looking away from the other. But he took another step from her, because he was so off-kilter that he wasn't sure what to do. Maybe something crazy like reach for her again, because touching her had been like every aching fantasy he'd ever experienced.

She moistened her lips. "What exactly happened?"

"I don't know. But I found out that your name is Elizabeth."

She gave a nervous laugh. "I have amnesia, but when you touched me, you brought some of my memories back."

"Yes."

"Did that ever happen to you before?" she asked.

"No. To you?"

"No." She laughed again. "At least I don't think so. The only personal things I remember are what you gave me."

There was no logic to what she'd just said. And she might have been lying. But he didn't think so.

He saw the challenge in her eyes and heard it in her voice. "We could try it again. Maybe you can bring back more of me."

"I can't."

"Even when I'm alone and desperate?" she asked in a low voice.

Her words and the pleading look in her eyes made his throat tighten. More than that, when he touched her, he sensed that she was a good person. She didn't deserve what had happened to her, although he knew objectively that being good or bad didn't have anything to do with what people endured.

Like the guy next to him getting shot. Jerry had been a good person, too. But anyone could lead an exemplary life and end up being killed by a stray bullet that came through the living-room wall.

Dr. Delano pushed the disturbing images out of his mind and managed to say, "It wasn't just memories. At least for me. There was another aspect to it."

He saw her flush. "Not just memories," she agreed, then looked down at her hands. "Sexual arousal," she whispered.

"But that was completely inappropriate. I'm your doctor. There can't be anything personal between us."

She took her lower lip between her teeth. "Even if your touching me makes me remember? I mean, isn't that…medically beneficial?"

"I'm afraid I can't stretch the definition that far."

She played with the edge of the sheet again, pleating it between her thumb and finger. "That last scene—where the guy dragged me out of the car. I don't think he was trying to help me. He looked relieved to have caught up with me—but not in a good way."

"I think that's right."

"I think he was following me, and I was trying to get away. That's why I crashed into a lamppost. I was desperate to escape from him and the other guy—the one who was driving."

"Do you remember it that way?"

Frustration flared in her eyes. "Not on my own. I think that's what you picked up from me, right?"

He nodded.

"So, odd as it sounds, it must be true, because you saw what I couldn't."

"Yeah."

"Probably it would be a good idea to avoid running into him again. If I knew who he was and why he wanted to hurt me."

"Yes."

Her eyes narrowed. "You sound like a computerized therapy program, agreeing with everything I'm saying but not adding anything—besides what you pulled out of my head."

He felt his chest constrict. "I'm sorry."

"How am I going to stay out of that guy's clutches when I don't even know who I am or who he is?"

He wanted to help her, but his hands were tied because of the professional demeanor that he was forced to maintain. In the end, all he could say was, "I'm sorry. I don't know."

He stopped talking when he realized Elizabeth was staring at someone standing in the doorway behind him.

Chapter Two

Matt turned to see that Polly Kramer, one of the nurses, had come into the room behind him.

"Dr. Delano."

"Yes," he answered, relieved that someone else had intervened to break up the intensity of the encounter between him and Elizabeth but also wondering how much of the conversation the nurse had heard.

She must have picked up on something, perhaps the tone of their voices, because she asked, "Is there some problem?"

He was wondering what to say when Elizabeth answered from the bed. "Basically, still my memory." She cleared her throat. "But while Dr. Delano was examining me, a name popped into my head. I think it's my real name."

The woman's face lit up. "Why, that's marvelous. What is it?"

"Elizabeth." She waited a beat. "I only got the first name."

"But that's a start."

"I was hoping that Dr. Delano could help me dredge up some other facts about myself."

Kramer looked at him. "Can you help her?"

"I'm afraid not. The name came to her. It wasn't anything I did," he protested, not sure that he was actually telling the truth but totally unwilling to explain. He'd done something, but he'd only touched her, and he wasn't going to do it again.

The nurse nodded, then changed the subject. "Is Elizabeth ready to be discharged?"

"If I knew where to send her," Matt muttered. "Nobody's come forward looking for her?"

"I'm afraid not."

His gaze flicked to the woman on the bed, and they were probably both thinking, given her memory of the aftermath of the crash, that might be an advantage.

"Do you have any suggestions?" Elizabeth asked.

"I might," Nurse Kramer murmured, shifting her weight from one foot to the other.

Matthew waited for her to say what was on her mind.

After a long pause, the nurse said, "I have a spare room that I haven't used since my daughter got married and moved away. I was thinking that…Elizabeth might want to stay with me until she remembers who she is."

IN HIS DULANEY VALLEY mansion, Derek Lang leaned back in the comfortable leather chair behind his desk. He was a tall man, and the expensive chair was specially designed with a comfortable headrest. His dark hair was tamed by a four-hundred-dollar haircut. His well-muscled frame was clothed in a thousand-dollar suit. And he was currently having a facial massage administered by Susanna, one of the gorgeous young women he kept around the house. He liked them to have useful skills, in addition to being good in bed. And Susanna was a perfect example.

When she finished and stepped away, he picked up a hand mirror and inspected his face. At forty-five he still looked fit—because he took good care of himself with daily sessions in the gym on the weight machines and ellipticals. And he'd also had some nips and tucks by one of the most expensive plastic surgeons in the city.

"Thank you, honey," he murmured.

"You're welcome, Mr. Lang."

He gave her a long look as he thought about asking her to take off her halter top and miniskirt. Per his instructions, she wouldn't be wearing anything under either one, and she could stand in front of him while he ran his hands over her. Then he could pursue a couple of interesting alternatives. Like having her kneel in front of him. Or having her sit with her legs open at the edge of the desk.

Enjoying her services was a tempting prospect, but he had some urgent business to take care of. He flicked his eyes to her face, knowing she was following his thoughts and waiting for him to make a decision. He liked the power he had over her and everyone else who worked for him— either voluntarily or involuntarily. Susanna was one of the latter, of course.

He repressed a sigh. Business before pleasure. "Tell Southwell to come in."

"Yes, sir."

As she turned away, he patted her butt, then pulled his chair up to the desk. Moments later one of his best men entered and stood respectfully in front of the desk.

Gary Southwell had been a high-school football star, and Derek had recruited Gary at the end of his senior year because of his bulk and menacing appearance. Since appearance wasn't enough, Derek had Gary specially trained both in martial arts and on the firing range.

The man was adept at hand-to-hand combat and was an excellent shot. And he was grateful for the good salary he earned, the comfortable accommodations and the women he could shag anytime he wanted. All of that made him loyal to a fault. And anxious to please.

"Do we have a report on the Elizabeth Forester situation? Is she still in the hospital?" Derek asked. His men had been keeping tabs on her for weeks and closing in for the kill when she had wrecked her car, drawing too much attention from witnesses. Derek didn't like it when his plans went sour.

"She's still in the hospital," Southwell answered. "Her

physical condition is okay, but they're keeping her because she's lost her memory."

"You think that's true?"

Southwell shrugged.

"If it is, I wonder if it's because she'd rather not remember," Derek mused.

"That could be part of it," Southwell agreed. "And it's good for us, isn't it?"

"At the moment, but how long is that going to last?" Derek Lang asked.

"No way of knowing."

"If the memory loss were permanent, that would solve our problem. But I don't want her suddenly remembering why she's been so busy over the past few weeks and then calling in the cops."

"She didn't do it before."

"Because she knew that was dangerous, but getting hit on the head could have affected her judgment which could make her reckless now."

Southwell nodded.

"You went to her house after the accident," Derek said. "Anything I should know about?"

"We tore the place apart and didn't find anything on paper, but there were computer files with information you wouldn't want anyone to read."

Derek sat forward. "And?"

"We took out her hard drive and smashed it."

"Good. But that's not enough. We have to shut the woman up for good."

Southwell waited for instructions.

"I understand why Patterson couldn't get to her earlier," Derek said, thinking aloud. "There were too many people around the crash scene, asking her questions, trying to figure out who she was. Wait until the shift change at the hospital. They don't have as many people on at night."

"Got it."

He considered his options. "I don't want you to take care of her there. I mean, she's in a hospital, and we could get into trouble with the cause of death. Bring her to me. I'd like to ask her some questions about why she's been nosing around in my business, starting with what put her on to me in the first place. Maybe I can think of something that will jog her memory."

"Yes, sir."

Southwell left, and Derek leaned back in his chair, thinking of the methods he'd use in his basement interrogation room. In the movies, tough guys held out against torture. In reality, everybody ended up spilling their guts. And he was pretty sure that with a woman like Elizabeth Forester, it wouldn't take long. After he got what he needed, he'd have some fun with her before he killed her.

ELIZABETH'S HEART LEAPED at the offer from Mrs. Kramer, but she still forced herself to ask, "Are you sure it wouldn't be an imposition?"

"Of course not, dear."

"Thank you."

The woman had just solved one of her biggest problems—by offering a place to stay. But there was still the basic problem, with totally unexpected complications.

She'd been lying in this hospital bed trying to dredge up a memory—any memory—until the man standing across the room had put a hand on her, and everything had changed. At least for the few moments when they'd been touching.

She had a little sliver of herself back, courtesy of Dr. Delano's touch. Now she recalled the first day of nursery school. Playing field hockey. What had seemed like a college classroom.

Of course there was the little problem of the sexual arousal that had flared between them. His and hers. But she understood that he was a man with high moral standards, and he wasn't going to let himself get dragged into an inappropriate relationship with a female patient, which was why he'd flat-out refused to touch her again.

He'd opened a door in her mind just a crack and slammed it shut again. She'd alternated between being angry that he wouldn't help her and wanting to plead with him to give her more of herself back. But she'd understood where he was coming from and had kept from embarrassing herself any further.

Then that nice nurse who had taken care of her earlier had showed up and thrown her a lifeline to deal with her present day-to-day situation.

"I'd be very grateful to stay with you, but I insist on paying you—as soon as I find out who I am. I mean, assuming I'm not indigent or something."

"You're too well cared for to be indigent," the doctor said. "It's obvious that you were living at least a middle-class lifestyle."

"Okay." She looked from him to the nurse, wanting to be absolutely sure the woman had thought through her offer. "You're certain it's all right?"

"I'd love the company."

The doctor left, and the arrangement was settled quickly. Probably the hospital was anxious to get rid of a patient who couldn't produce an insurance card, even if she was living a middle-class lifestyle.

"I'm going off shift in half an hour," Mrs. Kramer said. "Once you get dressed, I'll get a wheelchair and take you down. I can meet you in the waiting area near the elevator."

Climbing out of bed, Elizabeth stood for a moment holding on to the rail. She'd been lying down too long, and her legs felt rubbery. Or maybe that was the result of having a concussion.

When she felt steadier on her feet, she crossed to the small bathroom and turned on the light. She'd deliberately avoided looking at herself until she was ready. Now she raised her gaze to the mirror and stared at the woman she saw there. She wasn't sure what she had expected, but the face that stared back might as well have belonged to a stranger.

Disappointed and unsettled, she stood for a moment, composing herself. Trying not to look in the mirror again, she washed her face at the sink and brushed her teeth with the toothbrush the hospital had provided.

Doggedly she focused on the simple tasks in order to keep from thinking about anything more stressful—like how she was going to figure out who she was and why she had crashed her car. The easy answer was that she'd been speeding. As she pictured herself driving, she realized she knew the part of town where they'd told her the accident had occurred.

That stopped her. She'd come up with another memory—this time on her own. Well, not a memory of anything personal.

The observation about Baltimore—that was the city she was in—brought up another question: What else did she know? Maybe not about Elizabeth Doe specifically but about the world around her.

She stopped and asked herself some questions she imagined would be standard for someone in her situation. She couldn't dredge up the correct date. But she knew who was president. And she knew... She struggled for another concrete fact and came up with the conviction that she could make scrambled eggs that tasted a lot better than what the hospital had served her this morning.

"Your clothes are in the closet," Nurse Kramer said through the bathroom door. "Do you need help?"

"I think I can do it myself," she said, because she wasn't going to depend on other people if there was a chance for independence—even in small things.

By the time she stepped back into the room, Mrs. Kramer had gone back to her duties and Dr. Delano wasn't there, either. She felt a stab of disappointment but brushed it aside. Probably he was wishing that some other doctor had examined her. And staying as far away as possible from her was probably the way to go, from his point of view.

After crossing to the closet, she took out the clothes that someone had hung up for her. Dark slacks. A white shirt and a dark jacket. A very buttoned-up look, except that the outfit was a little scuffed around the edges from the accident.

She looked at the labels of the garments. They were from good department stores. Not top-of-the-line but good enough. Another piece of information that she found interesting.

She'd been wearing knee-high stockings and black pumps with a wedge heel. Not the shoes she'd wear if she had wanted to impress someone. These were no-nonsense footwear. Did that mean she walked a lot as part of her job? Or maybe she had bad feet.

There was also underwear on the hanger, and that was more interesting than the exterior clothing. She'd been wearing a very sexy white lace bra and matching bikini panties. Apparently she liked to indulge in very feminine underwear. She took everything back into the bathroom, then decided that she might as well take a shower before she left. It would feel good to get clean. Too bad she didn't have a change of underwear.

She thought about her name as she stood under the shower. *Elizabeth.* A very formal name. Did people call her Beth? Betty? Liz? Or any of the other variations of the name? She didn't know.

But she noted that she'd washed her hair before soaping her body, and it had been in the back of her mind that she'd better do that first—in case the hot water went off and she was caught with shampoo in her hair.

An interesting priority. Did it mean she lived in a house

or an apartment where there was a problem with the hot-water heater? Or had she traveled abroad like Dr. Delano?

She clenched her hand around a bar of soap, annoyed with herself for switching her thoughts back to him. He'd made it clear that there couldn't be anything personal between the two of them, and she understood that. Yet, at the same time, she couldn't stop thinking of him as her lifeline to her own past.

After turning off the water and stepping out of the shower, she reached for a towel and began to dry herself. There was no hair dryer, so she worked extra hard on her hair, rubbing it into fluffy ringlets.

Was that the way she usually wore it? She didn't think so, but it would do for now. Her coiffure was way down on her list of priorities. It didn't matter what she looked like if she didn't know who she was and how she'd gotten herself into deep *kimchi*. Because it was clear from the memory Dr. Delano had dredged up that she'd done something to bring trouble on herself. Was it something she deserved? Or something that wasn't her fault?

She made a small sound of frustration as she tried to work around the holes in her memory, then stopped and started again. It was more like her entire past was a great void—except for the memories Matt Delano had brought to the surface. With that nagging side effect he hated, she reminded herself.

Well, that probably wasn't true. She was pretty sure he didn't hate the sexual pull between them. He'd responded, after all, but he was determined not to cross a line with her.

She clenched her fists in frustration. If she couldn't fill in all the blank places in her mind, they were going to drive her crazy.

Chapter Three

At the nurses' station, Matt was thinking about the moral issue that was tearing at him. Because he was very conscious of the sexual awareness between himself and Elizabeth Doe, he should stay away from her. But at the same time, how could he refuse to help her?

Mrs. Kramer came down the hall, her strides purposeful, and he looked up questioningly when he found her standing in front of him.

"Yes?"

"Do you get the feeling that Elizabeth is in some kind of trouble?" she asked. "I mean not just the memory loss."

"Yes."

"Perhaps she was fleeing from someone. There was a report of a man dragging her out of her car at the accident scene. Maybe he took her purse."

Matt nodded.

"Would it be all right, do you think, if I didn't tell anyone that I was taking her home with me? Well, I mean, anyone besides you."

"If someone is looking for her, wouldn't that make it harder to locate her?" he said.

"But I'm thinking, it's likely to be the wrong kind of person, and it might be better for him not to find her."

"Or it could be her husband, frantic for information."

"You think she's married?" Kramer asked.

"No," he answered immediately, then tried to assess his

firm conviction. His certainty came from her mind, but he couldn't tell that to Kramer. Instead, he said, "No ring."

As the nurse nodded, he took his private speculation a step further. The best he could figure was that he hadn't gotten any hint of a husband from her memories. Or any indication of a current relationship. Just from that brief trip into her mind, he thought that she was like him—disconnected from any meaningful relationship. Only for a few moments, the two of them had connected in a way he'd thought impossible for himself.

He clenched his teeth.

"Is something wrong?" Kramer asked.

Quickly he rearranged his features. "No."

"You look tense."

He wished she hadn't noticed.

When he didn't speak, the nurse said, "I'll let you know how she's doing."

"Thanks."

He did care, more than he should, but he couldn't admit it or anything else that would give away the out-of-kilter personal involvement that had flared between them. He turned and left the ward before Elizabeth came out, and he did something he knew he shouldn't—like touch her again.

Thinking about it made his nerve endings tingle, but he ignored the sensation as he headed for the other end of the hall.

POLLY KRAMER WATCHED Dr. Delano stride off. She could tell he was trying to react on a strictly professional level, but he wasn't succeeding. Which was interesting. Since he'd come to Memorial Hospital, she'd thought of him as closed up. Maybe even a cold fish. But something about the woman with no memory had created a change in him. He seemed to really care about her, although he was trying not to show it.

Probably he thought any personal feelings about Elizabeth were inappropriate. But was there some way to change that? He'd been cautious of involvement with her because she was a patient. But she wouldn't be a patient after she left the hospital.

Polly smiled to herself. Here she went again, trying to match people up. Because she'd been so happy in her marriage. And she wanted the same thing for other young couples.

A voice broke into her thoughts. It was Cynthia Price, one of the other nurses on the floor.

"I couldn't help overhearing you and the doctor talking. Are you really taking that Jane Doe woman home with you?" Price asked. She was a slender brunette in her mid-thirties, and as far as Polly could tell, she had the right nursing skills, but she didn't have much empathy for the patients.

"Yes."

Polly's colleague fiddled with the ballpoint pen she was holding. "I don't like to interfere, but isn't that taking a chance?"

"What do you mean?"

"She could be…" The woman raised a shoulder. "She could be a thief or Lord knows what."

"I think I'm a good judge of character, and I don't believe she's a thief or a murderer. But Dr. Delano and I both have the idea she's in some kind of trouble."

"Yes, I heard you discussing it. What do you think it is?"

"When she gets her memory back, we'll know." Polly paused for a second. "I think it would be better if you don't tell anyone she left with me."

Cynthia considered the request. "What if her family comes looking for her or something? What if they're worried sick about her?"

Polly thought for a moment. "Don't tell anyone where she's gone, but get their name and number and call me."

"You sound like a character in a spy novel."

Polly laughed. "I'm being cautious is all."

The conversation was interrupted when she saw Elizabeth look out of her room toward the nurses' station.

"Here she comes now." As Elizabeth focused on them, Polly said, "Thanks for your help," wondering if she could rely on Cynthia's discretion.

ELIZABETH LOOKED INTO the hall. Once again she'd been hoping to see Dr. Delano. He wasn't there, and she was annoyed with herself for fixating on him and feeling disappointed. But that was logical, she told herself. He'd been the only link to her past. Deliberately she ordered herself not to dwell on the rest of it.

Polly Kramer smiled as Elizabeth came down the hall, then asked, "How are you feeling?"

"Physically, okay."

"Good. Let's leave."

"Mrs. Kramer..."

"Please call me Polly."

"Polly, I appreciate what you're doing for me."

"I wouldn't do it if I didn't feel good about it myself."

Polly helped her into a wheelchair and then into the elevator where, she gave Elizabeth a studied glance. "You look very professional in that outfit."

"I was thinking the same thing. I'm very buttoned up."

"You obviously have a job that requires a polished appearance."

"The shoes are a little dowdy."

"They're practical."

"What do you think I do for a living?"

"You could be a lawyer."

Elizabeth contemplated the answer. "Perhaps."

"What do *you* think?"

"A teacher would be closer, but that doesn't quite work for me, either."

As they exited the elevator and Polly wheeled the chair out the staff-only door, she said, "Your outfit gives you the look of authority, but it isn't exactly comfortable for relaxing. I was thinking we could stop at a discount department store, and you could pick up a few things."

Elizabeth felt her chest tighten. A line from a play leaped into her head. Something about relying on the kindnesses of strangers. "I don't have any cash, and I'm already imposing on you by staying at your house."

"Nonsense. I'll be right back." The nurse got her vehicle and drove to the curb, where Elizabeth got in.

"I hate the idea of your spending any money on me," she said when she was settled.

Polly made a tsking sound. "I'd feel like I was abandoning you if I just left you twisting in the wind."

"Do you take in stray dogs and cats, too?"

Her companion laughed. "No. I'm more people oriented."

They stopped at the automatic gate where Polly inserted her card, then drove out of the hospital parking lot.

"Does any of this look familiar?" she asked.

"I'm not seeing anything that jumps out at me," Elizabeth answered.

"Well, let's try something more specific." A few minutes later, she pulled into a suburban shopping center and led Elizabeth inside the discount store, where they picked up a cart. "I thought we'd try the drugstore section. Why don't you walk around and see if you can spot products that seem familiar?"

Elizabeth gave her a grateful look. "That's a fantastic idea. Thanks." She grabbed her own cart and began wheeling it up and down aisles until she spotted a brand of makeup that she thought she might have used. Also shampoo and deodorant.

"We need to keep track of what I spend, so I can pay you back," she said again.

"If that makes you feel more comfortable."

"Of course it does."

Elizabeth chose a lipstick and some moisturizer, as well. "Did it look like I had on much makeup when I came in?" she asked.

"Maybe a little eye shadow."

She selected a packet that had a couple shades of gray. "Fifty shades," she muttered.

"What?"

"Isn't there a famous book called *Fifty Shades of Grey?*"

Mrs. Kramer laughed. "More like infamous than famous."

"Why?"

The older woman flushed. "I believe it's some kind of sex thing."

"Oh. I guess I didn't read it."

"Neither did I. I'm just repeating what I heard." Polly changed the subject quickly. "Let's go look at the casual clothing."

Elizabeth might have protested about spending more money on herself, but she wasn't going to be borrowing any of the other woman's shorter and wider clothing.

Maybe Polly was following her thoughts because she said, "I have some big old T-shirts you could use to sleep in."

"Good. One less thing I need to worry about," she answered, thinking that this was certainly a surreal experience—although it didn't quite come up to the standard of touching Matthew Delano and getting into his mind. Or the other part—the sexual part.

Trying to put *that* out of her thoughts, she hurried to the ladies' department, where she found shelves full of inexpensive T-shirts. She selected three—deep blue, turquoise and purple.

"Perfect for your hair and skin tone," Mrs. Kramer approved.

"I guess I know my colors."

She shuffled through the piles and pulled out size eights,

which turned out to fit her well, along with a pair of jeans and a three-pack of panties, figuring she could wash them every other day. And the bra she had on would be fine.

"Get some socks and tennis shoes," her guardian angel advised.

Again she felt her stomach clench at the idea of spending someone else's money so freely, but she couldn't think of an alternative.

On the groceries side of the store, Polly asked, "What do you want to eat?"

Another memory test. "Will you let me do the cooking?"

"If you're not too tired."

She selected a package of ground beef, canned kidney beans and salsa, pleased that she could come up with a set of ingredients that made sense. "Do you have onions, chili powder and cumin?"

"I believe I do."

"Then I'll make us chili."

"Do you need a recipe?"

She thought about what would be involved in making the dish. "No, I can do it."

"You like to cook?"

"I think so."

"One more thing you know," Mrs. Kramer said.

Elizabeth nodded. It was like playing a game where she didn't quite know the rules. But some of them came back to her—basically what she considered ordinary things. Or general things. The part that dealt specifically with her own life remained a mystery.

As they drove to Polly Kramer's house, Elizabeth kept looking behind her.

"Is something wrong, dear?" the older woman asked.

"I can't shake the idea that somebody is following me."

"Do you see anyone you recognize?"

She sighed. "No. I'm just nervous about it." She didn't

want to say why. That, when she'd touched Matthew Delano, she had had a memory of someone following her and that trying to get away had caused her automobile accident.

They pulled into Polly Kramer's driveway.

She lived in a redbrick rancher in a close-in suburb, probably built in the 1950s, Elizabeth thought, wondering how she'd placed it in time. There was a low chain-link fence around a half-acre yard and a carport instead of a garage.

"My husband and I bought this house forty years ago," Polly said as they pulled into the driveway.

"Is he home?" Elizabeth asked, looking around for another car.

"He died a few years ago."

"I'm sorry."

"It's one of the reasons I'd love to have some company. The house isn't all that big, but sometimes I feel like I'm rattling around inside."

"I understand," Elizabeth said automatically. Because of personal knowledge of loss? she wondered. Or because she was good at getting in touch with people's emotions? Which would be strange if she basically felt disconnected from everybody.

"Dan was an engineer. He made a good living and had a nice pension, and I still collect most of it. Plus we paid off the mortgage years ago. I don't really have to work at the hospital, but I like the contact with people. So don't worry about my paying for a few things you need. We'll get it sorted out later."

"Thank you," Elizabeth answered, overwhelmed by the kindness of this woman she barely knew. Was Elizabeth the type of person who would do the same thing for a stranger? And was that how she'd gotten in trouble? The question stopped her, and she thought she caught the edge of a memory, but she wasn't able to pull it into her mind.

"You come in and get settled," Polly was saying. "You

probably want to rest awhile, and there's no need to start dinner for a couple hours."

Elizabeth nodded. In fact, the brief shopping trip had taken a lot out of her.

Polly showed her through a living room, furnished in a comfortable contemporary style, to a pleasant bedroom in the back of the house. "I keep the sheets fresh," she said. "Go on and lie down for a bit."

"You're sure you don't need help putting the groceries away?"

"We only got a few things. You just relax."

"Thank you." Elizabeth took off her slacks, jacket and shoes, and laid down, thinking she'd get up in a few minutes.

MATTHEW DELANO COULDN'T shake the feeling of guilt that hung over him as he finished making his rounds, then went down to his office on the first floor, where he entered some information into the computerized patients' charts. On Tuesdays and Thursdays he saw patients in the hospital clinic, but he had the afternoon free today. And he couldn't stop thinking about Elizabeth Doe.

She was in trouble, and he'd walked away from her because he was uncomfortable with the sexual heat that had flared between them when he had touched her. But he felt like a bastard for abandoning her when she wasn't in any kind of shape to fend for herself.

He told himself ethics cut both ways. What if something terrible happened to her that he could have prevented by helping her bring back the memories she needed?

He was silently debating what to do when a knock on his office door interrupted him.

"Come in," he called.

A man wearing dark slacks and a navy blazer over a white dress shirt stepped into Matt's office. The stranger looked to be in his late twenties, and he had broad shoulders, a muscular build and large dangerous-looking hands. His face wasn't particularly remarkable, although perhaps he had broken his nose sometime in the past.

The overall impression he gave was negative, although Matt couldn't exactly explain why. Just as he'd gotten the feeling that Elizabeth Doe was a good person, he sensed that this guy was "bad." There was something behind his eyes that told Matt his mood could turn deadly in an instant.

"Dr. Delano?"

"Yes," he said, still sizing up the man.

"I'm Bob Wilson. I understand you saw a patient with amnesia?"

"I'm not at liberty to discuss my patients."

"Yes, of course. I understand completely. But I think she might be my sister."

"Why?"

"She told me that she was coming over yesterday, but she never showed up."

"And you haven't heard from her?"

"No."

"The woman I treated was listed as Jane Doe. What's your sister's name?"

"Elizabeth Simmons."

He hoped he didn't show any reaction. The Elizabeth part was right, but was that really her last name? And why did he doubt this guy? "Do you have her picture?"

"Of course." The man opened his wallet and took out a photograph that looked like it might have been taken for a college yearbook.

"Yes, that's her," he reluctantly said. There was no way out of the admission because, if he lied about it, it was easily exposed since his having treated her was a matter of record.

Wilson's face lit up, but not in a way Matt liked.

"Thank God. Do you know where she's gone?"

This lie was easy. "Sorry."

"You're sure you have no idea?"

"Sorry," he said again. "I can't help you. I'd left the floor before she was discharged."

The man's expression turned hard. "If you do hear about her, I'd like you to call me." He took out a business card that read Bob Wilson and handed it over. There was a phone number on the card but nothing else besides the name.

"What do you do, Mr. Wilson?"

"I'm in sales."

"Why don't you have that on your card?"

"I'm between jobs."

Matt wanted to ask, "Then why have a card?" but he kept the question to himself.

Wilson gave Matt a penetrating look, and Matt had the feeling that he wanted to say, "You're in big trouble if you don't call."

But he said nothing more.

THE RINGING OF THE phone woke Elizabeth, and when she looked outside, it was getting dark.

She dressed in her new clothes, then hurried into the living room, hoping it might be Matthew Delano on the phone. But it sounded like Polly was talking to someone else. She had a pad of paper and a pencil in her hand and was writing something down.

When she hung up, she looked at Elizabeth. "A man came to the nursing station asking about you."

"Who?"

"He said his name was Bob Wilson and that he was your brother."

"Bob Wilson," she repeated, saying the name a couple of times aloud.

"Does that mean anything to you?"

"No, but that's not surprising. I mean, nothing has come back to me except—" She stopped abruptly.

"Except what?"

"Except the part about my name," she said, unwilling to relate that, when Matthew Delano had touched her, a whole slew of memories had come flashing back to her. But telling Polly about that would sound strange. Really, Elizabeth wouldn't have believed it herself if it hadn't happened to her.

And she didn't want to make her benefactor think that Elizabeth Doe had lost her marbles as well as her memory. "This Bob Wilson person spoke to someone at the hospital?" she asked.

"Yes."

"Who?"

"Cynthia Price. She's one of the other nurses on the floor. She heard me and Dr. Delano talking about my taking you home."

Elizabeth felt her stomach knot. "But she didn't tell him where I'd gone?"

"No."

"Why not?"

"I asked her not to."

"Why?"

"Because Dr. Delano and I both agreed that you're in some kind of trouble, and it's best to find out what it is before revealing your location."

"Thank you," she breathed, a feeling of relief settling over her.

In the next second, it popped into her head that the normal thing to do in this situation would be to call the police, but she dismissed that idea as soon as it surfaced. It simply didn't feel right. Which was a hunch she didn't much like.

She folded her arms across her chest and rubbed her upper arms.

"You look worried," Polly said.

"I can't help wondering if Cynthia told him where I was."

"I understand, but she's very reliable. Why don't you start dinner? I've got something I need to take care of."

"If you'll show me around your kitchen first."

Polly led her to the back of the house, where she gave her a quick tour and got out some of the supplies that Elizabeth was going to need, including a big pot.

"You know how to use an electric stove?"

"You have to wait a moment for the heat to go up or down."

"That's right. Will you be okay for a while?" Polly asked.

"I think so."

Mrs. Kramer left, and Elizabeth put the pot on the stove, then used the knife and cutting board to chop the onions.

She put them into the pot with the ground beef and began to sauté them, soothed by the simple act of meal preparation. It was familiar, routine work, but it was also reassuring doing something useful and comforting that she had no problem remembering how to do.

When the meat began to stick to the bottom of the pot, she turned down the heat and added a little water, stirring as she watched it change from red to brown.

Should she add the spices while the meat and onions were browning or wait until she got the salsa into the pot?

She let the task of cooking dinner completely absorb her, breathing in the smell of the chili when she had all the ingredients in the pot, including a can of tomato sauce she found in the pantry because she needed to supplement the salsa. She was just tasting the seasonings when the doorbell rang.

Elizabeth went rigid, then glanced toward the back door. That guy who'd come to the hospital had found out where she was, and she had to get away before he came in here.

Chapter Four

When Polly opened the front door, Matt stepped into the living room. "Thanks for calling me."

"I didn't mean to drag you over, but thanks for coming," the nurse said.

"I was telling myself it was unethical to keep seeing Elizabeth. Now I think it's unethical not to, if I think she's in trouble."

Mrs. Kramer nodded. "That makes sense."

"Where is she?"

"In the kitchen. Cooking dinner. I thought it would give her something to do."

Matt took an appreciative sniff. "Smells good. Did you have to help her, or did she remember how to fix a meal?"

"I just showed her around the kitchen, and she got busy all by herself."

"Good."

They walked to the back of the house and stopped short when they saw the kitchen was empty, a simmering pot was on the stove, and the back door was open.

"Where is she?" Matt asked, feeling his stomach knot.

"She was right here," Polly murmured.

Matt looked toward the open back door and cursed under his breath. "Did you say something that would frighten her?"

"I told her a man who called himself Bob Wilson had been asking for her at the nurses' station. That was before

I called you, and you said the same guy had been to your office."

Matt clenched his fists as he walked to the back door and looked out at the darkened yard. "She must have heard the doorbell, assumed the worst and ran. You look through the house in case she changed her mind and ducked back inside. I'll look outside."

"I'm sorry. I should have warned her that you were coming over," Polly said.

"We'll find her," he said, to reassure himself and Mrs. Kramer. As he stepped onto the cracked patio, a security light came on.

"Elizabeth. Elizabeth, it's me. Matt Delano," he called.

When she didn't answer, he looked around. Polly's yard butted against the property in back of her and to the sides. Elizabeth would have to climb over several fences to get far. His gaze landed on the metal storage shed just inside the range of the security light.

Quickly he hurried to the door and thrust it open, although he didn't charge inside, because his experiences in Africa had taught him not to rush into an enclosed space if he didn't know who might be in there. Lucky for him. He jumped back as a baseball bat came swooshing down. It missed his head by less than an inch.

The woman holding the weapon stared at him. "Oh, Lord, Matthew. I'm so sorry."

"It's okay. Polly told you someone called the nurses' station, right?"

"Yes."

"I think the same guy came to my office after he tried to get information from the staff. He said you were Elizabeth Simmons."

"That doesn't sound right. I mean the last name."

"Why not?"

She shrugged, looking so lost and helpless that his heart

turned over. But she wasn't exactly helpless. Instinct had told her to run when she'd heard the doorbell ring. And she'd been prepared to defend herself.

He had vowed not to touch her again, yet the desperate look on her face drew him forward. Unable to stop himself, he reached for her, pulling her into his arms, holding her close as he stepped into the shed.

"She's not inside. Did you find her?" Polly's voice called from behind him.

"Yes. She's fine. She's in here. We'll be right there," he managed to say, amazed that he sounded so rational when his brain and his senses were already on overload.

He said they were coming back, but he didn't move, only absorbed the reality of Elizabeth's body molded against his.

He had been trying to stay away from her. Now he knew that was an impossible goal. Not when they already meant more to each other than anyone had ever meant to either one of them. It was a crazy evaluation. How could two people who had just met mean *everything* to each other? But he knew it was true as he wrapped her more tightly in his arms.

In the hospital he'd barely touched her—just his hand on her arm at first—and the memories had come. Then holding her closer had been enough to trigger additional memories and so much more. Now they were alone in a dark, private space where it was impossible to pull away from each other. At least that was the way it felt.

Her own arms came up and locked around his waist, holding him close, and he was lost to everything except the woman in his arms. Her sweet scent, the feel of her silky skin, the crush of her body against his.

The same thing happened as before. Memories flooded through him. Her memories. And he knew she was picking up things from him—things that he had tried hard to forget. He was traveling through the backcountry, and he had come to a village that looked deserted. But the smell rising from the huts told him a different story.

He forced himself to look in one, seeing the mangled bodies of a mother, a father and three children piled on the floor. He backed out, retching, unable to understand why anyone had felt compelled to slaughter innocent civilians who were just trying to live their lives as best they could. Had the rebels done it or the government? He didn't even know.

He thrust away the horrible images and slammed into one of Elizabeth's memories. An early recollection that had always torn at her. She was in an elementary-school classroom. He saw bright pictures on the wall, pictures painted by the students. And words that might be the spelling lesson for the week.

She was sitting in a chair, watching as other children leaped up and ran to their parents. It must be some sort of special school day, and everyone was hugging and interacting. But Elizabeth sat in her seat, and her mother was standing near the door. Finally Elizabeth got up and ran to the woman, the way the other children had done. But it wasn't the same. Elizabeth knew it wasn't the same, and so did her mother. They were separated in ways that Elizabeth didn't understand. She wanted desperately to bridge that gap, but she didn't know how.

The scene was an echo of his own memories. His parents had been well-off. They'd wanted the best for their son— and they'd given Matt everything they could. Even love. And Matt had tried to respond, but he simply couldn't give them what they craved from him. What he craved, if he were honest about it.

And now he suddenly had what he had always been searching for, from a woman who was a stranger.

In her memory, he saw another scene. She was an adult now, bending over a bed, comforting a young and beautiful Asian woman who turned her head away and wouldn't look her in the eye.

All of the memories—his and hers—made him sad. It was much more gratifying to focus on the here and now—on the woman he held in his arms.

His head had started to pound, but he ignored the pain as he moved farther back into the shed, taking her with him. The door was at an angle that made it close behind them, shutting them inside. In the dark, they clung to each other for support and a whole lot of other reasons.

He hadn't admitted it, but he had needed so much more from her since the first moment he had touched her. Now, here, he couldn't resist the pull. Unable to stop himself, he lowered his mouth to hers for a kiss that was almost frantic. His lips moved over hers, and he smiled when he realized she'd been tasting the dish she was cooking on the stove.

But he stopped thinking about the chili as he stroked his hands up and down her back. Seeking more, he lifted the hem of the T-shirt she was wearing and slipped his hands underneath, flattening them against her warm skin, loving the feel of her and the contact that was so much more than he could put into words.

He knew he was arousing her, just as she knew she was arousing him. Holding her, kissing her, touching her was so very sexual, even with the underlying layers of memories from her past and his.

He'd made love with women before, looking for something that he was sure he wasn't going to find. Sex had always been physically satisfying, but there had invariably been something missing, the same disappointment that had dogged his life.

Again he knew it was like that for her. Searching and never finding. Until now.

I didn't go out and sleep with a bunch of guys.

I know. I was just thinking how it was the same for you. Disappointing.

The exchange stunned him. Neither of them had spoken aloud, yet he'd clearly heard her respond to his thought. And he had responded to hers.

That was enough of a shock to make him drop his hands and step back. What was he doing? What were they doing?

And he was glad he had broken the contact when the door of the shed opened. Whirling, he found himself staring at Polly Kramer.

"Oh, I'm sorry."

"No. We were just coming back to the house," Matt managed to say, hearing the thick quality of his own voice and not quite able to meet the older woman's eyes.

"Are you all right?" Polly asked Elizabeth.

Elizabeth ran a hand through her hair. "Yes."

Polly turned back to the house, and Matt waited a beat before asking Elizabeth, "Does your head hurt?"

"Yes. What do you think that means, Doctor?"

He laughed. "I can speculate, but I don't know."

By mutual agreement, he turned and walked out of the shed, and she followed. He didn't have to see her to know she was walking behind him.

He wanted to talk about what had happened between them. The sexual pull. The memories. And something even more startling. Actual words exchanged in their heads.

"You heard what I said?" he asked.

"Yes."

There was no need to explain he was talking about the silent exchange.

"I turned the chili down," Mrs. Kramer said when they stepped into the kitchen.

"Thank you," Elizabeth answered. She went straight to the pot, stirred it and tasted.

"How is it?" Matt asked, his voice still sounding not quite normal.

"Good."

"We should eat," Mrs. Kramer said. "You two sit down, and I'll serve."

"I can get us all a glass of water," Matt said, thinking it was a lame comment. But everything felt stilted now except the intimacy of being with Elizabeth.

"We can serve ourselves from the stove," Mrs. Kramer said.

They all did, then sat at the table, which would be a perfectly normal thing to do, except that nothing would ever be normal again.

That was a pretty exaggerated way to put it, but Matt knew it was true.

"Where are you from?" Elizabeth asked him, startling him by breaking into his overblown thoughts.

He struggled to deal with the question. "New Orleans."

"What did your parents do?"

"My dad was an oil company executive. My mom sort of did the country-club thing. They live in Santa Barbara, California, now."

"Were you an only child?"

"Yes," he answered, thinking that his mother had told him she'd had a lot of trouble getting pregnant. She'd been torn between wanting another child and not wanting to go through the rigors of a fertility clinic again. Although that had been her decision, she'd made it clear that he hadn't been the loving son she'd wanted. But he didn't tell the women he dated any of that.

"Did you grow up down there?"

"Yes."

Elizabeth was staring off into space.

"What?" he asked.

"New Orleans."

"What about it?"

"I remember stuff about the city. I mean I can picture… Jackson Square," she said.

"You've probably seen pictures."

"I think I've been there. And the French Market."

"Okay."

He waited for her to give him more information, but she only shook her head. "Maybe I'm wrong."

"We'll assume you're right."

"If it's true, it gives us something in common."

He nodded, wondering if it was important, and why it might be.

"Do you know how to cook *pain perdu?*" he asked.

"French toast?"

"Yeah."

"That's easy."

"What about gumbo?"

"I have a general idea of what's in it, but I'd have to look up a recipe if I wanted to make some."

"Most people would, I think." He looked at Elizabeth. "Where are you from?"

The answer to the question lurked below the surface of her mind. "Nice try," she murmured.

"I thought I'd give it a shot."

They were all silent for several moments while they ate.

"Well, this chili is delicious," Mrs. Kramer said, as she spooned up more of the beans and beef mixture.

"Thank you," Elizabeth answered.

Again they resumed eating, and Mrs. Kramer broke the silence once more as they finished the meal. "How did you get so far north?" she asked Matt.

"I went to medical school at Hopkins. After…" He stopped and glanced at Elizabeth. "After Africa, I decided Baltimore was as good a place as any to practice medicine."

"You intend to settle down here?" Mrs. Kramer asked.

He involuntarily glanced at Elizabeth again, thinking that everything they said had a double meaning or a subcontext that only the two of them could really follow.

"I...don't know." He cleared his throat, changing the subject abruptly as he looked at Elizabeth. "Do you want to try hypnosis?"

"What?"

"With many people, it can help recover memories."

"You mean now?"

"After we finish eating."

"You know how to do it?"

"I had a class," he said. "We could try it."

Elizabeth gave that some consideration. "Okay. What do you want me to do?"

"Just sit in a chair and relax."

"I can clean up," Polly said.

"You shouldn't have to," Elizabeth protested. "You already have a houseguest."

"You cooked us a delicious meal. I'll do the cleaning. That's only fair."

Matt and Elizabeth got up, carefully avoiding touching each other. They went into the living room where she glanced around, then settled into an overstuffed chair, looking apprehensive.

"What should I do?"

"Like I said, get comfortable."

"That's difficult."

For a whole lot of reasons, some of them having to do with her situation and some with him, he knew.

He sat down on the sofa, trying to relax and not having perfect success.

"Lean back. Look up at the line where the wall meets the ceiling."

"Why?"

"It puts your eyes at the right level."

She did as he said, and he kept speaking to her in a soothing voice. "Relax now. Relax now. Relax now."

He saw some of the tension drain out of her features.

"How do you feel?"

"Good."

"There's nothing to worry about. We're just going to see
if we can bring back more of your past."

"Yes," she murmured.

"And when I tell you to wake up, you will. Do you understand?"

"Yes."

"We can start with a little mental vacation. Let's go somewhere where you'd like to be."

She thought about that. "I'm not sure."

"Most people like the beach. Does that work for you?"

She waited a beat before answering, "Yes."

"We're at the beach. You're on a chaise, lying in the sun.
It feels good on your face and body. The waves are rolling
up across the sand."

"Um."

"Let's go a little deeper into relaxation. You go back to
the resort where you're staying. You go inside, and there's a
flight of steps. You go down, one step at a time."

"Okay."

"Every step takes you deeper into relaxation." He could
see from her face that it was working.

"What's at the bottom of the stairs?" he asked.

Her body jerked.

"What?"

"Women. They're frightened."

"Why?"

"They're a long way from home." Her body jerked again.
"I don't want to be there."

"Okay."

Her eyes blinked open, focusing on him.

She looked so lost and alone that every instinct urged him to cross the room and take her in his arms again, but he knew that wasn't such a great idea, given what happened every time they touched.

"Yes," she murmured.

"You know what I'm thinking?"

"It's all over your face."

"Sorry I'm so transparent."

"Not to most people, I think."

"I want to ask about that memory."

She shuddered. "It's nothing good."

"Is it something recent?"

Her vision turned inward. "I think so."

"But you aren't sure?"

"I'm betting it has to do with that man who was following me. Maybe I saw something I wasn't supposed to. And the mob is after me."

"The mob?"

"You have a better explanation?"

"I wish I knew, but the part about your stumbling into something sounds right." He thought for a moment. "What kind of women?"

"Young and pretty."

"What race?"

"Why are you asking?"

"You had a memory of an Asian woman before."

"These were Caucasian."

"Okay. Do you think it has anything to do with your job?"

"Good question." She shook her head. "Maybe it would help to try word association."

"I think we shouldn't try to push this any further tonight. You've had a tiring day—coming off a mild concussion."

"Yes, probably pushing to come up with any more answers right now is a waste of time."

"I don't want to leave you and Mrs. Kramer alone, with that Wilson guy out there."

"I think we'll be all right."

"But you took off out the back when the doorbell rang."

She shook her head. "Yeah. I'm jumpy, but that doesn't mean it's logical."

He wrote down his cell phone number and set it on the coffee table. "Call me if anything worries you. Or if you have any memories."

"I think the latter's more likely when you're around."

He nodded, looking at her hand. It was so tempting to reach out and touch her. They'd get memories, all right. And a lot more.

She looked up at him and away, and it was obvious again that she knew what he was thinking.

"I'll tell Mrs. Kramer I'm leaving."

Elizabeth was still in the living room when he returned, and he had to force himself not to stop and touch her. And force himself to leave, for that matter. He'd forged a connection with this woman who didn't even know her name, and he wanted to strengthen that connection. But nothing had changed as far as his ethics were concerned. He still had no business coming on to her.

Chapter Five

Matthew had been right. Elizabeth was exhausted. She dropped off again almost as soon as she crawled into bed. For a few hours, she was able to sleep. But sometime in the small hours of the morning, a dream grabbed her.

She was on her way to work. And a car was behind her, inching up. There were men in the car, and she knew they wanted to hurt her. Because…

Her hands clenched on the steering wheel as she struggled to grab on to the answer. The only thing she could remember was "the women."

She'd been trying to help the women. She had to remember that. It was an important clue. But there was no time for clues right now. She had to get away because the men were going to kill her if they caught up. She wasn't sure why she thought so. But she knew it was true. Well, they were going to question her first, because they wanted to know how she had found out about the women.

She pressed on the accelerator, desperate to escape, weaving down an alley before shooting out onto the street. A truck was in the way, and she slammed into a lamppost.

This time, she woke with a muffled scream, wondering where she was.

Then it came back to her. At least the past day. She glanced at the clock. It was four in the morning, and she knew where she was—at Polly Kramer's house, the nice woman on the hospital nursing staff who had brought Elizabeth to her home, a woman who couldn't even remember her name.

At least she knew her first name. *Elizabeth.* She'd gotten that when she had touched Matt Delano the first time. Something happened whenever they touched. A flood of memories—his and hers. Was she fixated on him because she couldn't remember anything else about herself?

It was an interesting theory, but she knew it wasn't true. Whatever had transpired between them was real—and unique. The exchange of information and the startling sexual awareness that pulled them together every time they touched. And then the speaking to each other, mind to mind. She shouldn't forget about that.

She squeezed her hands into fists. He could help her, but that sexual connection was keeping him away because of his strict code of morality.

Movement at the door made her tense and glance up. Polly Kramer was standing there, staring at her.

Elizabeth relaxed when she saw who it was.

"Are you all right, dear?"

"Yes. I had a nightmare. I'm sorry I woke you."

"I'm a very light sleeper. Are you okay?"

"Yes," she lied.

"Was the nightmare a memory?"

"Maybe." She related the dream.

Polly lingered for a few more moments. "And that's all you remember?"

"Yes," she answered, again making the decision not to tell her about what else Matt had pulled from her mind.

When Polly had gone back to bed, Elizabeth lay in the dark, thinking about the broken recollections—trying to force herself past the blank wall before the car chase.

What had she been doing when she got herself into trouble?

Matthew had said all hypnosis was self-hypnosis. Did that mean she could try to do what he'd guided her through before?

She considered the idea, then rejected it. What if she couldn't wake up and nobody was here to pull her back?

She made a frustrated sound. Every which way she turned led to some new dead end. No, not really new. Just another manifestation of the same old sense of defeat.

She tried to go back to sleep, but that was beyond her. Finally she heaved herself up and went down the hall. Hoping she wasn't going to wake up Polly, she prowled around the kitchen, checking ingredients in the refrigerator and the pantry. Polly had the makings of a vegetarian minestrone soup. Well, vegetarian except for the chicken broth.

Yes, she could make that and put it in the refrigerator for later.

She stopped and laughed out loud. Was cooking what she did to relax herself?

She didn't know, but it was something to occupy her mind while she tried to get the rest of her life back.

CYNTHIA PRICE WAS back at the nurses' station in the morning when another young man showed up. Last time it had been a guy who had said he was Elizabeth's brother, although Cynthia had wondered if it was true. This time it was a different story.

"I understand you had a woman here who doesn't remember her name or anything else," he began.

"Yes," Cynthia answered cautiously.

"She didn't have any identification on her?"

"No purse."

"She was in an auto accident. Did the police check the car's registration?"

"That was a dead end. The car belonged to someone else who's on an extended trip outside the country."

"Your patient's a mystery woman."

"Uh-huh."

"I was thinking I might be able to help her."

"Who are you?"

"Oh, sorry. I'm a newspaper reporter with the *Baltimore Observer*."

"Never heard of it."

"We're an online publication. That gives us the flexibility to get the news up quickly."

Cynthia waited for him to say more.

"If I did an article about the woman—Jane Doe—someone might come forward to, you know, claim her."

"We don't have a picture of her."

"But do you know where she went?"

Cynthia hesitated, weighing the upside and the downside. Polly had said not to talk about Elizabeth, but this was a newspaper reporter who might be able to help her.

"She went home with one of our nurses," she finally said.

"One of the nurses from this floor."

Cynthia swallowed. "Yes, but if you get someone who thinks they know her, you can call me, and I'll contact her."

"You can't give me her name?"

"I'd rather not."

"Okay. And what else can you tell me? Can you give me a description of her?"

Cynthia thought for a moment. "She was in her late twenties or early thirties. Her hair was short and dark, curly. Her eyes were blue. Her face was oval-shaped. She's about five feet five inches tall and weighs about 110 pounds. Does that help?"

"That's excellent."

Cynthia was starting to wonder if she had done the right thing. "What did you say your name was?"

"Jack Regan."

"You have a card?"

He handed her one with his name and a phone number.
She bent it back and forth in her hand.

"I'll call if I get a lead," he said.

"When will the article be out?"

"I'll let you know."

The man left, and Cynthia looked toward the phone.
Should she call Polly? Or should she just act like nothing
had happened? In the end she didn't make the call.

ELIZABETH WAS THINKING that she would have never in her
life have considered finding herself in this helpless situation.
Then she laughed because she was making up the "never in
her life" part. The truth was that if she had imagined this,
she didn't know about it because the memory was missing.

She showered and dressed, and spent a restless morning
flipping through TV channels.

Over two hundred channels and nothing held her interest.
As she looked out the back window, her gaze roamed over
Polly's weedy garden. If Elizabeth went out and worked in
it for a few hours, at least she'd be doing something con-
structive.

This was one of the days Polly didn't go to work. At least
that's what she'd told Elizabeth, who hoped the nurse hadn't
made special arrangements to stay home and watch over her.

SO FAR SO GOOD, Derek Lang decided. Hank Patterson, who
had posed as Jack Regan, returned with valuable information.

"Elizabeth Forester is staying with a nurse who was on
duty yesterday."

Derek swung to his computer and consulted one of the
many databases he had access to.

He quickly came up with the personnel files of Memorial Hospital and found out who was on the nursing staff.
Next he used a hacker program to get into the hospital work

schedules and was able to zero in on the medical unit that had treated Forester.

A few moments later, he looked up from the computer. "There were three nurses on duty in her area. We know it's not the Price woman. That leaves two others." He gave Patterson the names. "You and Southwell check them out."

When Patterson had gone, Derek went back to the computer. It might be good to know what doctors had been on duty, too.

ELIZABETH FOUND POLLY folding laundry in the bedroom.

"I'm going to be out back, doing some yard work."

"You don't have to do anything like that."

"I want to."

"All right, dear."

"Do you have some gardening gloves?"

"In the shed."

Elizabeth took a plastic grocery bag from the kitchen. She could stuff weeds inside it and then periodically empty the bag at the side of the shed. And then she could ask Polly what she wanted done with the mess.

She slipped out the back and stood on the cracked concrete patio for a moment before crossing to the shed. As soon as she stepped inside, she started thinking about what she and Matthew had been doing in here last night.

Banishing that intimate scene from her mind, she located the gloves, exited the shed and looked around. The garden had been laid out with several flower beds, although it seemed that Polly had lost interest in keeping the place up. But really, it could look much better. Elizabeth crossed to the far right corner, got down on her knees and began pulling at the various weeds that had taken over. She didn't know the names of them, but she knew which were the plants that were choking out the flowers.

She'd been working for a half hour when the back door

opened. Expecting to see Polly, she looked up. Instead of the nurse, a man was standing in the doorway staring at her. A man with a gun that had a strangely long barrel.

She gasped.

He gave her a smile that didn't reach his eyes. "Let's go."

"No."

"You want me to shoot you here?" he asked.

She raised her chin. "You won't. You want information from me."

His face registered surprise and annoyance. "Yeah, but what if I shoot you in the kneecap?"

"Are you going to risk it?"

Chapter Six

Elizabeth was shocked at her own audacity, yet in the back of her mind, she had been expecting something like this all along. Men had been chasing her, and she'd been sure they were looking for her. Now she wasn't really surprised that one of them had caught up with her. They'd been desperate to find her, and it had been bound to happen.

A horrible thought struck her. The man had come through the house, and Polly had been in there. Had she hidden from him, or had he found her? And what had he done to her?

She clenched her teeth, holding back the questions. Perhaps he hadn't seen Polly and she'd gotten to the phone to call 9-1-1.

Stalling for time, she said, "What if I still don't know who I am?"

"We'll find out if you're telling the truth."

The light behind the man changed, and she saw another figure standing there. Was it the other man who'd been chasing her in the car? Then he shifted to the right, and she saw it was Matthew Delano.

Her heart leaped—with relief and fear. Matthew had arrived, but what good was that going to do either one of them against a man with a gun?

She tried not to look directly at Matt, tried not to give away that there was anyone behind the man.

Matt was staring at her with intense concentration on his

face, and she realized with a zing of recognition that he was trying to tell her something.

Mind to mind. They'd done that once before, when they were touching. Now he was ten feet away and struggling to send her a message.

She strained to understand what he was trying to tell her. It was fuzzy. Half-formed, like a radio transmission full of static. She struggled to focus on the words while she kept her gaze on the man with the gun. And finally a message solidified in her head.

If you hear me, raise your shoulder. Then drop to the ground.

As soon as she got the message, she did as he said, raising her shoulder, then dropping down, out of the line of fire.

"Wha…"

That was all the man said before Matt was on him, throwing him down where he stood.

The gun went off, a silenced sound as the guy fell. She dashed forward and lashed out with her foot, kicking him in the face. He screamed, and Matt grabbed his hair, lifting his head and smashing it against the concrete patio.

The man went still, and Matt heaved himself up.

She turned to him. "What are you doing here?"

"I tried to stay away, but I couldn't. Come on, we have to get going."

"Where's Polly?"

Matt's expression turned grim. "I'm sorry. She's dead."

Elizabeth felt her chest go tight, hardly able to process the words. "Dead?"

"Yeah." He paused for a moment before saying, "He shot her. Used a silencer so you wouldn't hear it."

She moaned. "But…"

"I know. It's awful, but we have to get out of here."

"Where are we going?"

"I don't know. Away."

He grabbed her hand, and she felt the familiar jolt of sexual awareness. Struggling to ignore it, she let him lead her into the house, but she stopped short when she saw blood trailing out of the laundry room. Following it, she found Polly lying in a crumpled heap in the door to the laundry room, a pool of blood under her.

"We were just talking about garden gloves," she whispered.

"I'm sorry," was all he could offer.

The reality of everything that had happened in the past few minutes jolted her. "Did she fight him?"

"I can't tell."

He turned toward the wall phone, picked up the receiver and punched in 9-1-1.

"What is the nature of your emergency?"

"There's been a murder at 2520 Wandering Way," he said, giving Polly's address.

"Stay on the line and…"

He hung up. "We can't stay around."

"But…"

"We have to be out of here when the cops get here," he said with conviction. Picking up a dish towel, he wiped off the phone. "You bought some clothes. Where are they?"

"Bedroom."

He strode down a short hall and came back with the bag from the discount store. "Let's go."

When she couldn't manage to move, he took her hand again, leading her out the front door. In the distance she could hear the wail of a siren.

They climbed into the car Matt had parked at the curb and drove away, while Elizabeth looked back over her shoulder.

"She was a nice woman. She was just trying to help me, and look what happened to her."

"It shows what kind of men you're dealing with."

She nodded numbly, trying to take in his words and the

implications. She'd thought she was in trouble. She'd had no idea how much trouble. "Where are we going?"

"I don't know. But I don't think we can risk going to my apartment."

"Why?"

"They probably know I treated you. They could be looking for me, too."

She gasped. "I've gotten you into bad trouble."

"Not your fault."

"Polly's dead, and thugs with guns are after…us."

"We'll figure it out."

"How?"

"I don't know yet." He kept driving, putting distance between Polly's house and themselves.

"You sent me a message—mind to mind—and I got it."

"Yeah. Lucky thing, because I couldn't risk hitting him when he had the gun pointed at you."

"Telepathic communication," she whispered.

"Probably it only worked at that distance because it was an emergency."

She would have liked to test the theory, but not now.

Glancing at him, she asked, "You're leaving all your stuff in your apartment?"

"In Africa, I got into the habit of carrying essentials with me, in case I had to get out of a tight spot in a hurry. I've got an overnight bag in the trunk."

"Okay."

She tried to stay calm as they drove toward the suburbs.

He stopped at an ATM and got a wad of cash, then stopped at another and got more.

"What are you doing?"

"I may not be able to use my credit card after this. I want to make sure I've got money."

"Why are we running from the authorities?"

"Because we don't know the situation. The cops could be in on it."

"That's a cynical way of thinking."

"I've learned to be cynical. And I think you agree."

"Why?"

"Did you go to the cops when those guys were chasing you—or try to run away?"

"I guess I tried to run away."

He put twenty miles between Polly's house and themselves before pulling into the parking lot of a motel chain.

"Stay here. I'll be right back. And slump down in the seat so you're not so visible."

She didn't question him as she slid down and watched him disappear into the lobby. He was back in under five minutes with a key card.

"I asked for a room away from the highway," he said as he drove around to the back and pulled up in front of one of the units.

They both climbed out, and he unlocked the room. She'd held herself together in the car, but as soon as they were inside, she started to shake, leaning her shoulders against the door to stay upright.

"I'm…I'm sorry…" she managed to say through chattering teeth.

"None of this is your fault."

He reached for her, pulling her into his arms, and it was the most natural thing in the world to mold herself to his rugged frame, letting her head drop to his shoulder.

He held her close, stroking his hand up and down her back.

She knew what he was thinking. He was cussing out the bastards who had put her—the two of them—in this position. And he was determined to figure out what the hell was going on.

But she felt his coherent thoughts—and hers—slipping

away, overwhelmed by the sexual need zinging back and forth between them. It had been there from the first moment he had touched her in the hospital, a doctor thinking he was going to do a routine exam and being shocked by the results. The connection between them was stronger now, no doubt jolted up by her fear and his concern for her.

"I SHOULDN'T," HE WHISPERED. "I'm taking advantage of you."

"Do you really believe that? I mean, you can read my mind." She had to keep from punctuating the comment with a hysterical laugh.

I guess that's right."

There was more she could say, but she chose to demonstrate her feelings—and his—with actions, not words.

Twenty-four hours ago, he'd been a stranger. But that was only a technical matter. The connection between them was stronger than with anyone else she'd ever met. Since they had first touched, she'd ached to be alone with him in a bedroom. And now they were here.

The moment their mouths collided, it was like an old-fashioned kitchen match striking a rough surface. Unbearable heat flared, and she knew there was no going back—if either one of them was going to hold on to sanity. Their lips feasted on each other as his hands roamed her back.

They kissed like two lovers at the end of the world who had thought they would never see each other again. And then each of them had stumbled around a corner and found the other standing there.

Joy flooded through her. After all the long lonely years, she had found someone who...

She couldn't even put it into words. All she knew was that she and this man were on the same wavelength, both absorbed in the magical reality of being in each other's arms and each other's minds. It was so wonderful, except that the pounding in her head—which she'd felt when they had kissed in the shed—was back. "What is it?" she murmured.

"The headache?"

"Yes."

"Could be something bad."

"Or what's bad is stopping."

He made a sound of agreement, pulling her to him, deepening the kiss, angling his head to drink in everything he could.

His thoughts were there for her to read. He had wanted her for what seemed like centuries, and it was gratifying to hear that silent admission.

She moved closer, her arms creeping around his neck as she kissed him with intensity. When he finally lifted his head, they both struggled to drag in a full breath.

He reached behind her, and she knew he was turning the door lock, then slipping the safety chain into place.

They swayed as one, clinging together to keep from toppling over.

"You're putting your trust in my hands," he whispered.

"Who better?"

He must have read the invitation in her mind because he bent his head, stroking his face against her breasts, then turned to brush his lips against one of the hardened tips poking through both her thin bra and the fabric of her T-shirt.

Just that touch made heat leap inside her, and she knew that she had to get the damn shirt and bra off.

She pulled the tee over her head and reached to unhook her bra, tossing them onto the floor. By the time she'd finished, he'd pulled off his own shirt and flung it to meet hers.

Then he reached for her again, clasping her in his arms.

She cried out as her breasts pressed against his chest. The sensuality of his naked flesh against hers took her breath away.

"I don't think I can stand up much longer," she whispered.

"Likewise."

He slung his arm around her and led her to the bed, letting go of her to pull down the covers.

Then they were on the mattress, clinging, rocking in each other's arms.

He bent and swirled his tongue around one of her hardened nipples, then sucked it into his mouth.

Heat shot downward through her body, and she could only sob at the intensity of what she felt.

Yet the headache hovered at the edge of her pleasure.

"We could be heading for a cerebral hemorrhage," he muttered.

"I don't want to hear from Dr. Delano right now," she said.

And she knew he was thinking that they'd gone too far to stop.

To make that perfectly clear, she struggled out of her jeans and panties. As he caught her thoughts, he got rid of his remaining clothing. When they were both naked, he pulled her back into his arms, making her cry out again.

He slid his lips along the tender place where her ear met her cheek, dipping down to nibble along the line of her chin and then the side of her neck, before bringing his mouth back to her breast, taking one nipple into his mouth and drawing on her while his hand found its mate, using his thumb and finger to gently twist and tug, building her pleasure to fever pitch.

All her senses were tuned to him, to his masculine scent, the beat of his heart, the feel of his hair-roughened legs against her smooth ones.

Ripples of sensation flowed through her as his free hand slid down her body toward the hot, quivering core of her. Her hips moved in response, and she knew he was in her mind, sensing how good it was for her.

He rolled to his back, taking her with him, looking up at her. "You set the pace."

Maybe he still had a tiny sliver of doubt, and he was giving her the chance to back out.

She leaned in for a long, deep kiss, then raised her head so she could look down at him as she straddled his hips.

She felt the breath freeze in his chest as she lowered her body to his. She didn't need to guide him into her. They both knew where to find the right place.

For a long moment, she stared at him, overwhelmed by the intensity of her feelings. And his.

And then she began to move above him, around him, her eyes locked with his.

There was no question of hanging on to control. The pace started off fast and grew more frantic as they both pushed for climax.

The pain in her head peaked, and then it suddenly was gone, as she took them both higher and higher, and felt his hand pressed to her center to increase her pleasure.

She came undone in a burst of sensation so intense that she lost herself for a moment, but she felt him follow her over the edge, his shout of satisfaction echoing in the room.

As she collapsed against him, clinging tightly to him, he wrapped his arms around her, holding her where she was. And she was content to stay there for the next century.

Yet she couldn't. In that surge of intimacy, everything had changed.

FAR AWAY, IN LAFAYETTE, Louisiana, Rachel Harper stopped in the middle of planting flowers around the cottage where she and her husband, Jake, spent part of each week, when they weren't in New Orleans. Rachel had a boutique there, where she read tarot cards. And Jake had several businesses, including restaurants and antique shops. The cottage was on a plantation that belonged to Gabriella Boudreaux, where three couples had established a small colony. They all had something important in common. All of them were telepaths who had found each other after years of loneliness.

Recently they'd been on the run from men who wanted to use them or destroy them. Now they were living in safety and making a life for themselves. Their powers varied, but Rachel had a special ability—to send her mind over long distances. Because of that, she was always on the lookout for more couples who had hooked up. She wanted to offer them the safety she and Jake had found. Yet at the same time, she was always cautious about approaching anyone new, because the first man and woman like themselves that she and Jake had met had tried to kill them.

The last time she'd detected another couple, Jake had been with her. Now she was alone in the garden. Tension coursed through her as she looked around. When Jake didn't come rushing out, she knew he hadn't picked up on her sudden awareness that another man and woman had bonded. The other couple were far away. Somewhere on the East Coast, she thought, although she wasn't sure of the exact location. But since she was the only one here who knew about them, she could keep the information to herself and decide what to do about it later.

Chapter Seven

Elizabeth Forester, Matt said into her mind.

    Thank you for that—and the rest of it.

    Do you know why those men are after you?

    I'm still not sure.

    We'll figure it out.

He clasped her to him, holding her in place, and she was content to lie on top of him, still marveling at the way they had traveled together to an undiscovered country.

"This is what we were meant for," he murmured, absolute conviction in his voice.

She understood what he was saying.

    Always incomplete.

    Until now.

    Why did it happen?

    The loneliness or what happened when we touched?

    Both.

"We have to find out," he said aloud as he stroked her arm.

She gave a short laugh. "You're saying we can't just enjoy it."

"Is that what you want to do?"

She considered the question. "No. I want to understand. And of course we still have to figure out why those men want to question me—then kill me."

"There's that."

She raised her head, looking around the room. She had barely noticed it when they'd come in. Now it had taken on meaning. It might be a typical motel room, but it was a magical place—where she and Matthew Delano had forged a connection neither one of them had ever dreamed of.

When she shifted off him, he sat up and looked around, and she knew he was following her thoughts. And she knew he was thinking about something else, as well.

Naked, he got out of bed and reached for the remote beside the television set. Then he slipped back under the covers and began flipping through the channels.

It didn't take long to find what he was looking for. The afternoon news was on several of the local channels. When he stopped at one, a reporter was standing in front of the house where they had recently escaped from Polly's killer.

"Polly Kramer, a local woman who worked as a nurse at Memorial Hospital, was found dead in her laundry room. Responding to a 9-1-1 call, police arrived to find the victim alone in the house. Wanted for questioning are Matthew Delano and a woman known only as Jane Doe, who was admitted to the hospital with amnesia. Ms. Kramer volunteered to take the discharged patient home while she tried to regain her memory. Apparently the Good Samaritan gesture led to her death."

Elizabeth stared at the television screen in shocked silence.

Matt pulled her close. "It's not your fault."

"Of course it is. She'd be alive if she hadn't volunteered to help me out."

"Don't blame yourself. You had no idea what was going to happen."

"But I knew I was in some kind of danger."

He rocked her as she shivered in his arms. "If you want to assign blame, think about how they knew where to find you. It wasn't through Polly, and it wasn't through me. It must have come from one of the other nurses."

"But why?"

"Maybe she thought she was being helpful."

Elizabeth wanted to believe she wasn't to blame, but she couldn't stop her physical reaction. "We have to find out what's going on. We have to turn him over to the police."

"But why didn't you go to the police in the first place?"

I wish I knew for sure. Maybe I didn't have enough on him. She dragged in a breath and let it out. *What if we just turned ourselves in?*

Not a good idea. If they take us into custody, we can't figure out what's going on.

NOT TOO FAR AWAY, in the home of Derek Lang, Gary Southwell and his boss were watching the same newscast.

Lang was sitting in a comfortable chair in his TV room. Southwell was standing a few feet away, shifting his weight from foot to foot and keeping his hands at his sides—away from his battered face.

"Tell me again how she got away?" Lang asked.

Gary cleared his throat, hoping his nerves didn't show. "I had a gun on her. Then she threw herself to the ground, and a guy jumped me from behind."

"Curious that she knew to get out of the line of fire."

Gary had thought about that. "He must have given her some kind of signal."

"Which would mean they had something prearranged."

Gary nodded.

"And you weren't aware of him in back of you?"

"No, sir. I had killed the old lady, and I didn't expect anyone else besides Forester."

He could see Lang thinking about the answer. He was wondering if Gary had made a mistake, or were they dealing with someone very clever? There was no use trying to persuade him either way. He'd make up his own mind.

"The police still don't know who she is, or they're not saying, which gives us an advantage," Lang mused.

"And I think she still doesn't know, either. At least I got that impression from talking to her."

"Why?"

"The look in her eyes," Gary answered promptly.

"Okay."

With any other employer, Gary might have asked a question like, "What's our next move?" but he kept silent because he knew Lang would give him further orders when he had a plan in place.

He watched his boss thinking about his options before he said, "Stake out her house. If she figures out who she is, she'll go back there."

"Yes, sir," Gary answered, relieved to have a new assignment, one he wasn't going to screw up.

"And another thing. The cops are looking for the doctor who treated her, the one on shift the morning she was released. Unless we have contradictory information, we have to assume that he's the guy who came up behind you. And we have to assume the two of them are together. Keep a man on his place, too, in case he's dumb enough to go home."

"Yes, sir."

"I'll check his credit-card records and his background. Where was he before he was in Baltimore? We may get a lead on where he's gone."

Gary left the room, feeling like he'd made a lucky escape. Other men who had worked for Derek Lang had disappeared. They might have moved on to other jobs, but Gary didn't think so.

MATT KEPT HIS ARM around Elizabeth. At the same time, he sent her soothing thoughts. It was a strange way to communicate, but he knew it was working as he felt her shivering subside.

"Let's think this through. Make some plans."

She caught a thought sliding through his head. "And you want to have a hamburger while we're doing it."

He laughed. "I can't help it. I haven't had much to eat today, and I think we both need to keep our strength up.

"Okay."

Her agreement came with what she was really thinking—that after seeing the news report, she wasn't sure she could eat.

"Inconvenient to be getting so many of your stray thoughts," he murmured.

"Yes."

"There are a ton of fast-food restaurants around here. I can go out and bring the burgers back."

"Okay," she answered, and again he picked up more than she was saying. She didn't love the idea of being left alone, but under the circumstances, it was safer. "I know," she murmured aloud.

He nodded and got dressed. "Back in a flash."

When he stopped short, she gave him a questioning look, then said, "You're worried that the cops could be looking for your car."

"Yeah."

"What are you going to do about it?"

He knew she was following all the options running through his head. He couldn't just go rent a car because he'd have to use his credit card. And stealing a car wasn't in his skill set—or his ethics set, either.

He finally said, "I read a spy novel where the hero changed a letter on his license plate with electrical tape. I'll see if I can pick some up."

When she nodded, he said, "Will you be okay?"

"Yes."

Wishing her answer were closer to the truth, he stepped outside and looked around to make sure nobody was paying him any particular attention, then drove at a moderate pace to one of the fast-food chains that were clustered in the same area as the motel complex. He bought double burgers, fries and milk shakes, because he figured both of them could use the calories.

When he returned to the room twenty minutes later, Elizabeth had dressed and had made the bed. She was watching the news again.

"Anything new?"

"No. I guess that's good."

"Yeah. Let's turn it off."

After setting the food on the table, he clicked the TV off with the remote and sat down. She took the seat opposite.

When he'd taken a few bites of his burger, he said, "I was thinking about why we're the way we are."

"So was I."

"I wonder if there's something in our backgrounds that's similar."

She laughed. "That would be easier if I *knew* my background."

"Yeah. About all we can tell is that we both felt cut off from other people." He chewed and swallowed. "Well, I'm from New Orleans. And you said you remember being there."

She nodded. "That's not much to go on. But I was thinking, the reason could be genetic. Or we could both have been exposed to some chemical—or radiation."

"Before or after we were born?"

"Did you have any major illnesses?" she asked.

"Nothing special. Only the usual."

She looked at him. "You said your mom went to a lot of trouble getting pregnant and that she went to a fertility clinic. Do you know where it was?"

"Houma, Louisiana, I think."

"That wasn't so common thirty years ago. I wonder if her

going to the clinic had something to do with it. Which leads to the question, what about me?"

"I don't know. But I can do some research in the medical databases."

"Looking for what? I don't think you're going to find telepathic abilities. Or more precisely—telepathic abilities triggered by…"

"Physical contact. With sexual relations cementing the final breakthrough."

"Very scientific."

He grinned. "I guess a medical background doesn't hurt." Sobering again, he added, "Of course, figuring out how we got telepathic powers is not our immediate problem. The way I see it, there are three things we need to do right away. Since we know your name, we can go to your house. That would help with getting your memory back. But I wouldn't suggest doing it until we have a better idea how to protect ourselves."

"With guns?"

"With our minds. When that guy was holding a weapon on you, I told you to duck, and you did it. We need to find out if we can do more stuff like that. Not just talk to each other."

"What else?"

He turned his palm up. "Did you read many science fiction stories when you were younger? There are a lot of paranormal abilities we can explore."

"I do remember *Star Trek* reruns."

"Another blast from your past."

He saw that she "heard" what that thought had triggered.

"You think we can use our minds to…blast someone?"

"I don't know. But if we can, it's a lot more convenient than having to pack a six-shooter. And stealthier, too. Who would suspect an innocent-looking woman like you of being the Terminator?"

She laughed. "Didn't the Terminator use brute force?"

"Yeah."

"Let's finish eating and try some target practice."

"Where?"

"Somewhere secluded." He waited a beat to see if she'd come up with something. Then he said, "We might drive out toward Frederick. There should be plenty of open space out there."

She took small bites of her hamburger.

"If you're not hungry, drink the milk shake."

"That's strange nutritional advice from a doctor."

He shrugged. "If we're going to try blasting something, we're probably going to use up some calories."

"I guess that's right." She took off the top of the bun and ate some of the meat and the bottom bun, then picked up the milk shake. "I can drink this while we drive."

"Do you often multitask?"

"Apparently."

"Well, eat more of your burger in the car, too."

He bundled up the trash and threw it in the wastebasket, then hesitated as he walked to the door.

"You're thinking that maybe we shouldn't come back here?"

"That could be right."

"But you're going to run out of cash if you keep renting rooms for a few hours."

"Yeah. I guess we can make a decision later."

He looked through the blinds before opening the door and ushering her to follow. They both got into the car, and he drove to the closest shopping center, which happened to have a home improvement store.

Inside, he bought electrical tape and a pair of scissors, then found a secluded part of the lot and looked at his license plate. One of the letters was an *L,* which he was able to change into an *E.* Stepping back, he looked at his handiwork. Not too bad, unless you got on top of it. But on the highway it should work. And he'd better not call attention to them by speeding.

They headed northwest on Route 70 and got off in a rural area. He found a state park where nobody else seemed to be taking advantage of nature, and they both climbed out.

"How are we going to do it?"

"Let's start with some mind-to-mind communication experiments."

"Like what?"

"When I called out to you to drop to the ground, I was about ten feet away."

"But now we've got a stronger link."

"Right," he said, and they both knew he was thinking about their lovemaking. "Let's see how far away we can do it."

"I think we have to be touching to *do it*," she teased.

"You know what I meant."

She nodded, and they first stood on opposite sides of the car.

Do you know the names of the trees? he asked.

She looked around. *I see maples, oaks, white pine.*

Good that you know them. Let's try it a little farther apart.

They each walked a few feet from the car and tried the communication again. It seemed to work until they were about twenty yards away, which was apparently the limit of their mind-to-mind communication skills.

At least for now, he said.

What do you mean?

As you pointed out, our abilities got stronger after we made love. I think that we can make everything we do stronger—if we practice.

Practice making love? she teased again, and he knew she was making an effort to lighten the situation.

That, too.

They joined up again and walked down a trail through the woods.

"It's so peaceful here. I hate the idea of destroying anything."

They came to a footbridge across a stream, where large rocks poked up through the water.

"Let's just see if we can do something to a rock," he suggested.

"How?"

He shrugged. "I don't know for sure."

She leaned on the rail, looking downstream, then pointed to a large boulder sticking above the water line. "We can aim for that one. And we don't want to work against each other. I think it might be best if one of us focuses on the rock and the other one tries to add power to the focus."

"That sounds right."

OVER A THOUSAND miles away in New Orleans, a man named Harold Goddard hunched over his computer. He was retired now, but once he'd worked for the Howell Institute, a D.C. think tank that had funded some very interesting projects over the years—like undetectable chemical weapons and torture methods that left no marks on those being interrogated.

Bill Wellington had been the director of the institute, and Harold had worked closely with him. Wellington had died in an explosion at a secret research lab in Houma, Louisiana, and that had raised Harold's interest.

The lab had been owned by Dr. Douglas Solomon, who'd run one of Wellington's pet projects, thirty some years ago. Only it hadn't quite panned out the way they'd hoped. Not one to double down on a bet, Wellington had pulled the doctor's funding, and Solomon had gone underground with a bunch of different experiments.

Had the two men kept in contact over the years? Or had Wellington found out something about the doctor's most recent activities? Harold might never find the answer to that question because Solomon and Wellington had both been killed when the doctor's hidden research facility had blown up. The authorities had concluded that the cause was a gas leak. Harold had his doubts—especially in light of subsequent events.

The lab explosion had gotten him interested in Solomon again.

He'd gone poking into old records from the clinic and had come up with a list of very interesting people—all of whose mothers had had the doctor's special treatments.

Over the past few months, Harold had brought a number of them together. Several men and women had ended up dead in bed together—apparently from cerebral vascular accidents. And then two of them, Craig Branson and Stephanie Swift, had vanished into thin air—after some very alarming incidents. Incidents that had made Harold cautious about approaching other people on the list.

Now here was one of the names—Matthew Delano, currently AWOL from his job as a house physician at Memorial Hospital in Baltimore and wanted for questioning in a murder investigation.

Harold scanned the article, noting that Dr. Delano had treated a female patient with amnesia. One of the nurses on the unit had volunteered to take Jane Doe home and had been shot to death in her own laundry room. By Delano and the woman? Or by someone else?

That was an interesting question, and one that gave Harold pause. His men had gotten caught in the cross fire when Branson had kidnapped Swift from the fortified plantation of her fiancé, John Reynard, just before the wedding ceremony.

And now here was another dangerous situation in the making, starting with the murder of the Good Samaritan nurse. Harold was tempted to send someone up to Baltimore to investigate, but perhaps it was prudent to stay away from the couple. Maybe it was best to keep tabs on the situation and make a decision later.

Yet it was hard to simply drop the chance for another experiment. He thought back over what had happened at the Reynard estate. Was there some way to protect himself from Delano and the woman—to prevent what had happened before?

ELIZABETH TURNED TO MATT. "Let me try to do the focusing."

"Because you still have a lot of memory gaps, and you want to be effective at something?"

"You read me so well."

"We already know you're effective at cooking."

"I'm not going to do in our enemies with a soufflé."

"You can make a soufflé?"

She considered the question. "Maybe not. I think I'm into more prosaic dishes—like last night's chili." The statement stopped her. "A lot has happened since last night," she murmured.

"Yes. And I also think we're stalling about trying out our powers."

"Right."

Cutting off the extraneous conversation, she looked at the rock she'd picked, thinking of a laser beam.

Or maybe lightning. And I'll try to lend a power assist.

She narrowed her eyes, concentrating—trying to do something that she had no idea how to accomplish.

Matt moved in back of her, pressing close and clasping his hands around her waist, making himself part of her.

She could feel energy flowing between them, gathering strength. It was a wonderful sensation, if she could only figure out how to use it.

Raising her hand, she stretched it toward the rock, imagining beams of power coming out of her fingers.

And suddenly, to her surprise, there was a flash of light

that streaked out toward the rock. Lightning crawled across the surface, and the water around it crackled and boiled.

She heard Matt make a strangled exclamation.

"You didn't think we could do it," she accused, "and you hid that from me."

"You think it was the wrong thing to do?" he challenged.

"No. I might not have tried if I'd known you were waffling."

"Right." He stroked his hand along her arm. "Hiding our thoughts is another skill we need to practice."

"Uh-huh." *For a whole lot of reasons,* she thought and knew he'd caught the silent comment.

She turned back to the rock, focusing on delivering another blast. This time it was easier, and the damage was more severe. She saw small chips of stone fly up into the air and land in the water. But she noticed that Matt's earlier observation was right. Blasting something took energy.

"Let's switch roles," she suggested.

He agreed, and they changed places, with her behind him clasping his waist and peeking around him to watch the rock. At the same time she tried to send him the kind of energy that he'd sent her.

She was tired, and it wasn't easy to do, but she finally felt the flow of power from her to him.

A stream of fire shot from his hand, and the rock blasted apart. She pulled him down, ducking behind the bridge rail as shards of stone flew into the air.

"Nice," she said.

"But dangerous. We need to figure out how to regulate the power," he answered.

"Can we bring it down to a little sizzle?" She pointed to another target, a tree stump that had gotten lodged in the water between two boulders. "Try to just tap it," she said. "Maybe you don't need me to do that."

Matt focused on the stump, and she felt him concentrating. After a few seconds, she saw sparks striking the surface of the bark.

"Nice," she said again. "If it were a person, I wonder how it would feel."

"Discomfort? Disorientation?"

They stayed on the bridge, leaning against the rail, both of them marveling at what they'd been doing. A few days ago, such an ability would have been unthinkable. It was empowering to realize what they could do together, but it didn't solve Elizabeth's basic problem.

"Let's go back to where we started," she said. *Memories.*

She turned so that she faced him. He wrapped her in his arms, and she leaned into him, closing her eyes as she tried to grab on to something from her past.

She knew Matt was keeping the exchange directed away from himself, trying to help her dig out nuggets from her past.

The easiest memories to reach were from her childhood. And not all of them were bad. She remembered being enchanted by a trip to the zoo with her parents. She remembered a trip to Disney World where she'd insisted on riding the Space Mountain roller coaster. She remembered being the best girl basketball player in her high school class. And then she remembered the time she had missed a shot and lost a playoff game for the team.

Matt rubbed her arm. "Don't focus on that."

"I felt horrible. I had finally found something that made me valuable to the other kids, and I blew it."

"We all have stuff like that."

The next picture that came to her knocked the breath from her lungs. It was like when Matt had hypnotized her. She saw young women huddled together. Only now she felt their fear and knew that she was the only one who could save them from a horrible fate.

Chapter Eight

Who are they? Matt asked.

"I don't know," she almost shouted in her frustration as the mental image faded. "But they're depending on me, and I have to help them."

"Okay," he answered, giving her his full support. "But how do we do it?"

"First I have to figure out who they are—and where they are." She swallowed hard. "And I think there might be something at my house that tells me."

He gave her a long look. "You think it's safe to go to your house? You might not know why those men were chasing you, but it's a given that they know your name. Now that you've escaped from them twice, they probably have your house staked out—hoping you'll come back."

"I know that." She dragged in a frustrated breath and let it out. "But I think I have to. I mean, I can't just keep running away. I have to figure out what's going on."

"Inconvenient," he answered in a dry voice that might have fooled her if she hadn't already learned a lot about him.

"I probably have records on my computer."

"And somebody probably already got to them—after the car accident, when you were out of commission."

She nodded, hating that they were in this bind. She needed to know more about herself, and she knew she couldn't do it alone. She also knew that Matt was following her thought processes.

"We have your address, and we can get there."

"We'll go back there, but we have to be cautious," he said.

It was instructive to see the way he thought as they drove toward Arbutus, a middle-class community, where her house was located. He stopped at a drugstore and bought them both Orioles baseball caps, which they pulled down low to hide their faces. He also bought two Orioles T-shirts. Hers was oversize, and hung far down her arms and body, but it certainly created a different look for her. A roll of duct tape completed his purchases.

When they'd returned to his car and she'd put the shirt over her clothing, he said, "Lie down in the back."

She didn't have to ask why. She knew he wanted anyone watching to think that a lone man was driving through the neighborhood.

Prone on the backseat, she couldn't see any details of the passing scenery, but that didn't matter because she didn't remember the details, anyway.

"I just drove past your house," he informed her.

"What's it look like?"

"It's a two-story. An older home with a porch and new vinyl siding. The front yard is nicely planted, and there's a man sitting in a car across the street, keeping an eye on the place."

"Great."

"It's the thug who killed Polly."

She sucked in a sharp breath. "Oh, Lord."

"We expected him or someone like him."

"Too bad we can't tell the cops he's here."

"Yeah. But it would just be his word against ours. And I have the feeling he'd lawyer up and get out before we could blink."

She nodded, then said, "He was alone when he came to Polly's, but he's not going to make that mistake again. I'm sure there's another guy out back."

"And we can't drive up the alley, because we could get trapped."

"Right."

He turned the corner and parked near the end of the alley. They both got out, walking back. She didn't even know which house she lived in, and it was strange to have Matt be the one to direct her.

He pointed. "Your place is about halfway down."

The yards were about thirty feet deep, all of them with three-foot-high chain-link fences.

She spotted the other man when they were about twenty yards away. He was sitting on her back steps, partly screened by low bushes.

We have to get close enough and disable him before he can alert his friend out front.

I don't suppose you remember who lives in the house next door.

Sorry. But in this neighborhood, they're probably at work. Let's hope.

Before they turned in at the house to the right of hers, they planned their attack. As they walked toward the back door, Elizabeth could see the guy on her back steps flick them a look, but apparently he didn't recognize either one of them.

When they reached the door, Matt pretended to get out his keys. She pressed close to him, giving him energy as he raised his arm toward the intruder on her back steps.

Is this going to work? I mean, he's not a rock in a stream.

We'll find out.

She felt Matt gathering power, then sending a bolt of energy toward the man on her back steps. It made the guy go rigid, then slump to the side. Matt was already charging down the steps and vaulting the fence into her yard.

Instead of continuing with the superhero route, he socked the guy in the jaw, then took the gun from his shoulder holster, checked that the safety was on, and stuffed the weapon into the waistband of his jeans, under his Orioles T-shirt.

She helped pull the thug into the bushes, where they taped his hands and feet together and slapped a piece of tape over his mouth. They also took his cell phone and wallet.

Matt took the battery out of the phone, then pawed through the wallet. The guy had a wad of cash, but no identification.

"The money will come in handy," Matt said, as he stuffed the bills into his own pocket. "Do you keep a key to the back door somewhere?"

"I wish I knew. Maybe a neighbor has a key, but I don't recall."

She pushed aside a flowerpot and moved a couple of large rocks but saw nothing.

"We may have to break in." Matt climbed the steps and tried her door. When it turned out to be unlocked, she drew in a sharp breath.

"Obviously the bad guys have been inside and didn't bother to lock up. Stay here until I make sure nobody's inside."

He drew the gun and held it in both hands. Before stepping inside, he studied the threshold, looking for trip wires, then cautiously entered.

Matt had asked her to wait for his all clear, but as she stood with her heart pounding in her chest, she knew she couldn't make herself stay outside. This was her house—an important key to understanding herself. And really, would the bad guys have someone in here, when they already had a man at the front and back?

When Matt saw she was following him, he made a rough sound, but he didn't order her out.

"Wait downstairs while I go up."

"Okay."

Again, waiting was hard.

All clear, he told her as he came down the stairs.

But I see from your thoughts that it's a mess up there. Sorry.

She had expected it from what she saw on the first floor. As she looked around, she grappled with mixed reactions. She was anxious to see the place where she lived. Apparently her taste ran to the whimsical, with touches like bright cloths on horizontal surfaces and ethnic pottery—not much like that sober black jacket and slacks she'd been wearing when she had had the accident. It seemed she liked to kick back when she got into her own environment.

But at the same time she was thinking about her taste, she was taking in the destruction. Someone had been through the house, searching and not caring what kind of mess they left.

She hurried to her office, which was a long, narrow room at the side of the house, and gasped when she saw her computer. The screen lay smashed on the floor and the processor had been taken apart, presumably to remove the hard drive.

The room was divided into two sections by a bank of filing cabinets. Behind them was an area she'd blocked off as a storage closet where she'd piled cardboard boxes purchased from an office supply store. From the mess on the floor she gathered that some had held old tax information and financial records, while others were for books and storage of out-of-season clothing. After looking at the area behind the cabinets, she walked through the main part of the office, where files and papers lay all over the floor.

As she looked toward the stairs, she was suddenly able to picture her cozy bedroom. She'd painted it blue and white, and continued the theme with the curtains and bedspread. She knew it was better not to go up and look at the mess, and better not to go up there and get trapped.

With a grimace, she returned to the kitchen, picked up a set of measuring spoons from the floor and looked around. Oak cabinets. Ceramic tile on the floor and some kind of fake stone on the countertops. The room looked like it had been renovated in the past five years, but it was as wrecked as the office. Cabinet doors hung open, and food had been emptied out, as though someone had thought she might hide important information in a cereal box.

Matt joined her.

"Sorry. It looks like they would have found anything of value."

"Maybe not," she muttered.

The searchers had taken apart all the obvious places, but was she clever enough to have thought of somewhere they wouldn't have considered?

Like, would she have hidden something in a box of tampons? Probably not, because every spy knew that old trick.

After returning to the office, she looked around and saw a bulletin board. Excitement leaped inside her when she saw several name tags from conferences hanging on pins.

"I'm a social worker," she breathed.

"Looks like it."

She swallowed hard. "I guess we have that in common— taking jobs where we could help people, because that was the only way we could connect."

"Yeah."

She picked up a framed diploma from the floor. "And I have a master's degree from the University of Maryland."

"Which might mean you grew up in the area—or not. It could be that they had the kind of program you were looking for."

Matt walked into the closet area. When she heard him open the window, she poked her head around the filing cabinets.

"What are you doing?"

"What I learned to do in Africa. Making sure there's an alternative exit if we need it."

GARY SOUTHWELL LOOKED at his watch. He and Hank Patterson had been staking out Elizabeth Forester's house since he'd gotten his new orders from Mr. Lang. They were supposed to check in with each other every half hour, and Patterson hadn't phoned. Which was unsettling because the man had been punctual as clockwork until this time.

Southwell clicked the phone one more time, trying to get his partner. Finally he gave up and wondered what he should do. Not call Lang. His boss was already annoyed by their lack of progress in apprehending Elizabeth Forester. The woman had determination—and grit. He'd give her that. And apparently she'd found a guy who wasn't going to leave her twisting in the wind.

Had they known each other before she landed in the hospital or what? If not, it was shocking that the doctor was laying his life on the line for a woman he'd met only a few days ago. Gary sure wouldn't do it. He laughed. Or for any other broad. They simply weren't worth it.

He slipped out of the car where he'd been sitting for hours and looked around as he stretched, then started down the block, glancing back at the house before turning the corner. If Forester and the doctor were in there, he was giving them the chance to get out the front, but on balance, he had to risk it.

In the alley, he hurried to the back door, where Patterson was supposed to be stationed. He wasn't there, but as Gary approached the house, he heard a muffled sound of distress in the bushes. When he cautiously approached, he found his partner lying on the ground, taped hand and foot.

Gary pulled the tape off his mouth. "What the hell happened to you?"

"They got the drop on me."

"You mean Elizabeth and that doctor?"

"Yeah," Patterson said as Gary freed his partner's wrists and started working on his legs.

Patterson shook his hands and kicked his feet to get the circulation going.

"What happened, exactly?"

"I'm not sure. It was like…" He stopped and glanced at Gary. "Like they hurled a thunderbolt or something at me."

"That's impossible. Maybe they had a Taser gun."

Patterson considered the idea. "I don't know what it was. I'm just sayin', be damned careful if you get near them."

"Were you unconscious?"

"Maybe for a little while."

"Okay," Gary muttered, wondering what they were going to do now and thinking about that five-minute window when he'd left his post and headed back here—to find Patterson.

Could they have gotten away while his partner was out?

"Did you see them leave?" Gary asked.

"I don't think so."

"Then we'd better assume they saw me out front, which means they wouldn't go out that way." Gary glanced at Patterson. "You steady on your feet?"

"Steady enough to kill those bastards."

"Waste the guy. The boss wants to do the woman himself."

"You mean do her—then kill her?"

"Yeah."

IN THE OFFICE, Elizabeth picked up some of the papers scattered on the floor and thumbed through them. "These are records of some of my clients."

After righting the desk chair, she sat down and started to read one of the cases. "This woman was living in a flophouse in Baltimore. It looks like she came into the country illegally."

"I know you want to understand what you were doing, but I think you don't have time to read cases now."

She gave him an exasperated look. "They could be clues

to what was going on—when those thugs tried to grab me after the accident."

"Maybe you can take some with you. We've got to get out of here pretty fast."

She nodded but didn't move.

"There's got to be something here," she murmured as she looked around the shambles that had been her office. "Something they missed."

"How do you know?"

She shrugged. "I just do. And maybe you can help me figure it out."

Standing, she reached for Matt. Pulling him close, she molded her body against his as they stood in the middle of the mess. His arms stroked up and down her back, and as she held on to him, she felt the familiar merging of their minds that had so quickly become necessary to her existence.

Yes, he silently agreed.

She wanted to simply revel in the special closeness they shared, but she knew there wasn't time for that now. What she had to do was search for the memories he'd brought back to her. Not something long ago. Something recent.

Eyes closed, she mentally looked around the room trying to figure out what she couldn't remember on her own.

Her mental gaze shifted to the bulletin board. There were several whimsical things stuck to it including a couple greeting cards, a Mardi Gras mask, two cocktail swizzle sticks and a key ring with a small flashlight attached.

Matt followed her thoughts as she stepped away from him and reached for the key ring. She had just taken it down from the board when an unwelcome noise made them both go still.

In the quiet of the house, they heard the front door open.

Chapter Nine

Matt froze. He'd known all along that coming to Elizabeth's place was taking a chance, but he'd also been desperate to help her get more information about herself. Now it appeared that they'd run out of luck. He looked at Elizabeth, seeing the terror on her face—and also the anger. These guys kept coming after her like a relentless robot killer in a science-fiction movie, and now one or more of them were in the house with them.

Stealthy footsteps crept slowly down the hall.

What are we going to do? Elizabeth asked.

Get out the escape hatch.

Thank God you thought of one.

He ushered Elizabeth behind him. *Climb out the window.*

What about you?

I'll block them, then follow. Head for the car.

He knew she wanted to argue about the hastily conceived plan, but she silently acknowledged there was no alternative.

Stepping around the filing cabinets, she headed for the open window.

He pulled out the gun that he'd taken away from the guy they'd encountered out back. What had happened while they were inside, exactly? Had Polly's killer found his partner and set him free? Or had the guy out front come around back? And did whoever was out there know Matt was armed?

Matt tensed as the footsteps came closer, his attention divided between Elizabeth and the invaders. In his mind he could see her climbing out the window and dropping down to the narrow space between her house and the one next door.

When he knew she was outside, he breathed out a small sigh. She was safely out of the house, but he knew the man who had killed Polly Kramer wouldn't hesitate to do the same to Matthew Delano.

"We know you're in there," one of the thugs called out. "Come out with your hands up, and you won't be hurt."

Oh, sure.

Could they really know he was in here? Or were they guessing? Apparently they didn't remember there was a back way out of the room. But Matt couldn't just run for it. If they came through the door, they could catch him on the way out and drill him in the back.

To give himself a few extra seconds, Matt fired through the doorway.

Curses rang behind him—the voices telling him there were at least two guys out there—as he ducked into the area behind the filing cabinets.

One of the men in the hall fired an answering shot through the door.

Matt reached the window and was thankful that Elizabeth had pushed it open farther. Climbing halfway out, he returned fire before hurling himself through the opening.

He wasn't surprised to find Elizabeth waiting for him on the ground. Even without reading her thoughts, he knew she wasn't going to take off and leave him there.

Thank God. Her exclamation of relief rang in his head as he pressed his shoulder to hers.

He didn't waste his breath or his mental energy upbraiding her for staying in the path of danger. Instead, he focused on the window, knowing she was following his thoughts and lending him power. When a head appeared above them, Matt hurled a bolt of energy at the man, who made a wheezing sound and dropped back inside.

Come on.

With Elizabeth right behind him, Matt ran down the narrow side passage, then climbed over the waist-high fence between the two houses, reaching to help her over.

They sprinted through the yard, through the back gate and down the alley.

No shots followed, presumably because the guys weren't going to take a chance on a gun battle outdoors in a residential neighborhood. Or maybe they were worried about Matt's secret weapon.

But he and Elizabeth weren't exactly home free. Before they'd reached the end of the alley, a police siren sounded in the distance.

"Someone must have heard the shooting in your house," he said as he slowed his pace, walking at normal speed toward his car.

Moments later, they were inside the vehicle and on their way out of the neighborhood, leaving the cops and the thugs behind them.

Elizabeth sat rigidly in her seat, and Matt knew what was in her mind. He was torn between escaping and giving her the reassurance they both needed.

He turned onto a side street, made another turn, and pulled up under a low-hanging maple tree that partially hid them from the street.

When he cut the engine, she turned to him with a little sob that was part relief and part frustration. He slid his seat back and reached for her, pulling her into his arms, holding tight as he ran his hands over her back and shoulders, thankful that they had both made it out of her house alive.

Her apology rang in his mind.

I'm so sorry.

Not your fault.

You said it was too dangerous to go there.

But I also said we had to do it. We both knew it was necessary.

They almost caught us.

But they didn't.

As they silently spoke, she brought her mouth to his for a frantic kiss. And his response was no less emotional. If they hadn't been on a public street, he knew they would have been tearing each other's clothing off in the next moment and making frenzied love.

But here in the car in a residential neighborhood, all they could do was clutch tightly, kissing and touching and silently proclaiming how glad they were that they'd found each other and how relieved they were that they'd escaped from Derek Lang's men.

The name jolted through both of them. He knew that the heightened emotions of the moment had made it pop into Elizabeth's head. But he also knew from her thoughts that she was sure it was right. He was the man who'd sent the thugs after her—when she'd crashed her car, then later at Polly Kramer's house and now. She looked at Matt, and he caught the swell of victory pounding through her.

Derek Lang. That's his name, she shouted in his mind.

Yes.

The next question is, what did I do to him?

I hope we've got the answer.

She nodded as she reached into her pocket and pulled out the small flashlight that she'd taken from the bulletin board. The men who'd searched the house had ignored it as just part of her kitschy office decorations, but when she'd unscrewed the top, she pulled out the thumb drive hidden inside.

"They got the hard drive, but they didn't get this," she said. "Hopefully it duplicates what was in the computer."

"Clever of you."

She grinned at him. "Yes, if I do say so myself."

"Let's hope it's got what we need. I'd like to figure out what's going on."

"But we need a computer." She smiled as she caught his next thought and murmured, "Your laptop is in your trunk."

"Yeah."

"Clever of *you* to bring it along."

"I thought it might come in handy."

She didn't ask where they were going because he knew she saw the picture of the motel room that had formed in his mind.

She scooted back to the other side of the car. He slid his seat closer to the wheel again and drove away, being careful to stay under the speed limit.

Matt slowed at the row of fast-food restaurants where they'd bought lunch.

"We just used up a lot of energy with that mental stuff. We should get something to eat," he said.

She tipped her head toward him. "That might be what came out of your mouth, but you were thinking about something else."

"I guess I can't hide that X-rated image of the two of us in bed. But we've got to keep our priorities straight. Food, work and then pleasure. What do you want for dinner?"

When a picture of a large pizza, loaded with cheese, vegetables and meat, leaped into her mind, he said, "Excellent choice."

They bought the pizza along with soft drinks and brought it back to the motel.

MATT DROVE THROUGH the lot before he stopped, but as far as he could tell, nobody suspicious was hanging around. Still he had Elizabeth wait in the car while he retrieved the laptop from the trunk.

After he'd ushered her inside, he set the computer and

the food on the table, then locked the door and checked out the bathroom.

"There's a window in here," he announced.

"In case we have to make another quick getaway?"

"I'm just being cautious."

"It was lucky you were being cautious at my house."

They looked at each other for a long moment. *We have to practice restraint and discipline,* he forced himself to say.

Opening the box, he selected a slice of pizza and put it on a paper plate while he booted up his computer.

He looked over and saw Elizabeth watching him.

"You can just eat like that—after someone's tried to kill you?"

"That's the best time for a hearty meal."

She shook her head and reached for a slice, pulling her chair around to his side of the table so she could look at the screen while she ate.

"Okay, this is good," she admitted.

He inserted the thumb drive into the USB port. They both ate pizza and sipped their drinks while they waited for the start-up routine to complete.

"What do you think is on the drive?" he asked.

"I don't know. Too bad it's not my biography."

"Since we know your name, I'm sure we can get an approximation. There's probably a bio of you at the place where you work. Maybe one of the county or city social service agencies."

"I didn't think of that. But let's read the thumb drive first."

He switched the computer's attention to the external drive and got a list of files.

"Which one's first?"

"Might as well start at the top."

The first file contained snapshots of women—all of whom looked like they might be of Eastern European origin.

Next was a picture of the Port of Baltimore and one of

the huge containers that was often taken off ships and set directly onto tractor-trailer trucks.

They both stared at the pictures.

"It might seem far-fetched, but I think I understand the connection between the pictures," Elizabeth said. "Does it sound crazy to think that Derek Lang is using cargo containers to smuggle women illegally into the country?" She swallowed hard. "And then something bad happens to them?"

"Well, we know something big is going on. Big enough for Derek Lang to want you out of the picture."

"As in—dead."

"You must have found out about it. But how could you stumble onto something like that?"

She shook her head in frustration.

They opened more files. Some contained dates and times. Others were lists that looked like order forms.

They kept looking through the files, but there was no more information that helped Elizabeth unravel the mystery.

"We have to help these women," she murmured. "Which means we have to figure out where they are."

"And we have to help ourselves, because we're not going to be safe unless Derek Lang is off our backs." He turned toward her. "I wonder why you didn't just go to the police."

"There has to be a reason."

WHEN ELIZABETH LOOKED at Matt, she knew he had caught her thoughts about how to come up with more information about the women.

The first time I remembered anything about myself was when you touched me. I think we need to try that again.

He nodded, but she was pretty sure it was going to take more than simply holding hands.

Keeping her eyes on him, she stood up and kicked off her shoes and watched him do the same.

"You think we're going to be able to focus on what we're supposed to be doing?" she asked.

"I guess we'll find out. Keep your shorts on to make it harder to go too far."

"A good precaution."

She pulled off her shirt, bra and jeans, leaving on her panties, and when she pulled back the covers and slipped into bed, he followed her, wearing only his briefs. He drew her to him, both of them longing for the contact and both of them knowing that they couldn't give in to their own needs—not yet. They had to focus on dragging out the information that had to be in her mind.

She brushed her lips against his, then pillowed her head on his shoulder, while his hands stroked over her arms, and up and down her back.

Maximum contact, he silently murmured as he lifted her up and stretched her out on top of himself, only two layers of fabric separating her center from his erection.

The intimacy was like a jolt of heat, and she couldn't stop herself from moving against him. After a few moments, he quieted her with his hands and thoughts.

Stay still, or we'll end up making love instead of pulling information from your mind.

Hard to remember that's what we're supposed to be doing.

Yeah.

Knowing he was right, she settled down, letting the simmering sexual heat pull their minds deeply together. The first time they'd touched, the transfer of memories had been unexpected. Now they had a much better idea of what they were doing—like when she'd found the thumb drive hanging in plain sight on the bulletin board.

And now he wasn't just inviting her memories. She felt him lending her energy, the way he'd done when they were out in the woods hurling thunderbolts at rocks, and then again when they had disabled the guy who had staked out the back of her house.

As she pulled the power into herself, another picture formed in her mind.

She was at a row house in Baltimore, checking out how things were going with a young mother named Wendy, who'd adopted a child from Romania. They had been talking for about five minutes when another young woman slipped in the back door.

Elizabeth looked up, taking in the woman's frightened eyes and pale skin. The newcomer and the mom exchanged glances.

"This is Sabrina. I met her when I was out walking the baby. I saw her a few times, and I knew she needed help. I told her you'd be here today—and that you could help her."

Elizabeth nodded, wondering at this unorthodox approach to social services. But in her profession, she had to be open to people in need, even when they didn't necessarily go through normal channels.

Wendy picked up her baby and went upstairs, leaving Elizabeth alone with the other woman.

"How can I help you?" she asked.

Sabrina licked her lips and spoke haltingly in heavily accented English. "Pardon me if I don't speak too good."

"You're doing fine."

"I thought to come to this country because there is nothing for me back home." She stopped and swallowed hard. "I had some money saved. I paid it to a man who said he could get me into America—and get me a good job."

When she stopped talking, Elizabeth prompted her. "And what happened?"

"He got me here. Me and other women. We traveled in a big shipping container."

"My Lord."

"It wasn't so bad. We had light in there, and food and

toilets. But then we got to Baltimore, and I found it was all a big lie. Men were here to meet us. They took us to a house where they forced us…" She stopped then started again. "Forced us to be prostitutes."

Elizabeth sucked in a sharp breath. "I'm sorry."

"They had us under guard, at a house way out in the country, but I was able to escape."

"How?"

"A man wanted to take me home for the weekend. He paid a lot of money for that, and I hit him over the head, stole some of his money and got away. I know that attacking him and stealing from him was wrong, but I had to do it."

"What he was doing was wrong."

Sabrina nodded. "Yes."

"But why is this happening in Baltimore?"

"Some of the girls had relatives in the city. That's why they came here. We had talked about this area, and I knew the part of the city where people from my country lived. I found this neighborhood. I was starving on the street, and Wendy helped me." She gave Elizabeth a pleading look. "I need to hide out from the man who is in charge of this shameful business. And I need to get the other girls out of that house."

Elizabeth was shuddering as she came back to the present. Tears leaked from her eyes as she looked down at Matt.

He rolled to his side, cradling her against himself. "You were investigating the smuggling ring."

"Yes."

"And it led you to Derek Lang."

"Yes. Sabrina had picked up his name at the bordello."

"Why didn't you turn him over to the cops?"

"Because I went to a fancy reception where he was. I saw him with a man who's high up in the police department, and I knew he was paying the guy off to look the other way. I was afraid that if I just turned him in, I'd end up dead."

"Which looks like it was the plan anyway."

"Obviously Lang found out I was poking into his business. I was staying in a motel room near home, while I figured out what to do." She made a low sound. "I left some of my stuff there."

"Like what?"

"Clothing. Toilet articles." She thought for a moment. "I guess nothing that would help them find me now."

"Right."

"When you didn't come back, the management probably went in and cleared it out."

"Did they save it, do you think?"

"Is there something important in your stuff?"

She laughed. "I did have some money."

"We'll have to think about whether it's worth trying to retrieve it—and paying your back rent."

"If we explain that I lost my memory, maybe they'll be… charitable."

"Maybe, but we've got more important issues."

"Yes. Like my car crash." She shook her head. "It's not my car. Susan, one of my coworkers, lent it to me because she was going out of the country and wouldn't need it."

"When this is over, we'll figure out what to do about that."

"I suddenly remember a lot more stuff."

"Good."

She gave him a direct look. "Well, it's not exactly coming at a convenient time. I mean I want to explore what I know about myself, but we can't while we're stuck in this mess."

"You remember something specific that you think is important?"

"Yes. You said your mother went to a fertility clinic in Houma, Louisiana."

"Yes."

"Would you believe, I remember *my* mother talking about it?"

"You do?"

She nodded. "That's the link we've been looking for between us. It can't be a coincidence. It has to have something
to do with our abilities."

"But first we have to deal with Lang and his thugs."

"Yes. I know they would have gotten me when I crashed
the car, but I think there were too many people around." She
dragged in a breath and let it out. "And now what are we
going to do—about us and the women?"

DEREK LANG RARELY permitted himself to be worried. He was
a visionary, but he was also a cautious man, with a firm handle on any situation into which he ventured. But this thing
with Elizabeth Forester was getting out of hand.

Lang had investigated Dr. Delano and found out he'd done
several years as a medic in Africa—during which he'd had
a number of hair-raising escapes from death. Apparently
those experiences had taught him how to defend himself.

He looked at Patterson, the man who'd been tasked with
guarding Forester's back door.

"How did they get past you?" he asked.

"They zapped me with something."

"Zapped?"

"Something like a Taser."

Derek's brow wrinkled. A Taser wasn't exactly a long-
distance weapon.

He asked for an account of the rest of the screwed-up
mission, listening as Southwell related finding Patterson
and then they both went into the house after the fugitives,
one from the front and one from the back.

"And how did they get out of that?"

"The doctor opened a window while they were in the
office."

Lang thought of saying that every exit should have been
covered, but of course, there had only been two guys on

the scene. Even so, he wanted to lash out at these men who had come back to him with bad news, but he wasn't going to waste the energy. And he'd better start looking for a replacement for Southwell. The man was simply making too many mistakes.

"Double the guard on The Mansion," he said.

"Yes, sir."

"And tell Susanna to come in here," he ordered.

She would do what she could to calm his frayed nerves.

Chapter Ten

"I'm thinking," Matt answered.

He didn't have to say more, because he knew Elizabeth was tapping in to his mental processes.

She went very still, when she realized what he had in mind. "Find the house?" she asked.

"Yeah."

She pressed her hand to her mouth, her face a study in concentration. "I…don't know where it is." Panic bloomed on her features. "Oh, Lord, Matt. What if all this has been for nothing?"

He wasn't going to simply give up. When he held out his arms, she hesitated for a moment, then came into them. He could feel her panic subsiding as she leaned into him. *Is the house in the city?*

I don't think so.

But you saw it?

Yes. I'm pretty sure I snuck up on it.

Let's go back there.

They both closed their eyes, and he pressed his cheek to hers, flooding power into her the way he had learned to do. For long moments he felt her frustration, until a picture of a large dwelling formed in her mind.

It was a Victorian mansion with three floors, a wide front porch and a newer wing on either side. It was painted a tasteful beige with darker trim. At one side he saw a paved lot where several high-end cars were parked. A brick path led from the lot to the front door. And the grounds around the house were nicely landscaped with azaleas, dogwoods and other typical local greenery.

That's it?

Yes. You'd never dream it was anything but a pretty rural residence. She gave a harsh laugh. *Or maybe an upscale bed-and-breakfast.*

How did you get close?

I waited until it was getting dark, then parked down the road and came through the woods.

You didn't get inside?

No. But I looked in the windows.

She stayed with the scene, and he got more than visual effects. From inside the house he heard soft jazz drifting toward him. It was accompanied by another picture that came to him of young pretty women wearing dressing gowns. Some were standing, others sitting in a nicely furnished room where men in sport shirts and slacks relaxed with drinks.

One of the men stood and held out his hand to a blond woman. She swallowed hard, then got up and walked ahead of him out of the room. He saw the man caress her bottom through her gown, saw her wince, then caught a glimpse of the couple climbing the stairs before they disappeared from sight.

He picked up the disgust in Elizabeth's memory as she backed away from the house and hurried across the neatly trimmed lawn. Turning around, she looked at the building again and froze. For the first time, she spotted a security camera she hadn't seen earlier. With a little gasp, she ran for the woods at the side of the house. But knew it was already too late.

"They must have seen you," he said aloud.

"Yes. I wasn't thinking about cameras. I only wanted to make sure that Sabrina was telling the truth." She made a soft moaning sound. "Oh, Lord, and I thought I was being so careful."

"Go back to the scene," he said.

He felt her resistance. She didn't want to go anywhere near the upscale prison where young women were being forced to service men who were willing to pay for the pleasure, but she did it because they were trying to save the women. Her head lay on his shoulder, but her mind flashed back to the memory, and he saw from her point of view as she ran frantically into the darkened woods. It took a few moments for her eyes to adjust to the gloom, and she stepped into a patch of brambles that tore at her clothing.

She wrenched herself away and veered to the left as she kept running, madly fleeing the house. And now he heard the sounds of heavy footsteps crashing through the underbrush after her.

"There she is."

"Don't let her get away."

Fear leaped inside her and kept her running as fast as she could. When a tree root snagged her foot, she almost crashed to the ground but caught herself against a tree and kept moving. She was breathing hard when she reached her car, opened the door with the remote and threw herself inside.

She gunned the engine and sped out of the woods, skidding as she turned right, then hurtled down the road, but Matt and she both knew she hadn't been in the clear.

When he felt her trembling, he soothed her. "It's okay."

"I made a mess of that."

"No. You got a look at the bordello—at what was going on in there."

Silently he asked her to return to the vision once again. She shook her head, hating to revisit the scene.

I think we can get information we need.

How?

Try it again. Get back into the car—when you were speed-ing away just now.

She put herself back into the vehicle. When she was sure she'd lost the pursuers, she slowed. Coming to a street sign, she saw she was on Sparks Road, and the cross street was York Road.

He squeezed her shoulder. "I think you've got it."

"Yes."

When she caught what was in his mind, she went rigid. "No."

"Yes. We have to make sure it's still business as usual out there."

"Then what?"

"I think I know what will work, but we have to make sure about the place."

He held her for a few moments longer, pulling her closer.

They'd both wanted to make love, yet now that she re-membered the fate of the women Lang had forced into sexual slavery, neither one of them was in the mood for lovemaking.

And again they didn't have to discuss anything out loud. They each knew what the other was thinking.

Finally he slipped away from her and sat up. "Come on." He felt her terror and also her determination. "You won't be alone."

"After everything that's happened, it's the only reason I can do it, I think."

Matt went to his computer and looked up the roads he'd seen in her mind.

They were in Harford County, and he mapped a route to the York and Sparks Roads.

He knew she didn't want to go back there, but he also un-derstood she had steeled herself to do what was necessary to bring down Derek Lang.

They drove north, and he followed her previous route in reverse. The farther they got up York Road, the more he could feel her tension. But she said nothing as he drove past the entrance to the house, which was on a two-lane rural road off Overbrook.

They came to a long drive with a small sign that said The Mansion. The house itself was up a long driveway, and you could barely see the house through the trees.

"Nice and private for the men who like to get their jollies here," he said.

"And hard for the girls to escape. They probably don't even know how close they are to the city." She shuddered. "I can't imagine how it is for them. They pay money to get out of their countries, and they're full of hope, thinking they're coming to something better. Then they end up *here*."

"You're going to get them out of the mess they're in."

"But Lang didn't just start with this shipment. He's been bringing in women for years. How many others did he lure here? And what happened to them?"

Knowing she was having trouble coping with the pain of the revelations, Matt reached over and covered her hand. "We can only deal with the situation that exists now."

"I know."

Getting back to practicalities, he said, "Last time, you parked on the other side of the property."

"Yes."

"Then let's go in from this side."

"Do you think they'll be looking for us?"

"Hard to say. Since you returned to your house, you could have your memory back. But they smashed your computer, so they may assume you can't find this location again."

"Let's hope that's what they think."

He pulled onto a dirt track and under some low-hanging trees that hid the car, then turned to Elizabeth.

"We need to make sure it's business as usual there. And we need to make sure nobody sees us, because if they do, they may well move the women."

"Yes."

It was getting dark, as it had been the first time Elizabeth had come here. This time they walked cautiously through the woods, being careful to make as little noise as possible.

Matt looked back the way they'd come, thinking that they might be in a hurry on the return trip.

When they got to the edge of the trees, he squeezed Elizabeth's hand.

"How far is the range of the cameras?" she asked.

"Probably not far, since they want to concentrate on the grounds near the house."

They were about fifty yards away, and they both stayed in the shadows under the trees as they looked toward the well-maintained structure.

"Quite a setup," Matt murmured.

"Nothing but the best for Lang's guests. Do you think he's actually here?" she asked.

"Probably not. He may steer clear of this place. I'm going to have a look. You stay here."

"Okay."

He caught the ambivalence in her mind. She hated sending him closer, yet she didn't want to get near the house herself.

Lamps were on all over the first floor. As in Elizabeth's earlier memory, light jazz drifted toward them. As he moved toward the house, he looked up and saw the nearest camera. Focusing on it, he sent a burst of energy toward it. When he heard a zapping sound, he knew he'd taken care of that problem.

Still he waited for any sign that he'd been spotted. Like on Elizabeth's previous trip, he had a good view in through the windows. He saw casually dressed men looking like they were at a party, a well-dressed older woman who must be the hostess, and women in nightwear who looked out of place in the expensively furnished rooms.

Having confirmed that this was the right location, he

was about to turn around and head back to the woods when he heard Elizabeth crying out a warning inside his mind.

Watch out.

But it was already too late. In the next moment, a rough voice ordered, "Hold it right there and raise your hands above your head."

With a silent curse, Matt stopped in his tracks, upbraiding himself for being too focused on the view inside the building.

"Turn around," the rough voice ordered.

There was no real choice, since running for it would only get him a bullet in the back. He turned and found himself facing a bald man dressed in a dark shirt and slacks. It wasn't anyone he recognized from his previous brushes with Lang's thugs.

"We're going inside," Baldy said.

Matt eyed him, thinking that he could send a bolt of power at the guy, but that was dangerous with the man's finger on the trigger of a gun pointed at Matt.

And then he heard Elizabeth's voice in his head, telling him what he'd told her back at Polly Kramer's house.

Drop to the ground.

She was fifteen yards away, and he didn't know if she could reach the guy from there. But he did what she said, watching the man with the gun gasp and topple over. And luckily, he didn't alert anyone else by pulling the trigger as he went down.

Elizabeth sprinted out of the woods. Matt clicked the safety on the gun and set it on the man's abdomen. Together they dragged the guy across the lawn and under the trees.

Matt turned to look back the way they'd come. As far as he could see, no one else had noticed the capture.

Thanks, he said to Elizabeth.

I should have seen him sooner, but I was focused on you. She looked down at the guy, who was about Matt's height, with bulging muscles and a swarthy complexion. *What are*

*we going to do? You said that if anyone saw us, they might
shut down the operation out here.*

Yeah. I'm thinking.

Can we...zap his brain or something?

It might do him permanent damage.

Do you care?

He considered the question. He was a doctor, dedicated
to treating illness and injury. But in Africa he'd gotten used
to the truth that if someone was trying to do you harm, you
might have to beat him to the punch.

No, he answered.

How do we do it?

Aim a blast at his head, he said, then considered the answer more carefully.

"We don't want him to come out of this like a vegetable."

"Why not?"

"Better if he just has a memory gap. If it looks like he
had a stroke, they might take him to the hospital and find
something...off."

"Then what do we do instead?"

"Blast his hippocampus."

"Which is?"

"One of the areas of the brain that governs short-term
memory. The other is the subiculum, which is next to it, but
that's only for *very* short term."

He knew that they didn't have time for a medical-school
lecture, but he sent her a picture of the brain, showing her
the hippocampi, which were actually two horseshoe-shaped
structures, one in the left-brain hemisphere and the other
in the right.

"It takes in memories and sends them out to the appropriate part of the cerebral hemisphere where they are retrieved
when necessary."

He knew she was studying the picture he'd sent.

The hippocampus. It's kind of at the bottom.

Yeah. He pulled at the limp body of the unconscious man, arranging him so that his knees were under him, his butt was in the air, and the back of his head was facing upward at an angle.

He didn't have to tell Elizabeth to give him power. She simply did it, and he felt it gathering inside himself—before he directed a thin stream of lightning at the back of the man's head. The guy's body jerked, and he fell over on his side.

Did that do it? Elizabeth asked.

Let's hope so. And there's one more thing we'd better do.

He picked up the gun, wiped it off with his shirttail, and put it into the man's hand.

Elizabeth tugged at Matt's arm. *Come on. Let's make tracks.*

Right.

They both headed back the way they'd come, making a wide circle around the man they'd left lying on the ground.

When they reached their car, he wanted to stop and pull her close, but he knew that the first thing they had to do was get away—before more of Lang's thugs came after them.

They both got into the car, and Matt drove off, thankful that nobody was shooting at them.

I'm hoping life isn't going to be a series of narrow escapes, she whispered in his mind.

We'll be a lot safer when Lang is out of the picture.

Chapter Eleven

Tony Verrazano rolled to his back trying to figure out where he was and what had happened to him.

He was outside. Yeah. He'd been on patrol at The Mansion.

But now he was lying on the hard ground with his head aching like a son of a bitch. His gun was in his hand, and he didn't remember drawing it. In fact, he couldn't call up any memories from the past few minutes.

How had he gotten here?

He struggled to pull anything recent into his mind, but nothing would come to him. In a panic, he sat up too quickly and winced at the stab of pain. After checking the safety on the gun, he stuffed it into his shoulder holster, then pulled up his knees and clasped his hands around his legs. Pressing his cheek to his knees, he ordered himself not to start shaking.

Something frightening had happened, and he didn't know what it was. Worse, he didn't even know how he'd gotten here. Yeah, he'd thought that before, hadn't he?

Still clenching his hands around his legs—he carefully went back to the last thing he did remember. He'd had a meal in the kitchen of the whorehouse where Lang kept the girls he'd imported from Eastern Europe. Then he'd gone out on patrol.

He'd been walking the ground, and something must have happened to him.

But what?

Had he seen something in the woods? Gone in here to have a look? And then what?

Nothing like this had ever happened to him before, and he struggled to tamp down the fear coursing through him.

Should he tell someone? What if an intruder had invaded the property? Like the woman who had been here a week ago. She was still on the loose, and the boss had ordered all the guards to be extravigilant.

But he didn't think she was here now. Or at least he didn't want it to be true. He got up and brushed off his clothing, feeling a lot of dirt on the back of his pants, like he'd been dragged into the trees. Could that be true?

Fear trickled down the back of his spine as he scrambled to come up with an alternative scenario. Maybe he'd been investigating something in the woods, tripped over a tree root in the dark, fallen down, hit his head and knocked himself out.

Clumsy of him.

Well, he wasn't going to say anything about it and risk getting fired from what he considered a very good job.

"Now what?" Elizabeth asked as they put distance between themselves and The Mansion.

"We shut the place down."

"I hate the idea of letting that house of horrors operate for even the rest of today, but there's another reason we can't just go to the police. Those women are in the U.S. illegally. Probably they'll all be deported if we just call the cops."

"Yeah, even if they were brought here under false pretenses, they could be caught in the system."

She sighed. "I wish I knew more about it. I don't want to get them deported because I'm trying to help them." She thought for a moment. "Maybe my best bet is going back to Sabrina and seeing if there's some way her friends in Baltimore can shelter them."

He made a rough sound. "We're getting ourselves in deeper every time we turn around."

"I know. But I want those women out of there—then to find a way to destroy Lang's whole operation."

"That's a tall order. How long has he been in business?"

"I don't know exactly." She gave him a pleading look. "I realize this whole thing is a mess, but I want to see it through. Not just for me. Polly died because I was stalking Lang."

Relief flooded through her when he said, "Okay."

"I think we have to go find Sabrina."

He tightened his hands on the wheel.

She put her fingers on his arm, and she knew she didn't have to speak out loud for him to pick up what was in her mind. He turned off onto a two-lane road and slowed, finding a clearing where he could pull off the blacktop.

"You want to talk about how we're going to work it when we go back to the house?" he asked.

"Yes."

"What was your original plan?"

She flung her arm in frustration. "I wish I knew. Probably I hadn't come up with anything definite, which was why I hadn't acted."

"But you're thinking about something that might help."

She grinned. "You read me so well."

When he'd cut the engine, she unbuckled her seat belt and leaned toward him. Reaching for her, he pulled her close. They clung together, both of them thankful that they'd gotten away from The Mansion.

She pulled away so she could look at him. *What if we have a technique we can use?*

He knew she was thinking about a book she'd read—about a girl whose parents had been part of a government drug experiment in college. The people who survived came away with superpowers. For example, the girl's father had been able to influence the actions of others.

Did you read it? she asked.

Yes. It's by Stephen King.

In the book, the father called his power "giving people a push"—influencing their actions and perceptions.

And you think we can do that? Isn't that a little grandiose? he asked.

We won't know until we try it.

"We'd have to practice to make sure we could do it," he said.

"Of course."

"Who do we practice on?"

"I don't know yet."

He switched topics and asked, "Do you know the part of Baltimore where you met with Sabrina?"

"Yes. I think that's where I was going when I crashed my car." She gave him directions, and they drove back to the city.

"But you don't know exactly where to find Sabrina," he said as they got closer to the right part of town.

"I think I only knew her through Wendy—the woman who adopted a child and was one of my clients."

"Then we'll start there."

They drove to a neighborhood of typical Baltimore row houses, some with brick fronts and some faced with a man-made material that was supposed to resemble stone but looked more like something from a kid's construction set. Elizabeth had always wondered why anyone would want to put that stuff on a home.

"You know which house?" he asked.

"No. But I think I'll recognize it when I see it."

He drove up and down several blocks, and she scanned the facades, looking for some kind of clue.

Finally she saw a house with a planter full of geraniums beside the marble steps. "That's it!"

Matt found a parking space around the corner, and they walked back, then climbed the steps.

After ringing the bell, Elizabeth waited with her heart pounding because she didn't know what the woman inside looked like, but she was pretty sure she'd recognize her when she saw her.

The door opened, and Wendy stood on the other side of the storm door, an expression on her face that was a mixture of astonishment and anger.

"You said you'd come back days ago," she accused. "Where have you been? We've been waiting and worrying. I called social services, and they said you had...disappeared."

Elizabeth swallowed hard. "I'm sorry. Can we come in?"

Wendy looked like she was about to refuse.

Matt pressed his shoulder to Elizabeth's, and she suddenly knew that he was going to use the technique they'd discussed. *Don't turn Elizabeth away. She had a good reason for not coming.*

Elizabeth fought to keep her gaze on Wendy. They'd only speculated about trying this, and Matt doing it now had taken her completely by surprise. But had it worked? Especially since she hadn't even thought about giving him extra power.

"Is there a good reason why you didn't come back?" Wendy asked.

"She was in the hospital. I'm her doctor."

"Oh, I'm sorry," Wendy said. "You'd better come in."

They both stepped directly into a small living room with a bay window that looked onto the street. The room was cluttered with toys. When Wendy knelt to sweep some blocks into a pile, Elizabeth bent down also to help her, remembering the little girl who was so lucky to be living here.

"How's Olivia?" she asked.

"She's doing great. She's already in bed."

Elizabeth picked up a floppy stuffed rabbit from the sofa and stroked it. "I remember this room," she said.

"What do you mean?" Wendy asked.

"I had amnesia. That's why I didn't come back. Matt—Dr. Delano is helping me recover my memories."

"Oh, you poor thing," Wendy said. "Where are my manners? Please sit down."

Elizabeth and Matt sat together on the couch. Wendy looked at Matt, then Elizabeth, then back again. "You look more like her lover than her doctor."

Elizabeth flushed at the directness of the statement.

"We've gotten to know each other pretty well," Matt said. "Elizabeth was on the way here, to your meeting, when she was in an automobile accident."

"I didn't know."

"She was banged up, but the main problem was the amnesia. It took a while for us to put you and your friend Sabrina back into the picture."

Wendy nodded.

"We've been working on her memories, and she finally recalled enough to come here."

Again Wendy nodded cautiously.

"But there are things we can't piece together."

"Like what?"

"Sabrina said that friends of hers are being held at a house owned by...."

Wendy glanced toward the door, like she expected thugs to come charging in. "Derek Lang," she whispered.

"Yes. I didn't know how much I'd told you," Elizabeth said.

"A lot of it. Not everything."

"We need to talk to Sabrina."

Once again, they met resistance.

"I don't know," Wendy said. "It was hard enough for her to come here the first time. That Lang man is dangerous."

"Believe me, I know," Elizabeth murmured as she gripped the floppy rabbit she was still holding.

Beside her, Elizabeth heard Matt's silent suggestion. *Why don't we try again to influence her?*

All right.

She looked at Wendy. "I'm really sorry that I couldn't get back here sooner. Just now, Matt and I went out to the property and confirmed that the women are there. We need Sabrina's help to get them somewhere safe."

"You mean to the shelter where she is now?"

"Yes." Elizabeth had forgotten that Sabrina had hooked up with a secret welfare organization that was willing to take in illegal aliens. Thankful that problem had been solved, she silently urged Wendy, *Get up and call Sabrina. Tell her that I've come back, that I was in an accident, that I had amnesia and couldn't make it here sooner.*

She felt Matt adding power to help her project the unspoken message. Her pulse was pounding as she waited to find out what would happen. After a few seconds, she saw Wendy's face change.

"I guess it's not your fault that you didn't meet up with us."

This time it was Matt who sent the message. As soon as she heard it, Elizabeth sent him power to help project the suggestion.

Yes, that's right. Tell Sabrina to come right over. Tell her we need to speak to her.

Wendy stood up. "Let me go phone her."

"Thank you," Elizabeth answered. *We got her to change her mind,* she said to Matt.

But we don't know how effective we were. All we know is what she did. She could have made the decision on her own.

But she was reluctant to even let us come in before you... pushed her.

We'll see.

HAROLD GODDARD HADN'T forgotten about Matthew Delano. He had a service checking for any mention of the man's name—in print or on the internet—and so far it was like the doctor had disappeared off the face of the earth. Harold would have liked to think that no news was good news. In this case, he couldn't convince himself it was true.

So he kept checking and waiting for the other shoe to drop. Like what was going on with the woman named Jane Doe? Who was she really? He had a pretty good idea. Not her specific name. But he wouldn't be at all surprised to find out that her mother had been treated at the Solomon Clinic.

There was no proof of that yet, but he was willing to bet there would be.

And if there was one thing Harold didn't like, it was losing control of a situation. He'd deliberately thrown other couples together so he could watch what happened. Now he was pretty sure two others had gotten together on their own, and there was no telling where they were or what they would do. But he had the feeling he'd better be prepared for trouble.

Chapter Twelve

Matt and Elizabeth sat tensely on the sofa, waiting for Wendy to return. Elizabeth wanted to get up and follow her down the hall, but she suspected that the woman had deliberately left the room to give herself some privacy.

Too bad we can't amplify hearing, Matt murmured inside her head.

She answered with a small nod.

Their tension mounted with every minute Wendy was away, and Elizabeth started imagining all sorts of scenarios—like Derek Lang walking in the front door.

But finally Wendy returned with a cautious smile on her face.

"Sabrina's coming over."

Just then, a wailing cry from upstairs made Elizabeth jump.

"That's Olivia," Wendy said, "probably telling me that she needs her diaper changed."

She departed again, but this time Elizabeth felt relieved. They'd cleared one hurdle.

Ten minutes later Wendy was back, holding a one-year-old girl.

"Do you remember Miss Elizabeth?" she asked.

The little girl pointed to Elizabeth. When her mother set her down on the floor, she crawled toward the sofa and pulled herself up, grabbing on to Elizabeth's knee to steady herself.

"I'll be right back with a bottle," her mother said.

Elizabeth offered the little girl the bunny, and she snatched it away, hugging it.

This was familiar and bringing back more memories. She remembered that Wendy was a good mother—and willing to help the women who'd ended up in Derek Lang's clutches.

When Wendy returned, she unfolded the playpen by the window and set her daughter inside.

Olivia lay on her back, kicking her feet in the air as she held the bottle and sucked. Elizabeth watched the baby, thinking how sweet she was. But was she bringing danger to this family just by being in this house?

Lang doesn't know we're here, Matt said, and Elizabeth knew he'd caught the drift of her thoughts.

We should get out as soon as possible.

When the back door opened, she jumped, but she relaxed when she saw Sabrina striding down the hall. She was a woman of medium height, with short blond hair and cautious eyes. She looked delicate, but obviously had inner strength—and the courage and determination to get herself out of a bad situation.

When she spoke, it was with the thick accent Elizabeth remembered. But the words were not what Elizabeth had expected to hear.

"Are you the woman who was staying with that nurse when she was murdered?"

Elizabeth sucked in a sharp breath. "How do you know about that?"

"It was all over the news. And Wendy said that you claimed you had amnesia."

"I didn't claim. It's true."

"You're not just saying it to get out of helping us?"

Beside her Elizabeth could feel Matt sending the newcomer soothing thoughts.

*It's all right. You were expecting Elizabeth to help you.
You were scared and angry when she didn't come back. But
now she's here, and she's going to help you like she promised.*

Elizabeth saw Sabrina relax fractionally.

"I'm sorry I left you in the lurch," Elizabeth said.

"But you were staying with that nurse?"

"Yes. Are you going to call the police and tell them where
I am? If they drag me into the investigation of Polly's death,
then I won't be able to help you get your friends away from
Lang."

Sabrina answered with a small nod.

"Lang's men were chasing me the day I was supposed
to meet you. That's why I crashed my car, hit my head and
ended up with amnesia. I couldn't meet you because I didn't
remember anything."

Sabrina struggled to hold back a sob. "I waited for hours."

"I'm so sorry."

"I thought you'd changed your mind. Or…or you were
too scared to do it."

"No. I still wasn't sure how to get in there, but now I have
a plan," she said.

She knew Matt caught her thoughts when his hand closed
around her arm. "No," he said.

"Can you think of anything better?" she asked.

After long seconds she felt his acquiescence and looked
back at Sabrina. "Matt's going to get in there by pretending
to be a customer. And I'm going to slip in the back way and
mingle with the women. While Matt keeps the men away,
I'll get the women out."

"You wanted to shut down his operation," Sabrina pointed
out.

Elizabeth nodded. "I don't know if we can go that far.
But we can rescue the girls who are there. And after every-

body's out, we can burn the house down. That will set him back while we figure out the next step."

Sabrina looked torn. "I want him in jail for what he's done to me and the others."

"I do too, but it might not be possible." She changed the subject. "And you have that secret welfare organization ready to take them in and hide them until they can get new identities?"

"Yes." She turned her gaze on Elizabeth. "Can we go get my friends tonight?"

"It's better if we have everything planned. You need to get the welfare group ready with transportation, and Matt and I need to rehearse our roles," she answered.

Sabrina's expression turned fierce. "You want me to get a rescue operation organized tomorrow. How do I know that you're not going to disappear again?"

Elizabeth felt her heart squeeze. "I can't absolutely guarantee what's going to happen tomorrow night," she said. "But Matt and I plan to be there."

It was the best she could do, and she let out a sigh of relief when Sabrina nodded. "Where are we going to meet? How are we going to do it?"

Elizabeth hadn't thought about all the details, and because this woman was pressing her, she felt like the room was closing in on her.

Matt gave Sabrina an angry look. "I know you're worried about your friends, and I know you're anxious to get them out of Lang's clutches, but Elizabeth has already been through a lot because she committed herself to helping them. She's almost gotten killed more than once."

As he spoke aloud, Elizabeth knew he was sending Sabrina a soundless message. *Don't lean on Elizabeth. She's doing everything she can. She'll be ready tomorrow night. All you have to do is have a van ready to take your friends away from The Mansion.*

She saw Sabrina take a breath and let it out. "I'm sorry," she whispered. "I know I'm not making this any easier for you."

"It's okay," Elizabeth managed to say, then cleared her throat. "I told you that I had a memory loss when I crashed my car and everything hasn't come back to me yet."

Sabrina nodded.

"I need to ask you some questions. You might have answered them before, but I don't remember some details."

"I'll answer what I can."

"There are men at The Mansion who act as guards, but who is it that greets guests?"

"Mrs. Vivian."

"Where will she be?"

"Probably mingling with guests. She might also be near the door."

"I saw men eating and drinking."

"The Mansion orders a lot of prepared food. And the bar is always stocked."

"Is there any place the women aren't allowed to go?"

"They usually stay in the front."

"I'll be dressed like one of the women, but I'll probably have to come in through the kitchen."

"You could say you were getting a snack for a patron."

"Okay."

"How many bedrooms?" Matt asked.

"Eight."

"So each girl doesn't have her own room?"

"No. They bunk together, and use the nice bedrooms for entertaining guests."

"How many women will be there?" Matt asked.

"Twelve to fifteen."

They discussed more of the layout, before Elizabeth asked, "Will there be a problem getting the women to come with me?"

Sabrina's brow wrinkled as she considered the question. "Mention my name, and tell them I sent you to get them out."

"But there could be women you don't know."

And one of them could give her away, Elizabeth was thinking, but she didn't say it aloud because she didn't want to make it sound like she was coming up with objections.

"Are there guards inside the house?" she asked.

"In a guard station down the hall from the kitchen. They watch TV screens there."

The monitors for the cameras, Matt said.

Yes. Finally she knew that she'd gotten all the information she could before actually going into The Mansion.

"We should leave now," Matt said. "Can you give me the address of the shelter where you're going to take the women?"

Sabrina gave him an address several blocks away.

"We'll meet there at seven tomorrow night," he said, then stepped to the door and scanned the street. When he saw nothing suspicious, he ushered Elizabeth out.

They walked around the corner to his car, and she dropped into the passenger seat.

"Thank God I've got you," she whispered. "How did I ever think I could do this myself?"

"You had the courage to do it, but you didn't count on the lengths Lang would take to get you out of the way."

"Stupid of me."

"Of course not."

"I guess I didn't realize how ruthless he is."

"Because your background and training make you think about helping people—not hurting them."

When she started to speak, he leaned over and pressed his lips to hers. *But you do have me,* he said. *And we'll do it together.*

She wrapped her arms around his neck and leaned into the kiss.

They embraced for long moments, and she thought again how lucky she was to have found this man who was strong and determined—with the survival skills she lacked.

She knew he heard that when he smiled against her mouth. *I'm so open to you,* she silently murmured.

Likewise.

When she caught the thought in his mind, her breath stilled.

I love you.

Oh, Matt.

You had to know it was true.

But I never expected it—not ever in my life. I was always so alone.

And you know I was, too.

"I love you," she said aloud, knowing there was no need to speak. But she wanted to say the words because they were important to her.

She would have been overwhelmed by happiness, yet she couldn't allow herself that joy. Not yet. "We have a job to do," she whispered.

"And when we're finished, we can figure out what we're going to do for the rest of our lives."

"It will be easier if we can prove we had nothing to do with Polly's death," she said.

"I'm hoping that we can get evidence after we take care of Lang." He pulled away from the curb, heading for the motel.

"We still have to practice the skills we're going to need to pull off the rescue operation at The Mansion."

"And it's not going to be as easy as persuading two women who wanted to believe our story."

"I wouldn't exactly call Sabrina easy," she argued. "She was upset—and that made her angry with me."

"But I want to work on a person who isn't involved with us, and get him to do something totally against their best interests. Like in a restaurant."

She caught what was in his mind. "Is that fair?"

"This is love and war. And it's not like we're robbing a bank."

She understood his logic, but she still didn't like what he was planning.

When they returned to the vicinity of the motel, Matt drove around the restaurant area, looking for a place that was a cut above the fast-food restaurants with drive-in windows. He found a small Italian restaurant that didn't appear to be part of a chain.

"Do you want to do try and influence the counter men, or should I?" he asked.

"In this case, I think a guy will be more persuasive. If you can do it at all."

"Just give me some psychic energy."

They walked into the dining room, which had a central aisle and tables on either side. Framed scenes of Italy decorated the stuccoed walls. At the back was a counter with a menu above it. Two young men with short dark hair wearing white uniforms were behind the counter.

"Help you?" one of the men asked.

Matt studied the menu, and Elizabeth felt him getting ready to tell a whopper. "We have one of your certificates for a free meal," he said.

"We don't…" The man stopped in midsentence, looking confused.

Elizabeth could hear Matthew furiously projecting false information. *You believe me. I have a certificate that gives me a thirty-dollar free meal. It's a new offer, and I'm the first customer to cash it in.* He opened his wallet, took out a business card he'd gotten from a colleague and held it up. "See, here's my certificate." *And you don't need to take it away. You just need to look at it,* he added without saying anything aloud.

Elizabeth held her breath as she waited to find out what

would happen. Giving away food was so clearly against the restaurant's best interests that it seemed impossible that the guy would go along with Matt's suggestion.

The counterman eyed the card and nodded. "I am not familiar with it, but I guess it's okay—since you got this thing."

She could feel Matt relax a little as he turned to her. "What do you want, honey?"

She looked at the food that had already been prepared. "A calzone would be good."

"Make it two," Matt said. "And add a couple of sodas."

While the man was packing up the order, Matt made a silent suggestion. *We haven't spent near thirty dollars. Why don't you suggest that we take a couple cannolis?*

His audacity took Elizabeth's breath away, but she stood without speaking beside him, waiting to see if it worked.

"You haven't used the whole thirty dollars. How about two cannolis for dessert?" the counterman asked.

"Great idea," Matt agreed.

Elizabeth shot him a look as she waited for the man to come to his senses, but he cheerfully packed up the food and drinks and handed over the bag.

"Thanks," Matt said as they strolled out.

Elizabeth was in more of a hurry and had to keep herself from running to the car.

Once inside, she breathed out a deep sigh. "I guess if we ran out of money, we could work as con artists."

"It's only a temporary necessity—I hope. I mean until we get out from under the Lang problem and clear our names."

As they drove back to the motel, she could hear ideas flashing in Matt's mind. He was thinking about the next evening's raid on The Mansion.

But as soon as they entered the room and closed the door, he set the food down on the table and reached for her.

She came into his arms with a small sob.

"I'm sorry. I know you hate all this. You don't like stealing food, and you don't like the plans I'm making."

"I'd like to forget about them right now," she said.

He lowered his mouth to hers for a kiss that told her that he'd been wanting to be alone with her for hours.

She wiped everything from her mind but the feel of him, the taste, the emotions running wild between them. And when he pulled back the spread and took her down to the surface of the bed, she held on to him, then rolled far enough away so that she could tear off her slacks and panties.

He was doing something similar, only his pants didn't come all the way off. She pushed the sides of the zipper away and pulled his briefs down, freeing his erection. With his legs trapped, they didn't have many options. She straddled him, bringing him inside her before she began to move in a frantic rhythm that brought them both to climax almost immediately.

She collapsed on top of him, and his arms came up to fold her close.

As they clung together, he whispered, "It's going to be all right."

"We'll be walking into danger."

He asked the question she'd asked before. "Can you think of a better plan?"

Of course she couldn't. She hadn't been able to do that in the first place. And now the moment of reckoning was coming all too fast.

"We should eat before the food gets cold."

"Eat our ill-gotten gains?"

"Uh-huh."

"We should pay for it."

"We'll send the restaurant some money—when this is all over and we have access to our bank accounts."

"If it's ever all over." She gave him a fierce look. Tomor-

row they were going to do their damnedest to take care of
Lang's operation.

"Then on to the next problem," he said. They both knew
that was solving the puzzle of how they'd ended up with
powers that had only become accessible when they'd touched
each other.

Chapter Thirteen

Derek Lang balled his hands into fists, then ordered himself to relax. It seemed like Elizabeth Forester had dropped off the face of the earth. It could be that she'd cut her losses and cleared out of town, but he wouldn't bet on it.

When he'd figured out that she was poking into his business, he had started digging up everything he could about the nosy bitch. One thing he knew was that she was persistent. Once she got a notion in her head, she wasn't going to let it go. Which meant that he'd better be prepared for whatever she had in mind.

He called in Gary Southwell, noting the way the man fought to hide his case of nerves.

"Did you get a report from The Mansion?" Derek asked.

"Yes. Everything's normal out there, except one of the cameras malfunctioned."

"Why?"

"We don't know."

"There's no chance someone could have tampered with it?"

"Not unless they climbed up on the roof."

"Who was on duty at the time?"

Southwell named several men, including Tony Verrazano.

"Any of them report anything unusual?"

"No, sir."

"Well, I want everyone extra-alert."

ELIZABETH AND MATT spent the day preparing for their invasion of The Mansion. After breakfast they both went to a local department store where Elizabeth bought a negligee like the ones she'd seen the women wearing. None of them had been wearing underwear. But because she hated the idea of walking around in a gown so revealing, she also purchased a chemise she could wear underneath.

Matt bought a sport coat and slacks on sale, an outfit that would make him look like the bordello's upscale patrons.

"We'd better stop at a drugstore," she said when they were finished with the clothes shopping. "I need some cosmetics, or I'm going to look out of place in there."

She'd already bought gray eye shadow and lipstick. She added foundation, eyeliner, blusher and mascara, going for products that weren't too expensive and hoping she'd be able to apply them artfully.

She and Matt brought lunch back to the motel room and spent the next few hours discussing various scenarios, but it was clear they could only go so far with the plans. Neither one of them knew exactly what was going to happen when they arrived at the bordello, and all they could do was outline several contingencies—which basically involved Matt keeping the management busy at the front of the house while she got the women out the back.

"How are you going to get away?" she asked.

"The same way I got in."

"You may need me to reinforce the messages you're sending. I can…"

He gave her a grim look. "Once you get the women out of there, you will not go back in."

She knew she had to agree, and she worked hard to keep him from realizing that she might not be able to keep her word.

"Get some sleep," he told her as she paced the motel room.

"I don't know if I can."

He closed the drapes, then lay down in the bed with her, cradling her in his arms.

They were both too keyed up to sleep, but it was a comfort to have him hold her.

Finally it was time to start getting ready.

"We should eat. I'll get more burgers and shakes."

"This isn't exactly a healthy diet."

"But it will have to do for now."

When he came back with the food, Elizabeth could barely choke any down. Finally she gave up, changed into the chemise and gown she'd bought and went into the bathroom to start playing with the cosmetics.

She began with foundation, then went on to lipstick, eyeliner, blusher and eye shadow. Standing back, she studied the effect, astonished at how different she looked. Then she finished it off with two applications of mascara.

When she came out, Matt did a double take.

"Wow."

"You like the effect?"

"You know I do." He eyed the gown. "I guess you fixed it so you can't see through it."

"I hope so."

She slipped her feet into mules, then reached for the light raincoat she'd bought.

Glad it was already getting dark, she crossed to the car and got in. And then they were on their way to the rendezvous spot.

When they arrived, Sabrina was pacing back and forth, looking anxious. As they pulled up, she visibly relaxed.

"I wasn't sure you'd come."

"I understand, but I had no intention of backing out," Elizabeth answered.

Sabrina introduced them to a woman named Brenda who worked at the shelter.

"Thank you for doing this," she said. "We can give them a

safe harbor once they come to us, but we're an underground organization, and we can't call attention to ourselves."

"I know that," Elizabeth answered. "But we'll get them to safety."

Brenda nodded, and Elizabeth wondered if the woman thought she could really pull this off.

As it turned out, Brenda was part of the operation. She would drive the van, and Sabrina would come along to help calm the women and keep order.

Matt would have to go in his own car because he'd be arriving at the front door like any normal customer.

She saw the tension on his face and knew he was worried about her. "I'll be okay."

"Just be careful." He turned to Sabrina. "Can you give the names of some of the men who…you were with in the house?"

"I don't know any of their last names."

"Give me some first names."

"There was Harry. Another one was Martin."

"Okay. I can use that. And you said the woman who runs the place is Mrs. Vivian."

"Yes."

"Then we're all set," he said, projecting confidence. He turned back to Elizabeth. "See you soon."

She gave him a fierce hug before climbing into the van. She could still feel his worry as Brenda drove away, and she kept up the connection with him as long as she could. When it snapped off, she clenched her fists, feeling suddenly very alone. She had gotten used to reaching for his mind, and now the connection had been cut off. But she'd get it again, she told herself. He'd be following in his car, and he'd arrive twenty minutes after she did.

She refocused her attention on her current reality.

"Don't head straight for the house," she told Brenda. "Drive past, and I'll show you where to park."

She directed Brenda up a dirt road into the woods to the place she and Matt had used when they came to check out The Mansion.

"Do you want me to come with you?" Sabrina asked.

"I appreciate the offer," Elizabeth told her. "But I think you should stay at the edge of the woods. That way, I'll be alone and less conspicuous."

She saw relief flood Sabrina's features. Although she knew the other woman had been prepared to go in if necessary, she also knew that the worst experiences of her life had taken place in that house. And the idea of stepping back into The Mansion terrified her. Elizabeth also knew Sabrina would have done it if Elizabeth had asked.

They made their way through the darkened woods, using the lights from the house as a beacon and circling around so that they were opposite the kitchen door.

Elizabeth and Matt had discussed how to handle the cameras. They'd already disabled one, and doing it again might put the security staff on alert. They'd decided her best bet was to keep her head down and walk to the back door. She wouldn't be visible until she was close, and hopefully anyone watching would think one of the girls had just slipped outside for a minute.

She watched for the guards she and Matt had seen. Just after one walked across the lawn between her and house, she strode across the lawn and made it to the back stoop, where she stood shaking, waiting for someone to burst outside and grab her. After more than a minute had passed, she breathed out a little sigh.

She'd gotten this far without any problems, but now came the real test.

Cautiously she tiptoed to the window beside the back door and looked in. A man who was probably one of the security staff was in the kitchen helping himself to food from the refrigerator, and she waited with her heart pounding while he loaded a plate.

Don't sit down at the kitchen table, she told him over and over. *Take the food where you'll be more comfortable.*

Her breath was shallow as she waited to see what he would do. He stood in the kitchen for endless seconds, holding the plate, before finally walking out of the room with the food.

When he was gone, she remembered to breathe again. She wanted to get this over with, yet she was glad that she'd had a little more time before she had to go in there.

She turned the knob and pushed the door open, then stepped inside and quietly closed it behind her.

Taking a few steps forward, she looked for the back stairs that Sabrina had told her about. She also saw a short hallway and knew it led to the guard station. She didn't want to go there, but it had to be a priority.

"Get it over with," she ordered herself, then crossed to the hallway and tiptoed farther into the house. At the end of the hall, she could see a small room with monitors flickering. The man who'd gotten the food was sitting with his back to her, looking at screens showing various views of the grounds. The plate was on a table beside him. Apparently he'd left his post and hadn't been looking at the monitors when she'd crossed the lawn.

Gathering her power, she sent a beam of energy to the back of his head, holding it as long as she could, hoping she'd put him in a coma.

Because tying him up would be too suspicious, she left him there and headed back toward the steps. She paused at the top, getting her bearings.

From the shadows where she stood, she saw a middle-aged man and a young brunette woman step out of a bedroom, and she pressed herself against the wall. But the guy wasn't paying any attention to her. His attention was focused on his companion.

He gave her a familiar pat on the rear, then strode to the front steps. The brunette was achingly young looking, and Elizabeth could only imagine what the poor girl had been through since leaving her own country.

She stood staring after her customer, a resigned expression on her face, then glanced up as Elizabeth hurried toward her.

Her expression turned to one of surprise as she stared at the woman who had materialized in the hallway.

"Who are you? Are you new here? Did you come in with another shipment?" she asked in heavily accented English.

"No. I'm helping Sabrina. I'm a social worker from Baltimore, and I met her there. I told her I'd come back here for the rest of you."

The statement was met with astonishment. "We haven't seen Sabrina in months."

"She's fine."

"Truly?"

"Yes. She and I worked out a plan to get the rest of you away from this place."

Fear and uncertainty flooded the woman's face. "You can't get us out of the house. We're guarded."

"Sabrina got out. You can too," Elizabeth answered, silently projecting the idea that escape from this hellhole was possible. "What's your name?"

"Maria."

"I'm Elizabeth."

"You're sure we can get away? And they won't kill us?" she asked in a shaky voice, her accent thickening with her mixed emotions.

"Yes. Do you know how many…guests are in the house?"

"Not many. It's still early."

"I need your help, Maria," Elizabeth said, projecting calm and certainty. "We need to get the other girls together."

Hope warred with fear on the woman's face. "Yes, all right. But some of them are downstairs, waiting for patrons."

"Get the ones up here together," Elizabeth said, knowing that they would have to wait for Matt to arrive to complete the mission.

MATT PULLED INTO the long drive and headed for the parking spaces at the front of The Mansion. There were only a couple cars already on site, and he was glad there wouldn't be too many civilians to deal with.

He got out, straightened his jacket and walked confidently to the front door, where he rang the bell.

After a few seconds, a nice-looking middle-aged woman opened the door. She was the woman he'd seen through the window when they were here the day before. Tonight she was wearing a beaded black dress and stylish pumps. She tipped her head to the side as she stared at him, obviously wondering who he was and how he'd gotten there.

"May I help you?"

"Mrs. Vivian?"

"Yes," she answered cautiously.

"I'm a friend of Harry's. He highly recommended this place if I wanted some relaxation."

"Harry who?"

"Harry," he repeated as he projected silent messages toward her. *I'm a friend of Harry. You trust Harry, and you trust me. You're so happy to have a new customer. You're glad Harry referred me. Let me in.*

He saw Mrs. Vivian wavering and poured on the reassuring messages.

"Come in," she finally said.

He stepped into the front hall, which was furnished with expensive-looking antiques. The hostess led him from there into an opulently furnished parlor. The rug on the polished wood floor was a palace-sized Oriental. The tables and chests were classic period pieces, and the sofas and chairs were comfortably modern.

"Harry told you our fees?" Mrs. Vivian murmured.

"Yes."

"You pay in advance."

"That's fine."

Five young women wearing negligees much like the one Elizabeth had donned were standing at one side of the room. They had been in various relaxed poses. When they saw him, they straightened, all of them arching their backs so that their breasts were thrust toward him.

So how did guys behave when they got here? Did they take some time to relax, or did they get right to business? Too bad he didn't have any experience with high-class bordellos. Or sex for hire.

He walked toward them, pretending he was trying to decide which one he wanted.

Unfortunately he couldn't just take all of them upstairs with him and disappear out the back way.

"What are your names?" he asked, stalling for time until he knew Elizabeth had gotten the first group out of the house.

They answered in turn, their English much like Sabrina's.

"Blossom."

"Daphne."

"Tara."

"Belinda."

"Jasmine."

"And what are you particularly good at?"

All of them flushed, but they began to name various sexual activities.

UPSTAIRS ELIZABETH WAITED in the hall. She'd heard the doorbell ring, and she prayed that Matt had arrived.

When she reached for his mind, she found him and breathed out a sigh of relief.

Everything okay? he asked.

Yes. I'm going to take a bunch of women down the back stairs and into the kitchen. If the coast is clear, I'll send them to Sabrina. She's waiting at the edge of the woods.

There are five women down here. I'll see if I can get them to the back of the house.

She broke off the voiceless conversation with Matt as Maria hurried back with six more women. Some looked frightened. Others doubtful.

"Everything's going to be all right. We'll go down the back stairs. The way I came up," Elizabeth said.

She debated whether to get them dressed in something more suitable for the outside, then decided that the better alternative was to get them away from the house as quickly as possible.

She put a finger to her lips in the universal symbol for quiet, then led the way down the stairs, pausing at the bottom to make sure that none of the guards had come back to get a snack.

The coast was clear, and she motioned for the others to follow.

The women peered around fearfully as they stepped into the kitchen, all of them looking like they expected a slave master to materialize out of nowhere and punish them for being downstairs.

It's all right. Everything's all right. You're perfectly safe. You're going to get away from here, Elizabeth kept assuring them. At the back door, she repeated the procedure she'd used when she arrived, waiting for a guard to pass. As soon as he had disappeared around the corner of the house, she opened the door and pointed toward the section of trees straight back from the door.

"Nobody is watching the video monitors. Sabrina is over there waiting for you. Go to her. She'll get you to the van."

The first woman cautiously stepped outside and started

across the lawn. The rest followed, and Elizabeth watched them go. She breathed out a small sigh as she saw them make it to the shelter of the trees. From the shadows Sabrina waved, and Elizabeth waved back.

Now they just had to get the women out of the parlor, and they'd be home free.

She turned and made her way toward the front of the house and stopped short when she saw Matt.

I'm here, she said.

I'm going to tell Mrs. Vivian that I'd like to take this group of women into the kitchen.

Will that work?

She's been completely cooperative so far.

But that could be problematic.

We'll see.

She heard Matt switch his mental attention to the hostess.

I love cooking. I'm taking the girls into the kitchen for some treats.

"What?" the woman said aloud.

"We're just going back to the kitchen to whip up some brownies," Matt said, madly projecting the message to Mrs. Vivian that what he was doing was perfectly normal.

"Come on," he said to the women.

None of them moved.

You get them to come with you out the back door. I'll keep Mrs. Vivian in line until you tell me they've all made it to the woods.

They had just started across the room when Matt heard a car pull up in the parking area.

Damn. It would have been better if they hadn't had to deal with another guest.

As that thought flickered through Matt's mind, the front door opened.

Another guest?

It was apparently someone so sure of his welcome here

that he didn't need to ring the bell or knock. The footsteps in the hall gave Matt a bad feeling.

He turned to see a tall, broad-shouldered man who appeared to be in his late forties stride into the room with the confidence of someone who knew no one was going to challenge him.

He stopped short when he saw Elizabeth, and a smile spread across his face.

Chapter Fourteen

"So good of you to show up here," Derek Lang said as he and the man next to him both drew handguns. The other man pointed his weapon at Matt. Lang covered Elizabeth.

Elizabeth's body went cold. This was the thug she'd been running from for more than a week, and she'd just put herself into his clutches.

Above the buzzing in her brain, she heard Matt switch his attention to Lang.

It's all right. Everything's okay. We're not doing any harm. We're going to walk out of here with these girls. And you're glad to see them go. None of them was working out, anyway.

Elizabeth knew she should add her power to Matt's mental assault, but for long moments, she simply couldn't manage it. It was all she could do to lock her knees and keep standing there in front of the man who had been repeatedly trying to kill her.

And apparently Matt's mental suggestion wasn't having any effect on Lang.

Help me, he shouted in her mind

She pulled herself together and added her strength to Matt's, but Lang's will must be strong. He acted like he hadn't heard the powerful suggestions they were now both aiming at him, and she realized that they should have simply zapped him instead of trying to convince him of something so against his best interests.

But it was already too late. He slammed Elizabeth against the wall, making her head ring as he fixed her with a murderous look. "You're going to be sorry that you ever got involved in my business."

He kept his hand on Elizabeth as he turned to the tough-looking man standing next to him. "Southwell, lock them in the basement."

He stopped and thought about the order. "No, wait. There's something strange about these two. They keep getting away, and I can't explain why. I want them separated. Leave Ms. Forester with me up here, and put Dr. Delano in the basement."

Elizabeth was still trying to clear her head, and she understood why Matt hadn't zapped Lang. The man was holding on to her, and if Matt hit him, he'd hit her, too.

Southwell flicked the gun at Matt. "Come on, let's go."

Elizabeth wanted to scream, but she wasn't going to show Lang that she was terrified. She watched the minion hustle Matt out of her sight.

It's okay. Everything's going to be okay. Matt sent her the reassurance over and over, but she didn't believe it. How could they possibly get out of this?

When Southwell and Matt were out of sight, Lang looked toward Mrs. Vivian, who was watching the scene wide-eyed.

"How did that guy get in here?"

"He said he was a friend of Harry."

"Harry who?"

"I...don't know."

Lang snorted. "We'll discuss that later. I want the girls upstairs out of the way. Elizabeth will stay here with me," he said, tightening his hand on her arm. "Bring me some rope."

"Yes, sir." Mrs. Vivian turned to the women. "You heard Mr. Lang. Go upstairs to your dormitory."

She followed the young women out of the room, leaving Elizabeth alone with Lang. He looked pleased with himself as he kept the gun on her and inclined his head toward a straight chair near the wall. "Sit down there."

With no other choice, Elizabeth sat, struggling to calm the pounding of her heart. She'd understood that sneaking into The Mansion was dangerous, but she hadn't anticipated that Lang was going to show up.

Mrs. Vivian was back all too quickly, holding a coil of rope.

"Tie her arms behind the chair back. Then tie her legs to the chair legs."

Don't do it. Don't tie me up, Elizabeth silently screamed, still fighting the fuzzy feeling in her head and trying desperately to project the message toward the woman who was standing meekly beside the chair.

When Mrs. Vivian hesitated, Lang's reaction was immediate and furious. "What are you waiting for? Tie her up, if you don't want me to shoot you."

The woman made a low sound and hurried in back of Elizabeth, pulled her arms back and began to wrap the rope around her wrists.

Don't make the bonds tight. Give my hands some circulation, Elizabeth said, not sure if that was going to do her any good. But maybe if the bonds were loose enough, she'd have a chance of getting free. Or maybe she'd get clearheaded enough to zap Lang, although she still couldn't risk it when he was holding the gun on her. And what good would that do if she was tied up?

THE HARD-FACED MAN named Southwell, who'd already tried to kill Elizabeth and Matt, marched Matt out of the room.

As soon as they were out of sight, Matt started to send his captor a message that he should let him go. Before he got out more than half a thought, the man raised his gun and brought the butt down on Matt's head.

He dropped to the floor, desperately trying to cling to consciousness.

"That's for all your tricky plays," the thug said, his tone understated. "You got me in a lot of trouble with the boss, and I don't much appreciate that. You're lucky I don't kill you now. But I think Mr. Lang wants to talk to you. I'm hoping he gives you to me when he's finished."

Matt heard the tirade through the fog in his brain.

"Get up."

When he was slow to comply, Southwell grabbed Matt's arm and dragged him toward the kitchen. He was aware of being pulled across the tile floor. They stopped as the guy opened a door. Then Matt was being dragged down the steps, his limp body thumping against the risers as they descended into the cold and dark room.

The guy reached the bottom, hoisted Matt onto his shoulder and carried him across an open space to a small room. He tossed him inside like a sack of rice. Matt hit the floor and lay still.

Southwell crossed the room and kicked him in the ribs, sending a wave of agony through his side.

"You'll be damn sorry that you made the mistake of hooking up with Elizabeth Forester. I'll be back when the boss wants to have a crack at you."

The thug closed the door behind him, leaving Matt dizzy and disoriented on the cold floor.

IN ONLY A FEW MINUTES, Elizabeth was tied to the chair, but Mrs. Vivian had at least done what was requested. Elizabeth thought she had a little bit of wiggle room at her wrists, and maybe if she had some time alone, she could get away.

Lang walked over, studying her. "I see the little social worker looks more like a prostitute. The outfit becomes you. Maybe as part of your punishment, I can let my men have some fun with you."

Elizabeth fought not to react.

"You know, the way your hands are tied thrusts your breasts toward me." When he reached down and cupped one in his hand, she tried to cringe away, but the chair and the ropes stopped her.

He pinched her nipple hard, and she couldn't hold back a gasp.

"What possessed you to get involved in my affairs?" he asked in a conversational voice.

She forced herself to raise her head and looked at him. "I couldn't leave those poor women here against their will."

"You're a real angel of mercy."

She didn't bother with a retort.

"How did you learn about this place?" he asked.

Thinking she'd made a mistake by answering his first question, she pressed her lips together. No way was she going to tell him about Sabrina. Oh, Lord, she thought suddenly. Sabrina was in the woods across the lawn, and the guards were still outside patrolling the grounds. Could she send Sabrina a message? Warn her?

All that was racing through her mind when Lang asked his question again.

"Where did you learn about my private business?"

When she didn't answer, he slapped her hard across the face.

IN THE BASEMENT ROOM, Matt scooted backward so that he was propped against the wall. It was almost pitch dark, and he could see nothing.

He tried to reach out to Elizabeth, but his brain was too fogged to make the connection.

Was she all right? What was Lang doing to her up there? The pictures in his mind terrified him. He had to get out of this room, but he had no idea how.

But first things first. Southwell had roughed him up, but

was there any serious damage? Quickly he began to take a physical inventory. His head hurt where the thug had clunked him, and he knew he was going to have bruises where he'd thumped against the stairs and been kicked in the ribs. But as far as he could tell, nothing was broken, and he had no internal injuries, thank God.

He stayed where he was for several minutes, then pushed himself to his feet and felt the surface behind him. It was a wall made of brick, because the house must have been built before the age of cinder-block construction. Next, he walked along the wall, turning a corner where new cinder block met the old brick, making him wonder if the room had been constructed as a cell. For what? To discipline women who didn't want to cooperate?

He grimaced as he thought about that but kept walking carefully and holding out his hands in front of him so that he wouldn't smack into anything.

When his shoulder brushed something different, he stopped. He'd reached the door where he'd been thrown in here. Positioning himself in front of it, he began to feel his way over the surface. It seemed to be made of wood, and when he thumped his fist against it, it felt very solid. Not one of those hollow-core jobs, yet somehow he had to get out of here.

If he could only see the room, he'd have a better idea of how to escape. But there was no light source except for a thin line at the bottom of the door, making him as good as blind.

In frustration he smashed his fist against the door. Then he realized he wasn't thinking straight at all. He wasn't going to break out of here in any conventional way, but he and Elizabeth had used bolts of energy to zap rocks and then the men coming after them. Couldn't he use that power to free himself?

He backed across the room and braced his shoulders

against the wall, then tried to send a bolt of power toward the door. All he got was a massive jolt of pain in his head.

He cursed aloud in the little room, then took several breaths, gritted his teeth and tried again.

UPSTAIRS, LANG BACKED away from Elizabeth and stared at her, studying her like a rat he'd cornered in the basement.

"You think you can keep from spilling your guts to me?" he asked.

When she said nothing, he shook his head. "What if I told you I was going to poke a knife into your eye? Would that help to loosen your tongue?"

Fear leaped inside her, but she kept her voice even. "If you were going to do that to me, I'd know you were planning to kill me. And what would be the advantage of telling you anything?"

"There are many ways to die, some a lot more painful than others," he answered.

From the side of the room, Mrs. Vivian was watching and listened to the unfolding scene with a sick look on her face. Elizabeth would bet that she'd never anticipated anything like this when she had signed up to run Lang's bordello.

Elizabeth switched her attention away from the woman when she saw movement in the doorway in back of Lang. Afraid it was the henchman coming back, she braced herself.

But it wasn't the man who had taken Matt down to the basement. It was the guy they'd called Baldy, whom they had encountered outside when they had scoped out the place a few days ago. The man Matt had disabled with a jolt of energy to his brain.

DOWN IN THE basement room, Matt marshaled his energy. He hadn't been able to blast the door, and that wasn't an acceptable outcome. He had to get out of here because Lang had Elizabeth upstairs, and the man had already been angry with her. Now that he had her in his clutches, there was no telling what he would do.

Matt clenched his fists, gathering his will, putting everything into his effort to escape. Coldly he told himself there was no room for failure as he aimed a blast of power at the lock on the door. This time he felt the mental energy shoot out of his mind and hit the door with such force that he would have been knocked backward if he hadn't already been standing with his shoulders against the brick wall. The door rocked on its hinges but stayed in place. Matt redoubled his efforts, keeping up the stream of power, praying that it was enough to get him out of here.

The lock finally gave, and the door burst open, slamming against the outer wall.

For a moment Matt couldn't move. The effort had taken so much out of him that he could barely stay on his feet, but he knew that he had to get to Elizabeth. Finally he summoned enough energy to stagger out of the room. As he passed through the doorway, he felt a jolt of heat and realized that the door frame was smoldering.

In the outer part of the basement, he crossed the floor as quickly as he could, heading for the stairs. Looking back, he saw that the door frame was now on fire, and the flames were creeping toward the joists of the floor above.

He and Elizabeth had talked to Sabrina about burning down the house, but not while they were still in it.

Chapter Fifteen

Elizabeth saw that Baldy's face was strained, and she had the feeling he hadn't been doing so well since their encounter outside The Mansion.

She and Matt hadn't been able to influence Lang's actions, but this guy was another matter.

She focused on him, using every ounce of power she possessed to send him a message.

The man in front of you is an enemy invader. You have to disable him. He's holding me captive. You have to disable him so I can get away.

She watched Baldy's visage. Confusion and doubt chased themselves across his features as he tried to figure out what was true and what wasn't.

Lang saw that she was staring at someone behind him and turned.

Enemy. He's an enemy, Elizabeth silently screamed. *Disable him.*

Baldy blinked.

"Tony, what are you doing here? Is your shift over?"

So his name was Tony.

His mouth opened and closed as he stared at his boss, puzzlement on his face.

Elizabeth frantically continued to send him false information.

The man in front of you is an enemy. He's here to attack The Mansion. Disable him.

Tony pulled out a gun and pointed it at Lang.

"What are you doing, you fool?" the crime boss shouted.

In the next moment, Tony pulled the trigger and Lang went down.

From in back of the shooter, another man appeared, and this time it was the guy named Southwell who had taken Matt away.

"Watch out," Elizabeth shouted at Tony. "There's another invader."

The man whirled, just as Southwell pulled the trigger of his own gun.

Tony went down, but Southwell jumped back. And as Elizabeth stared at the scene, she caught the scent of smoke wafting toward her. It could be a malfunctioning fireplace, but she didn't think so.

She glanced at Mrs. Vivian and saw the woman's eyes were wide with panic. "The house is on fire. Help me get untied."

The woman didn't move.

Help me! You have to help me!

MATT STARED AT the flames, knowing he didn't have a lot of time now. As he hurried to the steps, he heard the sound of gunfire upstairs.

Oh, Lord, had Lang shot Elizabeth?

Matt had put his foot on the first riser when he saw a figure at the top. It was Southwell, the man who had locked him in the cell down here—no doubt coming to finish him off. But he was staring into darkness, and apparently couldn't see what had happened in his absence.

Matt jumped to the side, waiting for the man to come down. When he reached the basement, Southwell started for the cell, then stopped short when he apparently spotted the burning door frame. Matt leaped on his back, taking him down to the cement floor.

Southwell grunted, struggling, and Matt knew he had to finish this quickly. He was in bad shape, and there was no way he could match this guy in a physical fight.

Smoke was filling the basement now, and both men began to cough.

The thug flipped Matt over and tried to bring his gun hand up.

Mustering every shred of power he had left, Matt tried to send a thunderbolt toward the guy, but it was like a fire-cracker that failed to go off.

Just as the man yanked his arm free, he went rigid above Matt.

He looked up to see a woman at the top of the stairs. It was Elizabeth, and she'd apparently done what Matt couldn't—zapped Southwell.

Matt yanked the gun from the thug's limp hand and bashed him on the head with it, then bashed him again. Shoving himself up, Matt staggered toward the steps.

He and Elizabeth met in the middle, clasping each other tightly.

"Thank God you're all right," they both said at the same time.

Matt forced himself to ease away. "We need to get out of here. And the women, too."

"You're hurt," Elizabeth breathed as he wavered on his feet.

"I'm mobile," he answered, because he had to be.

Clinging to each other, they made it to the kitchen. Just as they stepped onto the tile floor, water started gushing down from the ceiling.

"The sprinkler system kicked in," Matt said. "Maybe it will put out the fire, but the place is still full of smoke."

"The girls are upstairs," Elizabeth told him.

"We can't leave them here," he answered. When he started up the back stairs, Elizabeth followed. There was no water on the stairs, but as soon as they got to the upper hall, water started pouring down on them again.

"They met you already. Tell them the situation," Matt said.

"Lang's dead," Elizabeth called when she reached the upper floor. "And the house is on fire. We have to get out of here."

For long seconds, nothing happened.

As Matt started down the hall, a door opened and one of the women stepped out, water pouring down on her and a lamp base in her raised hand. It was clear she intended to use it as a weapon. When she saw Matt's battered face, she drew in a quick breath.

"The house is on fire. We have to get out of here," Elizabeth repeated, sending that message to the woman in the doorway and hoping it was reaching the others who must be in there.

The door opened wider, and more faces peeked out.

"Come on," Elizabeth shouted. "Your friends who were up here are already out of the house. They're safe."

As she spoke, she heard a roaring noise behind her and saw flames shooting up the back stairs where there were no sprinklers.

Matt turned and saw the fire. "We have to get out the front door," he said.

Women soaked to the skin hurried out of the room, and Elizabeth ushered them to the stairs. At the bottom, they stopped to stare at the bodies on the living-room floor.

"The bad man," one of the girls confirmed.

"And one of those evil guards," another added.

Matt brought up the rear, herding the women away from the bodies and to the front door. Then from outside, Elizabeth heard the sound of gunfire and knew that the guards were out there—determined to keep everyone in the burning house.

Behind her, she heard Matt issuing hasty instructions.

"No," she gasped as she looked from him to the line of

three men who were about thirty yards away, all facing the door with weapons drawn.

"Can you think of anything else?" he asked, his voice grim.

Nothing came to her, but she still protested. "You're in no shape to do anything like that."

"I am if you help me."

In back of them, water poured down and smoke billowed, making everyone cough. They might all die of smoke inhalation if they didn't get out.

We couldn't influence Lang.

His will was too strong. These guys are just hired help.

"Here goes nothing," Matt muttered as he swiped a hand over his wet face, then stepped toward the door.

"This is Derek Lang. Cease fire," he called out. "I have to get these women out of here." He reinforced the words with a silent command, broadcasting the message to the guards outside, and Elizabeth did her best to help, lending him power.

For a long moment, nothing happened. Then someone called, "Mr. Lang?"

"Yes. We're coming out."

Elizabeth's heart was in her throat as Matt stepped out, still sending the voiceless message. She continued to help him, praying that the men outside would believe the illusion he was projecting—and that the women behind them wouldn't question what was going on.

Matt stepped out onto the porch, then turned and gestured to her and the others. "Come on."

At first, nobody moved. But then a crackling sound on the stairs behind them made them jump. Like the back stairs, the front ones were not protected by the sprinkler system and were burning.

Still projecting to the men outside, Matt walked down the porch steps, and the women followed, with Elizabeth ushering them along.

Then she saw something that made her catch her breath. Figures moved behind the line of men on the lawn. And as she watched, Sabrina and some of the other women sprang from the shadows, moving in unison. Each of them carried a club made from a tree branch. One of them brought the makeshift weapon down on the head of a guard who had kept them from escaping. Others clubbed them as they went down, whacking them on the backs and shoulders The men didn't have time to fire as they all succumbed.

Matt rushed forward, grabbing automatic weapons from one of the men and then another. Elizabeth snatched up the third gun.

"Get them to the van," Matt shouted as he stood and covered the women's escape. "You, too," he told Elizabeth.

This time she wasn't willing to go along with his plan. She waited with him.

When one of the guards started to get up, Matt shot at the ground in front of the man, and they all went still. She and Matt backed away. As they got to the trees, they turned and ran.

Elizabeth led the way to the van. As soon as they were all inside, Brenda gunned the engine, and the vehicle rocketed off.

The shelter had brought blankets in case the women needed them, and it was definitely true now. Matt, Elizabeth and the other women who had gotten showered wrapped themselves to keep warm.

They drove around to the road, and as they went past The Mansion's driveway, they could see that the sprinklers had put out most of the fire, but smoke still poured into the sky.

"I guess The Mansion's ruined," Elizabeth said.

"And Derek Lang is out of the picture," Matt added.

"One of his own men shot him," Elizabeth said, not explaining that she was the one who had made the voiceless suggestion. And she wasn't completely sure how she felt about that.

She knew Matt caught her thought as he slung his arm around her and pulled her close.

I left Southwell in the basement, he told her privately. *He probably didn't get out. What about Mrs. Vivian?*

I don't know, and I don't much care. If she's still alive, she's out of a job.

Elizabeth rested her head on Matt's shoulder, glad that they were both out of Lang's line of fire. Matt slipped his hand under her blanket and stroked up and down her arm, reassuring her as they drove away from the scene of what could have been a total disaster.

"You need medical attention," she whispered.

"Dr. Delano says I'm all right," he answered.

What did Southwell do to you?

Kicked me around a little.

He told her about being locked in the basement cell. And she tried to tone down the scene of being tied to the chair and threatened. But Matt caught the gist of what had happened.

The bastard.

He's dead.

And with the fire out, the cops will be able to figure out that one of Lang's own men killed him.

Elizabeth looked up to see the other passengers watching them.

"I didn't think you could do it," Sabrina said.

"Elizabeth wasn't going to let you down," Matt answered. "She was going to rescue you or die trying. And I think you all know it was a close call."

There were murmurs of agreement around the van.

"I think I forgot to say 'thank you,'" Sabrina whispered.

"I'm just sorry it took so long to get everyone out," Elizabeth answered.

They pulled up in back of the shelter, and the women poured out. They all went inside, and the director, a woman named Donna Martinson, came up to them.

"I can't thank you enough for what you did," she said.

Elizabeth looked down at the blanket and the wet flimsy gown she was wearing. "Actually, there is something you can do. I'd like to dry off and put on something more suitable," she said.

"Of course. We have clothing ready for the women. You can use the downstairs bathroom."

"I have my own things. I just need to get them."

She and Matt both went to his car, where he got out his computer and she got her suitcase. In the bathroom, she quickly took off the negligee and tossed it onto the floor, then put on a bra and panties before donning jeans, a T-shirt, socks and running shoes. When she was dressed, she stuffed the negligee into the trash can and jammed it down, then stood for a moment with her fists clenched. She'd been in Derek Lang's house of horrors for about an hour, but the women there had been through a much longer ordeal, although they hadn't been tied up and threatened with torture. At least she hoped not.

She stood for long moments, struggling for calm. She'd been through a lot of terrible experiences in the past few days, but the most recent one was the worst.

When she came out of the bathroom, Donna was waiting for her. "How are you feeling?" she asked.

"Better."

"Dr. Delano is using one of the offices," the director said, leading Elizabeth down a short hall.

"Thank you."

She went in and closed the door. Matt had also changed into the clothes from his bag in the trunk. He had been sitting at the desk with his laptop. He stood quickly, and she looked at the bruises on his face.

"How are you?" she asked.

"Fine."

She knew the answer was automatic as he came around the desk and took her in his arms.

He didn't have to ask how she was doing. She knew he was listening to her thoughts. And she was doing the same with him.

They clutched each other tight, both thankful that they had made it out of The Mansion.

I never would have gotten through this without you, she told him.

Yeah, well, I can't imagine...

He didn't finish the thought, but she knew what it was. And she felt the same. Neither one of them could imagine a life that didn't include the other.

"Are we going to be able to live our lives?" she asked. "I mean, the cops still want to talk to us about Polly."

"We'll make sure we can," he answered with conviction, and she wondered if that was simply wishful thinking.

He caught the question and answered. "I was just writing an email to the Baltimore County detective who was investigating Polly's death—a guy named Harrison. Unfortunately explaining what's been happening is a little tricky. But we lucked out with the sprinkler system. The house didn't burn up and destroy all the evidence."

He returned to his seat, and she pulled up a chair next to his, reading the message he'd started writing.

From Matthew Delano to Detective Thomas Harrison:

You may be aware of a murder and fire in Harford County at a mansion that was being used by mob boss Derek Lang as a house of prostitution.

He paused and looked at Elizabeth as she kept reading.

An investigation of the scene will determine that Lang was shot by one of his own men, someone named...

"Tony," she supplied.

"No last name?"

"Not that Lang said."

"Okay."

She went back to reading.

Tony, who was shot in turn by another one of Lang's operatives, a man named Southwell, who subsequently ran into the basement. I also believe you will find, when you examine Southwell's gun, that it was the same weapon used to kill Polly Kramer, who was sheltering Elizabeth Forester, the woman known as Jane Doe when she was brought into Memorial Hospital suffering from amnesia.

He stopped and looked at her. "All right so far?"

"Yes."

As a social worker for the city of Baltimore, Elizabeth Forester had discovered a pattern of abuse involving Derek Lang. When he learned she was investigating him, he sent men to apprehend her. As they were pursuing her through the city, she was involved in a one-car accident. She was taken to Memorial Hospital suffering from amnesia. When she could not be identified, a nurse at the hospital, Polly Kramer, volunteered to take Elizabeth home.

I became involved in the case because I was the physician on call. Lang's men tracked Elizabeth down at Mrs. Kramer's house. Elizabeth was able to escape, but Mrs. Kramer was unfortunately killed by Lang's man, Southwell.

He stopped again. "Does that make sense?"

"Yes."

"Now comes the tricky part."

"Because there's no way we're going to betray Donna Martinson and the women we rescued," Elizabeth supplied.

Matt nodded.

Lang was trying to kill Elizabeth because, through her job as a social worker, she had discovered that he was forcing women into prostitution, and he wanted to keep her from acting on that information. We are confident that the results of the ballistics test will clear up the questions about Mrs. Kramer's murder.

He signed it Matthew Delano, MD.

"I guess we have to wait for a response before we can do anything else," he said.

"Do you think that will get us off the hook?" she asked.

"I hope so."

He continued silently. *The problem is that we can't give away the location of this safe house or the identities of the women.*

Yeah. That could be a deal breaker.

THEY DIDN'T HAVE long to wait for a reply. A demand came back pretty quickly that Matt and Elizabeth surrender themselves.

They politely declined. And the detective must have expedited the ballistics test, because it was only six hours later that they were given confirmation that the same gun had killed both Polly and Tony. Once that was established, Harrison asked to meet them at a neutral location.

"He could be lying to us," Elizabeth said. "On the TV shows, they don't have any compunction about saying whatever it takes to get people into custody—or to confess."

"Yeah, but you're forgetting we have an advantage. We can sway his thinking."

She gave Matt a worried look. "It didn't work with Lang."

"Unfortunately."

"Do we know why?"

"Maybe because his own nasty image of himself was so much a part of him that he wouldn't listen to anyone else."

"I hope that's true. And I hope it's not true of Harrison."

They negotiated through email for several hours and finally agreed to meet the detective early in the morning alone in the parking lot of a shopping center where they hoped they could make a quick getaway, if necessary.

MATT AND ELIZABETH said goodbye to the women they'd rescued and also Donna Martinson.

The women from The Mansion were still adjusting to their new freedom, but Donna took Elizabeth and Matt aside with a worried look on her face.

"Can you keep them out of any investigation?" she asked.

"That's what we're trying to do," Matt answered.

"But it might not be possible," she countered.

"I think it is," Matt said, praying that it was true. "In any case, we won't be coming back here."

They left Donna still looking worried.

In the car, Matt picked up on Elizabeth's troubled thoughts. "We can only do our best."

"Which better be good enough."

On the way to the shopping center, they discussed how they would handle the detective.

"The first question is—can we trust him?" Elizabeth asked.

"I think he's gotten a pretty good idea of what kind of people we are," Matt answered.

"Not telepaths."

He laughed. "No. Innocent victims caught in a mess they didn't make. And he's going to want to go to bat for us."

"We hope."

"We're going to reinforce that."

They stopped in an area where a few cars were parked and watched the place where they'd said they would meet.

Harrison kept his word and drove up alone in an unmarked car across from a fast-food restaurant.

Matt and Elizabeth made him wait for ten minutes before pulling up nose to tail with his vehicle.

The driver of each car rolled down his window so they could talk.

The detective began with "You know I don't usually do this kind of thing."

"We understand, and we appreciate it."

"Why the cloak-and-dagger stuff if you're innocent?"

"We told you Derek Lang was running a house of prostitution," Matt said.

"And bringing women illegally into the Port of Baltimore," the detective added.

Matt winced. He hadn't disclosed that information, but Harrison had figured it out. "We were hoping to leave out that part."

Elizabeth jumped into the conversation. "His death has stopped the traffic, and we don't want to involve any of the women, but we want to make sure we're not murder suspects. That's why we're meeting like this."

Leave the women out of it, Matt said, projecting the suggestion to the detective. *Leave the women out of it. They don't have to be involved. Lang's dead, and Delano and Forester were innocently involved.*

He repeated the silent words over and over, and they watched the man's face, both of them praying that he was going to come to the right conclusions.

"What exactly happened at Lang's bordello last night?" Harrison asked.

Chapter Sixteen

The tricky question, Matt thought.

"We went to rescue the women. Lang caught us there. He tied Elizabeth up and started torturing her. He had the guy named Southwell take me away to the basement."

"And how did you get away?"

"I was able to escape when the shooting started upstairs," Matt said. "Elizabeth was tied up when one of Lang's guards came in and shot him."

"Why?" Harrison asked.

"No idea," Matt answered.

We were there at the wrong time, Matt silently added. *We must have walked into a dispute between Lang and one of his men. We were lucky to escape with our lives.*

"I guess you were lucky to get out of there alive," Harrison said, and Matt breathed out a little sigh. The guy was buying it.

"The guard named Tony shot Lang. Southwell shot Tony."

"And how did you get away?"

"I untied Elizabeth, and we fled."

"How did the fire start?"

Matt shook his head. "No idea."

We were lucky to get out alive, Matt repeated. *You don't want to punish us for rescuing a bunch of women who were in a terrible situation through no fault of their own.*

Harrison looked at Elizabeth. "You had amnesia. How did you get your memory back?"

"Bits and pieces started coming back to me." She cleared her throat. "Dr. Delano helped me by using hypnosis. Finally I remembered enough to know about Lang."

"And why didn't you come to the police?"

"I'd seen Lang at a reception talking to a police official."

Harrison's eyes narrowed. "Which one?"

"I don't remember."

Harrison snorted. "Convenient."

You know we're good citizens. You want to help us, and Lang's death closes the case, Matt suggested.

"I think Lang's death closes the case," the detective said. "But I'd like an official statement from both of you about your involvement."

"At the station house?" Matt asked.

"Yes."

If we could just disappear, I'd go that route, Matt said to Elizabeth. *But it's kind of inconvenient not being able to get to our money.*

And having a criminal investigation hanging over us.

Still he wished to hell he could read the man's mind. This could be a trap, or it could be the key to getting them out of trouble, but they'd still have to dance around the part about the women.

They followed Harrison to the station house, agreeing on what they were going to say as they drove.

There was a bad moment when they went inside, and Harrison took them to separate rooms.

Matt saw the look of panic on Elizabeth's face.

Just tell him what we agreed on. And if we have any questions, we can confer.

Harrison asked them each to write an account of what had happened since Elizabeth had crashed her car into a lamppost. He wrote about treating her, having Polly take her home, and Lang's thugs coming after her.

And he silently checked in with her several times, seeing

that she was writing a similar account without using exactly the same words.

The part with the women was tricky, but Elizabeth pled client confidentiality, and Matt said she had given him only minimal information about them.

HARRISON CAME IN to read Matt's account and ask a few questions.

"So we're cleared of any involvement in Mrs. Kramer's murder?" he asked.

"Yes."

He let out the breath he'd been holding. "Thank you for taking care of this."

"I can't shake the feeling that I'm being manipulated," Harrison said.

Matt kept his features even. "We've just told you what happened to us."

"Uh-huh. Are the two of you planning to stay in the Baltimore area?"

Matt hesitated. He had been thinking about what they had to do next, but he didn't want to share that with the detective.

"I think we're going to try to decompress," he said. "But we haven't made any firm plans."

"And while you were with Elizabeth, the two of you hooked up."

"Yeah," Matt clipped out. *And I don't want to discuss it.*

To his relief, they were out of the police station a couple hours after they'd entered.

HAROLD GODDARD HAD checked his clipping service and his online sources four times day, looking for any item that might pertain to Matthew Delano and the woman named Jane Doe. He knew the doctor and his patient had disappeared after the woman who'd taken in "Jane" had been murdered.

He also scanned through the online version of the *Baltimore Sun*—where an interesting item caught his eye because it involved Dr. Delano. A crime boss named Derek Lang had been shot to death in a bordello he owned outside the city. One of his own men had turned on him, for unknown reasons. And another one had taken out the killer.

Interestingly he'd been using the same gun that had killed Polly Kramer, the nurse who had taken in Jane Doe. And there was another piece of information at the end of the story. The woman who had been known as Jane Doe was actually named Elizabeth Forester.

Harold went to his Solomon Clinic database and looked up the Forester woman. He wasn't surprised to find out she was on the same list as Matthew Delano—the list of babies born as a result of fertility treatments by Dr. Solomon.

As he read that piece of information, the hairs on the back of his neck prickled. He'd been putting together men and women from the clinic, and here were two of them who had found each other all by themselves.

What were the odds of that? What were the implications? What were they going to do next?

He started digging for more information and found out where each of them lived, although he was pretty sure that he wasn't going to find them in separate dwellings.

They'd be together.

From the article it wasn't clear exactly how they'd been involved with the crime boss, but it seemed they'd escaped from a dangerous situation.

What was their next move?

He didn't know these people, but he had a good guess about what they were going to do. Swift and Branson had gone to Houma to investigate their backgrounds. He'd bet his government pension that Delano and Forester would do the same. Did he have to kill them? Or could he head them off?

Perhaps his first move was to send someone to search her house and his apartment.

"I GUESS WE CAN get back to normal life," Elizabeth murmured, as they headed for the car.

"What's normal?"

"If you put it that way, I don't know. But we should start by telling Donna Martinson that she and the women are in the clear."

"Right."

They made the call, both of them happy to relieve the director's mind.

"What now?" Matt asked.

"I want to go back to my house and get some clothes. And now that I've got my memories back, I thought of something else. My baby book. Maybe it has some clues."

"I guess it's all right to go there."

"You're not sure."

"Old habits die hard."

They drove to her neighborhood and parked out front, then walked to the back.

"I know you wanted to look at some of the papers in the office, but I think we should skip that for now," Matt said as they approached the door.

She answered with a little nod. "But I should get a spare key, so that we can lock up when we leave."

She went to the office, opened the middle desk drawer and took out the key she kept on one side.

"At least they left it. You know, I'm going to have to do stuff like get a new driver's license."

"Yeah. Maybe they've got you in the computer, and you just have to call up, explain what happened and ask for a new one."

She grimaced. "First I'd have to prove who I am."

"You have a point."

She looked at the name tags she'd saved from conferences. "I guess they're not going to accept those. But that gives me an idea. If I stop by work, they'll know me at the office."

"And as your doctor, I can verify that you were the woman I treated for amnesia at Memorial Hospital."

"I hope all that's going to work."

"Let's get your clothes and get out of here."

"And that baby book."

They climbed the stairs, and Elizabeth took a suitcase from her bedroom closet. She opened drawers, taking out T-shirts and jeans. Then she took some clothing from the hangers in the closet, glad to have some of her own things.

"The baby book is in a box at the top of the closet—on the left," she told Matt. He reached up to the shelf and brought down the book. It had a padded exterior covered with faded pink silk. In gray letters it read My Little Girl.

He handed it to Elizabeth, and she held it carefully.

"I guess my mom was excited about having a baby."

Opening the cover, she flipped through the pages. In the front was her birth announcement and then congratulatory cards.

She could sense Matt's restlessness as she went through the contents.

"Bring it along. We'll look at it later. I want to get out of here while the getting's good."

The words were just out of his mouth when they heard a door open and footsteps on the first floor.

They both froze, and she gave him a panicked look.

Did you lock the door behind us? Matt asked.

Yes. Do you think it could be one of Lang's men down there?

I'm betting they got out of town—the ones who could still travel.

So who is that?

I'd like to know. But we've got one thing going for us. He's taking his time. He must not know we're here.

They listened as whoever it was pawed through kitchen drawers, then ambled down the hall to the office. After he rummaged around in there for a while, he headed for the stairs.

It sounds like only one intruder.

Unless he's got a lookout down there. Get behind the door.

Elizabeth flattened herself against the wall, waiting tensely as she read what Matt had in mind.

The man apparently didn't know his way around the house. When he reached the second floor, he walked into the guest room, stayed for a few minutes, then headed for Elizabeth's bedroom.

As he walked through the door, Matt hit him with a bolt of power. He staggered back, but he stayed on his feet and pulled out a gun.

Chapter Seventeen

Elizabeth was in back of the intruder.

"Over here," she called out.

When he whirled, Matt hit him with another bolt, and Elizabeth added her strength.

This time the man went down.

Matt leaped on him, stepping on his gun hand, making the intruder scream. And Elizabeth picked up the lamp on the bedside table and brought it down on his head. He went still.

"What do you have that we can use to tie him up?"

"What about duct tape—like we used before?"

"Yeah."

She hurried down the hall to the guest room and came back with a roll of tape, and Matt used it to secure the man.

He groaned and blinked.

"Whaa…?" he asked.

"What are you doing here?"

When he pressed his lips together. Matt kicked him in the ribs, and he let out a yelp.

"You'd better tell us what's going on, if you don't want worse."

Elizabeth made a silent suggestion. *Maybe we can use the persuasion technique on him.*

Matt focused on the man. *You don't want me to hurt you again. You want to tell us what's going on. You want to tell us who sent you.*

The man looked confused as Matt continued to project the message.

"Who sent you?" Elizabeth asked.

"I don't know."

"What do you mean, you don't know? How did you end up in this house?"

"A contact told me the job came from New Orleans. That's all I know."

New Orleans! Matt echoed. *What about New Orleans?* he silently pressed.

"What about New Orleans?" Elizabeth echoed the question.

"Someone down there wants the scoop on you. That's all I know. I swear."

Matt gave him another treatment, but he didn't come up with any more information.

I think that's all he's got.

She nodded.

"How were you going to get paid?"

"I was supposed to leave a message at a phone number. Then I'd get the money from PayPal."

Matt snorted. "Criminals are using PayPal?"

The man shrugged.

They left him on the floor and stepped out of the room.

"Hey," he yelled, "you can't just leave me here."

"Watch us."

Elizabeth put the baby book in the suitcase along with the clothing, and they hurried downstairs.

"Better leave the door unlocked so the cops can get in," he said.

When they were outside, Matt pulled out his cell phone and dialed Detective Harrison. The call went straight to voice mail, which was a relief to Matt.

He left a message saying, "We went to Elizabeth Forester's house to get some of her clothing, and we were surprised by an intruder. We restrained him, and you can find him in the master bedroom."

"Is that legal?" Elizabeth asked.

"I hope so. But I'm not going to wait around."

"What if he says he was there for a legitimate reason?"

"Like what? You called him to fix the water heater?"

"I guess not."

"I'm hoping his fingerprints are in the criminal database. I'll check later with Harrison on that."

She sighed. "The cops are going to be all over the house."

"Do you care?"

"I guess not. After Lang's men came through, I don't think I can live there again."

He put his arm around her and pulled her close. "When this is over, we'll decide where to live."

She nodded against his shoulder, then caught what was in his mind. "We're going to New Orleans?"

"I was thinking we might poke into that fertility clinic. Now with this guy showing up, I think we have to."

"Yes."

She could see he was turning over possibilities. "You don't want to fly."

"I don't want our names on a passenger list that someone could check. Which means we should drive."

"All right. Then let's not push ourselves."

She knew he was anxious to get there, but he said, "Yeah, we can stop along the way to practice our skills. And do some research."

Elizabeth checked in with Social Services and told them she wasn't ready to return to work. It turned out she had months of sick leave she could use. And Dr. Delano was happy to say she still needed to rest. She also got a new driver's license, and Matt checked in with Detective Harrison. When they found out the guy who'd burglarized Elizabeth's house was a known criminal named Walter Clemens, they went down to make a complaint.

"You two seem to attract trouble," the detective said.

"We're hoping to change that," Matt answered.

"How?"

"We're going on a road trip."

"How will that help?"

"It will get us out of town."

Matt checked back in at Memorial Hospital and took a leave of absence.

"What if they won't take you back?" Elizabeth asked.

"There's always a need for doctors. I'll be able to get a job somewhere."

After they'd made their arrangements, they mapped out a route to New Orleans.

"It looks like about an eighteen-hour trip," Matt said. "We could shoot for six to eight hours of driving a day."

Their first stop was Roanoke, which had initially been called Big Lick because of the nearby salt lick that attracted wildlife. The town had been a major stop for wagon trains going west. Coal and the manufacturer of steam engines had made the city prosperous.

"Too bad we aren't here for the Big Lick Blues Festival or the Strawberry Festival," Elizabeth said as she looked up information about the city.

"I think we can have our own festival," Matt answered as he drove past several chain motels.

She grinned at him, letting the images in his brain warm her, still thinking how lucky she was to have found this man.

"The feeling's mutual," he said as he pulled into the parking lot of an upscale motel.

"How long were you going to keep the information from me?" Jake Harper asked his wife.

Rachel looked up from the table in her New Orleans shop

where she read tarot cards. They were in the city—where they spent about half their time, when they weren't at the plantation in Lafayette that Gabriella Boudreaux had established as a refuge for telepaths. Rachel raised her face toward her husband. "I guess I wasn't going to keep it from you for very long."

"Do you know who they are?"

"Her name is Elizabeth. His is Matt."

"You found them when they were on the East Coast. Are they still there? Or are they doing what other bonded couples have done—looking for their origins?"

She sighed. "I think they're on the way to Houma."

"And are they a threat to us? Like Tanya and Mickey." The first couple they'd encountered like themselves.

"I think Tanya and Mickey were unusual," Rachel said. "They didn't want anyone to share their powers."

"But you don't know for sure, because you always want to see the best in people."

"I can't help what I am."

Jake walked up beside his wife's chair and slung his arm around her shoulder. "I love what you are."

She leaned back against him, reassured by what they were together. She was impulsive. He was cautious, which was often a good thing for both of them.

"Is the same man after them who was after Stephanie and Craig?" he asked, happy they could protect the newcomers who had recently come to the plantation.

"They ran into some bad problems in Baltimore—that didn't have anything to do with the Solomon Clinic."

She opened her mind fully to her husband and let him see some of what had happened to Elizabeth and Matt.

He winced. "It sounds like they're lucky to be alive."

"Because they're resourceful. They'd be a big asset to our community. Especially since he's a doctor."

"An asset, yeah," Jake agreed. "If they don't want to wipe us off the face of the earth. Are they flying down here?"

"They're driving."

"That should give us time to prepare."

"For the worst?"

"You know I have to think of worst-case scenarios."

"But we know some important things about them. He risked his life treating patients in Africa. She was going up against a man smuggling women into Baltimore and forcing them into prostitution. That means neither one of them is selfish—like Mickey and Tanya."

Jake nodded. "Those are good signs."

In their motel room, after making wonderful love with Matt, Elizabeth finally turned to the baby book she'd brought from Baltimore.

There were records of when she'd first eaten solid food, when she'd taken her first steps, and her first words—which were "dog" and "doll."

"My mother was pretty compulsive about writing things down," Elizabeth commented.

She turned a page, and her hand froze. There was a picture of her standing in front of a building. The sign beside the door read Solomon Clinic.

Matt stared at the picture. "I guess that must be the place. But what were you doing there? I mean, you look like you were maybe three."

"Yes. And I don't know why I went back there."

"But we do know it's in Houma."

Clemens, the man who'd gone snooping in Elizabeth Forester's house, had gotten into bad trouble. He was in jail, and Harold Goddard didn't like it, but now he had no choice.

He was certain that Forester and Delano were on their way to Houma. He had checked passenger lists on flights from Baltimore and found nothing. That wasn't reassuring. It just meant that the couple was being tricky. Probably they were driving, so no one could track their arrival.

Harold had been thinking about how to protect himself. Now he put that plan into action.

ELIZABETH FELT THEY were finally getting somewhere, when she went to sleep. She woke with a start in the middle of the night, her whole body rigid.

Matt was instantly awake beside her. Rolling toward her, he took her in his arms. "What is it?"

"Someone touched my mind."

"What does that mean?"

"I mean, it's like when you and I communicate without talking. Only it wasn't you." She clenched her fist in frustration. "Well, it wasn't exactly someone communicating with me. They were…probing."

He sucked in a sharp breath. "You're sure?"

"I didn't make it up. I felt another mind…skimming mine."

"You were asleep. You could have dreamed."

"I don't think so. But that could be true."

When she started to tremble, he pulled her closer.

"Something else we need to worry about," she whispered.

"Was it a man or a woman?"

"I'm not sure. If I had to guess, I'd say it was a woman."

"Why?"

She laughed. "Because she was delicate…subtle."

"You don't think men can be subtle?"

"It's not the way they normally operate."

He stroked her arm. "I guess you're right.

Is this woman a threat to us?" He reached for her hand and knitted his fingers with hers, and she tightened her grip.

"I wish I knew."

"We talked about practicing our skills on this trip. I think shielding our minds should be one of our top priorities."

She nodded against his shoulder. She'd thought they were safe—at least for a little while. Now she was a lot less sure. And she knew she wasn't going back to sleep any time soon.

Matt packed up on the observation. "We can start practicing now."

"Because you know I'm worried?" she asked, although she already knew the answer.

"Because it's the right thing to do."

He sat up, and she did the same, pulling up the pillow and leaning against the headboard.

When he climbed out of bed, she gave him a questioning look.

Better if we're not touching.

You mean, easier.

He pulled on a T-shirt and his shorts, and sat down in the chair near the window.

I'm going to block my thoughts. You try to worm your way in.

A nice way to put it. How do you block your thoughts?

I don't know exactly. I guess we'll find out.

Chapter Eighteen

"I'm going to picture a wall and put it up around my mind," Matt suggested.

"Will that work?"

"I hope it's better than picturing a mud hole."

She laughed. "I guess so." She gave him a long look. "Okay, you put up your wall, then think of something you want to guard behind it."

She could sense the barrier going into place. She could even see it in his mind. It was made of cement blocks, and he put it together block by block.

Then she knew by his expression that he'd hidden a thought behind it.

She had very little trouble breaking through. And when she did, she laughed.

"You're thinking about the food we're going to get in New Orleans," she said.

"Yeah."

"Try again."

He gritted his teeth and went back to the wall, and this time she had a little more trouble breaking through. When she did, she gave him a long look. "You've switched from food to sex."

"I'm a guy, after all. Maybe I put them in the wrong order. Why don't we reverse the process, and you try?"

She focused her gaze inward, constructing a barrier out of sturdy upright metal pieces. When she had it in place, she put an image of a beautiful garden inside, then put herself in the picture, sitting down in a wicker chair, enjoying the sunlight slanting through the trees.

It was hard to keep the wall in place and keep the image of the garden at the same time, but she managed it for a few minutes until Matt came along and started pulling her stakes out of the ground.

"No fair," she said aloud.

"Everything's fair."

"Oh, is it?" She heated up the metal stakes, making them too hot for him to handle.

"Nice move," he said.

"We're just playing around."

"But everything we do is practice for when we need to use it."

RACHEL HAD ANOTHER report for Jake in the morning. "She felt me probing her, and she's trying to shield her mind."

He cursed under his breath. "That means they have something to hide."

"Don't jump to conclusions."

"Then what?"

"Suppose you'd felt an outside presence trying to read your thoughts, wouldn't you try to keep him from doing it?"

"That's one explanation."

"But you think they have evil intentions?"

"I want to keep you safe."

"You're always so suspicious."

"I guess it comes from my early childhood experiences."

She reached for his hand. Jake had grown up on the streets of New Orleans, and he'd learned never to trust anyone until he'd proved himself.

"Did you get into his mind?" he asked.

"She's more open."

"Why?"

"Like I said, he was a doctor in Africa. I think he learned caution on a lot of different levels."

"And they're on their way down here?"

"Yes."

"I guess we'd better be prepared."

"How?"

"Keep trying to figure out what they're up to."

"On the other hand, maybe it's better if I don't try to dip into her mind."

ELIZABETH AND MATT left the motel after breakfast and got back on the road, keeping up their practice sessions as they drove.

But there were some things Elizabeth couldn't hide from Matt. The closer they got to New Orleans, the more unsettled she felt, and he picked up on her mood.

"You think we're going to be in danger when we get there," he said, not bothering to frame the statement as a question. "From whoever that Clemens guy is working for."

"Unfortunately." She turned her head toward him. "When is it going to stop?"

"Soon."

"How do you know?"

"Because I think there's got to be a quick resolution. Like we came to with Lang."

"That's not exactly reassuring." She reached to cover his hand with her own. "I got you into a lot of trouble."

"You know damn well we're in this together."

She understood that as much as she'd understood anything in her life and pressed her palm more firmly against the back of his hand. "I wouldn't have gotten my memory back or gotten away from Lang without you, but now I'm wondering if we're making a mistake."

He waited for her to say more, although he probably knew what was in her mind.

"I think we should do some research before we get down there. You can use the web to look up that fertility clinic."

"Agreed."

WHEN THEY STOPPED for the night in Huntsville, Alabama, they had an early dinner at a ribs restaurant. Then they returned to their motel room, and Matt used his computer to get on the web.

Because the Solomon Clinic had been closed for twenty years, there wasn't much information about the facility. But it had been run by a Dr. Douglas Solomon, and there was a piece of startling information about him.

"According to a newspaper article, he had a research facility in Houma that blew up a few months ago."

"Did he die?"

"Yeah. He was inside at the time. Also one of the nurses that used to work at the fertility clinic died with him. And another man who apparently used to run a government think tank."

"What was he doing there?"

"No idea."

Elizabeth winced. "Do they know what caused the explosion?"

"The article says it was a gas leak, but I find it pretty jarring that just before we started poking into Dr. Solomon's background, he got killed."

"You're saying you don't think it was an accident?"

"I don't know what to think, except that we should be even more cautious."

She shuddered, wanting to say that they should just turn around and go back to Baltimore.

"Only we'll always be looking over our shoulder, waiting for something else to happen," he said.

She answered with a little nod, knowing he was right.

"First we'll go to New Orleans and poke around," she said, thinking that she was only postponing the day of reckoning.

"No. I think we're going to find something there," he said.

"Not the guy who hired Clemens, I hope."

"He won't know we're in the city."

"Unless he has some way of finding out who's checked into hotels."

"That would take a lot of digging."

They arrived in New Orleans the next day and found a charming bed-and-breakfast in the French Quarter, a place where Elizabeth would have loved to stay if they'd been here on vacation. But she was too restless to enjoy their antique-filled suite or the old-fashioned claw-foot tub in the bathroom.

Matt looked at her with concern. "Maybe we shouldn't have come."

"You know we have to. And I want to walk around a little bit and get a feel for the city."

They headed for Jackson Square, where they watched the street performers and wandered around the stands where artists were offering to do quick sketches of tourists, and women had set up card tables where they were selling tarot cards and palm readings.

"Do you remember it?" Matt asked.

"Yes. I guess it hasn't changed much in twenty-five years. But I want to see something else."

"Something you remember?"

"No." Elizabeth walked rapidly along one side of the square, then took a side street leading to Toulouse Street.

"If you haven't been here before, you seem to know where you're going," Matt commented.

She shrugged. "Not really."

"You're just…wandering?"

She knew he didn't think that was true. Perhaps she didn't, either. She scanned the shops along Toulouse and stopped at an inviting little storefront that offered tarot-card readings by a woman named Rachel Harper.

"You walked past the readers in the square," Matt said. "Why are you stopping here?"

"This woman interests me."

"Why? Do you know her?"

"No."

"Then what is it about her? Is she more insightful because she has her own shop?"

"She made enough money to buy it."

"Or maybe a rich husband set her up."

Elizabeth snorted and peered at the Closed sign in the door. "I wonder when she's coming back."

"We can try again later," Matt said. "If you think it's important."

"It could be. I don't know," she said uncertainly. "Or maybe it's nothing." She dragged in a breath and let it out. "It's weird. When I first met you, I didn't remember anything. Now I do, and I'm also…" She flung her arm. "I don't know what to call it. Having insights?"

"Maybe part of your mental abilities." He examined the door and window of the shop. "You'd think she'd let customers know how to get in touch with her. But there doesn't seem to be anybody here."

They kept walking through the French Quarter, both of them on edge, but still able to enjoy the colorful buildings, art galleries, antique shops and tropical flowers that were so different from Baltimore.

When Elizabeth stopped in front of a restaurant, Matt gave her an inquiring look.

"You want to eat here?" he asked.

"Not necessarily. But I'm getting the same kind of feeling I did from Rachel Harper's shop."

She stood on the sidewalk for a minute, then walked on.

"Or maybe I'm making stuff up because I want to have something significant happen."

"Maybe it's not going to happen in the city."

At breakfast the next morning, as they enjoyed beignets, strong Louisiana coffee and omelets with andouille sausage, Elizabeth said, "I'd like to go back and see if Rachel Harper is there."

"Not by yourself. Not until we find out about that clinic."

She nodded, knowing he was right. They were safer if they stuck together. But safer from what? She still didn't know.

They both walked back to Rachel Harper's shop, but the tarot-card reader still wasn't there.

A woman across the street stuck her head out of a doorway and asked, "Are you looking for Ms. Harper?"

"Yes."

"She's only here part-time—since she got married."

"Thanks," Elizabeth answered, feeling let down. Turning to Matt, she said, "We should go to Houma and see what we can find out about the clinic."

"I did some more research after you went to sleep last night," he said.

"And?"

"I told you that a nurse who had worked there died in the explosion with Dr. Solomon."

"But what?" She cut him a quick look. "You're keeping me from knowing what you're thinking."

"Good because the technique is working. There's another one of Solomon's staffers living at a nursing home in Houma. Her name's Maven Bolton. Maybe there's something she can tell us about Dr. Solomon's operation."

"Did you look up Houma?" Elizabeth asked.

"Yes. The population is around 33,000. You can book swamp tours and fishing expeditions, eat spicy Cajun food and walk bird trails in the wildlife park."

"The town's not all that large. I mean for someone to locate an important clinic there."

"Maybe he wanted a specific kind of environment. It has a long and proud past, and a historic downtown area. The Terrebonne Parish Courthouse is there, which would mean it was a center of local activity."

"Was there anything about the Solomon Clinic?"

"Actually I know where it used to be."

"I'd like to see it. How far away is it?"

"A little over an hour."

"We can have lunch in town."

They arrived on schedule and drove around Houma, noting that the historic center was probably much as it had been for years, with newer development on the outskirts.

As they crossed a bridge, Elizabeth said, "The place is full of rivers and bayous."

"Yes. It's almost like some of the sections of town are islands."

"It's got a lot of atmosphere, but just being here makes me feel…nervous," Elizabeth mused as they drove up and down tree-shaded streets where large old houses sat on generous plots. She was silent for several moments, then said, "Can you find Dr. Solomon's lab? The one where he was killed?"

Matt consulted his smartphone, where he'd put some addresses. "It's not too far from here."

He punched the street and number into the GPS, and they drove for a few more blocks, stopping in front of a large red-brick house that had been heavily damaged. Behind it was another building that was totally destroyed.

"Why did he have his lab in a residential area?" Elizabeth asked. "Did he live here, too?"

"Actually this was the home of the nurse who died."

"Which implied that they had some sort of close relationship. I want to get out," Elizabeth whispered. Even when she knew Matt thought it was a bad idea, she opened the door and exited the car.

Behind her, he pulled closer to the curb, cut the engine and followed her up the driveway. She stood for a moment, staring at the house with its boarded-up windows and blackened bricks, then skirted around to the real scene of destruction.

She could see an enormous hole in the ground, filled with debris. Pieces of wood, cinder blocks, medical equipment and furniture were scattered around the rubble.

"It looks like nobody's been here to clean up," she whispered as Matt came up behind her.

"Maybe there's a question of ownership."

She looked up and down the street at the well-kept houses and yards.

"They can't leave it forever," he said, following her thoughts.

She made a derisive sound. "There was a swimming pool in Baltimore that kids used all the time. I mean kids whose parents couldn't afford a country club. The owner tore it down, and we all thought they had sold the land for houses or apartments. That was fifteen years ago, and it's still sitting empty."

"But the pool owners didn't leave a mess, did they?"

"No."

Matt nodded and stepped closer to the pit, looking down into the tangle of debris.

"I see a lot of medical equipment—some of it expensive."

"Like what?"

He pointed. "There's a mangled X-ray machine. A couple exam tables. Cabinets that probably held drugs. An EKG machine. Centrifuges. A spectrophotometer. It looks like the doctor had plenty of money to spend on his research project."

"I wonder what he was doing. Do you think it was related to the clinic?"

"Or something new. It looks like it was paying off." He turned to her. "We shouldn't stick around here."

"I know. I just wanted to see what it looked like." She shuddered. "And try to figure out what happened. You think this place was really destroyed by a gas leak?"

"I don't know." He dragged in a breath and let it out. "I don't smell anything like explosives."

"It was a few months ago."

He picked up a stick from the ground, walked to a pile of debris and turned over some charred pieces of wood and paper.

"But the smell would linger," he said.

"What else could do so much damage?"

"I'd like to know."

She gave him a long look. "If…uh…somebody had a lot of time to practice, do you think they could blow up a building the way we've been zapping people and rocks?"

His head whipped toward her. "You're thinking people like us could have done it?"

"Could they?"

"Not just two people, I don't think."

She shivered. "What if…"

He waited for her to finish the thought, but she shrugged. "I'm not going there."

They returned to the car and Matt pulled away, checking in his rearview mirror as he turned the corner.

"You think someone could follow us from here?" Elizabeth asked.

"It could be under surveillance, and I'm not taking any chances."

He kept checking behind them as they headed for the business district where they found several restaurants and some antique shops.

"There's where the clinic used to be," Matt said, pointing to a building that looked more modern than many of those around it.

"Was it torn down?"

"I don't know."

"Maybe Mrs. Bolton can enlighten us. I guess it's time to talk to her." Elizabeth sighed. "I wonder why I want to put it off."

"Maybe you're afraid you're not going to like what we hear."

"Then let's get it over with and eat later. The more we know, the better off we are."

They arrived at the nursing home before lunch. The facility was an attractive looking one-story redbrick residence and nursing facility for the elderly.

"I hope we can get something out of this interview," Elizabeth said as they pulled into the parking lot and Matt cut the engine. "I mean, if she's in a nursing home, maybe her mind is going."

"Or maybe she's just not capable of living on her own."

Elizabeth nodded, trying not to dwell on her doubts as she scanned the building and grounds. "It's well maintained."

"It might be a nice place to retire," Matt said as they followed a winding path through well-tended gardens.

Just beyond the double doors was a reception area where a young woman sat at an antique desk.

Her name tag identified her as Sarah Dalton.

"Can I help you?" she asked in a gracious southern accent.

"We'd like to visit with Maven Bolton."

She tipped her head to one side, studying them. "Another couple to visit Maven. I wonder why she's gotten very popular."

"There have been other couples coming to see her?" Matt asked.

"Why, yes. Two others."

"Who?"

"I didn't know them. But Maven told me that one of the women was named Rachel."

Elizabeth tensed. "From New Orleans?"

"I don't know for sure. How do you know Maven?"

"We…we're old friends," Matt answered.

"They were, as well."

That sounds weird. Should we leave? Elizabeth silently asked Matt.

No.

But who were they? I mean, could Rachel have been the tarot-card reader?

Maybe we'll find out.

"I'm sure she'll be pleased to see you," Ms. Dalton said. "Maven should be in the dayroom now."

They followed the employee down a wide hallway with nature pictures on the walls, to a pleasantly large recreation room with windows looking out onto the gardens.

About twenty women and a few men were sitting around the room. Some were in wheelchairs. Others were in easy chairs watching television or at tables playing cards or working puzzles.

Ms. Dalton led them to a woman who was seated by the window with a magazine in her lap. She had short gray hair and a wrinkled face, and she was wearing a nice-looking black-and-white blouse and black slacks.

"Some people to see you, Maven."

The older woman looked up a bit apprehensively.

"We just stopped in to say hello," Matt said. They both pulled up chairs and sat down.

After a few moments the attendant left them.

The old woman silently studied the visitors. "Are you like that other couple?"

The receptionist had also said something similar.

"I don't know. What can you tell us about them?" Elizabeth said carefully, pulling her chair a little closer.

"They were both getting married. They wanted information about…the Solomon Clinic."

Elizabeth tried to keep her voice even and her face neutral while her heart was clunking inside her chest so hard that she was surprised her blouse wasn't moving up and down. "Why?"

"I shouldn't talk about it. It was supposed to be a secret."

Chapter Nineteen

Elizabeth looked at Matt, then back at the old woman who might be able to tell them what had really been going on at the Solomon Clinic.

But you want to tell us about the clinic. You worked there years ago. It's all right to talk about it now.

Maven looked uncertain, and Matt repeated the suggestion and added, *It's all right to talk to us. We won't tell anyone else.*

Elizabeth waited with her heart pounding for the woman to speak.

Maven lowered her voice. "Their mothers had fertility treatments from Dr. Solomon."

"That's not so unusual," Matt answered.

"Yes. But Dr. Solomon doesn't like me to talk about that. Not since the clinic burned down."

"It burned?"

"Why, yes. It was at night, so nobody was hurt, thank the Lord."

I guess she doesn't know Solomon's dead, Matt silently commented.

And from her tone of voice, it seems she was afraid of him.

"We won't tell anyone," Elizabeth repeated Matt's earlier assurance. She gently put her hand on the old woman's arm. "What can you tell us?"

Matt soundlessly reinforced the question.

"Well, you know, the doctor ran it like a fertility clinic.

That's how he got the babies. But he was really doing experiments on those children before they were born. He thought we didn't know, well, all except Dorothy. She was his pet."

"Experiments?" Elizabeth asked carefully. "What was he trying to do to them?"

"Make them supersmart," the old woman said as though she were confiding the nuclear-launch codes. "That's why he had the children come back for tests. But he was disappointed because they didn't seem any different from ordinary children."

"He was doing brain experiments?" Matt asked.

"Didn't I say that?"

"Not exactly."

"He was so excited when he started. He was sure his techniques were going to produce something extraordinary. Then he couldn't understand why they weren't working." The woman's expression suddenly closed. "I shouldn't be talking to you about any of this." She raised her head. "I should call Sarah."

"No need," Matt said. "We won't ask you any more questions."

She turned her head away, and Elizabeth looked up to see that some of the residents were staring at the scene.

We're attracting attention.

We'd better go.

She and Matt got up and left the dayroom, then hurried down the hall, retracing their steps.

"I think we found out what we wanted to know about the clinic," Matt said when they were back in the hall. "I think he was working with fertilized eggs, operating on the blastocytes, the first hundred cells that develop."

"Back then? Isn't that kind of advanced?"

"I guess you could say he was a genius."

"An evil genius. He was using eggs he had no right to. He was playing with people's lives."

"Obviously he thought the end justified the means. And he didn't care who got hurt in the process. But it didn't work out the way he thought it would. He was altering these babies' brains, but instead of making them smart, he created potential telepaths."

She nodded.

"And creating people who were doomed to lead miserable lives—unless they met someone else who was a product of the experiment."

"How many more of us are there, do you think?" Elizabeth asked.

"That's something we should try to find out."

"And it sounds like we're not the first couple that got together."

They both stopped short as they considered the implications.

"Let's say that the woman who was probing my thoughts is one of us," she said.

"That's a stretch."

"Who else?"

He shrugged.

"And let's say that, for some reason, she and her partner blew up Dr. Solomon's clinic."

"An even bigger stretch," Matt said. "But an important question is, are the other people friendly to each other or hostile?"

She sucked in a sharp breath. "Why would they be hostile?"

"I don't know. I'm trying to consider every angle."

"Like what?"

"Okay, then, who is it that was trying to get information about us—at your house? Some of the other adults who were born as a result of the project?"

"Or someone else."

They had reached the front door, and Matt pulled it open.

She grabbed his arm, stopping him from walking out on the porch.

"What?" Matt asked.

"There's a car next to ours."

"Another visitor."

"I don't think so."

As they watched, two men got out. Both of them were wearing sport shirts, casual slacks and what looked like football helmets.

Matt stared at them. *Football helmets?*

I don't like it.

When they saw Elizabeth and Matt they started rapidly up the walk toward the building, and the expressions on their faces weren't particularly friendly.

"What are we going to do now?" she asked.

"Find the back exit."

The receptionist looked up at them as they hurried down the hall in the direction they'd just come from.

"You can't just go back there again," she called.

Matt turned toward her.

Two men are headed this way. They're thugs. Keep them from following us.

Praying that the mental suggestion was going to give them a little extra time, Elizabeth kept pace with Matt.

He took a side hallway, then dodged into one of the rooms. A woman was in a hospital bed watching television. She looked up in alarm as two strangers charged into her room.

"Who are you?"

We're friends. Just keep calm. Don't tell anyone we were here, Matt instructed as he crossed to the window.

It was of the casement variety, and he turned the crank, then used his foot to knock out the screen.

"Go on," he said to Elizabeth.

With no other choice, she swung one leg over the sill,

then levered herself the rest of the way out, glad that it was
only a few feet to the ground.

Come on, she called to Matt.

*I wish I could close the window, but I can't crank it from
the outside.*

Just get out of there.

To her relief, Matt stuck his foot out the window, then his
head and shoulder. He lowered himself to the lawn, and they
looked around. The grounds of the nursing home were well
kept, but beyond them was a scraggly area that bordered one
of the bayous that cut across the town.

Can we make it to the car? Elizabeth asked.

Not directly. He looked toward the scruffy area, where
the trees and bushes would give them some cover. *Maybe
we can work our way around.*

You think there are just the two guys?

I wish I knew.

Why are they after us? Elizabeth asked.

*I'm guessing someone has a clue about the children from
the Solomon Clinic, and they want more information. Or they
are children from the clinic, and they know we could screw
with their minds—so they rigged up some protective gear.*

Unfortunately.

From inside the nursing home, they could hear running
feet and knew they didn't have much time to make a getaway.

Matt took the lead, moving alongside the building until
they were closer to the wooded area.

When the distance was as short as it was going to get, he
looked back at Elizabeth. *I'm going first. If I make it across
without getting shot, you follow.*

His thoughts confirmed that he hated putting it that way,
but he didn't see any alternative.

With her heart in her mouth, she watched Matt dash
across the open space to the scrubby patch of land beyond
the manicured lawn.

When he raised his hand and waved at her, she breathed out a little sigh of relief. In the next second, she saw his expression change to one of horror.

Before she could figure out what was wrong, a hand closed over her shoulder.

"Move and I'll shoot you in the kneecap," a harsh voice said.

RACHEL HARPER STOOD frozen in the living room of her cottage at the Lafayette plantation. When the door burst open, she whirled as Stephanie Swift charged through the door. Craig Branson was right behind her. They were both products of Dr. Solomon's illegal experiments.

A few months earlier, Stephanie had been trapped into an engagement to a man named John Reynard, a criminal who'd insinuated himself into New Orleans society. Then she'd met Craig Branson and had known she was about to make a horrible mistake by going through with that marriage.

When Reynard had whisked Stephanie away to his heavily fortified plantation, Craig had followed.

Rachel and Jake had helped them escape from Reynard's men—and also from thugs sent by someone else. And now they were all at the plantation owned by Gabriella Boudreaux, who was paired with Luke Buckley.

"It's the same man who was after me and Craig," Stephanie gasped as they rushed into Rachel's cottage.

"You saw what just happened?"

"Yes." She flushed. "I mean, I knew you were upset. You were broadcasting it like a television cop show."

They were followed very quickly by Gabriella and Luke.

Rachel turned as her husband, Jake Harper, came into the room.

"What's happening, exactly?" he asked.

"I wasn't sure what was going on until now," Rachel

breathed. "That other couple—Elizabeth and Matt—are from Baltimore. It's a long story, but they found a man burglarizing Elizabeth's house and got from him that he was hired by someone in New Orleans. They'd already started doing research on the Solomon Clinic and went to Houma. They found the same nursing home we did and talked to Maven. But thugs were waiting for them when they came out."

"They just grabbed Elizabeth," Stephanie added. "And they're wearing some kind of protective helmets."

"Helmets?" Jake asked. "Why?"

"Because they know we have mental powers, and the helmets must have some kind of lining that blocks us," Stephanie said.

Jake swore under his breath.

"We have to go there," Stephanie said. "We have to help them."

The men looked doubtful.

Rachel swung toward the other women, exchanging silent messages before focusing on Jake. "You guys may not be coming, but we have to go to Houma."

"If you think we're letting the three of you go there alone, you're crazy," Jake said.

"Is that a sexist opinion?" she asked.

"It's the opinion of a man who loves his wife and doesn't want to send her into danger."

"But we have to go," Stephanie answered.

Jake apparently knew when he was outvoted. "We'll take the van. And we'll make plans on the way. It's almost a two-hour drive."

"Will we be in time?" Stephanie asked.

"We can only pray we will be," Rachel answered.

Rachel's gaze turned inward as she tuned in on the scene in Houma.

Jake heard her gasp. *What?*

Maybe it's already too late, she said.

MATT STARED IN HORROR as one of the helmeted men reached for Elizabeth and pulled her against his body in a parody of an embrace.

"We've got your girlfriend," he called out. "If you don't want to see her get shot, you'd better come back here."

Stay away. Don't do it, he heard Elizabeth shouting in his mind. But how could he leave her with the men?

We'll think of something.

But what? He tried sending a mental suggestion to the man who held Elizabeth. *Let her go. You don't want to hold her. Let her go.* But the silent order had no effect.

Matt wanted to spit out a string of curses, but that wasn't going to do him any good. He understood the problem. The man knew what he and Elizabeth could do, and he was wearing that football helmet thing to block any messages Matt and Elizabeth might try to send him.

But the two of them could still communicate with each other. And although they knew a mental command wasn't going to make her captor turn her loose, there might be another way.

"Why do you want us?" he called out.

"It's just a job for me."

"Then let us go."

"No way. Turn yourself in if you don't want something bad to happen to her."

I'm going to look like I'm giving up, he said to Elizabeth. *When I get about ten feet from you, act like you're going to faint.*

Okay.

Matt's gaze flicked to the left and right. At any moment, the other thug could show up, and that would create a problem he might not be able to overcome.

His heart was pounding so hard that he could barely breathe as he started back the way he'd come.

Mary ...tion as one of the balcony... reached
for Elizabeth and pulled her against his body in a parody
of affection.

"We've got one survivor," she called out. "If you don't
want to see her get ..., you'd better come back here."

Stop now. Over ... to ... hitting at the
mind. But it was ... to take the next.

By ... of something.

But when I ... d scrabbling a mental suggestion to the

Chapter Twenty

Matt saw the tension on Elizabeth's face. He imagined that
his own expression was just as grim.

As he walked, he gathered his energy, and he felt Elizabeth preparing to aid him. He might not be able to reach the
man's mind, but that wasn't his only option.

He was about twenty feet from her captor when he silently shouted, *Now.*

Elizabeth went limp, as if the frightening situation had
made her legs give out. The man scrambled to get control
of her, but part of his attention had to stay on Matt. With
only a small window of opportunity before the guy was in
contact with her again, Matt shot out a jolt of energy, hitting
him in the shoulder.

He yelped and reared back.

Elizabeth regained her footing immediately and dodged
to the side, giving Matt another shot at the man.

The guy bellowed and went down. Elizabeth kicked him
in the face, marveling at her new attitude toward violence.
When he stilled, she bent to get the gun and took it out of
his hands.

Do we keep this? she asked as she drew up beside Matt.
He wanted to reach for her, but there was no time for anything but escape.

I'll take it.

He clicked the safety on and tucked the weapon into the
waistband of his slacks.

The two of them ran for the scraggly underbrush, disappearing into the trees. But a shout followed them, and Matt knew that the other man had seen where they went.

No, not just one man. There were two others now.

One stopped by their fallen comrade. The other stayed behind Matt and Elizabeth.

STEPHANIE TURNED TO Rachel. "Are you following what's happening?"

"Yes. They got away from the bad guys, but armed men are chasing them alongside the bayou."

Frustration bubbled inside Stephanie. She'd been in a similar situation not so long ago.

Craig put a hand on her arm, trying to calm her.

"Is there anything we can do?" she asked.

"We can try." Rachel closed her eyes, her face a study in concentration as the two other women reached out to touch her. Stephanie felt Rachel trying to direct a surge of power toward the pursuers to at least slow them down, but at this distance, the task was impossible.

"We have to get closer." Rachel said.

She looked toward Jake, but everybody in the van already knew he was driving at a dangerous speed.

"We can't fly. And we aren't going to be any use to them if we crash," he muttered.

MATT AND ELIZABETH plunged farther into the wilderness area, dodging around cypress, tupelo trees and saw palmettos. They splashed through areas of standing water, mud clinging to their shoes and making it almost impossible to run.

Both of them were breathing hard, and he wondered how long they could sustain the pace. But they had to keep going because behind them he could hear the men getting closer, making no attempt to hide their progress through the underbrush.

Elizabeth looked back in panic, then pointed to their right. *If we go farther into the swamp, maybe they won't follow.*

We can try.

Matt veered off in the direction she'd suggested, and they worked their way farther into the dense foliage.

When the sounds of the pursuers grew louder, they both went completely still.

"Where the hell did they disappear?" one of the men said.

Sounds like three men. The one who captured me must have joined the others again.

"You beat the bushes around here. We'll keep going. Widen the search."

They're splitting up.

Maybe that's good. Maybe we can take at least one of them out.

He thought of a plan, telling Elizabeth what he had in mind.

He could feel her uncertainty but also her determination.

He took up a position behind a tree, and she moved into a patch of low bushes.

"Matt," she called out. "Matt, I'm stuck. Help me."

Two of the men were too far away to hear her. The other stopped at once, reversing direction and moving cautiously toward the spot where she was standing.

Matt tensed, waiting for the guy to get closer.

"All right," the thug called out. "I see you. Come out with your hands up."

Elizabeth moaned. "My foot's stuck."

The man took a few careful steps closer, and Matt struck, sending out a bolt that hit him squarely in the center of the chest. He went down, and they both crouched over him.

Matt removed the football helmet and inspected the

inside. There was some kind of heavy foil lining, and he laughed out loud.

"What?"

"You know some paranoid mental patients think aluminum foil will protect them from outside influences probing their brains? Apparently it works—at least when we're the ones doing the probing."

The man was stirring. When he reached up and found that his helmet was gone, he gasped.

"Who are you? Why are you after us?" Matt asked.

"Following orders."

"Who wants us? And why?"

"I'm just doing a job," he said, repeating what the other guy had said.

"And why are you wearing a helmet?"

"The boss said to."

"Why?"

He looked away. "He said you had some kind of mind control rays."

Oh, great.

Too bad we can't read minds, Elizabeth said.

Too bad he doesn't have more information. But we can't waste a lot of time on him. The others could come back. He bent to the man. *Stop looking for us. Go back to your car. Drive away.*

The man looked confused.

Go on. Get out of here, before the man and woman do something worse to you.

The man gave them a panicked look. Pushing himself up, he began running back the way he'd come as if the devil were after him.

When he was out of sight, Matt and Elizabeth moved farther into the swamp. Ahead of them, Matt saw one of the bayous that cut through the area. They could run along the edge, or they could plunge in—which might or might not be a good idea, depending on whether an alligator was waiting to scoop them up.

In the distance, he saw a pier sticking out into the brown water. A couple boats were moored there.

Elizabeth followed his thoughts, and they both ran for the dock.

Behind them they could hear running feet. When a bullet whizzed past them, Matt whirled and returned fire, making the attackers duck into the underbrush.

That gave them a little time, but he knew he and Elizabeth would be sitting ducks when they went out onto the dock.

He slowed, trying to make a decision. *I'm going first.*

That didn't work out so well last time.

What's your suggestion?

We go into the water on the other side of the dock and climb into one of the boats.

Risky. But may be our only option. You go in. I'll hold them off.

They reached the pier, and both ducked to the other side. He took up a position at the end near the shore, ready to stop the bad guys from coming closer. Elizabeth went into the water, swimming along the pier where she was sheltered from the men who were coming cautiously through the trees.

From behind the cover of the dock, Matt got off a couple shots at the pursuers, making them think twice about coming closer. But the standoff couldn't last forever. There were still two pursuers left, and Matt had only the ammunition in the one weapon.

As he kept part of his focus on the men, he also followed Elizabeth's progress. She made it to one of the crafts, a speedboat with an inboard motor.

This one?

He answered in the affirmative, wishing he knew more about boats. But they had to get out of a bad situation, and the vessel seemed to be their best alternative.

Can you get in it?

I hope so.

It had seemed like a good idea at the time, but making it from the water into the boat was easier said than done. As she tried to heave herself over the side, he waited with his breath shallow in his lungs, wishing he could swim over and boost her up. But he had to stay where he was, holding off the pursuers.

ELIZABETH STRUGGLED TO pull herself inside, but it was clear that the side of the craft was too high for her to scramble over from her position in the water. Her only alternative was to set the boat rocking from side to side. When it was almost dipping into the water, she finally flopped over the gunwale, onto the bench seats, banging her hip and shoulder as she came down.

Wet and dripping, she lay there for a few moments, struggling to pull her thoughts together.

Now what?

You have to start it.

She began searching around, looking for a key. It wasn't under the dashboard, and it wasn't in any of the compartments around the craft.

Zap it. Like I zapped the door lock in the basement of The Mansion.

This is a little different.

She made a low sound, but began studying the controls, and Matt directed her to the starter.

She focused on it, giving it a mental jolt, then another. Nothing happened, and she thought they might have to abandon the craft and go to plan B—which was swimming across the bayou and disappearing into the swamp beyond—if they could make it across without getting shot before an alligator ate them.

When she was about to give up hope of starting the boat, the engine coughed, then sprang to life.

Good work.

TO KEEP THE THUGS from rushing forward, Matt got off a couple more shots. Then the gun clicked and he knew he was out of bullets. Abandoning his position at the side of the dock, he leaped up on the boards. As soon as he made a run up the boat, the bad guys started shooting. He ducked low, and he heard a gasp behind him. In his mind's eye, he saw what was happening. Elizabeth had turned and was hurling bolts of power at the men, pushing them out of range, giving him time to untie the boat from the piling and leap inside.

Elizabeth watched him jump aboard, then turned back to the wheel. As she pulled away, the men started shooting again. He and Elizabeth bent low, making themselves as small a target as possible while the craft roared up the bayou.

Matt looked back at the two men. One of them seemed to be in charge and was giving orders to the other. He pointed toward another motorboat moored nearby, and they ran to the vessel and jumped in.

Matt was pretty sure they weren't going to make the engine turn over with their minds. But it seemed they didn't need to. When he heard the craft start, he muttered a curse. Either they knew where to find the key or they had lucked out.

He cursed again as the boat took off after them, and it became clear very quickly that the other craft was more powerful.

"They're gaining on us. What are we going to do?" she shouted. "Can we goose up the engine?"

"I don't know."

He focused on the motor, trying to force it to put out more speed, but the maneuver didn't seem to be working, and all they could do was keep going.

The men in the boat behind them kept firing their guns, the shots becoming more accurate the closer they got. Bullets whizzed past, and some struck the hull. Matt looked down, seeing water rising in the bottom of the boat. They were sinking.

Chapter Twenty-One

"We have to bail out," he said. "Then dive below the surface and swim toward shore."

"No, wait." Elizabeth pointed toward a blue van that had turned onto the road beside the bayou and was racing along, keeping pace with the two boats.

He gave her a questioning look.

"It's them."

"Who?"

"The woman I told you about. The one who was prob-ing my mind."

"Is that good or bad?"

"I don't know."

From the van, a voice zinged toward them. *We're here to help. We're going to blow up the other boat. Add your energy to ours.*

Matt still couldn't be sure that the people in the van were on their side, but he knew for sure that the men in the other boat were closing in for the kill.

He looked toward the van, trying to see who was inside. Someone slid a window open, and he saw several people.

With a little prayer that he was making the right move, he fed power to the woman in the van.

He felt her building energy, and then a beam of tremen-dous force shot from the van to the pursuing boat.

For a moment it seemed to hover in the water. Then the gas tank exploded with an enormous boom. The boat disintegrated, sending a shock wave across the water, and swamping Matt and Elizabeth's craft. They went into the water, both of them gasping for air as waves from the shattered craft pounded them.

Elizabeth, Matt cried out in his mind. When she didn't answer, everything inside him went cold.

Still shell-shocked from the explosion, he tried to focus, tried to figure out where she was. At first he heard nothing. Then he picked up dim echoes from her mind. She was underwater, unconscious and sinking.

He dragged in a breath and held it, diving below the surface, swimming toward where he thought she was.

He could see nothing in the murky water, but he kept going, guided by his connection to her. His own lungs felt like they would burst, but he stayed under, because if Elizabeth died, he might as well die with her.

But finally, finally, his searching hand hit against her shoulder. He grabbed her shirt, trying to summon the strength to pull them both up. Then he realized that another man was beside him, grasping Elizabeth's other side and helping pull her upward.

They broke the surface, and Matt gasped for breath.

They pulled Elizabeth to shore and laid her on the bank. She was pale and lifeless, and Matt checked her airways before turning her over and starting to press the water from her lungs.

Water gushed from her mouth, and he screamed in his mind as he worked, *Elizabeth. For God's sake, Elizabeth.*

For horrible moments, she failed to respond. And then he caught a glimmer of consciousness.

He kept calling to her, saying her name, telling her how much he loved her.

Matt?

Right here.

What happened?

They blew up the other boat, and you went down.

He turned her over, clasping her to him, ignoring the crowd that had gathered around them. But finally their voices penetrated his own consciousness.

"Thank God."

"I'm so sorry. I didn't know that would happen." That was the woman who had directed the energy beam at the other boat.

"It's all right. You kept them from shooting us." That last comment came from Elizabeth, who was taking in the men and women around them.

You're like us, she marveled.

Yes. And we have to get out of here before someone comes to investigate the explosion.

Was it safe to go with them? Matt wondered.

Yes, Elizabeth answered, and he let her faith guide him.

The men and women helped them to the van. Like the night at The Mansion. Cold and wet in a van.

Matt pulled Elizabeth closer and tried to pay attention to where they were going, but it was still hard to focus. He knew that they stopped at a shopping center. Some of the newcomers stayed in the van. Others went in and bought dry clothing. First the men cleared out and Elizabeth changed in the van. Then it was Matt's turn.

The dry clothing did wonders for him, and he looked around at the people who had rescued them.

"How did you find us?" he asked.

"Rachel found you," one of the men answered. "We're all children who were born as a result of Douglas Solomon's experiments—using fertilized human eggs he acquired from his fertility clinic."

"We found out from Maven Bolton that he was trying to make superintelligent children," Matt said. "And, instead, he got us."

There were murmurs of agreement.

"And we are…what, exactly?" Matt asked.

"You probably figured that out, too. Telepaths who couldn't connect with anyone on a deep level until we met someone else from the clinic," one of the women said. "I'm Rachel Harper."

In turn, they all gave their names.

Jake Harper, Stephanie Branson, Craig Branson, Gabriella Boudreaux, Luke Buckley.

"You were probing my mind," Elizabeth said to Rachel. "When we were driving down here."

"I'm sorry if I alarmed you."

"Why did you do it?"

"Because we had to be sure you weren't enemies. The first time we met other people who had been altered by the clinic, they tried to kill us."

"Why?" Elizabeth gasped.

"They were selfish. They wanted to be the only ones with special powers."

"Nice," Matt murmured.

They turned onto an access road, then drew up in front of what looked like a large plantation house. "This is where I grew up," the woman named Gabriella said. "I've opened a restaurant here, but it's closed today. We can all go inside and relax."

Matt was still overwhelmed to meet this group of people.

We're on your side, Rachel Harper said.

Matt swung toward her. *Got to watch what I think.*

We all do. That's one of the little inconvenient things about us. But I know you've been practicing blocking your thoughts. You'll get better at it.

Inside Gabriella led the way upstairs to a sitting room on the second floor.

Matt and Elizabeth sat together, still coming to terms with their narrow escape.

"Who was after us?" he asked.

"We can't be sure who he was. Dr. Solomon is dead. And so is a man named Bill Wellington, who funded the project through a Washington think tank called the Howell Institute. That should have laid the past to rest. But it appears that someone else knew about children from the clinic. Either they knew what was going on back then—or perhaps they discovered it."

"Why were they chasing us? What do they want?" Elizabeth asked.

"They're after us because of what we are," Jake answered. "We've got powers they don't understand. Which makes us a threat, or maybe an asset that someone can exploit. Like a secret weapon."

Elizabeth shuddered.

"You have to admit that being able to send mental bolts of power at your enemies is a skill to covet."

Matt nodded.

"It's a lot to deal with," Rachel said. "And I'm sure the two of you want some time alone to think about what you're going to do."

"What are our choices?" Matt asked.

"You can stay here with us. Or you can go off on your own. It's up to you."

Elizabeth looked at Rachel. "You have a shop in the French Quarter. Where you do tarot-card readings."

"Yes."

"I went there. I mean, I was drawn there by…" She lifted a shoulder. "I don't know. I guess there was some kind of connection between us."

"I'm sorry I wasn't in town. It would have avoided that boat chase."

"Yeah, but the guys in the other boat would still be alive," Jake said in a hard voice. "It worked out."

Matt looked at him and knew that it was a lot better to be friends with Jake Harper than his enemy.

Jake answered with a small nod.

They talked for a while longer, each couple telling how they'd met and what had happened to them as a result.

Finally Gabriella said, "You must be worn out. There's an empty cottage on the property. Why don't the two of you go over there and relax? And we can all meet back here for dinner." She looked at her watch. "At six-thirty."

"Yes. Thanks," Elizabeth said.

Gabriella showed them to the vacant cottage.

Elizabeth looked around admiringly at the antique pieces and classic fabrics. "It's charming."

"Stephanie's the one with the visual smarts," Gabriella said. "She did the decorating, but we've all been going to country auctions and estate sales—picking up furniture for here and the main house."

Elizabeth nodded.

"I'll leave you alone."

When Gabriella had walked out of the cottage and closed the door behind her, Matt turned to Elizabeth.

"In my wildest dreams, I didn't imagine anything like this," she whispered. "People like us. Friends."

"Yeah. And the two of us—safe at last."

He reached for her, and they embraced. He wanted to take her straight to the bedroom, but they were still covered with dried bayou water.

She grinned at him, and he knew what she had in mind. They both headed for the shower, discarding their clothing as they reached the bathroom.

Matt turned on the water, adjusted the temperature and stepped under the spray. Elizabeth followed, and he reached for the soap, slicking his hands and running them over her bottom, her hips and up to her breasts.

She made an appreciative sound, leaning in to him as she soaped her own hands and caressed his back and butt, then clasped his erection, stroking up and down, making him gasp.

"Not like this," he muttered.

"You don't like it?"

"You know I do."

She turned him loose, and they kissed as they washed off the soap.

When she reached for the shampoo and began to lather his hair, he groaned at the delay. But he saw the smile in her mind.

Foreplay.

Are you trying to drive me crazy?

I'm enjoying the freedom I never thought we'd have.

Oh, yeah.

He returned the favor, washing her hair. They'd barely rinsed off when he scooped her up in his arms, cradling her against him as he fitted her body to his. Leaning back against the wall, he let her do most of the work, and they climaxed together in a burst of sensations. As he eased her down, she melted against him, and they stood under the rushing water, spent but happy.

When the shower began to cool, he turned off the taps. Both of them were almost too limp to move, but they managed to dry off and hold each other up as they staggered to the bedroom.

Under the covers, they cleaved together. Two people who had always been alone. But no longer.

The events of the day had taken their toll, and they were both quickly asleep.

SOME TIME LATER, Elizabeth woke and marveled at the way she felt. Safe and relaxed and free.

For the first time since she'd crashed into that light pole, no one was trying to kill her. *I'm still overwhelmed that we found each other.*

Yes. And it's not just the two of us. There are people who understand us.

She nodded against Matt's shoulder, taking in his thoughts, catching the edge of his sudden tension. Even though she knew what he was thinking, she also knew he was going to say it aloud.

He pushed himself up in the bed, and she did the same, pulling the covers up with her.

He cleared his throat and looked at her. "I'm finally free to ask. Will you marry me?"

"You know I will."

Reaching for her, he folded her into his arms, and they clung together.

"Being with you is a dream come true," she murmured.

"But it's real. And it's the beginning of our lives together."

She sensed another thought in his mind. "Getting married is a good idea before we have kids."

"You want them?" he asked.

"Yes, even though it makes me a little nervous. What powers will they have?"

"I guess we'll find out," he said.

"They won't be alone the way we were. They'll have us."

"Yes. And we have to make sure they have a safe place to grow up."

"Like here," she breathed.

"You want to stay here?"

"I think so. I feel so blessed that Rachel and the others found us." She squeezed his hand. "We should get dressed and go over to dinner—before they wonder where we are."

"They know," he answered. "But they're giving us privacy. They know how much we love each other. And they know we're going to want a lot of time alone."

He grinned at her, and she followed his thoughts.

"Not just for sex." She said it aloud.

"Of course not."

They climbed out of bed and began to dress, both of them loving the freedom to joke around and the freedom to plan the rest of their lives together.

* * * * *

He waited until she glanced up. The wary darkness had vanished somewhat, but not totally. "You okay being here?" he asked.

"I see the shooting when I close my eyes. It hardly matters if I'm here or back at the house."

Not that he could blame her. The latest shoot-out was on a slow-motion reel in his head, as well. "For a few hours last evening you seemed to forget."

She slipped her fingers through his. "And I plan to use that tactic again tonight."

"Never been called a tactic before." This woman could call him anything she wanted. Could do anything she wanted with him. They'd been on fast-forward since they met, and he did not want to slow them down.

Still, hand-holding at a crime scene qualified as unprofessional and borderline stupid, so Ben gave the back of her hand a quick rub then let go.

Even though every bone in his body begged him not to.

RELENTLESS

BY
HELENKAY DIMON

Published in Great Britain 2014
by Mills & Boon, an imprint of Harlequin (UK) Limited,
Eton House, 18-24 Paradise Road, Richmond, Surrey, TW9 1SR

© 2014 HelenKay Dimon

ISBN: 978 0 263 91356 9

46-0414

Award-winning author **HelenKay Dimon** spent twelve years in the most unromantic career ever—divorce lawyer. After dedicating all that effort to helping people terminate relationships, she is thrilled to deal in happy endings and write romance novels for a living. Now her days are filled with gardening, writing, reading and spending time with her family in and around San Diego. HelenKay loves hearing from readers, so stop by her website, www.helenkaydimon.com, and say hello.

To Laura Bradford and Dana Hamilton—
I'm thrilled to be working with both of you.

Chapter One

Jocelyn Raine walked under the wrought-iron archway and followed the path to her garden apartment. It was just after nine and the sun had disappeared behind the Annapolis, Maryland, horizon about a half hour ago. Lights inset in the pavers crisscrossed, highlighting the way as she turned right and jogged up the three steps to her front door.

Her cell buzzed at the same time she reached for her keys. While juggling her small purse, she almost dropped the phone. It slipped out of one hand but she caught it in the other before it hit the hard concrete of the small porch.

She swiped her finger over the screen. The promised check-in text from Ben Tanner greeted her. The guy had light brown hair in a short, almost military cut and the most compelling olive-green eyes she'd ever seen.

She could describe the color exactly because she'd stared into them all night across the dinner table on their first date. Add in the linebacker shoulders and that scruffy thing happening around his chin, and no sane woman could brush him off without a second look.

It all worked…except for the part where he carried a gun. She hated guns. She wasn't a fan of violence and despised being scared. She hadn't seen a horror movie since she was a teen. All of which explained why the guy had to ask six times before she finally agreed to go out with him tonight.

Didn't help that within the first two days of knowing Ben, she'd watched him run, shoot, dive, guard and wrestle a scary dude to the ground. All in the critical-care unit of the hospital where she worked, and all while sporting an injury. He'd been shot in the upper arm but that hadn't stopped him from setting up next to a guy in a coma, insisting the unconscious man needed a guard.

And that was why she had finally said yes to him. Something about the former NCIS special agent broke through her defenses. Just a few minutes ago he had insisted, in that respectful voice, that he walk her to the door. She had said no to avoid the awkward "to kiss or not to kiss" confusion, though he was a temptation.

She texted back that all was well and slipped her keys into the locks, first the dead bolt and then the standard one. A woman couldn't be too careful. She'd learned that the hard way.

Once inside, the three-inch pumps came off first. She sighed in relief when her feet hit the thick area rug. That would teach her to wear sexy shoes. Ben only saw them for a second anyway before she tucked them under the table, so she didn't get the point.

The light next to the couch bathed the open area in a soft glow. After resetting the lock and dumping everything but the cell on the table just inside the door, she headed for the family-room area to her right. Ben could text again, so why not be ready?

She looked around for the remote. The television provided background noise, but she had to turn it on first. Ducking, she checked the floor, then the couch cushions.

Spinning in a circle, she scanned the room. She always kept it in the basket on the center of her square coffee table. Her gaze went back to that spot, but it still wasn't there.

An odd chill moved across the back of her neck. She blamed the air conditioner she'd set lower than normal to battle the unusual June heat. But then her gaze came to rest on the magazines spread over the coffee table. She stacked them in a pile. Every day and always.

Some people called her obsessive-compulsive, or OCD. She preferred the term *overly neat*. Either way, she put stuff in its place, and things were not the way she had left them two hours ago.

All thoughts of her sexy date fled.

The chill morphed into a warning itch. She'd been in this situation before and this time she didn't ignore the alarm bells. With a quick look at her phone, she clicked on Ben's name and waited for it to ring on his end. The reaction might be overblown but—

She sensed movement. A change in the air in the room. Little things, almost imperceptible things. A heat—a presence—right behind her.

She spun around as her hand dropped and something brushed against her cheek. A sweet smell hit her dead-on and she shook her head to evade the pungent scent.

A scream died in her throat when a knife waved in front of her. She looked from the muscled arm to the face hardened by lines around the eyes and mouth. A man, tall, bald and dressed completely in black.

Light bounced off the blade. Her breath hitched in her chest as fear hammered through her, threatening to knock her down.

She glanced at the white cloth in his fist. The lingering smell triggered a memory. Nursing school…

chloroform. They no longer used it as an anesthesia in hospitals, but she had read about it in medical-history class and had a lab tech describe it in depth during a tour.

She knew through every quaking cell in her body what this man intended to use it for. She vowed right there not to leave this apartment with him, and that meant staying conscious.

"Who are you?" she asked.

"Don't make this difficult," he said in a harsh whisper. Every muscle in her body tensed. Her palm ached. She forgot about the phone until she looked down and saw her death grip on it.

The attacker knocked the cell to the floor and stepped toward her, filling the last bit of safe distance between them. The hand with the cloth went to her throat. His fingers squeezed and her breath was cut off.

She clawed and punched at his hands, walloping him with both fists while she turned her head away from the heady scent assailing her nose and throat. She kicked out but one forceful hit against his shin caused pain to vibrate from her bare foot up her back.

He didn't even flinch.

Just as she lifted her knee to slam into his groin, the knife flashed in front of her eyes again. The flat line of his mouth inched up on one side. The smile was sick, feral, and her stomach churned in terror.

He held the blade close to her eye. "Where is it?"

"What?"

"No games. I want it now."

She fought through the waves of panic shaking through her and tried to process the question. It didn't make sense. "I don't know—"

With a flick of his wrist, he shook her as if she were a rag doll. "Lying won't save you."

The back of her legs banged against the chair behind her. She rose on tiptoes to keep from losing touch with the ground. He had to be over six feet, and at five-five she didn't have the strength or the height to take him on.

"You have the wrong person." The words scratched against her dry throat and her fingers wrapped around his, trying to ease the punishing hold.

"I guess you want to do this the hard way. We'll see how sorry you are after a few hours of convincing." He threaded the end of the knife through her hair. "I am very good at my work."

His hollow laugh sent tremors running through her. The rush of blood to her head made her dizzy. But she had to stay on her feet. Had to think.

"Tell me what you want."

"Tsk, tsk, tsk." He waved the knife back and forth in front of her nose in time with the annoying noise. "Don't play dumb."

"Please." Begging, running—even with her energy reserves low she would try anything.

"You are done causing problems." He scraped the knife's tip over her skin.

She flinched and felt a prick. If there was pain, it didn't register. Not with the adrenaline coursing inside her.

But he just stood there, staring at her. Her fingers went numb from the desperate clenching around his arm. Her heart thudded hard enough to echo in her brain.

Lying. She went with lying. Her breathy voice barely rose above a choked whisper. "I'll tell you what you want."

"That's a good girl."

She pretended to cough. Let the rasp in her voice back up her lie. "Can't breathe."

As if she weighed nothing, he threw her into the chair. Her back slapped against the cushion and she gripped the armrests to keep from slipping down on the material.

The plan was to spring up and out of the seat again, screaming and flying at him as she attacked. Nails, feet, hands, she'd use them all and bring the lamp with her as a weapon.

As soon as she moved, he clamped a hand over her wrist. Trapped it against the chair and pressed down. Put his weight into it. The intense pressure had her crying out.

The knife flashed again. "Not one sound or I break it."

His head turned toward the door. One minute he was in front of her. The next she was up and he stood behind her with the knife touching her throat. "Sounds like we have company."

BEN SMILED WHEN he saw her number light up his phone. Putting the car back in Park, he let the engine idle as he stopped in the middle of her apartment complex's parking lot. "Change your mind about letting me come in?"

Silence greeted him. No, not silence. Shuffling and footsteps. And something that sounded like a muffled shout.

Everything inside him stilled as he strained to hear. All his years of training came roaring back, from the navy to NCIS to his current position with the Corcoran Team. He beat back the urge to race in, gun firing. He needed to know what was happening, if anything even was. And the nerve pulsing by his temple suggested it was.

More moving and a loud crinkling sound as if the

phone was breaking in two. After a few seconds her voice boomed through the confusing thuds.

Who are you?

Ben didn't bother to turn off the car. Reaching over the center console, he pressed his index finger in the lock reader, and the compartment next to his radio popped open. With a gun in his hand, he got out.

One in his hand. The other at his ankle. That should do it.

Without looking down, he hit a series of numbers on his cell and lifted it to his ear. After two rings, the line clicked and he started talking. "Apartment six. Now."

Without hanging up, he slipped the cell in the front pocket of his black pants. That would be enough. His teammate Joel Kidd would track the phone, and someone, or a whole group of them, would come blazing in. Until then, it fell to him to assess and rescue.

Crouched and running, he slipped down the pathway that ran through the center, stopping one apartment down. Constantly scanning the area, he looked for trouble. Except for the muffled voices from a television and the wail of a child a few doors up, everything stayed quiet in the comfortable suburban area.

Her door and the drapes to her front window were closed. He could see the light on inside. Everything seemed normal. He knew that wasn't true. And if he'd misread the scene, he'd apologize after. No way was he asking for permission or explanations first.

With a long exhale, he controlled his breathing, forced concern for Jocelyn out of his mind and put on the back burner the memory of how skittish she was to even go on a date. She would be okay. He would make sure of that.

Keeping his steps as silent as possible, he bounded

up the stairs. He picked up the low murmur of a male voice. With a light touch, he checked the knob. He had the element of surprise on his side and tried to plan the best way to use it.

Then he heard her scream, and all common sense vanished.

Raising a leg, he nailed his heel into the door right by the knob. The wood split and the lock broke. There was a huge crack as the door slammed open and a hinge snapped.

Somewhere in the distance, a dog barked but Ben ignored it. All of his focus centered on Jocelyn and the man pulling her out of the chair and wrapping an arm around her neck while he hid behind her like a trapped rat.

Ben took in the knife and did a quick glance around the room for a potential partner to this guy. Then he stared at her. The attacker had her long auburn hair pinned under his arm. His hold hiked up her skirt high on her thighs. Nothing torn or ripped. The disheveled state suggested she was thrown around but that the attack hadn't gotten as far as this guy planned.

Those huge blue eyes pleaded with Ben and her hands shook where she grabbed on to her attacker's arm. She wasn't crying or screaming. She stayed stiff and maintained eye contact.

Good woman.

Gun up, Ben moved into the room and kicked the pieces of what remained of the door shut behind him. Having an innocent neighbor wander by would only cause more trouble. Kids and families lived in this part of town. Someone might interfere. That meant the death toll could rise in a second.

Ben ran a quick mental inventory. The other man's

face didn't look familiar. He held a knife, not a gun, though he could have more weapons handy. Clear eyes and dark clothes perfect for a silent attack.

Yeah, this wasn't a junkie looking to steal jewelry. Possibly a professional, though that didn't make sense. Jocelyn was a nurse, not a field agent.

Something else was going on here. Ben would figure out the "what" later. Once the man no longer touched her.

"Step away from her," Ben said with his voice as steady as the hand holding the weapon.

The man's eyes narrowed but his arm tightened against her throat. "Who are you?"

Confusion and maybe a touch of worry. Ben knew he could use those to his advantage. "Put the knife down."

"You don't seem to understand who's in charge."

"I am." But Ben needed that blade away from her skin. She already had a nick where a small trickle of blood welled.

"You shoot me, you shoot her."

The man underestimated his opponent. Also a good sign in Ben's view. Bravado had taken down more than one otherwise strong man. "Actually, no."

The attacker ran his nose over her hair and the side of her face. The inhale was deep and exaggerated. "She is lovely."

Ben didn't say a word. Didn't so much as twitch. One sign of weakness and Jocelyn could get stabbed or worse.

The man pointed the end of the knife at Ben. "Is she yours?"

There wasn't a good answer, not one that would help her, so Ben continued to stay quiet.

"Ben." Her soft voice carried a wobble.

The attacker smiled in a way that promised pain. "Sounds as if the pretty lady knows you."

When Ben didn't respond, the man's mouth flattened and twisted into a look of pure hate. "Gun on the floor now or I will carve her into tiny pieces."

Her chest heaved and a strangled sound escaped her throat.

Ben watched the light fade from her eyes and knew it was time to act. "Okay, enough."

His gaze locked on hers. With a subtle bounce, he glanced down at her arm. Then he did it again. The heavy breathing forcing her chest up and down in rapid movements slowed and she frowned. He hoped she got the hint.

"Do it now." The attacker barked out the order.

Putting his hands in the air, Ben held up his gun. "Let's stay calm."

The attacker waved the knife around, getting far too close to her face. "Stop stalling."

"My arms are going down." Ben hoped that last attempt delivered the message to Jocelyn.

He had only seconds and a minimal window for error. With his knees bent, he lowered his body and hands toward the floor. The attacker scowled but his focus centered on Ben, right where Ben wanted it.

He set the weapon on the carpet and watched the other man shift his weight. Right when the tension eased, Ben put his palm near his foot, pretending to push up again.

"Now!" he shouted.

In one smooth move, he came up. His second gun slid out of its holster and arced through the air right as Jocelyn smashed an elbow into her attacker's stomach.

"Humph." The man bent over. When he came up

again, he roared with a sound of fury that bounced off the walls.

Ben's bullet struck the man's forehead and cut off the sound.

Jocelyn was tight up against Ben with her arms wrapped around his neck before the other guy hit the floor. Ben looked over her head. The bullet hole and trail of blood told him the attacker was dead. So did the look of horror frozen on his silent face.

Still, Ben didn't take any chances. Pushing Jocelyn behind him, he stepped over the attacker's legs and kicked the knife away. After a quick pulse check, Ben's heart finally stopped thundering.

"Is he dead?" Her voice shook.

When Ben turned around, he saw every one of her muscles quaking. Those eyes were wide enough to swallow her entire face. But she was on her feet and not curled up in the corner. She'd given him the assist without any training or lengthy explanation.

Man, he was impressed. "You did great."

"I think I'm going to throw up."

Okay, not his favorite response. "You're probably entitled to, but I kind of wish you wouldn't."

"Looks like I'm too late." Wearing jeans old enough to be faded near white and a dark beard from days without shaving, Joel stepped in the doorway.

Before Ben could make the introductions, Jocelyn bent down and grabbed the other gun. As she aimed it at Joel, the barrel bobbled from the trembling of her arm. "I will shoot you."

Joel's eyes widened and his hands went into the air. "Hold on there."

"Whoa, Jocelyn." Ben reached around her and lowered her arm with the softest touch he could manage in a crisis. "This is Joel Kidd—he's with me."

She glanced at Ben over her shoulder and a haze fell over her eyes. "Joel?"

She should recognize the name from the assignment Ben had been on when he met her. Joel never came to the hospital but Ben had mentioned him. He had talked about him again tonight when he spoke about a friend with a car fetish.

Joel flashed her a smile. "Ma'am."

If she was impressed with Joel and what most women seemed to find irresistible in him, she didn't show it. She spun around to face Ben again. All the color had drained from her face. "What is going on?"

That was exactly what he planned to find out.

Chapter Two

There were more than eight men in her apartment. Jocelyn couldn't give an exact number because she stopped counting when Ben's friends—he called them his team—arrived and the police showed up. Even a stray neighbor or two poked their heads in before being pushed behind the crime-scene tape.

Officers shifted in and out of her family room. A few took notes and circled every piece of anything left on the floor post-attack. They'd snapped photos and a Detective Willoughby asked her questions until her mind went blank.

Now they trampled over every inch of her floor as Ben talked with them, pointing from the door to the couch and explaining things she couldn't hear. They must have mattered to him because he kept up a steady stream of talking while two uniformed officers listened and nodded now and then.

Ever since Ben escorted her out of the fray and to the barstool in her kitchen, she hadn't moved. She didn't think she *could* move. Her bare feet balanced on the bottom rung, frozen despite the humid night. Ben had put a sweater over her shoulders but she couldn't feel the material against her skin.

The sirens had stopped wailing but the rumble of conversations continued all around her. She heard a clatter and creaks and looked up to see a crew in blue jackets file in with a gurney. There were evidence bags and a huge red stain under the head of the unknown man sprawled on her floor.

Something inside her brain started circling, around and around, and she almost fell over.

"Hey." Ben stepped in front of her, blocking her view of the chaos and holding her steady with hands on her forearms. "You okay?"

If anyone but him, any voice but that soft, reassuring tone, had asked the question, she might have lost it. The calm demeanor only held so long. With the adrenaline rush gone and the shock of what could have happened settling in, her mask slipped. She felt raw, as if someone had flipped her inside out.

She managed a half smile. It was forced, but she tried. "Do you want an honest answer?"

"Probably not." A policeman tapped Ben on the shoulder and he waved the officer away.

Suddenly desperate, she grabbed Ben's hand and pulled him back to face her. Through everything, he kept her centered. Focused.

His arrival had given her hope. He had sent her the signal when he needed her to fight off her attacker. Then he had saved her with a single shot.

For a woman who had seen so much pain and death on the job, it was the terror she'd experienced in her home this second time that threatened to break her apart. Smash her right into pieces on the floor.

After all those months of learning to handle her anxiety and dealing with the newfound issues of needing everything just so, she was plunged back into a cycle of spiraling fear.

But he, a guy trained to kill, the exact type she should have run from, had proved to be a lifeline. She searched her mind for the right words. When nothing came to her, she went with something heartfelt but simple.

"Thank you," she said as she squeezed his hand.

He leaned in as those intense eyes softened. "You saved yourself. You called and left the line open, which let me know you were in danger. You nailed him in the stomach when I needed the distraction to get the upper hand."

"I got lucky."

"No, you used your head." Ben warmed her hand in both of his with a gentle rubbing. "Without your fast thinking, this would have turned out differently."

"So, the urge to heave up my dinner will pass?"

He chuckled, rich and as soothing as a sweet caress. "Eventually."

A tall man with black hair and startling bright blue eyes walked over. He wore khakis and a polo shirt. Not a police officer but definitely in charge. Everyone certainly acted as if he was. He also looked familiar. Jocelyn knew the face, but the waves of exhaustion crashing over her now made finding the memory impossible.

He spared her a quick glance before launching into conversation. "You're going to need to do an inventory, but nothing obvious is missing."

Ben dropped her hand but rested his palm on her shoulder. "Jocelyn, do you remember Connor Bowen?"

Relief battled with the need to close her eyes as she leaned against Ben. The pieces from the past few months fell together—the hospital and the coma patient. Endless rounds of questions about when the man would wake up and how quickly the nurses could clear the floor if needed. "He's your boss."

Connor held out his hand and gave hers a shake. "That's how I like to think of it."

"No overturned drawers. Electronics are all here. I saw some jewelry." Another man walked up, reading from a list and ticking off each item. "The bedroom is painfully neat."

Yeah, that described her. Painfully neat. She decided to remind the guy she was sitting right there before he said anything embarrassing about how her underwear sat in stacks arranged by color. "Hello."

Ben pointed at the newcomer. "And this is Davis Weeks. He's basically the second in command at the Corcoran Team."

She remembered the company name. Sort of.

"Ma'am." Davis nodded, then launched right back into the rest of his speech. "There's no identification on the guy. There's a chloroform-soaked rag on the floor, so he came prepared and likely didn't expect a fight."

A bone-crushing tremor shook through her. "He tried that first, then went with the knife."

Ben swore under his breath. "The important thing is he didn't hurt you."

Scared the crap out of her, but didn't really touch her, unless you counted the small nick and the nasty bit of manhandling. His smell, the threats and the sick glee he took in saying them would stick with her for a long time. But as a critical-care nurse, she'd seen real injuries, blood spurting and watched as the life drained out of patients. Using that scale, she was pretty lucky.

She kept repeating that, hoping she'd come to believe it.

"You must have messed up his burglary plans," Connor said. "Good for you."

"No." The word slipped out before she could think it through, but she knew she was right. This went beyond taking a television or rummaging through her wallet for cash.

Ben stared at her with narrowed eyes. "What are you saying? Did you know him?"

"No, but he said he wanted me to give him something."

All three of them swore that time, but Ben said it the loudest. "Sick jackass."

Bile rushed up her throat at the thought, but she choked it back. "No, not that. Like, hand him something. Something he thought I had in my possession."

Squinting and closing one eye, she tried to push out the visual images of the terrible things that could have happened and focus on the attacker's words. But they wouldn't come to her. With all the panic bouncing around in her head, she didn't have room for much else. She wondered if she'd even remember the names of all the men she'd met tonight by this time tomorrow.

"Excuse me?" Connor asked the question in a rough tone. "Go back a second and explain."

She rubbed her forehead and tried to ignore the three sets of eyes boring into her. "He kept asking me to give him something."

Davis made a quick note in his small notebook. "What?"

"That's the thing. I don't know." She shook her head. "He never said."

They all wore matching frowns. Except for a bit of feet shuffling, they stayed quiet. The room whirled with activity behind them. It was like riding around and around on a carousel with all the noise and sights blurring around her.

Finally Ben turned to Connor. "Our phone connection was on during most of the attack. Have Joel play back the tape and you might be able to pick up something in the background. Whatever is on there was enough to have me jumping out of the car and heading for the apartment."

Davis nodded. "I have your car keys, by the way. You're lucky no one stole it with the way you left it."

"Like I care about a car right now."

The conversation leaped to a point that had her gaze bouncing between them. "Wait, go back. What tape?"

"Office protocol. All of our calls are taped in the event of an issue like this one." Connor made the comment as if it explained everything. As if it made sense.

The idea was like a whack to the center of her chest. She dealt with a high level of stress in her job, life and death all the time, but she never worried about being shot. At least not until she'd met Ben. "You mean this sort of thing happens to you guys a lot?"

"I wouldn't say a lot." He threw it out there and they all nodded.

Her head threatened to implode as she worked through all the facts. "And you tape everything. Even private calls?"

Davis frowned at her. Shot her one of those "how could you not be following?" looks men sometimes gave when they thought they were making perfect sense.

Wasn't that annoying?

"We only listen if there's trouble," he said.

"Who are you guys exactly?" Her voice rose and more than one head turned to look at her, including Joel, who shot her a wide smile.

Ben answered, "The good guys."

Again with the cryptic comments. That one explained even less than the last ones about the attacks and the tapes. Still, she was alive, and that meant she was willing to cut them some slack and ignore the more controlling parts of their personalities.

But only some. "Right now I'm inclined to agree, but maybe more information would help."

Ben opened his mouth but Connor started talking first. "The Corcoran Team."

These men needed some work on the concept of sharing. "And?"

"We're a private group. We assist in kidnapping rescues and conduct threat assessments, sometimes for the government and sometimes for businesses…and others."

She wasn't sure he'd actually explained. If anything, she was more confused. And there were some scary words in there. "By 'assist' and 'conduct' do you mean you do those things legally?"

Davis shrugged. "Okay. Sure."

Now, that was convincing. She almost rolled her eyes. "Do you think this was a kidnapping? Someone wanted me or some poor woman this guy thought was me?"

Connor looked over at the police milling around and nodded a hello to Detective Willoughby before turning back to her. "We don't know yet. Maybe."

Ben blew out a long breath. "A little tact might be a good idea."

"No, it's okay." She meant to wave him off but accidentally brushed her hand against his where it lay on her shoulder. Then she kept it there, letting him fold his fingers over hers. "I'd rather have the truth."

Connor looked from her face to her hand and back

again. "We're not sure what that is yet. I'm just happy Ben was close by to step in."

"I would guess Ben was happy, as well," Davis said.

She decided to ignore that but she did glance over. A strange whirring took off in her stomach when she saw Ben staring back at her. This time fear had nothing to do with the tingling sensation.

She cleared her throat. "So, when you were at the hospital, you were guarding someone you thought might get kidnapped?"

He sucked air through his teeth, making a hissing sound. "Uh, not quite."

"He was guarding a killer to make sure his killer buddies didn't take him out before we could question him," Connor said, filling in the gaps left by the silence.

"Well, then." She had no idea what to do with that bit of information. She settled for ignoring it. That was then and she had enough to deal with right now.

Ben shook his head. "Again, Connor. Tact."

"Ignoring that, to the extent I can, how did this guy get into my house? I have double locks and…" Davis smiled at her. Connor stared at the floor. She got the distinct impression he was trying not to laugh. "Now what?"

"You want to tell her?" Davis asked Ben.

This couldn't be good. "Someone should."

Ben turned her so that she saw only him. "Locks are easy to pick. You really need a specialized security system if you want a true warning system and a chance to get away or get help."

Her stomach plummeted to the floor. All those hours spent checking and rechecking the locks. Those nights she slept in the stale air because she was afraid to drift off with the windows open. None of it mattered because any sicko or criminal could just jimmy them open and walk right on in.

Well, wasn't that terrific?

She took a deep breath and counted to ten. Her heart still hammered and her hands shook, so she tried it again. The audience didn't help, but she would not let panic plow her under.

"Jocelyn?" Ben's concerned voice slipped through her misfiring brain.

She concentrated on the counting.

"You still with us?" Davis asked.

She tried to block them out and duck the embarrassment. These guys handled guns as if they were born holding them. She was halfway to a full-on screaming fit at the idea of an unlocked window.

"I'm fine." She strained to say the words and winced over the rasp in her voice.

"There's no need to panic. You know now." Davis glanced at Connor. "We can hook that up for her, right?"

"Of course," Connor said.

She needed a minute and wanted to tell them not to worry. From the wrinkled brows and joint staring, she knew she was too late with that assurance.

"Okay, that's enough safety talk for now." Ben clapped his hands together and all eyes went to him. "No more alarm discussion. Doesn't matter anyway because she's not staying here tonight or anytime soon."

The change in his demeanor from listening to taking charge stunned her. She'd seen him in the hospital as he chased down a guy with a gun, but when he talked with her, he had always kept his voice light and his mood friendly. He had flirted and stopped by the hospital and generally swept her off her feet with his charm until she had finally agreed to go to dinner. Since that had ended with a rescue, she was grateful, but the truth was she had no idea which version was the real Ben.

But she knew one thing that was not happening. Scared or not, she needed a bed. At this point she thought she could sleep right there on the barstool. "Well, I'm not sleeping in my car, so let's figure something out."

Ben's inviting smile reappeared. "I was thinking my house."

He had to be kidding. They'd had one date and it had ended in a bloodbath. Not exactly the best introduction for more time together. "What?"

"Not a bad idea," Connor said. "We need to do some investigating here and clean up. I can keep Joel with me."

Seemed to her they were skipping an obvious step, which was hard to understand, since hints were all around them. She held out her arm and swept it across the room full of people trampling through her stuff. "The police—"

Connor waved her off. "We'll back them up on this one."

"Why? This strikes me as being a bit out of your jurisdiction, and I'm saying that because I refuse to believe someone wanted to kidnap me." Every time the thought entered her head, she pushed it right back out again. "He had the wrong place or something."

Connor looked at her as if she'd lost her mind. "Possibly. We'll talk that through with Willoughby."

"Does it have to be him?" she asked.

"Detective Glenn Willoughby is the man in charge, or so he said when he introduced himself." Connor pointed at the man across the room in the dark suit and no tie. "He's new but doesn't seem that hard to handle."

She wondered if they were talking about the same

guy. The Detective Willoughby who talked to her had rapid-fired questions until Ben made him stop. "I'll trust you on that one."

"And for the record—" a smile spread across Connor's face as he talked "—we're stepping in because you're dating Ben. That makes your safety our concern."

"A major one," Ben mumbled under his breath.

"They're dating?" Davis's eyes widened. He glanced around, as if checking to see if anyone else overheard. "That's a definite thing?"

Before they could get carried away and totally lose focus, she tried to rein them in. "Date, as in singular."

Ben shrugged. "I thought it went well."

Wiping her hands over her face, she pushed her hair back off her shoulders and bit back a groan of frustration. "I can't even think right now."

"Put a bag together." Davis hitched a thumb in the general direction of her bedroom. "My wife will be happy for some female company in the house."

"I'm coming, too," Ben said.

Davis nodded. "Fine, but you get the couch."

Ben held up his hands as if in surrender. "So long as I'm in the building."

Speaking of trampling, they went off on a tangent and left her behind. Never mind they were talking about her life. Maybe that was what happened with the savior types. They tried to control everything. Not her favorite male trait.

"Gentlemen?" They kept talking and the arguments turned into a haze of mumbling she decided to ignore. To keep from knocking their heads together, she looked around the room, at all the men standing around and the few trying to act as if they weren't listening in.

Then she saw the blood puddle on her once-fluffy

beige carpet and the body bag next to it. Reality punched her right in the stomach as she realized life had changed on her again. "I don't get a say, do I?"

Ben stopped talking to his team long enough to look at her. "No."

Chapter Three

Jocelyn liked Lara Bart-Weeks immediately. She had shoulder-length brown hair with perfect blond highlights and a warm smile. Pretty and trim, and she practically glowed when she looked at Davis. Even now she made up the guest bed while keeping up a constant stream of welcoming chatter.

The place was as inviting as she was. The brick two-story town house sat on a tree-lined street just off the historic center of Annapolis. The inside had been gutted and renovated, a project that was ongoing by the look of the dismantled kitchen downstairs. But this room, with the blue walls and stacks of pillows piled on the high bed, screamed comfortable.

Lara stood on the opposite side of the mattress with a pillow hanging loosely from her hand. "Hey, you okay?"

"Not really." A thousand different emotions bombarded her, but Jocelyn couldn't seem to hang on to any of them long enough to find a steady center. But one thing she knew for sure—she was not okay.

Lara's smile turned sad. "It's all going to work out."

Rather than pretend to be fine or wave off the concern, Jocelyn slumped down on the end of the bed. She held out her hands and turned them over, stunned at the constant movement. "I can't stop shaking."

"That's normal."

"I don't feel normal."

Lara sat down next to her with a pillow tucked on her lap. "It's aftermath. Nerves bouncing around as you come down from the dramatic episode. Once the adrenaline is gone, the memories of the horror come rushing back. This is the hard part, but it will get easier. I promise."

Jocelyn still battled the need to double over and saw blood pooling on her carpet whenever she closed her eyes. Still, something in Lara's tone caught her attention. "Sounds like you talk from experience."

"Unfortunately." Lara sighed. "A time not that long ago, a man hunted me down and tried to kill me. When that didn't work, more men came."

Her comment touched off a new round of trembling. Scenes of the night tumbled through Jocelyn's mind as she glanced at Lara. "What are you talking about?"

"I had this job performing security-clearance checks for government agencies. I'd go in, ask questions, do the investigations." She tossed the pillow on the bed behind them. "One job went wild and ended up with this mess in the NCIS."

Memories clicked together. The news, the shooting, slim facts and a sense there was a piece of the story the public didn't know. Jocelyn knew about the scandal because anyone not buried underground knew. Between the headlines and cries of corruption, the NCIS story a few months back had been hard to miss.

Then there was the personal angle. The Ben part. That was what had Jocelyn sitting at her laptop and searching for more information for two weeks before she said yes to a date. "The murders and the deputy…something. I can't remember his title but it's the case where Ben testified against his boss about the corruption."

Lara frowned. "Did he tell you about it?"

"He didn't really have to. His name was all over the papers." The boss was an accomplice in an old murder, and the boss and his connected friends had tried to cover up a leak of information, leading to a long line of deaths and Ben leaving NCIS under a cloud of suspicion. "It's not very attractive, I know, but I started with the scandal, then did a few more searches under his name."

"Sounds smart to me."

Maybe it was the way she said things or how genuine she came off, but something about Lara had Jocelyn wanting to open up. She'd hidden parts of herself away for so long. After being scared and having no one believe her, fighting off a policeman stalker with all the power and reputation on his side, she had stopped reaching out for help.

After it all blew up and she changed her life around, the anxiety remained. She battled it by limiting contact and coming up with routines that comforted her. A few times the other nurses insisted she come out with them and she did, but she barely knew Lara.

Still, the words flowed and Jocelyn was helpless to stop them. "When Ben started asking me out, I thought I should figure out if the man I met at the hospital as a guard was as decent as he appeared to be, because I've met some who aren't."

"We all have, but he is. I knew it from the second he walked into Corcoran headquarters. Not that much later, without even thinking about it, he put his body in front of mine and saved me from being shot."

Apparently that sort of thing was a habit with Ben. "Sounds familiar."

Lara's smile came back, more subtle this time but definitely there. The kind that said she was about to go on an information-fishing expedition. "So, he *started* asking you out?"

"I made him work for it." Jocelyn ran her fingers over the outline of the flower print on the comforter.

"Good for you. When it's easy for them, their egos are unbearable." Lara got up and went to the dresser. She turned around with shampoo and other bathroom essentials in each hand. "Since I'm a bit of a bath-gel collector, we have a lot of choices, but you might like a few of these."

Figuring out which fragrance to use seemed so mundane after seeing a dead man on her floor. Jocelyn didn't know how to switch the fear off and go back to regular conversations. The idea of sleeping in a strange bed already had her insides jumping around.

She rubbed her hands together but stopped when she felt a burn on her skin and saw how red they were turning. "So, at some point I'll go back to not being terrified of being attacked again?"

Lara's arms dropped. "I won't lie to you. It will creep up on you now and then, but you'll get through it. And you're safe here."

"I can't exactly live in your guest room." Though Jocelyn had to admit she didn't hate the thought.

She winced at the idea of returning to her apartment. She'd considered it a safe place, her sanctuary. An easy walk to the water and a few miles from the heavy traffic of the touristy historic district and the Naval Academy. But no way could she stay there now.

"You're welcome to live here as long as you need." Lara handed her two bottles.

Jocelyn took them without reading the labels. "Aren't you guys newlyweds?"

"Almost three months, but we've known each other a long time. We were engaged before." Lara held up a hand as she rolled her eyes. "Long story."

That sounded better than talking about murder. "Apparently I've got time."

"Right now you need sleep."

She made it sound so easy. Jocelyn knew from experience it wouldn't be. "I'll never be able to drift off."

"I'll bet you a doughnut tomorrow morning that you will."

BEN SAT AT Davis's dining-room table and spun a water bottle around, watching it tip and using his palms to make sure it didn't fall over. The edges thudded until it came to a stop. Then he started again.

Davis reached over Ben's shoulder and snagged the bottle-turned-toy. "So you and the nurse are dating, huh? A guy goes on his honeymoon, misses one case and comes back to all sorts of changes."

Skipping the groan, Ben wiped his hands over his face then let his arms fall against the table with a slap. "You held that in longer than I expected."

"You know, if you had convinced her to let you into her apartment for some after-date time, the guy may have taken you out before you could have saved her." Davis shrugged as he sat down sideways in the chair across from Ben and stretched his long legs out in front of him. "So it's good she had no trouble resisting you."

There were times Ben hated the lack of privacy in this group. They were connected by the intercoms in their watches and phones. Joel tracked their movements and each had cameras in their houses that reported back to Corcoran headquarters and could be turned on in the event of an emergency call. It reminded him of his time in the navy—all structure and little alone time. Having been out for years, it was taking time to get used to the intrusions again.

"Are you doubting my abilities?" Because by the fifth time Jocelyn said no to coffee, Ben had started to.

Davis shrugged. "Just pointing out that Dating Ben might not be as on top of things as Agent Ben."

"Feel free to go to bed. I don't need conversation." But he would stand watch. Ben stared out the double glass doors to the backyard and into the darkness beyond.

He knew from hanging out there that the large rectangular space consisted of mostly mud in the middle covered with some boards, thanks to all the renovation work Davis and Lara were doing. They also refrained from building anything out there or working on the landscaping because Davis wanted a clear sight line and limited places for intruders to hide.

Not that the guy was paranoid or anything. Though the elaborate security system complete with heat and motion sensors and a secret door to the neighbor's yard suggested some trust issues.

All those precautions meant they should be fine staying there tonight. But almost anything could be breached, and until Ben knew if the attacker wanted him or Jocelyn, or was just part of some unlikely random event, he planned to be ready.

"I'm not going anywhere," Davis said.

"Worried?"

"Let's say confused."

It wasn't a surprise that Davis phrased it that way since he was the more serious one of the group. Much more than his younger brother, Pax.

Like Connor, Davis led by example and wouldn't hesitate to throw his body in front of any of them to make sure they survived. He ran them through drills to keep their instincts and skills sharp.

He demanded the best and gave the exact same back. That kind of dedication inspired loyalty. So when Davis showed signs of concern, they all did.

Ben gave a voice to the questions churning in his mind. "None of this makes any sense."

"Any chance the attack is about you?"

That was the worry. The one Ben wrestled with as guilt sucker-punched him. "The guy asked Jocelyn to give him something. Wish we knew what."

"Could be subterfuge. We've seen that sort of thing before. The guy fears he's caught and throws some nonsense out there to send us spinning in the wrong direction."

"It does seem convenient." That ticked Ben off. The idea he put Jocelyn in this position kept his mind turning to find a way to save her now.

"You start dating a woman and someone comes after her. It could be a one-plus-one thing." Davis wiped a hand across the wood top of the table. "I don't like it."

"You think it's blowback on the NCIS deal."

"There are some angry people out there who don't like that you spotlighted the corruption."

"Well, that's tough sh—"

Davis held up a hand. "Hold on there. I'm not one of them. You helped save Lara and put your neck out there to weed out the losers in an otherwise fine group. It's all pretty damn heroic to me. I'm just saying some of the crazier elements might not agree."

Three beeps cut off Ben's answer. He glanced around for a phone. "What was that?"

But Davis was already up and opening the small door beneath the cabinet holding dishes and other delicate things that looked far too easy to break for Ben's liking.

After pressing a few buttons, Davis took out a gun and another clicked against the table when he set it down. Next he took out his phone and talked in a low voice.

Two words: *stay upstairs*.

"Motion sensor," Davis said as he pulled out of the direct line of sight through the back doors and motioned for Ben to do the same.

"An animal?" But he didn't wait for an answer. Taking up position on the side of the opposite door, Ben peeked into the yard now bathed in a bright yellow light. Something out there had those shining through the trees.

"Maybe."

Ben checked the gun and prepared for battle. "So, no."

"Contact the team and I'll check on the women upstairs." Davis pivoted and froze.

"Too late." Lara and Jocelyn stood at the bottom of the staircase in sweatpants and T-shirts.

From their wild hair and big eyes, Ben guessed they'd gotten Davis's message on the way to bed and found clothes.

That wasn't good enough. Ben wanted them locked down. "You two need to get out of here."

"Agreed." A nerve ticked in Davis's cheek. "Lara, take Jocelyn to the safe room."

The beeps turned to a long, steady buzz. The alarm wound up, getting louder every few seconds.

Time was up. Rather than draw straws, Ben issued some orders. "You take them upstairs and I'll check it out."

"Another attack," Jocelyn said in a voice that sounded small and distant.

Ben shook his head. "Could be nothing."

"Lara, we're not debating this. Ben needs me down here. You go up. You know the plan." Davis turned to Jocelyn and his voice suggested neither woman argue. "You stick with Lara and do not come out of hiding unless you see a member of my team."

Jocelyn frowned. "I'm not even sure if I know all of them."

Enough talk. A shadow moved in the yard and Ben wanted it handled before whoever it was got closer to the house. "We need to move."

Davis pointed to the staircase. "Go."

With one last glance at Jocelyn's pale face, Ben took off. Skipping the glass doors, he headed for the one off the kitchen. It dumped into the side yard. He could circle around if he was able to stay hidden.

Tiptoeing over boards and around boxes, Ben headed for the door. He balanced on a box of tiles while he squeezed around the new dishwasher where it was lodged between the kitchen island and the freshly painted cabinets.

The place was like a war zone. He had to hope if anyone made it this far they'd fail to look around and get tripped up in this room.

When he reached the door, he crouched on one knee and listened for any noise on the other side. When the night stayed silent except for a few crickets, Ben turned to Davis. "No light."

Davis nodded and hit something on his black watch.

Ben didn't wait another second. Still kneeling, he lifted his arm and turned the knob. Slow and quiet, the door opened a few inches.

The scent of freshly mowed grass overwhelmed the room. He waited for footsteps or signs of a surprise attack. Nothing happened.

He squeezed through the small space and waited on the top step. His gray T-shirt wouldn't blend in well with the surroundings. That made him a target, so he'd have to move fast. He glanced over his shoulder and saw Davis's nod.

Time to move.

Stepping down the few stairs outside the door, he slid against the wall and scanned the yard. He picked up movement in the shadows, over by a group of shrubs under the tree diagonal from his position across the backyard.

Even sticking to the fence, circling around without being spotted would be tough. He couldn't see Davis, but he sensed he was out and running along the far side and directly into danger.

The goal was to draw any gunfire away from the house and catch whoever was out there. To try to cut the person off, Ben headed for the fence to his left. He had his guns plus the one Davis had given him. That should be enough firepower.

He held one now as he sprinted through the grass, dodging twigs or anything that would make noise. Keeping his breathing even, he turned and followed the fence line.

After a quick visual tour around the yard, his gaze landed on those shrubs again. He could make out a second shadow and hear grunting and shuffling.

Ben took off running. Blood pumped through him and his heart pounded. Not from the physical exertion. From the hunt.

Davis and a man dressed in colors so dark he blended right into the landscape rolled on the ground, wrestling and punching. One got the upper hand and leveraged his body to the top. Then the other.

Ben couldn't get a clear shot without running the risk of hitting Davis. Not at this angle or at this time of night.

"Hey." His voice cut through the night, freezing both men.

The second of hesitation was exactly what Ben needed. He grabbed for the attacker, pulled him off Davis. The guy went through the air and landed hard on the ground with a soft thud. Putting a foot on the guy's back, Ben aimed his gun at the man's head,

Davis lay sprawled on his back and panting. A trickle of blood ran down the corner of his mouth and he held his stomach as he rose up on his elbows. "Nice takedown."

They needed this guy alive. It would be hard to question a dead man. Ben repeated the mantra while he forced the energy racing through him to subside. No matter how much he wanted to shoot the guy, he couldn't. "You picked the wrong house."

The guy dug his fingernails into the grass. "Go to hell."

Ben almost smiled at the reaction. "Then we'll do it the hard way."

He barely got the sentence out when he got nailed in

the back. The hit knocked the gun out of his hand and stole the air out of his lungs.

The blow came from above. It was as if this one fell out of the tree. Might have been the case, since he'd made a soundless entry.

Something scraped against Ben's arm, and a knee slammed into his back. He was on the ground and kicking with what felt like three hundred pounds of furious male dropped on top of him.

They were all shouting and moving. In a mad scramble, Davis reached for his gun, and the attacker on the ground crawled toward the one Ben had dropped. Clothing rustled and someone yelled.

Ben took a dive and landed next to his dropped weapon just as the guy with him on the ground knocked into him. It was like hitting a wall. Ben swore as his body bounced.

That meant plan B. Swiveling around to his back, Ben grabbed for the weapon at his waist and fired up and out. The attacker on his feet got off a shot as he dropped to his knees, then fell face-first into the grass. Ben felt a burn across his shoulder as the man next to him roared.

"One inch and you join your friend." Davis's voice shook with anger.

Ben whipped his head around and saw Davis on his side with his gun aimed at the attacker struggling to his knees. With an arm wrapped around his midsection, there was no question Davis was ready to forget the questioning and engage in some rapid-fire action. Probably had something to do with this guy's mistake in coming onto Davis's property and breaking through the first line of defense.

"I'd listen to him before he kills you." Ben sat up, then

winced when every part of him screamed in agony. No doubt he was going to hurt something fierce tomorrow.

When the intruder shifted, Ben smashed the butt of his gun into the guy's temple. The attacker went down with both hands to his head and yelling as though he'd lost it.

Ben didn't wait around to see what he'd do next. Pinning him to the ground with his knee, Ben wrenched the guy's arms behind his back and tightened a zip tie.

"This one's dead," Davis said as he checked the pulse of the one who had done the face-plant.

Ben hadn't even seen Davis move, but he was on his haunches over the body and staring at Ben.

Ben still didn't understand how this guy had got the jump on Davis. He was not a small guy. "He get off a shot on you?"

"I thought he was watching you but he turned before I could adjust. Good thing you rode in when you did or my miscalculation could have cost us both." Davis nodded at Ben's shirt. "Speaking of which, you okay?"

Ben sat down hard on the soft grass. Looking down, he saw blood, which led to a shot of pain across his side and over his shoulder. Amazing how injuries didn't blare to life until you got a good look at them. Then they burned like hell. "Not my best work."

"You're alive, aren't you?"

Lights clicked on in neighbors' yards. Ben could hear doors banging and voices over the side of the high fence. The siren in the distance was most likely headed their way. "I think we're about to have company."

"I'll handle it. Better yet, I'll make Connor do it." Davis exhaled as he got to his feet. He looked down at the breathing attacker, the one muttering and swearing. "Can you drag this one to the garage?"

Ben nodded. "Yeah."

Davis stopped and took a longer look at Ben. "You sure?"

"Do I look that bad?" He touched his shoulder and hissed out a painful breath. "Man, that hurts like a—"

"Think positively, Jocelyn might find this sort of beaten-up-and-bleeding thing sexy in a guy."

Ben thought back to the look on her face at her apartment and knew she wouldn't.

Chapter Four

Light flooded the backyard. Jocelyn heard the shots and bolted out of the safe room before Lara could close the door and lock them in. No way was she going to sit upstairs and wait to see if Ben got killed. Not if all of this was about someone being after her. Not at all, actually. Guns scared her and the idea of being grabbed made her knees buckle, but she could pick up her cell phone and call the police.

She flew down the stairs and was in the dining room about to make that call when she saw Ben stumble out of the garage at the back of the property by the alley. He headed for the house but his usual cocky walk seemed less steady than usual.

Through the crashing fear and panic, she saw something dark splotched all over his shirt. He got closer and… *Blood.* Lots of blood. It stained his T-shirt on his side and painted his shoulder.

Before she could think about safety, and ignoring Lara's calls from behind her to stay down, Jocelyn opened the glass doors and stepped onto the small back porch. A wave of humid air smacked her in the face but she didn't care. All that mattered was the strong man walking up the yard as he stared at something on his hands.

He was no more than six feet away when he finally glanced up. His face went from pale and sort of blank to furious. His mouth flattened and his eyes grew dark.

He picked up the pace until he stood one step away, scanning around the yard as he went. "I told you to stay inside."

She wanted to throw her body into his arms and hold him to reassure herself he was fine, but his sharp tone stopped her. Falling back on her medical training, she pushed out personal concern.

She raised a hand toward his shoulder but stopped as she visibly assessed the damage. "You're hurt."

Ben glanced over her head to a spot behind her. "Davis is fine. He's talking to the guy next door."

Jocelyn peeked over her shoulder and was stunned by Lara's wide eyes. Guilt wrapped around Jocelyn. She had raced through the house panicking for Ben but Lara had to be crazed about Davis's safety. Not that she showed it. Except for the way she kept biting her lower lip, she appeared calm. Jocelyn had no idea how that was possible.

"Are the police coming?" She didn't know if that would be good or bad. Two incidents starring her, and they might jump to conclusions.

Ben nodded. "Likely on the way."

"I hear sirens," Lara said.

Jocelyn didn't understand why the entire town wasn't already in the backyard. Her whole neighborhood had come out at her place. Here, it was quiet in comparison. "You two live in the middle of town. How can people not be running in every direction?"

"Luck," Ben said.

"He means Davis is calming them down and will put Connor on the job as soon as he gets here, if he isn't already."

Jocelyn couldn't worry about that now. Ben listed to the side. She knew he'd go down soon. Careful not to jostle him, she shifted her weight and moved in beside him. She took some of his weight against her as she checked his shoulder.

"What are you doing?" he asked but let his body fall into hers.

Truth was she worried he'd go into shock, but she didn't share that. Something told her this protector by nature would not take that news well. "I want to check your wounds."

"I'm fine."

Lara stopped looking at the yard long enough to scowl. "Ben, let her look you over."

"See, everyone thinks you should give yourself over to me."

He let out a harsh laugh. "Now you offer."

"Ben's still standing?" Davis came up behind them with a gun still hanging from his fingertips. He gave his wife a wink. "Connor and Joel are here and handling questions and the guy two doors down who's demanding answers."

"Davis." Lara's eyes welled up as she breathed out his name.

"I'm okay, hon." Davis caught her when she leaped at him from the doorway straight into his arms. Ducking down, he buried his face in her hair and whispered something only they could hear.

The moment was so personal and intimate that it almost hurt to watch them. Jocelyn could feel the love pulse between them. She thought she saw Davis's hand tremble as he rubbed it up and down Lara's back. Heard the soft sobs as Lara nodded but kept her face tight against her husband's cheek.

Finally Davis lifted his head and his voice sounded gruffer than before. "Ben took the brunt of the damage."

Ben shook his head. "You got hit in the stomach."

"What?" Lara lifted Davis's shirt, revealing a flat stomach and an already blue bruise.

"Ribs. I'm more concerned about Ben's bleeding."

Ben waved him off. "Later."

Jocelyn could barely keep up. Each man pointed to the other as being injured even though they both looked rough.

She put a hand on Ben's chest, the only place not covered in blood. "We need to get you inside."

Davis nodded. "Listen to your woman."

She didn't bother to correct him. Ben stayed quiet, too, and she had no idea what that meant. Probably that he'd lost enough blood to be incoherent.

Without any fanfare, Jocelyn lifted Ben's shirt, or tried to. The caked blood made it stick to his skin. She hoped that meant the slash wasn't deep and had already stopped seeping.

"Where's our friend?" Davis asked as he wrapped an arm around Lara and pulled her in close for a kiss on the forehead.

The question drifted around Jocelyn. She heard it and it took a second before it registered. "Wait, who are you talking about?"

"We caught one." Ben jerked when her fingers brushed close to the stomach wound. "Careful there."

As far as she could tell, the man was skipping over some important information. "There was more than one?"

"Two." Ben started to turn and his hand shot to his bleeding shoulder. "The breathing one is passed out in the garage."

Davis picked that moment to smile. "Did you help him fall asleep?"

When Ben didn't answer, an eerie quiet settled on the night. Sirens wound down and she could see the flashing lights and hear an older woman's voice.

None of that mattered. Ben beating someone up and dragging him across the yard did. "Ben?"

"He shot me. Or his accomplice did. I can't really remember." Ben shook his head and his balance faltered.

"Yeah, he needs to sit down." Davis reached Ben first. Putting his shoulder under Ben's good arm, Davis got them up the last step to the back door and leaned him against the jamb. "I'll find Joel and send him in before I check on our guest."

Anxiety welled inside Jocelyn. Good guys or not, going after someone tied to a chair made what was left in her stomach sour.

"What are you going to do?" Not that she knew what she wanted the answer to be. Police made her wary. So did hiding a guy in the garage and knocking him around to get some answers.

"I hope Connor will be able to head off the police so I have time to ask our friend some questions."

"He's unconscious," she pointed out.

Davis shrugged. "He'll wake up eventually."

Lara stepped in front of her husband. "No."

"He's tied up." He acted as if that explained everything.

To Jocelyn it made the whole idea sickening. "Which is the problem."

Ben pushed off from the wall and stood up, wobbling slightly. "I'm going with you."

Jocelyn still couldn't wrap her mind around the conversation or what Davis planned to do. "Are you going to torture the guy?"

He frowned at her. "No."

Relief zoomed through her.

Then Ben opened his mouth. "He did try to kill us."

"That's not an excuse." He had to see that. She needed to know Ben understood that.

"We have medical supplies upstairs," Davis said.

Guns in the house, a safe room and football-stadium lights in the backyard. These guys were prepared for anything. "Of course you do."

"You know," Davis said, "it might not be bad to have a nurse around here."

Because that was what she wanted to do on her day off. Sew up this crew. "You guys need one a lot?"

Ben nodded. "More than you'd want."

And that was what scared her.

LITTLE MORE THAN a half hour later, most of the crowd had cleared out of the house. Police officers still wandered around the yard, and more than one neighbor came to bang on the door and complain about the lights only to get turned around by Davis. Not many people crossed him.

Ben watched the cars pull away, then walked through the house to the back porch. He stood there and rolled his shoulders back, trying to ease the stiffness working its way through him.

Big mistake. His muscles had locked up but the aches

settled in. He winced in pain as the bullet graze on his shoulder burned.

He wanted to let out a shout but kept his voice low because Jocelyn was right inside cleaning up. Though he wouldn't mind having her stand close and run her hands over him again, the last thing he needed was her rushing out and ordering him to bed. For rest.

But, man, he'd enjoyed watching her work. She turned bossy and took control, which was interesting, since Joel usually handled the minor medical stuff.

Between the two of them, Ben had stitches and bandages and a pocketful of painkillers. As a combined force, they would be hard to duck. If they thought you needed medical attention, you were going to get it.

He debated going inside and seeing if he could get Jocelyn to touch him again when Connor and Detective Willoughby headed up the backyard from the garage. Willoughby talked and Connor nodded his head. That usually meant Connor was collecting information, not giving it.

Once they hit the back porch, Connor broke the silence. "There was no identification on the dead guy."

"Figures." Ben wasn't surprised. The team rarely got that lucky.

If he had to guess, he'd say the attackers were professionals. Hired guns. That made it more and more likely he was the target, and all the blame for the deaths and injuries fell on him. He endangered Jocelyn. The realization hollowed him out.

"Gotta say, I've had better nights." Connor blew out a long breath. "Would have made things easier if we found a license."

The detective's gaze, wary and a bit defensive, traveled between Ben and Connor. "Anything you two want to tell me?"

Ben had loads of questions, and once he'd finished sizing the detective up, he might ask a few. Until then, he could only go on what he could see. Fortysomething and smooth. Maybe a bit too slick. If this Glenn had once been a beat cop, those days were long behind him. He looked more like television's idea of a detective. Dress pants and a gold watch. Made Ben wonder what kind of car he drove.

He made a mental note to have Joel run a check. "Like what?"

"I've been on the job for three months and despite your business's reputation and yours—" the detective shot Ben a quick look "—I've never met any of you until tonight, and now I've seen you twice in a few hours."

Connor screwed up his lips. "Weird how life works."

"Suspect," the detective said. "I don't believe in co-incidences."

Something they had in common. Neither did Ben. "They happen."

"I'm going to need statements from everyone in the house. They answered some questions, but we're not done here."

If the guy planned to make his career on this case, Ben vowed to shut it down. He already had reporters looking to him for the next headline and former NCIS friends who wouldn't take his calls. He vacillated between being invisible and being infamous, and he didn't like either extreme.

If it weren't for Corcoran, he'd totally lose it. Connor had taken him in when the NCIS case ended and Lara no longer had to look over her shoulder for danger. The whole team knew the story about how his boss had turned out to be a killer and a liar, but none of the guys put that on Ben. He'd worried they would see his choice to testify against his boss as a breach of office loyalty and not trust him to back them up. But they'd all made clear their support and given him to understand that they would have played it the same way.

Loyalty was not the same as sanctioning corruption. They got that. It was a shame his dad, the admiral, saw it differently.

But there was nothing Ben could do about the divide in his family tonight. The immediate goal was to figure out if the attacks now related to his decisions back then.

And he would ferret it all out but he needed some breathing room away from this detective to do it. "This was a home-invasion attempt. Very straightforward."

The detective folded his arms in front of him. "I'm beginning to wonder if any dealing with you is going to be that simple."

Ben had to give him that one. "Probably not." Since the distrust already ran pretty high, Ben decided they might as well add to it. "Did we mention there's a guy in the garage?"

The detective's head shifted forward. "Excuse me?"

"I'm sure I told the officers," Connor said.

Ben would bet money he hadn't. Delay was the only way to question the attacker without interference.

Corcoran ran under the radar. Part of their success relied upon being able to get in and out of situations without bureaucratic red tape. Not that the few minutes of questioning helped. The guy was not talking.

"One of the attackers survived." And Ben was starting to regret that. "So far."

If possible, the detective's mouth dropped even farther into a flat line. "We're going to have a talk about this."

"What?" Connor asked.

"Your team's decision making and protocol and how private companies aren't equal to law enforcement or immune from the law."

There was a time when Ben had bought into that kind of argument. Then he had stood on the wrong side of one of the "good guys" and realized the line between right and wrong needed to shift around sometimes.

"Your choice—a lecture or an interrogation," he said to the detective.

"I plan to do both."

Ben blew out a long breath. "Lucky us."

IT WAS WELL AFTER two in the morning before Jocelyn saw Ben again. She'd sewn him up and insisted he rest. Naturally, he went outside. Headed right for that garage and the man tied up out there. The only thing that kept Jocelyn from crawling out of her skin as she waited was seeing that police detective come out with Ben on one side and the bound man on the other.

That was twenty minutes ago. She still hadn't heard his footsteps on the stairs. And she listened for them. Kept her door open, careful not to wake Lara and Davis down the hall.

She paced the space between the chest of drawers and the end of the bed. Much more of this and she'd wear a hole right in the pretty cream-colored carpet.

"Hey." Ben poked his head in the doorway. "Why aren't you sleeping?"

She almost knocked against the wall mirror. At the last minute she managed to stifle a scream. Barely. "You're the one who should be resting."

For six feet of muscle, he sure could sneak around.

He wore sneakers, and the stairs hadn't so much as given the smallest creak as he came upstairs.

He tipped his head to the side and shot her that sexy smile that made her toes curl. "Still a little keyed up, so I walked the family room for a few minutes and re-checked the locks and alarm."

Of course he had. Sounded like him, but she refused to let that could-take-him-home-to-mother look win her over. "Did you kill him?"

"What?" He stepped inside and closed the door be-hind him. "You mean the guy in the garage?"

"Unless there are more bad guys lying around out there?" A chilling thought.

"What kind of man do you think I am?" All amuse-ment vanished from Ben's face. Tiny lines appeared around his mouth.

She thought they might be from stress. No wonder, since the entire evening was an invitation to a heart at-tack. "I have no idea."

"How about thinking I'm the guy who saved you?" He held up two fingers and stepped in closer. "Twice."

Without thinking, she moved back. When he frowned, she knew he'd noticed the shift away from him.

Guilt whirled around her. Despite the gun and the job, he'd never actually scared her. She'd been unsure of him and worried he hid a side that could rear up at any moment, but their date had been so freeing. So fun and relaxed.

Nerves had made her fold her hands on her lap to keep from fumbling and knocking over a water glass or something equally embarrassing at the table. But his charm and stories of life aboard a ship had made her laugh out loud.

Truth was she didn't really know him, and the past

few hours had her emotions whipping from grateful to wary. No sane woman fought off a man who saved her life. But the ease with which he accepted violence took her mind spiraling down a dark path.

She forced her feet to stop moving. "Look, I'm not trying to be a jerk about this and know I'm failing."

"You're just tired."

His hands landed on her shoulders and his thumbs massaged her joints. The gentle touch lulled her, reeled her in. She wanted to slip into his arms and forget her worries.

When she felt his breath across her cheek, she blinked. She was practically on top of him.

With a hand on his chest, she stepped back, breaking his hold. "Ben, I can't do this."

He held up his good hand, as if in surrender. "I won't try to kiss you. I mean, I want to and without the newest attack I'd planned to tonight, but the timing stinks."

She added his cute rambling to the list of things she liked about him. But the "con" list sent up a flashing red warning light she couldn't ignore. "I mean this, the violence, the shooting. Worrying you'll lose control and do something crazy. All of it."

His hands dropped to his sides. "What are you talking about?"

"I've lived through this before." The words ripped out of her, actually felt as if they tore at her throat as she admitted them. "I can't do it again."

"Lived through what exactly?"

On top of everything, she couldn't drag that baggage out and paw through it. "Can you stand there and tell me this—the attacks—aren't because of you?"

His face went blank. "I have no idea."

But she had her answer. He clearly thought he was

the cause. She'd seen him for weeks at the hospital as he guarded that other man. Watched him a bit too closely, but she'd seen the practiced look before. Blank meant he purposely wanted to hide his feelings.

Another con.

"We went out and I got attacked. We came here and attackers came again." It sounded pretty obvious when she spelled it out like that. "I'm a nurse who works long shifts and, except for the occasional drinks with the girls, lives a boring life. That's how I want it."

But did she? She'd been repeating the mantra in her brain so frequently for a year that she now wondered if she'd finally fooled herself into believing it.

The best part of the past few months had been flirting with Ben. At the hospital, on the phone. When he stopped by and just happened to be in the hospital cafeteria getting coffee during her breaks.

She'd started timing her life around those meetings. She realized that now. The attention flattered her. The thought of not seeing him for days, or longer, started an ache in her chest that weighed down her whole body.

She knew that made her a hypocrite or a tease, but she couldn't stop the battle between what intrigued her and what scared her witless. That left only one solution.

"You'll get the sense of security back. We'll figure this out." This time he didn't reach out, but his voice dipped low to the soothing level that made all the other nurses sigh.

"I said no to you five times because I wanted quiet. Peaceful." The second the words left her mouth, part of her knew they were a lie.

"Sounds boring."

"One date and all this happens. You can see where I'm reasoning out the cause and effect and—"

"Blaming me."

The word stung her. She didn't mean that. "Not blaming. Connecting the dots."

"Same thing."

She reached out for the brush on top of the chest because she needed something in her hands. Needed to find a way to keep from twitching because the way her insides jumped all over the place, it was inevitable that would soon show on the outside, too.

"Some women might find it all thrilling. I find it terrifying."

He lifted the brush out of her hands and put it back down. "What are you saying exactly?"

"Tomorrow I find somewhere else to go. Somewhere safe because I sure don't have a death wish, but somewhere away from all this." She rubbed her hands together then wrapped them around her middle. When that felt wrong, she dropped them to her sides again. "And then we end this before whatever is following you makes me collateral damage."

"Happy to know you're concerned about my well-being in this scenario."

Everything was coming out wrong. She wanted to drop her head into her hands. Maybe scream for an hour or two to work out all the frustration building inside her. "Don't you get it? I'm trying to get out before you mean too much."

His head snapped back as if she'd slapped him. "That's an excuse."

"I'm being realistic."

"You're being a coward."

In a blink, guilt turned to fury. Anger washed over her, heating her skin everywhere it touched. "How dare—"

"Let's try this." Without warning, he stepped in close

with his hands on her hips. "I'm going to kiss you. If you don't want me to, you need to say so."

This far away she could smell the soap on his skin. Something clean and fresh. If she reached out, she could brush a finger over that sexy scruff on his chin.

And he asked permission. It was all too much for her wavering self-control to handle. She couldn't speak. Couldn't breathe. She was pretty sure she'd forgotten how to do both. She may have nodded and she certainly didn't remember putting her hands on his forearms.

But she felt the kiss.

His head dipped and his mouth brushed over hers. Soft at first, gentle and undemanding. Then the second pass, bone-shattering and intense. Deep and full of need. His lips crossed over hers and a hand went to her hair. It drove on, unlocking something deep inside her that she'd shut down and forgotten.

When they broke apart, all she could do was stare into those rich green eyes. "Uh, wow."

"Tomorrow we'll figure out date number two."

Chapter Five

Gary Taub sat in his top-floor office in the nondescript office building away from the historically protected houses and expensive yachts associated with Annapolis. His business, Worldwide Securities, required anonymity and more security than a hundred-year-old town house with its faulty wiring could offer.

He looked around. The place might be new and state-of-the-art, but it was drab. If his wife were still alive, she'd drag in photographs and paintings. But he'd lost her a year ago to improperly diagnosed stomach cancer, six months after losing his brother to carelessness.

Without Marilyn's touch, from the unadorned beige walls to the beige carpet, it could be any office in any corporation, anywhere in America. The only nod to the subject matter of his work was the presence of three computers lined up around the utilitarian metal desk.

He'd set up the surroundings this way on purpose. The only way to hide what happened here was to make it boring, forgettable. He'd been conducting the same work, moving the money around, for ten years. No need to change his operation now.

And he knew how lucrative silence could be. He had the expensive modern waterfront home a few miles away to prove it. He'd earned it. As a businessman he demanded perfection—in his clothes and his technology. He thought it would be obvious he expected the same of his employees.

For the first time since he took his seat, Gary stared across the desk at Colin Grange, the man who had served as his security manager for over two years. Fifty and suffering from the syndrome where his pants got lower and his stomach got thicker every year.

But his credentials, first in the military and then with a defense contractor, made him the perfect choice for this position. So long as he didn't go soft or fail in his planning. Unfortunately, this time he had.

"How hard is it to grab a woman who lives alone and maybe weighs a hundred and thirty pounds?" Gary asked.

"There was a man there."

"I am aware." Gary had been receiving reports all night. He'd gone home and come back because the phone kept ringing. An attempt to remove the woman from her house, then a second attempt at some other residence in Annapolis.

Turned out Ms. Jocelyn Raine, reported loner without many friends or any family, had a savior. Finding that out after the fact ticked Gary off.

"Then you understand how we couldn't—"

Gary blocked the excuse with a simple raise of his hand. "I was told she was single."

Overprotective boyfriends tended to muck up everything. The body count was already two too high.

Gary had spent the past hour retracing every step and making sure nothing could tie the dead men littering the houses of Annapolis to him or Worldwide.

He'd been careful and neither man knew about Gary

or the reason they were being paid, other than to grab the woman. Still, that left a loose end or two. And from Gary's experience, someone always tugged on them.

"Explain." That was all he said. Colin had been with him long enough that he should have been able to pick up on the fury behind the word.

"At the apartment…this guy came out of nowhere."

Apparently Colin thought it was his job to sit in a car and watch. "And why didn't you step in and subdue him? I assume he wasn't so large that he was immune to a bullet."

Colin touched the two pens lined up at the edge of Gary's desk blotter and rolled them between his fingers. Even picked one up and twirled it around. "It was a losing battle."

When he toyed with the more expensive of the set, Gary slapped his hand against the pen and flattened it on the desk again. "Maybe I've failed to impress upon you how important this job is."

Colin jerked and withdrew his hand. "No, sir."

"I have two men down and another in police custody. Independent contractors, yes, but you can see where that might be a concern for me."

"I can get her."

The clock was ticking and Colin picked this time to be incompetent. Gary figured he'd need to handle that problem, but he wanted this job done first.

They had three days. Exactly three.

"There was nothing in the apartment?" he asked even though he'd watched the video surveillance of the search.

"No."

"Then first, take care of Jacobsen before he talks. Make it look like a suicide while in police custody or whatever will call the least attention to his death. Use our contacts for that. Clean up after. Delete files. You know the drill." Not that Gary trusted this sort of thing to his staff. He'd erased what he could find. He doubted anything else existed, but he needed Colin to think it was a matter of life and death—his own—if anything was found.

"He won't talk," Colin said.

"Not once he's dead." And that better happen soon or Colin would be next. "Then we need to come up with a solution for grabbing Ms. Raine that isn't a direct attack."

"Sir?"

The lack of common sense infuriated Gary. He felt his temper rise, but he strained to wrestle it back again. "We're trying not to raise suspicion, though I'm not sure how that's possible now."

"Why?"

The urge to kill him surged. "Because there are people involved with this job who are not going to be happy with the way you've bumbled your way through this so far."

Colin nodded and lifted his hand as if he was going to take another run at the pens, but stopped. "Right."

"And get me intel on the boyfriend."

Gary had names for the town-house ownership but there was surprisingly little to find. Looked like a dummy corporation of some sort.

That meant there was more digging to do. He wanted everything from credit reports to the second cousins' medical records on this guy. Every stone would be turned over, scrubbed for information and dumped.

Colin checked his phone then looked up again. "I don't have a name for the boyfriend."

And that fact intrigued Gary even more. If Ms. Homebody was seeing someone, people would be talking. Find the right nurse or neighbor, or even on-scene policeman, and this would all be resolved. Good thing Gary had an "in" there.

But he still wanted to check Colin's skill. See how far he could get. "Examine the police reports. Eyewitness statements."

"By when?"

"Tomorrow morning." Because there was a bigger concern at work here. Someone who disliked mess and surprise more than Gary did. "Whatever you need to do, do it before we both need to answer for this Ms. Raine and her ability to dodge capture."

THEY ALL GATHERED in Davis and Lara's kitchen the next morning. Three members of the team were out of town and had been for months. They were the traveling squad. The skeleton crew that manned the office every day in Annapolis was there, along with Jocelyn. Lara hadn't come downstairs yet.

Ben eyed the ever-present coffeepot in the center of the table. Before he could reach for it, Jocelyn grabbed it and poured a mug for herself and one for him. Straight-up and black for both of them.

In the stark light of day, Ben still didn't regret the kiss. She'd stood there babbling nonsense and acting as if he was some kind of criminal. Not because of NCIS but because of who he actually was inside and what he believed in.

The suggestion he somehow lacked humanity or would let her get hurt kicked him in the gut. It had ticked him off and kept him up most of the night.

But that kiss. That taste and feel of her turned out to

be even better than he imagined, and he'd been having some pretty hot dreams about her almost from the beginning. That hair, a deep rich red, and eyes a sky-blue.

She was trim with an athletic build. And when she wore that nurse's uniform, his brain flipped to autopilot and his lower half clicked on.

Being patient and giving her time to get comfortable was slowly eating away at him. He'd wait if that was what it took, but when she'd talked about cutting it off last night, he'd shifted into fast-forward. The relief that poured through him when she leaned into the kiss, meeting him touch for touch, not pulling back, still filled him today.

He leaned over and caught the scent of vanilla. Good grief, she smelled like cupcakes. A man could only take so much.

Joel swiveled his chair from side to side like a little kid. "You okay over there, Ben?"

Yes, but he planned to kill Joel later. "I was making sure Jocelyn remembered everyone. Yesterday was a bit crazed."

She smiled and pointed as she went around the room. "Joel Kidd, the tech wizard. Connor Bowen, the boss. Davis Weeks, my current landlord."

Pax nodded. "Nice."

She frowned at him. "But you I don't know."

"My baby brother, Pax." Davis dumped a tray of muffins on the table, then sat down with Connor across from Ben. "You'll find that Pax is annoying, but you get used to it. You kind of have to because we need him around here."

Pax leaned over Connor to snag a muffin. "I'm the good-looking one."

Connor rolled his eyes. "And so modest."

Ben noticed the Weeks brothers were alone when they usually had women by their sides these days. One absence was particularly notable, since she owned the house with Davis. "Where's Lara?"

Davis didn't look up from his coffee. "Sleeping in."

"Now that we're on the same page, we need to come up with a new solution." Connor opened a folder as he talked.

"That's why he's the boss," Joel joked. "Jumps right to the point."

"So will I." Jocelyn smiled as if she'd been waiting all night to drop this bomb. "I can stay in a hotel near the hospital."

Ben almost groaned. He knew she'd immediately pick a solution that made him nuts. Forget running from him—this was just dangerous. Yeah, she believed he was the target, but whoever was behind this knew her and associated her with him. That made her safety his biggest concern.

"You can't go to work." Admittedly this wasn't her field, but she had to know that fact. Seemed obvious to him. From the nods around the table, the rest of them got it.

"I have to."

For a very smart woman, she was slow picking up on this point. "Absolutely not. And you can frown at me all you want. It's not happening. It can't."

He glanced around the table looking for backup, and Davis jumped in. "Not a good idea, Jocelyn."

"I have bills to pay." She slid her fingers over the handle to her mug, back and forth over the smooth surface.

He was mesmerized by her lean fingers and trim, manicured nails. He blinked to break the trance. "Don't worry about those."

She made a face that suggested he needed meds. "How can I—"

"Whoa." Davis held up a hand "She can continue to stay at the house. Lara would like the female company. Apparently, I can be difficult."

"No." All eyes turned to Pax when he gave the curt reply.

Gone was his usual lighthearted banter. He wore a matching scowl to Davis's expression, and tension spilled through the room as they engaged in some sort of brotherly standoff.

Ben didn't understand what was happening. "Something you want to share with the rest of the class?"

Pax didn't break eye contact with his brother. "It's not my news."

"What are we talking about?" Jocelyn asked.

Pax folded his arms over his chest. "Davis, you know I'm right. It's not safe. You're offering because that's what you do, not because you think it's a good idea."

Whatever was going on arced back and forth between the brothers. The rest of them sat there watching the staring contest.

But Ben had to pipe up. "Someone took two shots at Jocelyn in one day."

A fact he still couldn't process. Men at her home. Others following her around town to this house. He expected danger in his job. Even though he watched Davis and Pax get ripped apart when the women they loved stepped close to danger, Ben never thought his work would bleed into his personal life. Lately that was all it had done.

His father blamed him, claiming after all his years of service he was suffering a backlash at the Pentagon for Ben's choices. Powerful people sat in jail awaiting trial. And Ben had walked away from a career that had once meant everything, only to have his name stamped on the front of every paper and as the lead in every news broadcast.

"Lara is pregnant." Davis made the announcement with a slap of his palm against the table. "Okay, that's the issue."

Everyone started talking at once. There were back-slaps and congratulations. Davis took it all in, nodding and thanking everyone even as his face grew more drawn.

"Why the secret?" Not that Ben knew much about babies, but he couldn't imagine a better set of parents than Davis and Lara.

"She's not far along, and because of what happened before with the miscarriage…" Davis blew out a harsh breath. "Well, we were being careful and preferred not to talk about it yet."

That explained it. Fear gripped Davis. Ben didn't blame him one bit. "Congratulations."

The only one not jumping up and down with good cheer was Jocelyn. For a few seconds she just sat there. "It's great news, but how could you let me in the house at all? Or Ben?"

Again with the theory that he was the devil's right-hand man. "I'm sitting right here."

Jocelyn gave him a "wait until I get you alone" glare, and not in the good way. "My point is that Davis strikes me as the kind of guy who might put his wife in a pro-tective shell when she's pregnant. And in this case, he should. We're talking guys with guns here."

"I would if Lara would go without yelling the house down. I'd take her to an island with a private doctor and hide out until the baby comes," Davis mumbled under his breath.

The click of Connor's coffee mug against the table had everyone turning. He didn't slam it down or yell. No, neither was Connor's style. He simply commanded attention and somehow got it without any fanfare.

He cleared his throat. "I'm not convinced this is a Corcoran issue but—"

"What does that mean?" Jocelyn asked.

"I think they—whoever *they* are in this case—are after *you*."

"Why?" Ben asked.

"I've been with Ben the whole time," she said at the same time.

"If someone wanted to take Ben out, they could have gone after him on the street or at his house. Why wait until you were around?"

Ben had walked through that argument in his mind and on paper. He came up with one reason. "Leverage. They know we're together and can use Jocelyn to get to me."

"Together, really?" Pax asked as he looked around the room. "That's news, right?"

"Then there's the problem with the records search," Joel said.

Ben groaned. He knew what that meant and it wasn't good. Background checks. Quiet checking. It all spelled trouble for Corcoran.

Jocelyn sighed. "Now you lost me."

"Joel has a warning system of sorts set up. When someone goes looking for information on us or our property or our backgrounds, it trips an alarm and Joel finds out." Ben found the whole thing spooky but he had to admit it had come in handy more than once in the short time since he'd begun working with the team.

"Last night someone started looking into the ownership of Davis's house." Joel made a few swipes on his tablet. "Thought maybe that detective was double-checking but it didn't trace back to him. This look came from someone skilled at hiding their digital footprints."

Davis swore. "That's great."

But it was what Joel and Connor didn't say that had Ben's nerves clicking to high alert. "No one checked on me."

Joel winked at him. "Exactly."

"Hello." Jocelyn waved a hand in front of Ben's face. "Still lost."

"No one is searching for my house, which is a brand-new condo, one I got since leaving NCIS." One whose ownership trail Joel and Connor had helped Ben bury through a corporation and a shell and whatever else they insisted on to keep his name off the title. "The search was for Davis's house, where you are right now. It suggests the attackers don't know about me and are fishing to figure out who you're with and why."

She winced. "But why me? I don't know anything."

"I have no idea, but we're going to find out." Connor glanced down at his notes. "We start with the clue about the first guy wanting something from you. That means we retrace your steps and, sorry to say, tear your life apart."

Her body stiffened and she almost bounded out of her chair. "What?"

Ben held her down with a hand on her thigh. The reaction combined with the cryptic comment from yesterday about this not being her first experience with danger

had him wanting to do some background searching of
his own. "We need to know what we're dealing with."

"Whatever it is just happened, so I'm thinking this is
about the last month, if it's about me at all."

Interesting how she defined the time parameter. Ben
knew that meant something. There was something in her
past she wanted to hide. With his personality, that was
exactly where he now wanted to dig.

She deserved privacy, and a part of him wanted to
discover things about her normally, like non-agents did.
Over meals and while watching movies on the couch.

But life had been rapid-firing disasters at them from
the beginning. He couldn't figure out how to slow it all
down now and double back.

And her past could hold the key to what was happening today. The way Joel eyed her, Ben knew he planned
to call upon all of his search skills, which were consid-
erable, to hunt this one down.

Ben wanted to be the one to find whatever was to be
found about her. Give her some dignity in not having the
whole group know, if that was her preference. So, he'd
try to get answers from her, and if that failed, he'd step
carefully and keep the search narrow. He owed her that.

"We'll circle back to what we need to check in your
past later." Connor's gaze traveled over the table. "You
know what else this means, right? We're on lockdown
protocol. Pax and Kelsey move in with Davis and Lara."

That was how the system worked. It was one of the
many fail-safes they put in place. They drew in close,
making it difficult for anyone to grab one of them. Ben
was surprised Connor wasn't insisting they all bunk
with him. That was the usual rule.

More than likely had something to do with the preg-
nancy announcement. Lara would want to be home and

tough-guy Davis would do backflips to make it happen. Connor's decision to carve out an exception allowed them all to skip the arguing step.

Jocelyn leaned closer to Ben. "Who's Kelsey?"

"Pax's live-in girlfriend."

Pax groaned. "She's going to love this."

"You want her safe," Connor pointed out.

"And she'll insist on opening her store." Jocelyn opened her mouth, but before she could ask, Pax filled in the blanks. "She owns a coffee shop not far from the City Dock. We live above it."

Connor's hand balled into a fist. "No one goes to work unless you're working at the Corcoran offices."

"Wait a second." Jocelyn pushed back her chair and stood. "Stop."

Joel smiled. "I'm surprised you waited until now to jump in and say that."

"I have nursing shifts. I can't just disappear or fall out of rotation."

Joel's grin didn't lessen one bit. "Use the excuse that you were attacked at home."

"Since it's true," Davis said.

They were using the wrong strategy. Ben had been negotiating meals with this woman for weeks. She'd stick up for others before she did for herself. He had finally got her to say yes to a date when he pointed out the hospital staff had taken up a pool to see how many times he'd get shot down. He had no trouble using pity for the first date. After that, pity was off the table.

But the reality was, he wasn't the only one on that side of the table with a rescue complex. "If someone is after you, they could follow you right to the hospital floor and endanger patients, other nurses, innocent visitors checking on sick relatives."

Joel made an explosion sound. "And he goes right for the gut shot."

She sat down hard. Clenched her teeth together, looking as if she wanted to yell at Ben for taking that route. "That's not cool."

He didn't budge. Didn't give her a way out of lessening the possible tragic outcome. If anything, he was tempted to start listing all sorts of horrible things that could go wrong. "But it's true."

She saved them all from hearing more. "Impressive argument…and also a winning one."

"I had a few hours last night to work on it." Long hours of not sleeping and a few worrying she'd shimmy out the window to avoid him this morning.

"That's enough information on your nighttime activities." Keeping his caffeine addiction up and running, Connor reached for the coffeepot again. "Joel will take the crash pad on the third floor of my place. Ben and Jocelyn will be on the second floor with me. All in separate bedrooms, of course."

Jocelyn rubbed her temples with her thumbs. "A lot of decisions are being made for me and no one is bothering to ask me."

And Ben could tell she was not pleased about that. It was another thing he'd learned. She was independent and any suggestion of needing to be coddled didn't go over well.

He liked that about her. The spirit. The way he first saw the dedicated nurse and welcoming smile, then the backbone underneath, won him over.

"It's for your own protection," Connor said.

Ben winced over the monotone delivery.

Jocelyn went a step further. "Do you know anything about women?"

"My wife would probably say no."

Jocelyn's gaze went to Connor's ring finger and the slim band he wore. "You have a wife?"

"She's out of town."

Not a good subject. Ben had forgotten to warn her on this one. Jana had been MIA for months now. Connor talked about a sick aunt and then about some work she needed to do out of town. Neither excuse sounded all that compelling.

They all liked Jana. She was warm and smart. She did some work with them and supported them all by opening her home and never complaining. But those last few weeks before she left had been rough. She'd turned quiet, as if her spirit was broken.

Now Connor kept up the pretense but they'd all come to the conclusion Connor and Jana had separated. Maybe Connor hadn't come to grips with it, but it seemed real. And the lack of communication from her couldn't be a good sign.

As if sensing the tension in the room, Jocelyn switched topics. "Oh, just so you know, I pretty much hate the protect-the-girlies argument."

Connor nodded. "I'll take that under advisement."

With the fight over, she slumped back in her chair. "Okay, I'll agree to most, but I go to work tomorrow to straighten out shifts and get coverage and do a last check on my patients."

Ben wasn't agreeing to that one. "No."

She didn't concede. "This is not a negotiation."

She was tight-lipped, her eyes flashing with fire. More than likely he'd spend every hour battling her on this one. It was a bad idea and he'd drive her insane, but if that was what it took to get her to turn in the paperwork, fine. "Then I go with you."

The color rushed out of her face. "You know that can't happen."

Now, that was insulting. "Take it or leave it."

"Where exactly do you plan to stand during surgery?" Pax asked.

Ben had forgotten they were all there, listening. Breathing so quietly they blended into the background. No one dropped a mug. None of the chairs squeaked. Complete silence was quite the feat for this noisy group.

He'd bang their heads together later. Right now he needed to make a point, even if he said it through gritted teeth and the words stung. "You're reassessing our dating life, fine. Well, not fine but not a topic for this meeting."

Her mouth dropped open. "Ben—"

"But no matter what, you get a bodyguard. You don't move without me being right there." And he would figure out how to spin that into more dates and, eventually, into an invitation to her bed.

She blinked what looked like fifty times. "That's ridiculous."

"It's what we do. I'm good at my job and I'm the only option you get." He said it like an order and hoped she wouldn't come firing back at him.

After all, it was not as if he'd tie her to the chair. She could leave. He just needed her to think she shouldn't. Because, really, she shouldn't. Not with the danger lurking out there.

"It's settled." Connor reached for a muffin. "See how easy that was?"

Chapter Six

Gary walked across the small park to the slim strip of land between the overhang of trees. The path led to the bike trail and a bench. He ignored the sun burning into his back through his dress shirt and fought the urge to loosen his tie. It was like standing in front of a hair dryer on full blast. Branches swayed and leaves rustled in the warm breeze but everything grew sticky. And Gary hated being uncomfortable.

This qualified as a ridiculous meeting place, out in the open in the middle of the afternoon. But Kent Beane had insisted, and the nervous bobble in his voice and the fact that he used the phone, which he'd been explicitly instructed never to do, had Gary reluctantly agreeing.

He sat at the opposite end of the bench and folded his hands on his lap. "You run a bank. You should be there."

"I got your message this morning."

Ah, yes. The order to turn over Jocelyn Raine's bank statements and any other information at Kent's disposal for use in tracking down this mysterious boyfriend. Gary had to admit the note he had left on Kent's desk had been…heated, what with the threats and a lengthy description of the knife work he wanted to try.

Not that Gary regretted it. They had an annoying

loose end and he wanted it tied off. "About that. I would remind you time is running out."

"We're on schedule."

"Yet you continue to fumble around. Makes me wonder if you really love your wife." The woman tied up and lying in a box in a warehouse a few exits down the highway. Once Gary had her, Kent had been more than willing to unlock his bank's door, open his records and share resources.

With a sharp intake of breath, Kent swiveled around to face Gary. Fear radiated off him. "You promised you wouldn't hurt her."

"I never said that." Gary could almost smell the desperation pouring off the man.

Gary looked into the trees in the distance and focused on the job ahead. On his revenge.

They had killed his brother by failing to notify him in time and now Gary would burn it all down.

"I've done everything you asked." Kent was pleading now.

The mix of panic and begging made Gary ready to end the meeting. "Except control your employees."

"Where is Pamela?"

Dead. "You don't really want to know."

The teller had had the misfortune to be in the wrong place and overhear too much. She should have been home that night a week ago since the bank had long since closed. But she'd gotten locked in when she hung back to check some financial records, fishing for transactions about her friend's cheating husband.

A privacy violation and reason to be fired for sure, but that didn't bother Gary. Maybe it was even a decent thing for her to do, but her nosiness had proved to be her undoing when she'd been found listening at the door to his private after-hours conversation with Kent.

It was a good thing he had thought to check the bank's security cameras. Gary hooked into Kent's system because that was part of the deal. He checked older video files because he worried Kent might get heroic and call in law enforcement. Then Gary had seen Pamela sneaking around and overhearing things that were not her business.

He'd kept scrolling and stopped at the next morning. Not knowing what she'd done, he walked into the bank during regular office hours and went to her station. Shock rolled over her face. Panic. Then he knew she recognized his voice from the meeting the night before.

That would have been bad enough to require her to be killed, but she had compounded the problem by handing a note to Jocelyn Raine. The person behind him in line. Now both women would die.

But first Gary needed to know what the note said and how much this Jocelyn woman knew about what was really happening in the building next to the bank.

"It's possible Pamela never tipped off the Raine woman." Kent had made that argument many times.

Gary ignored every one. He would not take the risk after setting up the operation and being so close to pulling it off. "I saw the security tape. She handed something to Jocelyn Raine. Your Pamela saw me and panicked, which was smart on her part."

"It could have been a receipt."

"Then there's the problem where Ms. Raine didn't exist until recently." Between the annoying detail of her lack of a history before a year ago and her ability to evade trained mercenaries, Gary needed her caught. "Put those facts together and my partner is concerned. I am concerned. That means you, Kent, need to be concerned."

"If she was going to call the police, they'd be here."

"Or they'd be waiting to catch us doing something illegal." Catch them transferring the money and releasing the data.

"But—"

"So far, we've done nothing." Gary remembered the dead bodies starting to litter the ground. "Well, almost nothing."

"You killed Pamela."

Gary once again glanced around to make sure they were alone in the secluded area running between the noisy park and the baseball field. "You should be more concerned about me killing Sharon."

"Please, let my wife go." Tears filled his eyes as Kent wrung his hands together. "I'm doing everything you want."

"She is pretty." Gary hadn't bothered to notice if she was or not.

"Don't touch her," Kent said in an unusual burst of strength. He shifted around, crossing his legs then letting them fall down. He was a breathing bundle of nerves.

Which was why Gary had blocked cell-phone signals to the spot and carried a handy little device to pick up on listening devices. Kent was clean. An embarrassing wreck, but not taping this conversation. "You are not in a position to give orders."

"I need a few more days."

Not possible. "You have one. I'd work fast if I were you."

"I'm getting everything in place."

"That's good because your Sharon is running out

of time…and air." Gary stood up and started walking, leaving the man sobbing behind him.

JOCELYN STOOD AT the nurses' station, scribbling notes in a folder. This was the one cleanup day she'd been granted before the team put her in hiding…or whatever they were doing. She'd spent a year of her life not being free to do what she wanted when she wanted. She'd vowed never to go back to that place, yet here she was.

She felt a presence right behind her. The body heat. The scent she recognized and could call up in her memory without trouble.

She didn't bother turning around because she knew who hovered. "Ben, you're making people nervous."

"You're alive. That's all that matters to me."

This time she did peek over her shoulder. Nurses and doctors shuffled in and out of the confined space in the middle of the hallway. An older woman stood a few doors down, crying while someone who looked as if he could be her son held her.

The harsh lighting, the smells of antiseptic and floor cleaner, the constant squawk from the speakers—Jocelyn let it all fall over her. It was familiar and cleansing. She thrived on the energy and no longer broke apart at every lost soul. She'd hardened because she had to, but in private she mourned each death.

Ben scanned the floor, his gaze never stopping on one thing. Some of the nurses had the opposite problem and kept sneaking glances at him. When a male nurse dragged a cart down the hall past them, Ben crowded in closer.

She fought off a smile. "I can see we need to talk about personal space."

"I'm not hanging back and pretending I don't know

you, so don't ask." He made eye contact, focusing the intensity he used to guard directly on her. "Most of these people have seen me before anyway."

"Sitting in a chair next to a coma patient."

Ben put a hand under her elbow and guided her to the small lounge area just down the hall. The room smelled musty and magazines spilled over every table. The television on the wall provided twenty-four-hour news coverage but no one was in there right now to watch it.

"Point is, I was on this floor on the assignment where we met. There are no surprises here," he said.

"I wouldn't say that." She noticed he hadn't let go. His touch was gentle and strangely reassuring. It also silently stated he wanted her right there.

The mix of commanding and charming continued to confuse her. Her stalker had possessed that. He could convince anyone, including his commanding officer, of his innocence while attacking her in private.

She assumed that was how it worked. The evil side was real and a guy like that could turn off the other side at will. But with Ben she hadn't seen evil and she wondered if it lurked under there somewhere.

Some of the strain left his face as he continued to stare at her. "Look, I get that you're scared."

He didn't even understand what had her emotions knocking around like Ping-Pong balls. "Which Ben is the real Ben?"

He frowned. "Excuse me?"

"The sweet-talker or the grumpy one who likes to issue orders?"

"Both." He hadn't even taken a second to think about it.

For some reason the answer eased some of her anxiety. "Well, at least that's honest."

He moved his hands to his trim hips. "Fill me in on what we're talking about."

She waited until the group of teenagers walking by in the hall and arguing about baseball scores moved on and then lowered her voice. "You change from one minute to the next."

He shrugged. "It's a job hazard."

That was exactly her fear. "Is that really your answer?"

"Do you know anyone who's happy all the time?"

"Are you kidding?" She threw her arms out wide and moved in a semicircle. "Do you see where you're standing?"

"The last year pretty much sucked. I had this job..." He blew out a tortured breath. "Well, it doesn't matter."

"NCIS." It was the one topic they'd always danced around. Through the getting-to-know-you talks and dinner, he had filled her in about work but only in general terms. More about older days in the navy and how he felt about service.

The light left his eyes. "I'm guessing you know the worst and have made up your mind about what happened and what I should have done."

She treaded carefully. She knew this one stung. From everything she'd read, he had taken on a horrible situation like an expert, like everyone should want him to do—with dignity and honor—and then got clobbered for it. His father, some military bigwig, had given a ridiculous quote about how "these things" should be handled internally.

Seeing the pain etched on every line of Ben's face made her ache for him. "Not to make things worse for you on this subject, but doesn't everyone? But you saved people. Lara told me you saved her."

"No, Davis and Pax did that. Pax has the bullet wound to prove it."

"I remember Pax from the hospital." Patients' faces sometimes ran together, but his had triggered her memory as soon as he'd said who he was yesterday. He'd been guarded around the clock and demanded to be released almost from the minute his back hit the bed.

"That sort of thing changes you. You think you know the rules and the parameters are clear, then something shakes what you believe in." Ben's gaze went to the window for a second before coming back to her. "You come face-to-face with what you think is the end, with the destruction of all you've worked for, and you can't walk away unscathed."

He was finally talking, and when he stopped, she held her breath waiting for more. "You believed in your boss."

"I believed in the system and in NCIS and lost all of it. People went to prison, but I went before an administrative board and got sanctioned for working without permission with the Corcoran Team to get the truth out. Had to listen to threats about betraying my country."

An icy cold washed through her at his words and flat tone. "What?"

"After being so sure and being so wrong, my perspective is off." His eyes closed for the briefest of moments before reopening with the dullness gone. "I worry I'll mess up. Guilt eats at me and fear tears me up."

Something in the way he held his body stiffly and his eyes drilled into her as if trying to will her to believe and accept had her resting a hand against his firm chest. "I can't imagine you being afraid of anything."

His hand covered hers. "Only an idiot doesn't know fear. It's how you work through it that matters."

"You honestly believe that?"

"Yes." Voices sounded in the hallway and he glanced over her shoulder to watch another group pass by.

The buzz of activity didn't diminish. A constant stream of calls sounded over the intercom. Still, her entire focus stayed on the compelling man in front of her.

"I've been stationed overseas and served on ships. After putting my life on the line over and over, I walked into a room and wanted to put a bullet through a man I once respected, a man who worked his way to the top of NCIS." He gave her fingers a squeeze before dropping his hand. "So, yeah, I believe in a healthy dose of fear."

The words made a difference. Him opening up, sharing and not holding back. His thoughts about danger and his honesty, even though she could see the storms inside him were ripping him apart.

She'd known fear. She had stood at her door and watched a policeman smash it down. She had listened when he told his superiors lies about how they'd been dating and had a small fight. He'd been a neighbor, then he became a nuisance when he wouldn't leave her alone and started commenting on her dates and her clothes.

He had built this fantasy about the two of them and sold it to everyone, until she never felt safe. Then one time he had gone so far that even his loyal partner had broken his silence.

No, Ben was nothing like Ethan Reynolds. Nothing at all.

She inhaled deeply and took the plunge. "Want to buy me a cup of coffee?"

The darkness cleared from Ben's face and that tempting grin slipped into place. "Now, there's a change of topic."

"Seems to me you've earned the right to move on from your past. A bunch of idiots on some board of review might have judged you one way. Everyone else sees you for the hero you are, or at least the ones that matter do. Me included."

He smiled. "You know how sexy that is, right?"

The scruff, the bright smile, those shoulders. Yeah, no question she was going down for the count. "What?"

"Acceptance."

Right answer.

To keep from jumping on him and trying another kiss right there, where people worried, prayed and mourned, she stepped back. "So, how about that coffee?"

He winked at her. "Sounds like a second date to me."

"Don't push your luck."

Chapter Seven

Ben held the door open for Jocelyn as they left the cafeteria. When he realized she matched her stride to his, he slowed down. Longer legs meant he ate up more space and he didn't want her running. The goal was to stay steady and keep her safe. Calm didn't hurt, either.

The thud of their shoes supplied the only noise between them. People passed and conversations swirled around them as the clanking of silverware from the cafeteria faded behind them. He hadn't said much. Well, not after verbally spilling his guts out upstairs.

He swore under his breath, unable to understand his uncharacteristic lack of control. He had no idea why he had gone off on the tangent or told her so much. He'd never been one to talk just because.

With his upbringing, he had learned to hold things in and overcome them. No whining. That was his father's motto. His father had not exactly been the cuddly type, and Mom dying before Ben hit elementary school hadn't loosened the guy up.

If Jocelyn wasn't afraid of him before, she would be now. Ben wondered if maybe she should be.

Every time he thought he'd found his emotional footing, something new knocked him off-balance. A follow-up story about the pending trial. Something his father said to the press. The way people looked at him when he walked down the street. He saved it up, didn't talk about it, but something about her icy blue eyes and the way they saw through him had him opening up.

She played with the lid of her cup, tracing her fingers around the outside rim. "You okay?"

Great, he could tell by the careful placement of her words she was back to pity. Just what he didn't want. "I believe it's my job to ask those questions."

She smiled up at him. "The bodyguard thing."

"That's why you're tolerating me, right?" Man, he wanted her to deny it. But if she mentioned the kiss, he'd be all over her, and that was a level of unprofessionalism that could get them both killed.

She shook her head instead. "Just keep walking."

He pulled her closer to him, pinning them against the wall as a large group of what looked like family passed in almost a straight line. They took up much of the wide space and didn't seem to care. Since the move gave him a second to be squished next to her, he wasn't complaining.

They started moving again. "Yes, ma'am."

"I like the sound of that."

He'd spent a lifetime saying it. The words rolled off his tongue without thinking now. "Came with the uniform."

"There's a reason women love those, you know."

He thought about the one in his closet and seriously considered offering to model it for her. He'd try anything to get her clothes off in bed with him at this point. "I believe my recruitment contract said something like that. The promise of many women wanting to pet my jacket if I put on the dress blues."

She nodded as that smile grew wider. "Nice image."

He'd lived his entire life by a strict set of rules. His father's career took him from base to base, city to city. He never stayed long enough to set down roots. Some psychologist would likely have a field day assessing why, after all those years of despising the constant moves, Ben had followed in his father's footsteps.

And now he listened for others.

Around corners and down hallways, Ben heard the soft tap of shoes behind them. When he tested his theory and sped up their pace, so did the echo behind him. By logic, whoever it was should have slipped by them when he pulled Jocelyn over to let the family pass. But that didn't happen.

Now as they turned a final corner and headed down the straight passage for the more open area of the elevators, Ben pretended to sip his coffee all while peeking up at the mirror set in the corner. "This tastes awful."

He spied the person immediately. With his nondescript expression, black clothing and bulge in his unseasonable jacket, the man was very similar to the guys who had been following and attacking Jocelyn.

They were all cut from the same pattern. Probably because whoever hired them bought their services at the same place.

Finding a mercenary for hire was far too easy, especially in this area, so close to Washington, D.C., where many disenchanted law-enforcement and military types lurked. Some of these guys did solid work, protection and security, but not the group coming after Jocelyn.

"I didn't promise you good coffee." Her voice still rang out sunny and strong.

That was good. He needed her calm and temporarily oblivious to the danger swallowing up the air around them. The sooner the guy behind them knew he'd been spotted, the sooner he would attack. Ben wanted to stall. He needed time to maneuver them into a less public position.

But Ben had to warn her. Give her a second to prepare for what he knew from experience could go haywire. "I need you to do something for me."

Must have been his voice, maybe the softer tone, that grabbed her attention, because she stared up at him. "Okay."

"This is easy."

Her smile faded as the seconds ticked past. "Name it and I'll try."

"No, no. Keep smiling and don't change your steps."

Her hand tightened on the cup, threatening to pop the lid off. "What's happening?"

"Probably nothing." Something. Oh, definitely something. When she started to turn around and look behind them, Ben touched her elbow. "No."

Coffee dripped down the side of her cup, running over her hand. The steam rose but she didn't even flinch. "Level with me. This is bad, right?"

"We're going to be very careful." He scanned the area up ahead. A few people milled around by the elevator. That meant he had to protect Jocelyn and take care of the civilians. Not an easy task when he had heaven knew how many weapons pointed at him right now and a two-hundred-pound bruiser to wrestle.

He studied the exits. Elevator banks on both sides and an emergency stairwell just beyond. Then he looked at the double swinging doors to the hallways of innocent people on the other side. No way could he lure the guy that way. Far too many chances for casualties and a low percentage of success.

"Want to tell me what's going on?" Her voice shook as she asked the question.

He thought about downplaying the adrenaline rushing through him but his heart hammered too hard for this to be a coincidence. "I think we're being followed."

He slowed them down, letting the four people hovering by the elevator get on and the doors close behind them before they reached that point. That took a few potential victims out of the way but left his biggest concern vulnerable. Jocelyn. He had to shove her out of the way and hope his shot hit.

One more test first.

They hesitated at the elevator doors. Handing her his coffee, he pushed the button. Stepping on there with the assassin guaranteed death. A confined space and no way out. Bullets would fly and the chances of not being hit were slim, if not impossible.

The man came up behind them. Close enough to violate their space but not right on top of them. He didn't shift or say anything. He stared straight ahead.

Ben kept his body between hers and the other man. When he saw the guy put his hand in his pocket and his gaze slide to the security camera above the elevator doors, Ben knew their time was up.

Pushing Jocelyn to the side, he moved her away from the elevator right as the bell dinged. Coffee splashed and the man grunted.

They'd gotten two steps closer to the stairwell when the man pivoted and followed them. No guessing now. He had the gun out and his arm rose.

Ben turned but Jocelyn was faster. She whipped around and launched both cups of coffee right at the guy. Looked as if she aimed for his head.

The liquid arced through the air. The guy threw up

his hand but the hot coffee hit him dead in the face, splashing over his body and streaming to the floor.

The man closed his eyes as drips hung from his hair and leaked into his eyes. He swore loud enough to send security running.

Ben didn't wait for a better time. "Move, Jocelyn."

He gave the order as he kicked the emergency door open and with a shoulder rammed into the guy's back shoved him through. The attacker spun and his gun dropped.

A ping rang out as the bullet left the chamber. The weapon bounced down the steps to the next landing as a woman screamed a few flights up.

Ben ignored the tearing along his recent wound and the pull at his waist as he hit the guy again. Another shot and he could go right over the metal railing to the bottom. Ben picked the gun instead.

With a hand on the guy's back, doubling him against the rail, Ben pressed the barrel of his gun against the guy's shoulder. Against his firing arm.

He was too close, right on top of the attacker. Ben knew if the guy could get his balance or wiped the burning coffee from his eyes, he might be able to perform a punishing tackle or throw. As it was, he just hung there, panting and heaving, but not saying a word.

The heavy door clicked shut behind them and Ben backed up to lean against it. The last thing he needed was Jocelyn coming through the door to rescue him. The coffee had been quick thinking.

Once again, she zigged when he worried she might zag. The zig had made all the difference.

"Who sent you?" he asked, not expecting a response.

The man lifted his head. Coffee ran down his face

and red streaks stained his cheeks. Those dead eyes were bloodshot and teary.

Score one for Jocelyn.

"Go to hell." The attacker no longer held a gun but he had a knife. Probably slipped it out of its sheath as he stood there trying to regain control over his breathing.

Ben remembered the other guy saying the same line and steadied his weapon. "Gun beats knife but try again."

Rather than take a swing, the guy turned and half slid, half ran down the stairs. His knees buckled and he grabbed for the railing. A squeak rang out as skin rubbed against metal.

Ben was on him. He grabbed the guy's shirt and they both went down. The bruiser took most of the impact because Ben kept him under him. Legs hit the walls and thudded against the steps. They rolled and the world spun until momentum slammed them against the cement block on the landing below.

Ben heard people talking as they walked up the stairs from the garage below. The door he'd come through creaked open above him. He remembered the attacker's dropped gun and felt the man beneath him move. Ben scrambled to his knees, trying to locate his gun, then gave up, reaching for the weapon by his ankle.

"Ben, no!"

Jocelyn's voice broke his concentration. Only for a second, but that was all the attacker needed. He went to his stomach, then used his hands and knees. With his right leg barely moving, he slithered down the steps and right into a crowd of nurses coming up.

They screamed and shifted out of the way, but he rammed right into them. Grabbed one and hid half behind her as he dragged her toward the ground. He looked out from behind her waist as she screamed in terror.

Ben lay half on his side, shifting the gun and trying to get a clean shot off. But there was no way to hit the guy without injuring the women.

He swore as the attacker turned the corner and kept going. Ben got to his feet and stared down the spiraling staircase in time to see the attacker dump the woman on the step, then run into another crowd of people.

Out of air and with energy reserves failing thanks to the repeated injuries, Ben fell hard on his butt and leaned against the wall. He blinked back the pain thumping in his side. Breaths dragged out of his chest and blood seeped out of the wound on his stomach again. He hadn't got the bad guy but he had managed to tear his stitches.

"Hands up!"

Ben looked up as Jocelyn ran down the steps, her shoes clunking against each step. A security guard followed right behind, trying to catch her, while two more came up from below.

They all converged on the same half floor of steps and watched Ben. Worrying someone might play hero and accidentally shoot him, he raised both hands. "Calm down."

Two guards stopped to help the women the attacker had knocked over like bowling pins. The guard behind Jocelyn wasn't giving in. He barreled down, gun up and ready to shoot.

Jocelyn's gaze locked on him. Ben doubted she saw the guy right behind her. She dropped down beside Ben and ran her hands over his shirt.

He felt her lift the material and look at his stomach. He wanted to reach out to her, but he kept his gaze on the security guard's gun. "Can you lower that?"

The cloud of fear cleared from Jocelyn's eyes. She spun around, then leaned over, putting her body in front of Ben's. "He's with me."

DETECTIVE WILLOUGHBY STOOD next to Connor in the nurses' break room. The small space had been cleared out and Joel and two uniformed officers manned the door.

More than an hour had passed since the newest attack and Jocelyn's knees still threatened to give out. She leaned the back of her thighs against one of the tables but that didn't help. The blood thundered so hard in her brain that every word anyone said came through muffled.

She wanted to sit down, maybe pass out for an hour or two. Exhaustion hit her out of nowhere and the relief at knowing everyone in the stairwell was fine had her breath hitching in her chest.

The attacker had gotten away. Stumbled right out into the afternoon sun without anyone grabbing him. The fact made her temperature rise and a wave of heat hit her face, but her biggest concern was for Ben. The way Connor stared at him, she guessed he was concerned, as well.

Once again Ben had protected and rescued. Stepped right into the line of fire. For her. He had a new set of bruises and injuries to prove it. If he wanted to convince her to take a temporary leave of absence, this sure did it.

She could go a lifetime without watching Ben scramble down the stairs as he wrestled with an armed maniac. The image would haunt her dreams.

He had tumbled and fought, without any care for his own safety. Even bloody, he had gotten back up and tried to catch the attacker. Only concern for the innocent people standing there had stopped him.

Yeah, he was nothing like Ethan Reynolds. He'd proven that over and over, and she finally got it.

And she had never wanted to sleep with Ethan, but she wanted Ben.

"Someone want to walk me through this again?" the detective asked even though she and Ben both had set out the whole scenario. So had the victims on the stairs and the security guards who had rushed to the scene. The hospital had finally settled back into its normal rhythm again.

Everyone agreed a guy dressed in black had fled the scene. For whatever reason, Glenn Willoughby didn't accept that as the full truth.

"Guy with gun attacked." Ben breathed in deeply, then wrapped an arm around his middle when he tried to exhale. "He got away. End of story."

The detective stared at Ben, hesitating and giving him the silent treatment for what felt like an hour, before he looked at her again. "Ms. Raine, I'm thinking this all connects to you."

"Brilliant deduction."

"Ben." She said his name in warning at the same time Connor did.

This was not the time to take on the police. She didn't like the detective, either. Something about the ever-present smirk and the know-it-all looks. Then again, she wasn't a fan of police in general. The idea of them, she loved. The reality of what she'd faced made her question the ones she'd seen on television and in movies.

The dislike seemed to run both ways. Detective Willoughby had made his position clear on Corcoran and his feelings on outside companies getting involved in crime solving, which Ben assured her was the normal reaction.

But the detective also stared at her when he should

have been looking at other things. Not in a sexual way.
More as a sneer.

He put his hands on his hips. "Any reason someone
would want to kill you?"

"We're working on that," Connor said.

That had the detective aiming his furious gaze in
Connor's direction. "I believe I explained to you that
this is police business."

"She's one of us." Ben delivered the words without
blinking. He could barely stand up straight, but his steely
gaze all but dared the detective to challenge.

Willoughby did anyway. "What does that mean?"

She wondered the same thing.

"We'll protect her," Connor said, backing up Ben.

The detective's smirk rose to full wattage as he turned
to face her again. "And who are you protecting exactly?"

Jocelyn felt the bottom drop out of her stomach. Slam
right to the floor, taking most of her insides with it.
The room buzzed and she would have gone down if
Ben hadn't grabbed her arm and leaned her against his
warm body.

"What are you talking about?" she asked.

"Care to tell them, Ms. Raine?" The detective lifted
an eyebrow. The dare was there in his voice and his expression. "I'd call you by your real name, but I don't
know it."

The bomb dropped. No one moved. Connor spared
her a quick glance but Ben didn't react at all to the cryptic information.

No way would she let this guy, this detective she
didn't know and who took far too much pleasure in her
discomfort, set the terms for her reveal. The news was
private and terrible and something she wanted to forget.

It would not become a line in his report or something he could play with to try to get the upper hand.

She lifted her chin. "Jocelyn Raine is my real name."

That wasn't a lie. She'd changed it legally. A closed-door, filed-under-seal case in another county, but she'd gone through all the legal channels once she was guaranteed the information would be almost impossible to find.

"What did it used to be?" the detective asked.

And she knew the guarantee about privacy had been blown. If this guy knew, Ethan might know. The reality of what that meant sent a tremor of fear shaking through her bones.

Ben's arm tightened around her. "You heard her. She gave you her name."

But Ben had to know what this meant. He was a smart man. The idea of him backing her up helped her spine stiffen again. She'd been through so much. She could get through this, too.

Faced with a wall of support against him, the detective's hubris dimmed a bit. "The woman you are so keen on protecting has some secrets. My guess is those secrets followed her to Annapolis. That makes them relevant to *my* case."

"That's not true." She refused to let that be true. Ethan Reynolds was in prison. He wasn't out and she knew because she checked every week.

"Then tell me who you really are."

She didn't move. "Jocelyn Raine."

Chapter Eight

Ben sat on the edge of the bed, the one in the second-floor guest room of the Corcoran Team building, also known as Connor's house. Ben had showered and changed into an extra pair of jeans and one of Connor's tees. Not his bedroom. Ben had slept here earlier, right after the NCIS scandal broke. He'd only recently moved into his own place when he moved from Quantico to Annapolis, but Connor's house provided security and Ben knew how vital that could be when everything blew apart.

Between rounds of questioning by Willoughby and a status report from Joel, it had taken hours to get everyone moved around and settled in.

The bottom story of the brick Federal-style building housing the Corcoran offices had closed down for the night. The second floor was alive with activity, or at least three adults sitting in three separate rooms.

Ben stayed in his assigned space, stewing and fighting back the urge to storm across the hall and knock on the door. He'd wasted precious time tonight getting fussed over by Jocelyn…or whatever her name was. She changed his bandages and re-stitched his stomach, all while Joel watched over them. Hard to get privacy with everyone milling around.

99

By the time Connor shut the lights off and declared work off-limits, Ben was itching to grab her. Being close to her for hours, while she wore an overly sunny smile and pretended the conversation with the detective hadn't happened, had worn down Ben's defenses. He fought back a nasty adrenaline rush and struggled to hold on to his temper.

In the past, when he raised his voice, she had shut down. He needed her listening and talking.

Whoever she really was.

He rubbed a hand over his face and groaned. Not that he cared if she'd made a name change. He understood if something in her past required it, but she knew they were facing down danger and to not share a piece of information endangered them all. He had no idea how he could protect her if she refused to trust him.

And that was what really ticked him off. She held back. Maybe fear no longer dulled the sheen to her eyes, but she kept him at a distance. He wanted in.

He was so lost in his thoughts he almost missed the light knock on the door. When it opened before he could call out, he stretched out and reached for the knife under the pillow. A new habit he'd picked up thanks to hanging around Davis. The man was an expert knife thrower, with Pax a close second.

But Ben wasn't thinking about either of them now. Jocelyn stood in the small space. The dark hallway cast her in shadows but Ben could make out the tiny T-shirt that didn't even reach the top of her shorts. A sliver of smoking-hot skin peeked out, giving him a look at her stomach. Vibrant red hair fell over those breasts.

He was a dead man.

"Can I come in?" she asked in a voice barely above a whisper.

He couldn't find his voice, so he nodded as he sat up again. He'd been thinking about her, letting his anger fester, only seconds ago. Now he saw her standing there, curling her bare toes into the carpet as she waited for permission to walk in.

His brain misfired. Every intelligent argument raced out of his head and took most of the blood up there with them.

She walked over and didn't stop until her knees tapped against his jeans. She stood so close he had to lean back to see her face when he looked up.

She smoothed a hand over his cheek and scratched her thumb over his stubble. "I wanted company."

No way was he going to survive this. The urge to wrap his arms around her legs and drag her down to the mattress swamped him.

He had to swallow twice before any words came out. "Now is probably not a good time to talk."

Hell, he couldn't even think. Seeing her, smelling her, having her so close he could touch her made his lower half pound with need.

That thumb skimmed over his bottom lip and she gave him a small smile. "Good."

Before he could mentally recite the alphabet or come up with mundane conversation, she lowered her head and her hair cascaded around her. It brushed over his cheek as she dipped in close and captured his mouth with hers.

There was nothing subtle about that kiss. She held the back of his neck and kept him close as her lips moved over his. When she lifted her head, he sat up straighter and brought her back down to him again.

His hands slid up the outsides of her bare thighs. Her skin warmed under his fingertips and his head pounded as he outlined the lean muscle running up her legs. Smooth and silky, as sexy as he'd fantasized she'd be.

She broke off the kiss and stared down at him with half-closed eyes. "Let me stay."

The request shot through him and his erection strained against the back of his zipper. He should be a gentleman and tell her about adrenaline in the after-rush of violence and how it sometimes hit like desire. How they should wait.

He should have but he was too busy dragging her down onto his lap.

Her knees fell to either side of his hips and her arms wrapped around his neck. As if reading his mind, she spoke up. "I know what I'm doing."

"Then tell me." His hands roamed up her back, slipping under the edge of the slim shirt and caressing the bare skin underneath.

"Being with you." She leaned in and kissed his chin, trailing a line to his throat.

He moved his head to give her access, but he had to ask, "Why?"

That hot mouth licked around his ear. "Do you want me, Ben?"

He shifted her on his lap until his erection pressed against her. The move had him groaning. "Do you have to ask?"

"I waited." She kissed his nose. "I tried to hold back." Then the space under each eye. "I don't want to wait anymore." She ended with her mouth hovering over his.

"Be sure." He balanced his forehead against hers as he fought to hold on to his control. "I want you so much it will kill me to stop."

He felt pressure against his shoulders and let his body fall. He dropped back against the bed, loving the way she asked for what she wanted. No games. No male/female garbage.

She straddled him with her palms pressed against the mattress on either side of his head. "I won't want you to stop."

The kisses got better each time. This one grew heated in a second. His hands traveled all over her, and her hair tickled his arms. He didn't care if he ripped out his stitches or Connor tried to break down the door and barge in with a shotgun, this was happening. She was strong and sexy and smart and she knew what she wanted. If that was him, he was not going to do something stupid to turn that off.

Right when he thought about rolling her over, getting her under him as he'd been longing to do since the first time he saw her, she sat back on her heels. With her fingers at the edge of her shirt, she stripped the material up and off. No bra. Just perfect breasts, round and high. He cupped them, teased them. His thumbs ran over the nipples until her head dropped back.

The sight humbled him. This was the trust he needed from her. Maybe not with her secrets, but with her body. She didn't hide or try to rush him. She let him explore her as her fingers went to his zipper.

A sharp ticking filled the room as she lowered it tooth by tooth. His erection spilled out and she wrapped her hand around him. His need for her swept over him like a wildfire.

When she lifted his shirt off, he didn't say anything. Just lay there and let her undress him.

For a second her body froze as her finger traced the outline of the slice across his stomach. "Does this hurt?"

"No." It wasn't a lie but he would have told one to get her to keep going.

She pressed her body against him, chest against bare chest. Their bodies met everywhere but the thin scrap of skin of his injury. She kissed the evidence of the bullet graze on his shoulder. The touch stung, but he kept his mouth shut, focusing on how good the rest of her felt.

"Wounds of a hero." She whispered the phrase as she kissed her way over his chest and up to his mouth.

He covered one of her hands with his and dragged her palm back to his erection. "This is what aches right now."

"Poor baby." She squeezed him until his eyes drifted shut. "I'll do most of the work."

He opened them again. "What?"

"Condom?"

"My bag." He had to move. At some point his muscles had turned to pudding except for the part of him that thumped to the point of pain.

She crawled off and rolled down those shorts. Nothing under those, either. When she turned back, condom in hand, she was naked and he shook so hard he waited for the bed to move across the floor.

She sprawled out, half on top of him, half next to him. Her mouth skimmed his shoulder, all around the wound. "You're injured."

"I'll be fine in a few minutes." He just needed to be inside her.

He felt a tug and looked down. She pulled his jeans off, then crawled back up his legs again. She wrapped her hand around his shaft as her body slid over him. Her mouth met his as her fingers went to work on the condom. She slipped it on and then straddled him again.

His body snapped to attention. Every muscle and cell on alert. He wanted to grab her and pull her down on him, but he let her keep the lead. A part of him sensed she needed to be in control this first time.

Fine with him.

"Ready for me?" She breathed the question against his lips.

He kissed her then so blindingly deep and long that his breath stuttered inside him. She moaned and he licked his tongue inside her mouth. Giving her every chance to slow him down, he put his hands on her hips and guided her to his erection.

Their bodies took over then. She slid down, her mouth opening and her eyes growing wide as she took him inch by slow, aching inch. When he was finally completely inside her, he threw his head back against the pillows and clamped down hard to keep from thrusting. His body pulled tight and his muscles strained.

She brushed her mouth over his ear. "Ben?"

"Huh." That was all he could say.

She smiled against his skin. "I need you to move."

Jocelyn stared up at the ceiling. They'd made love twice and the time ticked somewhere past one in the morning. The pale yellow light of the lamp on the dresser gave the room a soft glow. So did the heavy breathing of the man snuggled against her with his face tucked in her hair and arm balanced across her stomach.

She'd made a choice tonight. The right one. Thanks to everything that happened and the way she'd locked down her life, she hadn't been with any man in almost two years, but Ben was the right man.

She moved her leg along his calf. Even that part of him was solid. Not an ounce of fat on this guy.

His head popped up. The stormy pain that had lingered in his eyes when she first came in the bedroom was long gone. The stress lines no longer marked the area around his mouth.

Now she spied only satisfaction. And not a subtle hint of it, either. No, he wore the smile of a man who enjoyed sleeping with her.

Seemed only fair, since he looked at her and a healing warmth spread through her, relaxing every limb. Her body still tingled from the kissing and the touching.

Somewhere deep inside her, a light danced. He'd let her lead. Let her control their first time together. She had no idea how he knew, but he had, and that freedom to explore made her want to stay right where she was.

"Abigail Wyndam."

He shifted slightly and frowned. "What?"

"That's my real name."

He pushed up on an elbow and balanced his upper body over hers. When he winced, she pushed him onto his back and came up over his chest.

"Your injury." She whispered the reminder.

"Are you sure you want to talk about this now?"

The spin in the conversation didn't throw her. He meant the name. "I was a nurse nowhere near here when a male neighbor decided he owned me."

Ben's body stiffened under her hand. "Jocelyn... I mean..."

She continued to brush her fingers over his skin, touching his chest and his throat, loving the feel of him. "I legally changed it. Use Jocelyn."

He didn't say anything after that. Didn't pepper her with questions, even though he clearly wanted to. He somehow controlled his investigative nature and let her tell the story in her time.

She'd definitely chosen the right man.

"He started out friendly, then switched to a stalker.

He acted like we were dating, though we never did."
The familiar anxiety started twisting in her gut. "He
was a policeman, so I had nowhere to go. And I tried.
Believe me, I tried."

"You shouldn't have had to. He should have stayed
the hell away from you when you said no."

Ben went so still she worried his bone would crack.

She touched his face. Gently, with the back of her
hands. "What?"

The color drained from his cheeks. "I...I did that to
you. I followed you and didn't listen when you said no."

"No." She held his face in her hands. "Asking me
out is not the same thing. I admit at first I was scared."

"The gun. I showed up at the hospital." He closed
his eyes and when he opened them again the anguish
was right there.

"You are not him. You never hurt me. You never
threatened me." When Ben just lay there unmoving with
his body frozen, she leaned down and kissed him. "I
know you never would."

His arms wrapped around her and he pulled her tight
against him. Those lips went to her hair. "I'm so sorry."

"I wanted you. Even when I said no, I wanted you to
keep asking." She rubbed against him and felt his erection twitch.

He swore and shifted his body away.

She touched his hips and brought him back "It's okay.
Kind of flattering, actually. A natural reaction to our
closeness, not the words."

Ben dragged a hand through his hair. She could see
the battle waging inside of him. He protected people,
and this news had his head turning on the pillow.

His hand dropped. "I want to go pound this guy into
the ground."

Anger filled his voice but this time it didn't scare her. This was about keeping her safe. She kissed him to let him know she understood, but when she lifted her upper body again, she saw pain and regret still haunted his eyes. "The man is in prison. His fellow officers backed him up, and so did his boss, until the day he broke into my house for the fourth time."

Ben rubbed his hands up and down her arms. "What happened?"

"He tied me up." Her voice trembled and a nasty shiver shook her body until her teeth rattled. "He got a knife. Cut my arm when I fought him off. I can still see the blood and him pounding on me. The chair tipped over and he was right at me, kicking and yelling."

The images flipped through her mind. Just thinking about it had the power to transport her back there. Curled in the fetal position and crying so hard it hiccuped out of her.

Her emotions whipped around but Ben's gentle touch didn't change. His face flushed and his scowl deepened but his anger soothed her. Something in his fury eased the memories. If he had been there, he would have believed her.

She rushed to tell the rest. It was like poison sitting inside her, bubbling up and pouring over everything. She refused to let it ruin this night.

"A neighbor called and this time the ambulance got there first. The police couldn't hide it and the photos a fellow nurse took at the hospital helped buy my freedom. Even his partner stopped lying for him." She shook off the fears that knifed through her insides whenever Ethan's face swam before her. "He finally made a plea deal and I left."

Ben's hand inched into her hair as he caressed her scalp. "I'm so proud of you."

"What?" She didn't have the time or will to hide the tremor in her voice.

"You were amazing."

A tear escaped and ran down her cheek to puddle on his chest. "I was terrified."

"You survived. You figured out a way through it and took your life back." His hold tightened as his voice grew raspier. "My fighter."

All the pain and hurt broke loose inside her. The tears rolled but she didn't break down in paralyzing sobs like she used to. This was a freeing cry. A letting go.

The whole time Ben held her, he whispered words into her hair. She didn't even know what he said because it didn't matter. This was about the soothing tone and gentle touching.

Most of the tale ended there except for the behaviors. She'd developed them after Ethan's last attack. Her need for control and order. She'd been to the classes and talked with a therapist. She knew the subtle shift in what she could tolerate, the compulsive needs she had, had grown out of the attacks.

And being away from her house and her life ate away at her, but holding Ben washed some of the anxiety away. "I need everything just so."

"The toiletries," he said without judgment or surprise.

She lifted her head. "What?"

"I saw your bathroom. Your drawers back at the apartment when we were checking to see what was taken."

That meant Joel saw and probably Connor. The whole police force probably knew, including that blowhard, Willoughby.

Heat hit her cheeks. "Oh."

"One more way you overcame something horrible." Ben brushed the hair off her face as he kissed her forehead. "Don't be ashamed of it."

"It's under control. I use these behavioral techniques." She was babbling now, sounding like a complete moron, talking about things she never discussed with anyone.

"Do whatever you need to do. Whatever works, and don't apologize for it."

For a man who'd had his name dragged through a scandal and even now fought for his reputation, his ready acceptance meant everything to her. "Sex with you seems to have worked to take my mind off every bad thing that's happened the last few days."

His mouth broke into a smile. "Has it, now?"

"Definitely."

His hand skimmed down her back and traveled lower. "Then I say we keep doing it."

Chapter Nine

Gary ran the computer simulation one more time. He needed to know the exact amount of time they had to make the transfer. The government put the money in the undercover agents' accounts on a set day and time each month. During that short window, the pay would go in and the security protocols would relax. It was shorter than a second, but long enough for him to grab the information he needed.

No one had rushed to save his brother. Now they would know what it was like to be hunted.

"Sir, did you hear what I said?"

Gary looked up and saw Colin standing by the office door. Gary didn't remember him coming in and had no idea how long he'd been standing there. "No."

"We have an opportunity to catch Jocelyn Raine tomorrow."

The banking thing. He'd been hearing this theory for days. "She will not keep to her usual schedule. Because that would be stupid, and everything I've read about this woman suggests she's smart."

Colin stepped farther into the room. He held a tablet and had something cued on it. "I say she will."

The whole idea was ludicrous. That a woman who

HelenKay Dimon 111

had been attacked would stroll into the bank to take care of bills and deposits didn't make any sense. That she even used the bank the way people did twenty years ago instead of depending on online bill payments and other services was madness. He could only assume she had a reason to stay somewhat hidden and pay with cash.

But that didn't change the commonsense facts. "She's been shot at and chased in her home, in someone else's home and now at the hospital."

"You don't understand what I'm telling you."

The tone grated on Gary's nerves. Difficult and disrespectful. He waited to smash his security head until he'd heard it all. It would be so much more satisfying to let him spell it out in great detail, thinking he'd won over the boss, then knock him down.

Gary leaned back in his oversize chair. "Enlighten me."

"She sticks to a schedule."

"I'm sure that's true absent an emergency." There was no need to hear more. "You're wasting my time."

"I've watched the video. She has a significant problem with change. She has to do things the same way all the time." Colin set the tablet in front of Gary and turned it around to face him.

Time-lapse videos ran in the four corners. The times of day were close and the dates suggested the events spanned exactly four weeks to the day. Gary saw the so-called evidence but didn't see the obvious connection. "Meaning what?"

"She walks in the same bank door every time. Walks up to the center console, straightens the pens and all those paper slips." Colin pointed at the screen as he ran through the list. "She comes on the same day each week, around the same time. She uses the same teller."

Gary couldn't help but smile at that one. "Not anymore."

What with Pamela being dead and all.

"I think the Raine woman's got that disease."

Gary glanced down at the screen. He blocked out the noise of Colin's talking and watched the videos. Then he hit Play and watched them again. Same walk. Same amount of time at the counter. She even looked as if she wore the same outfit—hospital scrubs.

Maybe Colin had a point that was at least worth exploring. Gary almost congratulated him for holding on to his job for another day. But that was by no means assured yet. "You mean you think she has some sort of obsessive-compulsive issue."

"Exactly." Colin nodded. "She can't help it."

But there was still one problem. Ben Tanner, a man with nothing to lose, which made him very dangerous to Gary's plans. Leave it to loner Jocelyn Raine to hook up with the pariah who took down the NCIS. It would be a funny pairing if it didn't threaten everything Gary had set up and arranged.

Then there was the Corcoran Team, Ben's new employer. On paper, they helped corporations with risk assessments. Wanted to fly your company executives into some country no one had ever heard of? Corcoran would help you decide if that was a good idea and arrange for bodyguards to watch over all of them. If all else failed, they'd storm in and get the executives out.

All fine and not too problematic, except that the confidential memo Gary received told another story. If you drilled down, Corcoran sat in the middle of everything. The team worked with the police and government agencies and appeared to have a great amount of leeway in how it operated. Weapons, locked-down buildings, no trace of team members' properties.

And if Jocelyn was messed up with them, she very well could know what was happening and be planning to stop it. Didn't look as if she had the funds to hire them, but with Gary's luck they could have taken her case pro bono. That made her Gary's top priority.

"I'm not convinced the boyfriend, Mr. Top Secret, lets her out to go to the bank."

Colin pointed at the security-camera images and smiled. "She'll be there."

If it was even a possibility, Gary knew he had to follow the lead. "Set it up. This will be very public, during daylight."

"I know what to do."

Gary had seen Colin's proposal for handling the issue, so he knew the plan. "I'll call Kent."

"Yes, sir."

"And, Colin? No mistakes."

BEN HAD NO IDEA how he had let Jocelyn talk him into this. It was a desperately bad idea. Out in public, not far from the hospital where she worked. The Anne Arundel Medical Center's Hospital Pavilion sat just a few blocks up. If he squinted he could see the lobby doors.

With a hand on her elbow and his gun close, Ben steered her toward the inside of the sidewalk as a group of businessmen passed them. He eyed the street, the cars passing by and the light up ahead of them. He never stopped scanning for trouble.

No wonder Connor had almost passed out when Jocelyn announced her intention this morning at breakfast to run one last errand. He'd said no. She'd said yes.

Ben had watched the heated exchange and finally stepped in to agree with Jocelyn. He still remembered her bright smile when he threw in the support behind her plan.

The one concession he got her to make was to move the timetable of her usual visit. She said no until he explained how having a habit made it easier for someone to track her moves. She wouldn't pick another branch but the time bump happened.

He'd had to wait until she ran upstairs to shower, to explain about the compulsive behavior to Joel and Davis. Ben skipped over the facts about the policeman who had hurt her, telling just enough to give a flavor, because Ben still couldn't think about that without his body going into a full-rage shakedown.

Good thing the guy was in jail, because Ben wanted to put him in the ground.

The warm breeze of summer had kicked up, taking the edge of her floral shirt and causing the soft material to dance against her waist as she walked. He stared longer than he should have. And he wasn't alone. Two men passing by watched her walk and Ben almost growled.

This part of Annapolis consisted more of office complexes and buildings than waterfront. Everything was compact and tidy—hospital, bank, coffee shop and two restaurants, and that was just what he could see from this angle. Ben guessed the street grew up to serve the hospital and all the people shuffling in and out.

As far as urban planning went, it made sense. But not so great for protection. There were alleys and crisscrossing streets. Lots of places for someone to swoop in and get off a shot. Knowing Joel and Connor hovered nearby helped but none of them could stop a bullet. They'd all try if that was what it took to protect Jocelyn, but they had to see it coming.

"You haven't said anything since we left the car." There was a smile in her voice as she stepped off the curb and headed across the intersection.

He glanced back to where the vehicle was parked across the street, then looked up and down the road, searching the area for stray cars and trouble. "That's only a block."

"So, I'll take that grumbly voice to mean you're still moping."

Part of him was. He wanted her back at the house. Really, he wanted her back in bed, wrapped around him and making those noises he was now addicted to. She was so sexy and beautiful that letting his mind wander for even a second to last night broke his concentration. He needed all of his wits and none of them thinking about her body, so he skipped the eye contact and tried to shut down his brain.

He also ignored her comment. "That's nothing compared to how unhappy Joel is right now sitting in a car nearby and listening in while pretending not to."

Joel's amused voice boomed into the little silver discs in their ears. "I love my job."

"I can't believe it takes three of you and an elaborate microphone intercom system to escort me to the bank." She pressed her finger to her ear.

Ben touched her hand and lowered it again. Thought about holding it but discarded the idea. He needed his hands free. "Don't make it obvious it's there."

She screwed up her nose and made a face. "It's a weird sensation."

"You'll get used to it." There were other parts of this sort of surveillance that took longer to adjust to. Ben always forgot the audience. More than once he'd entered into a conversation forgetting there were ears everywhere. "And technically there are four of us, since Pax is handling logistics back at the office."

None of the other men said anything. That was the silent pact. The ones not directly guarding a client, in this case Jocelyn, stayed quiet. Or they did until one of them had something sarcastic to say and broke in anyway. That sort of thing was less likely with Connor on the line. The guy stressed protocol.

"It's all here in case something goes wrong." Because you never were prepared for when things went right. No need. All contingencies and all the practices were aimed at controlling the uncontrollable or at least finding a way to steer through it.

"You always assume things will blow up."

"Have I been wrong so far?" But the truth of her words struck closer than he wanted to admit.

He'd always been careful but never been negative. He didn't want to slip to that place. People fell there and wallowed. He knew because he'd lived with a man who excelled at it.

His father was an expert at measuring and finding everyone wanting. Nothing pleased him, not even his only son following him into the navy. Maybe things would have been different if his mother hadn't died, but she had. The what-if game didn't solve anything.

When they reached the front of the bank and walls of glass doors, Joel started talking. "Okay, kids. In and out. Let's go."

Ben headed for the closest set of doors but she shook her head and nodded toward the middle ones. This was her show, so he let her run it. The entry, anyway. The in-and-out and how fast they got to the car was up to him.

Those were the ground rules they'd set and Connor demanded. If Ben, or any of the rest of the team, heard or saw trouble, they moved out. She didn't balk. She listened and obeyed. *Obeyed*—not a word she was fond of. She cringed when she heard it. He got that. The word didn't do much for him on a personal level, but this was a life-and-death issue.

Even now, in the security of the bank, with its shiny marble floor and towering double-height walls, letting her get more than a few inches away from him made his moves jerky. She walked up to the table in the center of the room and skimmed her fingers over the edges of the piles. Well, they were loose pages of deposit slips when she started. Piles when she finished.

She looked around, shifting her weight from foot to foot. Not that he spent a lot of time watching her feet. The way her skirt swished kept grabbing his attention.

"Where's Pamela?"

It took him a second to realize she was talking to him. He leaned down to hear her better. "Who's Pamela?"

"My favorite teller."

Ben didn't even know the name of the guy who cut his hair. "Really?"

A man in his fifties dressed in a dark blue suit stepped up next to Jocelyn. He wore a broad smile and a name tag. Also carried a gun.

Ben almost jumped the guy. He settled for angling his body so he stood half in front of her.

The man smoothed his hand over his tie several times. "Good morning, Ms. Raine."

"Hello." What Ben really meant was *back off*.

"Ed Ebersole, head of security for Primetime Bank." The older man made the introduction, then turned his attention back to Jocelyn. "You're a little late today."

She smiled. "Got tied up."

"Understood." He nodded at the cashier windows. "You picked a good time. Small crowd."

"Where's Pamela?"

Ben still didn't know who the woman was or why Jocelyn cared so much. He did know this was taking too long. Someone on the other end of the intercom had taken to breathing heavy and not in a good way. As everyone's impatience grew, they could get sloppy.

The older man's face fell. "Pamela had to leave town."

"I talked to her last week and she didn't say anything."

"Jocelyn, the line is moving." Not that she had picked one, but Ben needed her to focus.

"Family emergency." Ed waved to someone near the front door. "I see I'm needed and you would probably like to get moving."

Ben was happy someone got the hint.

With a nod, Ed took off. "Nice to meet you."

Ben wasn't sure when that happened, but he was relieved the guy was moving on. "You too."

"Sorry," Jocelyn mumbled. "He's usually not so chatty."

Ben watched the man scurry over to the front of the bank and grab the door for some customers who were leaving. "Even the security guy knows you."

"Apparently most people bank from home."

"Count me as one of those." Ben tried to remember the last time he'd walked inside a branch. "Ever think of trying the ATM?"

She picked a line with four people that ended with an older woman teller of about sixty. Ben nodded at the woman. "Do you know her name, too?"

"If I did I wouldn't admit it." Jocelyn glanced at him

over her shoulder. "And for the record, I don't have a card for the ATM."

"Uh, why?"

"I prefer to pay cash for things and handle major transactions in person so I know they're done, including my rental to the landlord's account."

He was about to dig deeper when he caught a blur of movement off to his left. Two guys in black pants with matching black jackets. They kept their heads down and close together as if they were locked in an important private conversation.

Probably not unusual but this was Annapolis in June, which meant eighty degrees and sunny. Not exactly coat weather. And the body language: stiff, turned away from direct eye contact, backed against the far wall—it all suggested trouble. The combination not only raised a flag, but whipped it around in a frantic wave.

But only Ben seemed to notice. People walked by the jacket guys and said nothing. Didn't even glance in their direction.

Ben's gaze shot to the front door of the bank, then to the space inside the door where the security guy stood a second ago. He was gone and a quick scan of the area didn't turn him up.

An older woman walked into his line of vision and stumbled over something but kept going. Ben took a step, thinking to investigate, but a hand on his arm pulled him back.

"What's wrong?" Jocelyn turned around and wrapped her fingers around his elbow as she whispered the question.

He gave the response without thinking, with the ease that some people said hello. "Nothing."

Her nails dug into the skin of his forearm. "Nice try. Tell me."

Joel picked that moment to break in. "What's up?"

"Do you have eyes in here?" Ben kept his voice low and barely moved his lips. Anyone looking would think he was talking to Jocelyn, especially since she stared at him in frantic panic right now.

"Tapped into the security cameras." Keys clicked on Joel's end. "Scanning the floor."

A nerve at the back of Ben's neck twitched. The old instincts roared to life, letting him know something bad was coming. That feeling was rarely wrong.

Joel's voice whispered over the line again. "Get out of there."

Ben didn't know what Joel saw, but the warning was good enough to get him moving. Now on edge and ready for battle, he shifted his weight. Forget the worry about upsetting the other bank patrons. He wanted Jocelyn out of there and it had to be quick. The line kept shuffling forward and people mingled, looking at cell phones and filling out deposit slips.

It all seemed so normal, but he knew. A guy didn't devote every minute of his adult life, almost eighteen years, to service and rescue without picking up a few cues.

"Get behind me." This time he looked at her.

She had the same earpiece and heard the order, but whatever she saw in his expression had her shoulders stiffening as the color leached out of her face. "How bad is it?"

"I'm thinking pretty bad," he said as he dropped eye contact. The pale skin and wide eyes made him want to comfort her. But she needed his protection right now, not a reassuring hug. "Hold on to the back of my shirt and stay close. We'll walk to the door."

"Right."

"Do not stop."

"Robbery?" The word was little more than a puff of air on her lips.

In her stupor, she stumbled back and bumped into the woman in front of her. Ben mumbled an apology as he wrapped an arm around her and started to turn. In the whir of activity, with people coming in and out and walking around them, he saw the teller on the far end look up and go into a sort of trance. Ben followed his gaze to the jacket crew.

Now or never.

A sharp bang rang out, echoing off every surface and mixing with the screams of the bank patrons.

Too late.

On instinct, Ben dropped down, spinning as he went and dragging Jocelyn with him. His knees hit the hard floor as he took the brunt of their joint weight. Ignoring her yelp of surprise and the thud of her body rolling into his, he tucked her underneath him with his chest against her back and his weight balanced on one elbow.

"This can't be happening again." She whispered the words low enough for only him to hear.

The despair in her voice pulled at him. "We'll get through this, too."

"Promise me."

He couldn't say the words. Planted a quick kiss on the back of her head instead.

If this was the newest in a line of escalating attacks, this one blew the others away. Well planned and performed in tandem. They had doubled the number of attackers and dressed them up for show.

The risks skyrocketed with a move like this. Cars on the street and people with cells and alarms. It would be hard to get out now that they were in, especially since they weren't running up to the tellers and demanding cash.

But the fact that had Ben's gut twisting was it would be too easy to take Jocelyn out in this situation. Just make it look like part of a bank robbery gone bad, and quiet her before they figured out what it was she supposedly knew.

He vowed right then not to let himself get separated from Jocelyn. If that meant going out in a suicidal hail of gunfire, he'd do it. He just wished he'd spent a few minutes of their time together teaching her to shoot and how to defend herself.

Tomorrow. There would be a tomorrow and he'd do it then.

His hand hovered near the weapon hidden by his left ankle as his gaze shot to the door. The room fell into a shadowy gray as two men by the floor-to-ceiling front windows lowered the shades, blocking out the street beyond.

Ben had no idea where the masks and guns came from, but the men had both. And it all happened in less than ten seconds.

With a gun and a knife, Ben could take on a few of them. He counted four masked gunmen. No way could he win a shoot-out against that many without civilians getting hit in the cross fire. Joel and Connor and the police, whom Connor would've surely contacted, evened the odds, but they had to get inside to be useful.

Rather than risk drawing attention or starting a bloodbath, Ben ignored the weapons. For now. He thought about the small silver ball in his ear. "Joel, you getting this?"

"Yep."

"Everyone shut up." The gunman in the middle of the room held up his weapon as he shouted his order.

Shoes clicked against the floor as two more armed men circled around him, both with their faces hidden. They paced through the curled and crying bodies of bank patrons scattered around the floor and hiding behind any desk or counter they could find. Most people sat huddled in groups on the floor and soft wailing came from Ben's blind side.

The gunman by the front door swung his gun over the room and stopped on a businessman. "Everyone down now. Phones and wallets on the floor in front of you and no talking."

Clothing rustled and feet shuffled as the last of the bank patrons crawled to the floor. A fierce tremble ran through Jocelyn as she lay half on her side with her legs out behind her. Ben smoothed a hand over hers on the ground, hoping his touch would help calm her down.

"Get on your knees," he whispered right into her ear. The theory being, with her feet under her, he could get her up if the chance for escape presented itself. The gunmen had to load the money and soon if they wanted to make this quick, which was the point of a bank robbery. Which was not why Ben thought they were here.

Ben barely made a sound but the man in the middle turned toward him. In two steps, he was on top of them, sticking the barrel of the gun in Ben's face. "You got something to say, hotshot?"

Ben shook his head, bowing until his forehead almost touched the floor beside Jocelyn's prone form in what he hoped looked like a move of deference. He really wanted to hide his face and keep hers down in the event the men were here for them and hadn't picked them out yet. When the scuffed shoes finally disappeared from in front of his nose, Ben eased his chest back up and ran a hand through his hair.

"This, folks, is a robbery, and anyone who talks or moves gets killed." The man in the middle of the room turned around in a circle as he talked in a low, gravelly voice. "Anyone touches an alarm or yells, dies. You stay calm and you get to walk out of here in a few minutes."

Ben looked for bags, for any movement toward the counter to gather money. Nothing. The attackers stood, weapons up and ready, taking their time and staking out positions across the room. They forfeited speed and quiet in favor of getting the people on the floor and the visibility to the outside blocked.

With a nod from the guy in the middle, who clearly acted as leader, two of the men broke off and headed to the slim staircase that ran to the balcony above them. Ben saw an open landing in a square around the main part of the room. There were a few doors up and off to his right, but nothing else up there but a walkway.

Ben guessed the men could gain a strategic position from above, but they walked up the stairs and kept going until they hit the emergency door. None of their actions made sense. Ben expected sirens any minute. This type of crime only worked if the attackers made a rush for the money and then raced to a waiting car. Even then it was a high-risk operation in the middle of a busy business day.

And if they wanted Jocelyn, why not grab her?

He wasn't familiar with this bank but he could see the door to the safe right there on the main floor. He had no idea what could be upstairs that would warrant this kind of attention from gunmen who should want to grab and run.

But they didn't run. They didn't even move fast.

That nerve at the back of Ben's neck ticked. He recognized the pull for what it was—a fresh warning. Tension flooded through him with a kick of adrenaline streaming right behind. This was no in-and-out. No grabbing of the people in charge. These guys had something else in mind. Likely something that involved Jocelyn.

"What are they doing?" She asked the question to the floor, low and barely above a hum.

"No idea."

But he knew they were all in trouble.

Chapter Ten

Jocelyn was afraid to lift her head. If they came for her, she didn't want to make it easy for them to find her. She didn't want anyone else hurt, either. She heard a low hum on the mic in her ear. But it was the beating inside her ears that had her concerned. She could barely think over the incessant pounding.

The temptation was to turn this over to Ben and let him figure a way out. He was the professional and she was a nurse who kept landing in trouble. But the idea of waiting and hiding no longer appealed to her. Those days were behind her. Ethan Reynolds could not hurt her anymore.

And after the past few days, she no longer feared a little man with a big ego and even bigger fists. She'd outlasted and outrun men with guns who could crush Ethan. She used her wits and depended on the right people to help her through.

She would make it through this, too. She had to believe that.

One of the attackers crouched down and started looking through the wallets. He didn't take money. He flipped them open and…checked IDs. The pieces fell into place. Ben guessed this wasn't a robbery and he was right. It was a hunt—for her.

She watched the attacker scan photos and faces. He dumped purses and shifted the contents around until he grabbed only the licenses.

"They don't know what you look like." Ben whispered the words into her hair.

It took all of her control to hold her body still and not jerk at the impact of those words. "Yes."

"How can that be?" he asked.

Probably had something to do with her name-switching and lack of a background trail. She had a license stuffed into her front pants pocket. No purse and no wallet.

She'd come in and out of here every week since she took the job down the street. Pamela had stopped looking at her license long ago. Jocelyn only took it with her as a precaution and she kept it tucked away now.

"Anything?" The leader glanced at his watch when the other attacker shook his head. "Okay, I need all the women on the right side and men to the left. Be quick and don't try anything."

One man got up and tripped and the gun swung right to him. "Please, no," he pleaded.

"Enough stalling. Everyone move."

Her knee banged against the hard floor as she tried to get her weight under her so she could stand up. She hated the idea. The thought of being separated from Ben started a shiver racing through her that the warm day and Ben's hard body over her couldn't slow.

This manhunt was about her. She had no idea what they wanted or how they intended to get it out of her, but there was nowhere else to hide.

She shifted to get up before the attacker got upset and took it out on Ben. She attempted to stand, but Ben pressed harder, flattening her against the ground again. No question he wanted her down.

When she peeked at him over her shoulder, he shook his head.

Do not move. He mouthed the words this time.

"You've got two," Joel said through the mic.

She had no idea what that meant. She couldn't ask, so she hoped Ben understood the clue.

The lead attacker stuck his gun right in a woman's face just a few feet away from Jocelyn. "I said, move."

People started shifting. A woman sobbed as the other attacker dragged her off the floor and threw her where he wanted her. "Let's go."

The room exploded into movement. Most people crawled on the floor rather than stand up, but the game of musical chairs with people had begun. Men filed one way and women the other. Only she and Ben stayed still on the floor.

If the plan was for him to cover her and take the bullets while Connor stormed in the front door, she voted for another plan. Suddenly her fears switched from what these men might do to her, to what they *would* do to Ben if he didn't listen.

She tried to think about how she could cause a diversion, at least give Ben a chance to launch an attack of some kind.

"No."

That was it. One word whispered against the back of her head. She hadn't said anything out loud and there was no way he could feel the anxiety churning and bubbling inside her. Yet he knew.

"Hey, you two. Get up." The lead attacker stood right in front of them now. No more than five feet away.

She ducked her head and tried to peek up without the lead attacker getting a good look at her face. She saw his shoes, work boots of some kind. Saw him lift his weapon.

"You have two seconds before I start shooting."

"We're going." Ben's voice sounded thin and wobbly, as if he were terrified and too shaken with fear to get his legs to move.

No way. She knew it was fake. All fake. Whatever the plan, he'd put it in motion. She heard a countdown in her ear and knew Joel was helping from the outside.

Most of Ben's weight lifted off her. She tried to move but his legs kept her pinned. They were targets right there in the center of the floor. The room had split and no else sat with them. A man off to the side begged Ben to move.

He took his time. He reached behind him and got to his knees, all while the lead attacker watched.

When the seconds ticked on, the other attacker stepped closer. "What's happening over here?"

The room spun. Something slammed into her back, knocking the air out of her and pushing her tight against the floor. She covered her head as the chaos exploded around her. She heard screaming and saw a blur as Ben threw something with one hand and a single shot rang out above her.

The noise cut off her hearing as it burned through her. She smelled smoke and saw people running. Time flew yet moved in slow motion. She saw every tiny movement even as she knew it unfolded in rapid time.

"Ben!" She screamed his name but he was up and running.

The front doors burst open and Connor and Joel raced in with the police sirens wailing in the street behind them. Ben jumped over the lead attacker's still body.

Then she saw the blood and the attacker's open hand. His gun lay a few feet away but his body didn't move.

Blood covered Ben's arm and stained his shirt. She tried to yell and rush for him, but strong hands held her back. She threw her elbows and kicked her feet but nothing happened. The hold didn't ease.

Joel's voice finally penetrated the frantic screaming in her head. This time in person, not through the mic. "Stay still. He's okay."

"Blood."

"Not his."

Then she went down again. Joel pressed her against him, shielding her with his body as people filed around the room and ran for the doors in a wild frenzy.

Flat against the floor, she could see Ben and Connor reach the lone attacker leaning against the table in the middle of the bank. Something stuck out of his shoulder and his gun dangled from his hand.

Connor took that guy's mask off, and his face was a mask of pain as his head fell back. She wondered why he didn't slide to the floor.

Sounds were muffled and she didn't understand what she was seeing. A blur moved into her peripheral vision. She looked up in time to see one of the attackers come out of the door upstairs. He held a gun.

She didn't know where he aimed, so she screamed the warning. "Ben, move!"

He dropped to the floor in what looked like a slide into home plate. Her heart stopped when his momentum had him skidding into the knifed man. Shots echoed around the room and pinged off the stone walls. Ben slammed into the attacker's legs and the guy went down as shots slammed into his chest.

Through the fog and the ringing pain in her ears,

she heard a yell followed by a sickening thud. No one stood on the balcony above. A deadly silence fell over the room.

Her panicked gaze flew from one corner to the other. First to Ben where he sat on his butt still holding his gun. She followed his stare to the pile of black folded on the hard floor not that far from where she sat. Then she swung back to Ed. He stood near the front door with his gun still aimed at the balcony.

The doors slammed open again and police officers poured in, fanning out and covering the entire floor. The direction they pointed their guns shifted between all the men still standing. The innocent ones.

"Get down!" Different voices all said the same thing.

The command rang all around her and the room headed into a spinning nosedive. She refused to pass out, but when Detective Willoughby stepped into the middle of the fray, she did lower her forehead to the floor and let the cool stone ease the hammering inside.

He looked around at the blood and the bodies. "Arrest everybody."

IT TOOK CONNOR all of ten minutes to talk the detective down. No wonder Connor was the leader. He could stay calm and reasonable and get people moving his way before they knew they were agreeing with him.

Ben would have yelled his way through the situation. With his patience expired, he'd reached the end of being social and professional. The detective had proved to be nothing but trouble. He was no help and more of an actual hindrance. Always a step behind and full of accusations. Ben was done with all of it.

Every part of his body ached and the realization of how close he'd come to seeing Jocelyn captured or killed had adrenaline rushing to his brain. With the police moving in and out and investigators roping off the area, Ben didn't move. He leaned against the middle table with the deposit slips now strewn all over it and on the floor.

When he finally shifted, his foot slid on the paper and his gaze shot across the room to see who'd witnessed his near fall. Jocelyn stood there. He could watch her all day.

She nodded and talked to Joel. They were holding hands. No, that wasn't right. Ben forced his vision to clear—Joel was checking her arm. Squeezing and asking questions, then waiting for an answer. Ben had been through that routine a few times himself.

The images of the past half hour clicked together in his head. He'd pinned her under him against the floor, ignoring his weight advantage. He recalled the way he'd shoved her down to keep her out of the line of fire. Rough, but necessary. He hoped she understood, but that didn't stop the guilt from the thought of her being hurt without him even noticing.

He shot up straight and stalked across the room. He got three feet away when her face fell. Man, she looked a second away from crying and his heart stammered in response.

"Jocelyn?"

She launched her body at him. Despite the raw pain radiating from his shoulder and the fatigue pulling at his muscles, he caught her and held her close. His mouth went to the side of her head and then her cheek.

That wasn't enough. Turning, he held her face in his hands and kissed her. Right there in front of everyone with bodies on the floor and policemen whispering around them.

When he came up for air, he felt whole again. Somehow this woman had wormed her way into his soul and now he couldn't breathe without her near him. The realization of how far gone he was had him leaning against her.

"Are you okay?" She whispered the question.

With his body wrapped around hers, he almost didn't hear it. "Yes." He held her away from him, careful not to hit her arm.

"I'm fine," she said before he could ask.

"But Joel was—"

"My wrist is sore." She twirled it around as if to assure him it wasn't broken. "And that doesn't matter."

The security chief, or whatever his title was—Ben couldn't remember—came up beside them. In his tenuous mood, Ben wanted to push him away. But this was the guy who'd made the final shot to bring down the guy on the balcony. Ben owed him something.

"Ms. Raine?"

She slipped out of Ben's arms and gave Ed a smile. "You doing okay?"

"That was a heck of a shot," Ben said, wondering what kind of skills this guy had. Until now, he'd never thought of security guards as expert marksmen.

The shot was within normal range, but emotions had been running high and tension had flooded over everything like an oil slick. Still, the guy had maintained his composure and hit a moving target above him. Any way you sliced that, it was impressive.

"I had him clear in my sights." Ed glanced up at the spot where he took the attacker down. "I'm just happy that was as bad as it got. You're all lucky you weren't killed."

Jocelyn patted the man's arm before stepping back beside Ben again. "And you, too."

Ed shook his head. "Weirdest robbery I've ever seen."

Not quite the comment Ben expected. It wasn't what the other man said. It was what he left out and the steady tone. For a guy who'd come through a crazy situation, Ed seemed ready to head back to work without missing a step.

That made one of them.

"Was this your first?" Ben asked.

"No, but the robbers usually get in and out." Ed frowned. "What was your name again?"

"Ben Tanner." He waited for a response, but nothing came. People usually reacted. Very few gave him the blank stare like the one Ed left for him.

There were those who supported Ben and the NCIS outcome and offered something akin to praise. Those who didn't tended not to need words because their expressions or dismissals were clear, though Ben sometimes heard some awful things from them, too. Amazing how vocal the "anti" crowd always turned out to be.

But this guy showed no reaction. Could mean he skipped the news. That was the most likely scenario, but nothing about this case had fit into a reasonable pattern so far, so Ben filed the information away to chew on later. When he analyzed everything else, he'd look at that, too.

"Nice to meet you." Ed gave a quick nod and left.

He passed the bigger problem on the way in. "I hate to break this up, but I need to speak with Ms. Raine."

"Detective Willoughby." At this point Ben had his own nickname for the guy but he refrained from saying it because he'd probably get arrested.

The detective kept his attention focused solely on Jocelyn. "I would have bet money you were in the middle of this."

"I came in to pay a bill," she said.

"There are checks for things like that."

Ben had had enough of the macho act. Willoughby liked to stand too close and pin people with a dead stare. Two days ago Ben had found the whole routine annoying. Now he was done with all of it.

"She handled herself really well," Ben said, daring the other man to disagree. Any reason to land a punch at this point worked for Ben.

"I'm thinking she's had some experience."

Yeah, this guy just didn't take a hint. Ben decided to make his position a bit more clear. "You have a point, Willoughby? If so, feel free to make it to me."

"I'm talking to the lady."

Ben took a step forward and Jocelyn pulled him back. "It's okay, Ben. Detective Willoughby is doing his job and his tactics don't scare me."

Since she slipped her hand in his, Ben guessed whatever was jumping around inside her didn't match the cool detachment of her words. Ben gave her fingers a reassuring squeeze. "It's actually not okay."

The detective ignored everything except what he wanted to say. He pointed from Ben to Jocelyn. "I'm going to need a list of where you plan to go the next few days."

"Why?" she asked.

"So I can have an ambulance ready."

Connor picked that moment to step in. There was another man with him. "Detective."

"Connor Bowen."

"Are we only using full names now?" Joel asked as he joined the group.

Connor pointed to the other man. "This is Kent Beane, the bank president."

To Ben's mind the guy looked ready to throw up. Sweat dripped off his forehead and he kept folding a handkerchief and wiping his brow. Beane acted as if someone had stolen his personal bank account and his house along with it.

Of course, since no one had tried to steal anything, the guy had bigger problems. Someone had used his office as a staging ground to grab Jocelyn. That put him on Ben's list.

Willoughby ignored the introductions. "I got a call from my boss about you."

Connor smiled. "Tell Anne I said hello."

"I'm not sure who you think you are or why you're protecting Ms. Raine—"

"Are you in trouble, Ms. Raine?" Kent asked.

"But it ends here."

That qualified as one threat too many. Ben heard it, let it wind through him and feed the anger festering inside him. "Is that what your boss said you were supposed to do? Threaten women for no reason?"

The detective turned on him. "I'm betting the media would love to know what you're doing now."

Jocelyn let out a grumbling noise and shook off Ben's hand. "How dare you?"

Whoa. Ben grabbed the hem of her shirt and pulled her back before she tackled the guy. Leaving his hand resting there, he massaged her lower back, letting her know he appreciated the support.

Not many people stepped up for him. Knowing she would meant something. Meant a lot. But he didn't want her to make herself any more of a target.

He could handle the detective. "Is that supposed to be a threat, Detective? If so, you need to do better."

Willoughby shifted his attention back to Jocelyn.

"You have one day to come clean. You tell me who you are and what's going on and your boyfriend stays off the front page."

"What is wrong with you?"

Jocelyn asked it but Ben figured they were all thinking it.

"Well, now." Joel made a humming sound. "We've been throwing words around, but that statement is definitely a threat."

"And you're a bit late to throw out one about my life. I can't imagine what hasn't been printed about me." There was a strange freedom in knowing there was nothing left for people to say about him. Ben didn't find a lot of comfort in the thought but he did see himself as slander-proof.

"I'll take that as a challenge."

The detective stormed off before anyone could respond or Ben could shove the guy through the wall the way he wanted to do.

"Who was that again?" Kent asked.

"He's a jack—"

"Okay." Connor shut down Ben's honest response. "That's enough."

"Nice work today." Ben didn't know if it was true or not. He didn't remember seeing the manager anywhere during the attack. Joel's video would tell them, but Ben had the clear sense this guy had ducked the tragedy.

Kent shook his head. He kept alternating between swiping his brow and swallowing. "I missed it, I'm afraid."

At least he didn't try to lie. Ben didn't really count that in the guy's favor, but it was something. Now if he'd just stop leaking sweat. "You weren't in the room?"

"Stepped out for coffee. Dropped it all over the street when I saw the police cars."

Ben thought he saw some of it splashed down the front of the guy, as well.

Interesting story but awfully convenient. People broke into the bank at the exact moment the boss was out? It raised a red flag. From Connor's frown, Ben realized he was not alone in wanting to dig around more in Kent's story.

"Everybody is fine." Connor's voice wasn't much better than the skeptical look on his face.

Joel pointed at the body bags. "Except for them."

"Who are they?" Kent asked without looking.

It was the one question Ben knew the answer to, so he handled it. "The bad guys."

Chapter Eleven

With his sleeves rolled up and his hair showing the tracks of his fingers, Connor stood at the head of the conference-room table on the first floor of the Corcoran Team headquarters later that night and looked around the room. "Let's run this."

Jocelyn heard the phrase but was too busy keeping her head from falling and smacking against the table to get all excited about being included in an information session. The adrenaline kick had long worn off. Now she had the afterburn of exhaustion. But no way was she leaving the room.

The entire building fascinated her. On the outside it looked like any other historically protected brick town house in this part of the city. Stately and expensive. But the inside had been carved up into something very different.

The big country kitchen with the blue cabinets at the back of the house fit. The front double rooms filled with computers and files and a conference area straight out of a spy movie looked more like a war room than a place for the family hangout.

This was where the real work happened. The behind-the-scenes gritty digging for leads. On the monitors stationed around the room and behind the security system complete with handprint identification and key cards.

They'd given her a seat at the table and she was going to sit in it, even if she almost fell asleep doing it.

A tray with a coffeepot and clean mugs sat on the middle of the table. Joel slid into the seat across from her and took a laptop out from where it was tucked under his armpit. Opening it, he looked up with his usual smile. "I'm ready."

"We need security footage, along with the name and all the information you can find about every business on that street."

Ben's voice, firm and angry, contrasted with the way he smoothed his hand up and down her thigh. Not sexual so much as soothing, yet the touch still made her want to crawl up onto his lap.

She tried to concentrate on what was being said and add in her concerns. "And where does the door from the upstairs balcony at the bank go?"

"Good question." Ben nodded. "Look into the blueprints, then check out the bank president, Kent Beane, and the security guy."

"Ed?" She thought about the older man who always greeted her with a smile. He made it a point to know people's names and open doors.

Seeing Ed as part of some grand conspiracy struck her as a waste of time. And a little scary. If the bad guys could get that close to her without her knowing, nowhere was safe.

"He disappeared for the entire robbery." Ben's fingers curled around the inside of her knee in a gentle squeeze.

An unexpected heat swirled through her. Okay, maybe she wasn't so tired after all. "Not to point out the obvious but Ed did shoot one of the attackers."

"You're both right." Joel waved a hand in the air without taking his attention from the computer screen. "I'll track this Ed guy on the tape and we'll see where he went. Could be a case of nerves. You know, a hiding-in-the-closet sort of thing. Some folks can't handle pressure."

She didn't like that explanation any more than the other one. "How comforting."

"I have a list of suggestions from Davis and Pax." Connor shot a file across the table in Joel's direction.

"Suggestions?"

"Davis used a different word but I'm trying to be tactful."

Joel laughed. "Must be killing them not to be in on this hard-core."

"Davis needs to stay where he is. By now whoever is coming after Jocelyn has to know something about our team, since we keep showing up next to the dead bodies. That means Kelsey and Lara need to stay in a protected space, just to be safe." There was nothing light in Ben's voice. The words settled in Jocelyn's mind. She hated every one of them. Ben was right but the underlying reality stung. She'd brought all this danger to their doors. Her, not Ben and not his team.

The guilt and worry balled up inside her. These men knew how to protect but her being there could cost them everything they cared about. She tried to think of another place she could go hide but nothing came to her.

Maybe some space and an hour or two to think would help. "As fun as this is, I need a break from the terror and attempted kidnappings and never-ending need to throw up. I'm heading upstairs."

They all stared at her but Ben spoke up. "You okay?"

Clearly her voice had given her away. Either that or in

her need for sleep she'd said something she only meant to think. "Not really."

Ben's arm slipped along the back of her chair and his fingers massaged her neck. The slow circle eased the thumping headache and kick-started a twirling in her stomach.

Some of the fatigue seeped out of her body and a new sensation set in. It looked as though her fear of gun-toting, commanding, strong men might be gone thanks to Ben.

On the list of everything about him that made her smile she added his tendency for public displays of affection. He had no trouble showing he cared for her in front of his friends. He didn't embarrass her or violate her privacy. She couldn't help but sink into the intimate way he touched her, as if it was something as matter-of-fact and normal as drinking coffee.

"You did great today," he said.

His automatic support was pretty great, too. From him that meant a lot, but she wasn't exactly ready to collect a medal for bravery. "I was plastered against the floor hoping not to get killed."

Joel smiled at her over the top of the laptop. "You stayed calm and called the warning that likely saved Ben's life."

"Damn," Ben groaned. "I meant to tell you not to share that yet."

All exhaustion vanished as she sat up straight. "What?"

"The trajectory of the hit on the attacker next to Ben suggested the bullet was aimed right at Ben's…" Joel froze in the process of turning the computer around to show her whatever was on his screen and stared at Ben instead. "What?"

Ben slipped his hand under her hair and turned her face toward him. "I'm fine. Thanks to you."

No, no, no. She had almost sat there and watched him get shot, all for her annoying habits and need to have repetition and uniformity.

She almost doubled over. "Now I am going up to vomit."

"You're fine."

"Don't bet on it." She had to get out of there. Find a quiet minute alone. So much had happened and she hadn't found two seconds to process it all.

She stood up, planning to find a shower and maybe sit on the bathroom floor by the toilet for a few minutes just in case. "I'm thinking it's inevitable at this point."

Ben winced. "In that case I might wait a while before I head up to join you."

Something about the big strong man being afraid of a woman getting sick made her laugh. "Chicken."

Because she couldn't resist, she brushed her fingers through his soft hair as she walked by. She wanted to lean down and kiss him, but that could be too much. With the world spinning and someone trying to grab her every two seconds, they hadn't exactly had a moment to sit down and talk about a definition for their relationship…if that was what it was.

He struck her as rock-solid, but kissing him in front of the guys could be the move that finally made him go all anti-commitment-male crazy. She just couldn't handle that loss on top of everything else.

"Hey, what was the teller's name?" Ben asked her as she reached the doorway to the main hall.

"What are you talking about?" Jocelyn gripped the doorjamb as she turned around. "Oh, you mean Pamela?"

Connor's eyebrow lifted. "Last name?"

Jocelyn was still stuck on the last question. "You think she has something to do with this?"

"She's the teller you go to regularly. You see her, she disappears and during the same time frame your life goes haywire. Seems too convenient not to be suspect," Joel explained as he typed away.

Ben glared at him. "*Disappeared* might be a strong word," he pointed out.

Jocelyn's head had taken off in a full spin now.

"Don't worry," Ben said. "We'll find out."

As Jocelyn walked up the steps, she thought of all the things she wasn't supposed to worry about. Her emotional baggage just got heavier with each passing second.

BEN FELT THE SENSATION of being stared at and decided not to lift his head and face whatever bugged Connor. Studying the file of Davis's notes provided cover. Not that Ben could read it. He stared at the words and lines of blue blur. All he could think about was the woman upstairs who could even now be stripping off her clothes and getting into a shower.

His control shattered.

"What about you? You okay?" Connor asked, clearly refusing to be ignored.

"Sure."

"I meant the gunfire."

The amusement in Connor's voice had Ben lifting his head. The flat line on the boss's mouth didn't match the tone. Concern played there, too. In his eyes, in the way he leaned forward. This wasn't about Jocelyn. It was about injuries, and Ben figured he could handle that talk.

"Can't lie. That was a close one. I felt the bullet whiz by my head." He knew it sounded nuts, but he could see the thing move through the air. That shot had come close to ending it all.

His bulletproof vest wouldn't have stopped the bullet to the head he'd only barely sidestepped. "I thought that was it."

"You're taking a lot of knocks on this case. Still think you should head to the hospital to take care of that filleting of your stomach," Joel said. "Lucky for you Jocelyn has the skills to keep you mobile."

Connor nodded. "She's a good woman."

Ah, there it was. Didn't take Connor long to circle from gunfire to Jocelyn.

Ben cursed the ease with which he got sucked in. "Agreed, but why do I think I'm about to get a lecture about women and safety and how those things don't easily square with our work?"

Leaning back in his chair, Connor tapped his pen against his open palm. "She's got a lot of secrets."

"Don't we all?" The list went on for pages—the real story about the whereabouts of Connor's wife, everything about Joel's past and Ben's doubts about whether he had done the right thing in the NCIS case. And those were just the ones that came to him on the spot. Davis and Pax came from a family that defined dysfunctional. No one walked away clean on this one.

"You still have secrets?" Joel asked. "I'm thinking most of your life is on display right now."

Leave it to Joel to drill down to the point. He wasn't the type to tiptoe around anything, no matter how uncomfortable. The straight shooting tended to take the squirming out of most issues. This time Ben didn't mind. "Unfortunately, true."

"Just tread carefully with her." The intensity of Connor's voice suggested he wasn't kidding.

Even Joel glanced over at him. "You think she's a danger?"

"I think she's *in* danger and I'm guessing this isn't the first time." Connor's pen kept tapping. "But I think Ben knows that."

He knew most of the information but not all. That didn't stop him from wanting to go after the guy who terrified Jocelyn. Maybe he wouldn't jump in a car and drive to whatever prison the guy was in, but he could poke around and make sure the guy wasn't coming out anytime soon.

"There's a piece of crap who wouldn't take no for an answer from her and is now locked away." Ben stopped there. Jocelyn could fill in the rest if she wanted to.

Joel's jaw clenched. "Give me the name and I'll check in and make sure he's not instigating the attacks on her now. I'll refrain from arranging for him to get shanked in the group shower. Probably."

Connor nodded. "Focus on the check in part."

"Appreciate that." Ben knew they'd been outraged at the idea of some moron hurting Jocelyn or any other woman. Still, hearing the anger in their voices and seeing it in the way their shoulders tensed backed up what Ben already knew—regardless of how he'd ended up at Corcoran, he was in the right place.

The pen flipped fast enough for Connor to launch it across the room. "You've had a rough few months, so be careful."

"Are you giving him the rebound speech?"

For some reason Joel's words made Ben smile. "Good question."

"I'm saying the timing of a relationship with her is not ideal."

Joel snorted. "Connor means it stinks."

Ben thought the same thing at least ten times a day. "You're not wrong about that."

"But I'm thinking you're going to keep seeing her." Connor didn't ask it as a question.

"Yeah, Connor. That is definitely going to happen."

SHE SHOULD HAVE gone back to her room.

She went to his.

Jocelyn stood in front of the dresser and ran her fingers over the folded stack of T-shirts and thought about how they fit over Ben's warm skin. One, two…she pulled out the third and frowned at the way one sleeve stuck out of the side. Before she could stop, she refolded it. Tucked the edges in just so. Switched the order, top to bottom, from light to dark.

The constant movement of her hands soothed her. Fixing things *just so* eased the anxiety that pinged around inside her. She'd endangered people, set off a chain of events that left people dead, and she had no idea how. The not knowing had her fought-for confidence puddling on the floor.

"Got twitchy when I couldn't find you." Ben leaned against the doorjamb watching her.

The idea he went hunting made her heart go a little wild. "Were you afraid I left the building? Because I'm not even sure that's possible."

"I was more worried I'd get stuck sleeping alone." He stepped into the room and stood next to her, facing the mirror above the dresser. "For the record, that would be a very bad thing."

"Tragic even."

"I agree." He folded his hand over hers and wove their fingers together. "How are you really doing?"

"My crazy is showing."

"The shirts?" He flipped through them with his other hand. "You can touch my clothes, my stuff— me—anytime."

"This sort of thing doesn't scare you?"

"Having someone try to kidnap you scares me." He lifted their clasped hands and kissed the back of hers. "Watching you overcome what haunts you fills me with nothing but awe. You impress the hell out of me."

Sweet-talking hottie.

He let go of her hand and his palm went to the side of her face. "Does the organizing help?"

"Still shaky." But the touching had her mind switching gears to much more interesting topics. Being close to him, smelling him, watching him, it all calmed her nerves.

"I'd be worried if you were fine with all of this."

She could take anything. She'd learned that a year ago. She survived. But... "You almost died."

She clamped her mouth shut to keep the strangled sob from escaping her throat. Every time she closed her eyes, she saw him sliding across the floor. If he'd been hit, if she'd seen him go down... A dark, suffocating curtain fell over her at the thought.

She didn't know when or how he'd come to matter so much, but he had. Even when she'd pushed him away and given him every reason to move on to any of the other fifteen nurses who eyed him up, he'd never given up on getting to know her. He'd never gone for someone who might be easier to win over. And now he refused to walk away when any smart man would.

He turned her until they stood face-to-face and his hands massaged her upper arms. "I could have gotten hit, but I didn't. Focus on the latter."

The strength. She had no idea where he found it. He

kept calling up reserves and never swayed. She envied that even keel.

But truth was he'd been sliced and shot and now almost killed because of her. "How can you look at it that way? Just shrug it off like the danger almost doesn't matter?"

"There isn't another way to move on."

She didn't wait for him to draw her close. She stepped into the circle of his arms and rested her hands against his muscled chest. "You got lucky and you wouldn't have needed to if I hadn't insisted on going to the bank."

"Whoa, back up." His fingers threaded through her hair and tipped her head back as his gaze searched her face. "Don't take that on."

"It was my fault and—"

A lingering kiss stopped her sentence. "I agreed you should go to the bank. Connor and Joel agreed. We own that blame."

"Because I insisted." His smile caught her off guard. "What?"

"Don't get all feisty on me when I say this, but we wouldn't have gone if I didn't want to."

"Because you're such a big, tough macho man." She snorted as she said it to let him know she wasn't buying the he-man act. "Oh, please."

"Do you forget I carry a gun?"

"Never." Seeing it used to touch off a strangling panic. Now, knowing he controlled his anger and could handle his weapon, never turning it on her, she felt nothing but safe.

"While I admit I am no match for you when you pile on the charm and insist on getting your own way—"

Okay, now, that was ridiculous. She laughed. "When has that ever happened between us?"

"Even you could not topple the joint pressure of me, Connor and Joel." Ben's firm tone never wavered.

"You're saying you could have said no to me today?" That was not the way she remembered the conversation.

"I'm saying we're all grown-ups. The visit should have been fine and the fact it wasn't is one more piece of the puzzle."

Relief tumbled through her, erasing all those rough edges of guilt. She dropped her forehead to his impressive shoulder. "Dealing with this is so exhausting, and that's coming from a woman who is used to working brutal twelve-hour shifts on her feet."

"Hmm." That husky voice vibrated against her ear.

"What?" When she lifted her head again, she faced the bed and found her back balanced against the dresser. She didn't even remember moving.

His fingers traced the dip of the neckline of her T-shirt, skimmed over her collarbone and down to the tip of the shadow between her breasts. "I was kind of hoping you weren't tired."

Yeah, well, she was wide-awake now. "Subtle."

With a small tug, he lowered the shirt and slipped his thumb underneath. "I'm not sure I was trying to be."

His finger stroked over her nipple, making her gasp. "I bet I can be persuaded on this point."

"Oh, I will try very hard to convince you." Then he dropped his head and licked his tongue over the straining top of her breast. "Put every ounce of my energy into the task."

She forgot about guilt and fear. She forgot about everything but him.

Her hand went to the back of his head and she held him close. "Yes."

"We're never going to make it to the bed."

She didn't think they'd make it to the floor.

Chapter Twelve

Gary sat with his elbows balanced on the desk and his fingers steepled in front of his mouth. All of his focus stayed on the man across from him. The same one fidgeting as if he would jump out of his skin at any minute. Colin shifted and tugged on his pants. Even glanced around. None of it broke Gary's concentration.

They'd been back in the office for hours. The sun dipped and the night fell, and still they reviewed today's disastrous plan. The outcome cried out for punishment, but Gary refused to end Colin's torture that easily by killing him.

Gary sat and waited. He glanced at the clock on the wall and calculated the time since he last spoke.

Eleven minutes.

Colin crossed and uncrossed his legs, sending the chair into a symphony of creaking. When he opened his mouth, Gary broke in first. "I'm starting to believe Ms. Raine has some sort of power over men. Makes them stupid and sloppy."

"She brought the entire Corcoran Team to the bank with her."

"Not quite."

Gary had done his homework, or tried to at least.

Finding information on the team had proved difficult. They had no website, and the internet appeared to be scrubbed clean of any reference to the business being involved in any project anywhere. He could find only a general reference to the general work they did.

Yet, their doors remained open, which meant paying clients. The leader's name, Connor, showed up now and then with veiled references about corporate risk assessments but without any real definition of what that meant.

The only clue was Ben Tanner. There was a name even the best hacker could not make disappear. Turned on his boss, took down the upper levels of NCIS. Yes, Ben had been a busy boy and now he'd appointed himself Jocelyn Raine's protector.

It wouldn't be hard to make him disappear and shift the blame to any number of disgruntled military types. Gary smiled at the thought. Tanner was the type of man who could experience an accident and no one would be surprised. Media coverage would likely include a "what did he expect would happen?" quote from anonymous sources. The fingers would point in a lot of directions, but not in Gary's, and the police would quietly close the case because that was what they did with snitches.

"No one expected a gun battle today. It was a simple snatch job. The men were to make it look like a robbery gone bad without being obvious about taking one woman," Colin said.

Gary saw the comments as further proof of his employee's incompetence. "You should have known this could go sideways. I did and I warned you. The men protecting her are not amateurs."

"And neither were the ones I hired."

"Your mistake was in thinking you would be able

to control the situation when your dealings with this woman suggest anything but."

"You think the Corcoran Team knows about the data-and-funds exchange?"

There was no other explanation. They protected for a living and they were currently protecting her. Had been from that first night at her apartment.

Protecting her meant making his life difficult, and Gary was just about done with that nonsense. "It's beginning to look that way."

"What about Detective Willoughby? He's on every crime scene."

Gary lowered his hands to the desk. "I'm not worried about him."

"Really?"

Colin refused to learn. The last thing Gary wanted was a challenge to his authority. When Colin paid for his failures in this matter, Gary would lead with that one.

"My main concern now is blowback. Being implicated," he said, ignoring the question that started a tic in his jaw. "I need to know what can be traced to me, which means I need to know what Corcoran knows."

Right now he'd be happy to know *what* exactly Corcoran was.

"You going to plant a device in their headquarters?" Colin asked as his jumping around subsided.

Normally that would resolve the issue. Gary would devise a way in, have his best people set up the equipment and collect the data. But that didn't work with a company like Corcoran that thrived on playing the clandestine card. "I assume they'd find it, and that's under the assumption I could even get past whatever security they have and get it in there."

"Understood."

Gary doubted that. "No, I think there's only one way to get this done in the time we have left."

"How?"

Gary no longer had a choice. "I'm going to walk through the front door."

"What?"

"Better yet, I'm going to bring them to me. Tomorrow morning."

BEN COULDN'T SHAKE the tickling sensation at the base of his neck. The two-story drapes were drawn, blocking out the sun and the view to the street beyond. The bank stayed closed, which was a problem, since this was a local bank with few branches. The locked doors and police tape kept people out.

Being in this cavernous room the day after the attack explained part of his unease. Standing next to the counter in the middle of the room where he almost bit it didn't help. Neither did watching Jocelyn page through the deposit slips that once fanned over the top but now were stacked in neat piles.

She shuffled them, then straightened them again. The repetitive action seemed to soothe her. The neater the pile, the less her hands shook. That she'd figured out a way to quiet the demons inside her left him humbled. He knew how the noises and doubts could grow into a deafening thunder, but she kept them at bay. It just made him gut-sick that she had to.

He reached over and touched his fingertips to hers. Nothing too obvious. Not with Ed and Joel circling the balcony upstairs for clues and Connor questioning Kent at a desk a few feet away.

They were sleeping together and Ben wasn't about to hide it or lie about it. Kissing her at the conference-room table this morning with Joel and Connor watching probably ended any questions on that score. But he could hold off on a general broadcast of his preferred sleeping arrangements until they had the "we're exclusive now" talk, and he definitely planned on having that soon.

He waited until she glanced up. The wary darkness in her eyes had vanished somewhat, but not totally. "You okay being here?" he asked.

She looked over and around, taking in every inch of the first floor before answering. "I see the shooting when I close my eyes. It hardly matters if I'm here or back at the house."

Not that he could blame her. The latest shoot-out was on a slow-motion reel in his head, as well. "For a few hours last night, you seemed to forget."

She slipped her fingers through his. "And I plan to use that tactic again tonight."

"Never been called a tactic before." This woman could call him anything she wanted. Could do anything she wanted with him. They'd been on fast-forward since they met and he did not want to slow them down.

Joel broke the spell when he walked up beside her. His gaze stopped on their joined hands but he didn't say anything. Still, hand-holding at a crime scene qualified as unprofessional and borderline stupid, so Ben gave the back of her hand a quick rub and then let go.

"Anything upstairs?" he asked Joel.

"An old balcony. Ed says there used to be a second floor, and the architect who did the redesign put the balcony in for aesthetics and some sort of ode to the place's former glory." Joel pointed out the walkway above them as he talked. "We went up and the only way out is through an emergency door to the roof and then down a ladder to the outside."

Jocelyn grabbed the closest stack of deposit slips and tapped them on the table, lining up the edges with precision. "So, the robbers just went up there for a walk? Doesn't make sense."

"I think we've established they weren't robbing anything." Joel watched her but again had the good sense to stay quiet.

Ben hadn't shared the compulsive behaviors. He probably didn't have to. Joel had helped him check her bedroom that first night. Clothing lined up with the exact amount of space between each hanger. The color coding. The perfect edge where she lined up her shoes.

Having been in the military, Ben recognized the symptoms of post-traumatic stress disorder. She never used the term. He doubted she'd been diagnosed. She talked about behavioral adjustments. More than likely, she handled the whole thing herself.

"Let me ask this." Jocelyn had them both staring at her now. "If this wasn't about taking money or things out of safe deposit boxes, then why didn't they just grab me and run?"

There was only one answer to that, so Ben gave it to her. "Because they had to make it look like a robbery."

"That guy seem okay to you?" Joel leaned against the table and nodded in Kent's direction.

The man sat at his desk in full-on fidget mode. Sweat dotted his brow and he kept wiping his hand over his mouth.

Ben had noticed the nervous tics before. They struck him as even more pronounced today, which made no sense at all. The danger had passed. He should be celebrating living through it or at least look more relaxed.

"To be fair, his bank was robbed, kind of," Jocelyn said.

Joel nodded. "While he was out."

There was a clicking sound as Jocelyn tapped the pile of slips against the table. "Still thinking it's too convenient?"

"Connor will break him." Even now Ben admired Connor's work. He kept his voice low and his gestures smooth as Kent unraveled into a bucket of sweat.

"No question."

Ben turned around to agree with Joel and saw Ed usher a man in the front door of the bank. "Hey, you can't be in here."

That was the deal. They had all come to get the search done faster. That meant bringing Jocelyn outside the house again, and Ben had laid down a bunch of rules to make sure that happened. Being in the bank with only Ed and Kent was one of them.

The new guest walked right over, just a few steps behind Jocelyn. Joel moved to block the direct line to her and Connor came up out of his chair with his hand on his gun. Ben beat them both. Ignoring the pull of the stitches across his stomach and the tightness over his shoulder, he vaulted around the table and put his body right in front of hers.

"Not one more step." And he would put a bullet in the guy to back up his threat if he had to.

Forget the expensive black suit and successful-businessman trappings. The guy was fortysomething and fit and could be a killer for all Ben knew. He wasn't about to play wait-and-see on that one.

The man's eyebrow lifted. "Since my money is in this bank, I believe I can do whatever I think is appropriate."

Connor shook his head as he walked over and through the wall of tension. "Sir, you have to—"

"It's okay." Kent rushed in with his hands in the air.

Nervous energy radiated off him as he flailed. "This is Gary Taub."

Gary stood in direct contrast to the bank manager. A good five inches taller and totally put together. He frowned when he saw the sweat pouring off Kent, then dismissed him by turning to Connor. "I own the building next door."

"I'm guessing you don't mean the coffee shop," Joel said.

Gary didn't break eye contact with Connor. It was as if he knew who was in charge and refused to deal with anyone he deemed lower on the food chain. "Worldwide Securities."

"What kind of business is that?"

"Financial."

"What can we do for you, Mr. Taub?" Connor shifted away from the group and took the spotlight off the place where Jocelyn stood.

She hadn't said a word. She was too busy digging her nails into Ben's back.

"Gary, please." The man almost bowed as he said it. "I'm checking on Kent."

That made almost no sense in Ben's mind. If Kent weren't a complete mess, maybe. As it was, Ben couldn't imagine Gary hanging out with schlubby, balding Kent unless Gary needed something from him. Gary just seemed that type.

"Are you two business associates?" Ben asked.

"We share an interest in keeping the area safe." Gary's gaze finally landed on Ben. Did a quick flick over his shoulder to Jocelyn, then back again. "And you are?"

"Connor Bowen," he said before Ben could answer. "This is my team."

"Of what?"

"Investigators."

The corner of Gary's mouth eased up. "For the police?"

"Maybe we could ask you a few questions."

Gary folded his hands in front of him. "I notice you're not answering any."

"That's how this game is played."

A terse silence followed the verbal volleying. If this Gary guy wanted a battle, Connor was not the right guy to pick as an adversary. Connor didn't blink. Didn't call any attention to the rest of the team, which was good because if Ben guessed correctly, Joel was using that fancy phone, held low in his hand, to get a photo of Gary.

Gary finally broke the quiet with a quick nod. "Well, I can tell you what I saw on the day of the incident."

"You were here?" Ben ran through his mental roll call of faces from that day and knew this guy was not on it.

"Next door."

Connor stepped back and gestured in the general direction of Kent's abandoned desk chair. "Then have a seat."

Everyone pivoted. Ed took up his old position at the door while Connor sat with Gary and ran him through a series of questions as Kent watched. No, while Kent stared at the large clock on the wall by the safe. The guy didn't sit still. Gary must have noticed because more than once he glanced up and scowled at his supposed business friend.

It took Ben a second to realize he stood alone. He spun around and found Jocelyn back at the counter in the middle of the room with Joel hovering over her shoulder like the bodyguard he was.

Ben walked back to her. He was about to make a joke but he noticed her hands. She'd stopped straightening. She turned the slips over and studied the back.

He knew something ran through her mind. "What's wrong?"

"Something."

He balanced his palms against the edge of the table and leaned in, keeping his voice at a whisper level. "Can you be a little more specific?"

"The deposit slips."

He still wasn't getting it. "One more detail might help."

"What about them?" Joel asked.

"No one gave me anything except Pamela." Jocelyn held up a slip.

From what Ben could see, it was blank except for the preprinted blocks. "What are we talking about?"

"The first attacker talked about me having something." The slip flapped when Jocelyn shook it.

Ben remembered the question the first attacker had asked her. They'd all turned it over many times. The team took turns asking her about it, trying to get to the heart of it. Was it something from a patient or doctor that the guy was after? But none of their questions had gone anywhere. "I thought we decided that was some sort of line to throw you off."

"The last time I saw Pamela, I did some banking and she gave me the receipts. She put them in an envelope, just like she always did." Jocelyn smiled. "Don't you see what I'm saying? *She* handed me something."

"And now she's missing." It didn't take long to put two and two together and figure out Pamela was dead. When Jocelyn kept talking, Ben knew she hadn't made that leap yet.

"I forgot because it was so mundane, and I assumed the attacker was talking about something that happened at the hospital." Jocelyn's voice rose as she talked.

Joel answered her in a whisper. "I'm thinking we can now assume Pamela is dead."

The color ran right out of Jocelyn's cheeks. She morphed from excited to pale in a second.

Ben hated the look of defeat he saw on her face. "Joel."

"Being realistic here." He shrugged.

Jocelyn waved her hand in front of her face. "It's okay. I need to know."

"But do you have any clue where you threw this slip or whatever it was away?" Joel blew out a long breath. "I mean, the chances of finding it are…what?"

"No." Ben kept shaking his head. "She didn't throw it away."

"I have it," she confirmed.

It took Joel a few more steps to catch up. "At your apartment?"

Still ghostly-white, Jocelyn managed to smile. "At Corcoran."

GARY STOOD AT the front door, just inside the bank, and watched the Corcoran Team rush out of there. After a tap on his shoulder from Ben, Connor had listened and then hustled them all out of there. The man asked one wrap-up question and they were gone.

Kent rocked back on his heels. "They didn't act like they knew you. I don't think—"

"You shouldn't because you'd be wrong." Kent didn't see it, but Gary did.

Kent frowned. "What?"

"Up until five minutes ago, she didn't know she had

the note." From a few feet away, Gary had watched the realization dawn on her face. She went from mindlessly playing with the papers to holding one up. Her excitement spilled over until one of the men said something and then they mobilized.

She knew. In a few minutes, they would all know. Gary couldn't control what was in the note from the teller, but he could get his hands on it.

"How do you know what she knew and when?" Kent asked.

Gary didn't feel inclined to explain to a man who wouldn't survive until morning. "The look on the woman's face and the way they ran out of here."

"The transfer is in a few hours." Kent looked around but Ed was on the other side of the room. "You promised to let my wife go."

Whether he promised or not didn't matter because Gary had no intention of letting that happen. Neither did his silent partner, since Sharon had most definitely seen his partner's face when he grabbed her. That made her collateral damage.

Yes, the Beane family would not survive the night. They'd die and the attempted bank robbery would be linked back to Kent as an operation gone wrong. Sharon as the innocent victim unaware of her husband's money issues and schemes. In Gary's scenario, Sharon found out, a fight ensued and the resulting murder-suicide would stand as one more horrific tale of a marriage on the edge and a desperate man who took a terrible turn.

At least that was where the evidence Gary manufactured would lead the police to believe.

"I have a very small window in which to fix your mess," he said to the man who would provide access then soon be dead.

"I didn't—"

"Stop." Baiting this man proved quite enjoyable. "For Sharon's sake, you better hope I can do it."

Chapter Thirteen

Jocelyn drew the envelope out of her purse and put it on the Corcoran conference-room table on top of the files and papers and everything else they had thrown all over the place. She beat back the urge to organize it all. This wasn't their first job and they knew how to do their work, but still.

Joel grabbed the envelope as soon as it hit the table. "You kept a receipt from more than a week ago?"

"I keep everything." She snatched it back and waved it in front of him from across the table. "Sometimes being a woman on the edge helps."

Joel frowned. "Excuse me?"

She turned to Ben at his position next to Connor at the end of the table. For some reason she wanted Ben to be the one to see it first. "Here."

"In your purse." Ben shook his head. "No wonder the guy couldn't find it at the house. Also makes sense we missed it. I'd never think to tell a woman to dump her purse. Seems like a surefire way to get my butt kicked."

"We will from now on," Joel said.

Connor rested his hands on the back of her chair. "I'm not sure I knew she had it here."

"I keep receipts in my purse and reconcile every Fri-

day. I was attacked before I could." It sounded crazy
when she said it out loud.

Never mind how smooth and perfect they fit together
and how she had them lined up inside the envelope with
not one edge sticking out. Just when she thought she'd
come so far, she ran smack into evidence she had some
work to do.

Ben shot her one of his sexy smiles. "I love your need
for order."

One look at that mouth and her bones melted. After
living with the anxiety as a curse for so long, she had
her first moment of clarity. Maybe this one time he was
right and it saved her. "Right now I do, too."

She glanced down at the words on the paper. The
last two stood out to her as if they were set off in flashing lights.

Worldwide Securities transfer. Sharon kidnapped.

He read the words and Jocelyn jumped in with the
first question. "Who is Sharon?"

"Kent's wife." Joel sat down and started typing.
"Let's see where she is."

Jocelyn glanced at Ben. "More kidnappings."

"Yeah, I know." The sadness in his eyes translated
to a vibration of anger in his voice.

After a series of ultrafast clicking, Joel made a noise.
"Hmm, not good."

"What?" Connor asked.

"A teacher who, from what I can see here, is out on
unexpected temporary leave. Kent said she's very ill."

"Funny how he forgot to mention that fact." Ben blew
out a long breath. "Guess her being gone explains his
constant sweating."

That made three women—Pamela, this Sharon and her. Jocelyn's chest ached at the thought she might be the only safe one. "So, someone is planning to take money from the bank? I still don't get it. They were in the bank and didn't steal anything."

"It all comes down to Gary Taub, owner of Worldwide and our sudden visitor this afternoon," Ben said.

Joel kept typing. "Thought that seemed a bit too smooth."

"So did he."

Ben's dislike for the guy had been immediate. He didn't exactly hide his feelings, with all that grumbling at the bank. Jocelyn had chalked it up to his protective instincts and having someone break through their security barrier thanks to Ed. Now she wondered if Ben's anger went deeper. The instant hate could have something to do with his innate ability to sense danger.

If so, she wanted to know. "What was this Gary guy doing? Why walk in and risk giving himself away?"

Ben shrugged. "More than likely checking us out."

"Then we should be fine." One business guy against all of them. Add in Pax and Davis, and Jocelyn tried to imagine how quickly Gary would go down. Then she noticed the three of the guys in question staring at her... waiting. "Oh, come on. This team is scary. What sane person would take you all on?"

Joel burst out laughing. "Thank you, I think."

"Let's go through the blueprints, construction grids, anything that could connect these two buildings in physical ways." The usual stern thread moved through Connor's voice but the look on his face came off suspiciously like a smile. "Anything on the bank security tapes?"

Joel shook his head. "All wiped clean. The most recent is from three weeks ago."

"What did Ed and Kent say about that?" Ben said as he took the seat next to her.

"They can't explain it."

In a few moves, they all shifted into their regular chairs, her next to Ben and Connor at the head. It was so natural that she wondered if they secretly practiced the maneuver.

With the head seat came the power, and Connor immediately stepped into the role. "Maybe this Gary person can."

"You think he's planning a bank robbery?" she asked, because she still couldn't wrap her head around the attacks being separate from the pile of money that sat in the bank safe.

"He's next door to the bank, which appears to be the epicenter of whatever's happening there." Ben punctuated each word with a thump of his finger against the table. "I'm willing to bet that balcony leads to Worldwide somehow."

Joel paged through the papers and flipped the blueprints out and on top. "Not that I could see."

"What do we know about him or the company?" Ben asked Joel.

"Wealthy financial guy. High-end brokerage. Lost his wife to cancer and a brother in a freak accident overseas. There's no one else as far as I can tell."

"So, we've got a guy with nothing to lose. That's the worst kind." Connor snatched a folder off the desk behind him and opened it. "We missed something. I want it found in the next thirty minutes. Call Davis and Pax and get them in on this by video conference."

Ben was too busy swearing under his breath to look at anything. "Fine, but in thirty-one minutes I'm taking Jocelyn to the garage."

"Sounds dirty," Joel said without lifting his head from the blueprint study.

As if they had an extra few minutes to check out a car. But when no one explained, Jocelyn went searching for one. "Uh, why?"

Ben's head came around and he stared at her. "Gun practice."

The intense look shot right through her. His mood shifted to serious and the heat in his eyes told her not to argue. This wasn't sexual, as Joel joked. This was more like an order. For the first in a long time, the tone didn't make her throw up a solid emotional wall in defense.

"We're going to shoot cars?" she asked when he didn't cough up another answer. Leave it to Ben to go quiet all of a sudden, just when she needed more information.

"It's not really a garage."

Again he stopped and again she had to poke him until he said something helpful. "What is it?"

"A weapons depot of sorts—and you're not going to shoot. We'd need a range and we can't get to one without further endangering you. The plan is to work on aim, show you how the weapons work, get you comfortable holding one." Ben laid it all out, then leaned back in his chair.

It was as if he waited for her to scream or have a fit. She half expected those feelings to rush up on her, but they didn't. Anxiety bubbled inside her as it always did but the overwhelming need to flee didn't hit her. She chalked that up to progress.

Probably also had something to do with the emotional free fall she'd been in for more than a week. That had one source—Ben. He smiled, he frowned, he spoke to her in a quiet whisper or he clenched his jaw, like he was doing now, and her heart performed a happy little spin.

He'd gone from potential date to bodyguard and now to the man she wanted in her life. The change smacked into her as her breath whooshed out. This was more than a free fall—it was a falling-for-him kind of thing.

She shoved back from the table and almost put her head between her knees. Would have if she didn't have an audience.

When he frowned at her, she knew she wasn't hiding the realization all that well but suspected he thought she got nauseous at the idea of guns. Not at all. She got it now. Sometimes the good guys needed to be armed.

Right before he could say something, she collected her jangling nerves and forced out a question. "And why do I need these gun skills?"

Connor broke in. "He needs you to be ready."

Okay. That didn't answer anything. "For what?"

Ben's hand hit the back of her chair and he spun her so that she faced him. "Anything."

TWO HOURS LATER Ben watched Jocelyn massage her palm with her opposite thumb. She'd followed every direction without arguing or passing out. When he first mentioned the guns, he thought she'd slide right under the conference-room table. Not now.

No way was he going to resist kissing her. Seemed wrong what with everything brewing around them and her obvious distress, but the need started backing up on him and he wanted a release.

"You're pretty amazing."

She glanced up at him. Her bright smile came a beat later. "You're not bad yourself."

He put the last of the guns in the locked cabinet and closed the false wall. When he leaned back against the workbench, she stepped right into the space between his legs. It was as if the woman was made for him.

He curled a piece of her soft auburn hair around his index finger. "Strong, beautiful, smart."

"You are a sweet-talking man." Her fingers fiddled with the buttons on his shirt. She unbuttoned the top one and traced the collar of the white T-shirt underneath.

If they weren't standing in the middle of a pile of weapons, he'd be stripping that sexy tank top off her right now. He settled for something more G-rated. "I'd rather be the man you're kissing."

Her hand slipped up his neck to the back of his head. "We can make that happen."

With a gentle pressure, she brought his head down. Not that it took much to get him going. The start of an erection pressed against his fly and air hammered in his lungs. There wasn't a moment he didn't want her.

A loud beep came right before Joel's voice broke into the heavy breathing. "How is it going?"

Ben's head dropped right before their lips met. He looked up and shot his teammate a death glare. "Apparently it's not going to happen this second."

Joel smiled as he looked from Ben to Jocelyn. "Did I interrupt something?"

"No," she said but she didn't jump back or out of his arms.

That was the only thing keeping him from lunging across the room and strangling Joel. "Yes."

She let her hands slide down Ben's chest. When she turned around to face Joel, Ben caught her with one finger hooked through her belt loop. He was fine with her staying close. Plus, she hid a bulge that Joel would give him crap about for days if he saw it.

"What's up?" she asked with the amusement still evident in her voice.

"A missing fourteen feet."

Maybe it was a sign of what was going on when Joel burst in, but Ben couldn't make sense of the comment. "Excuse me?"

"Checked the blueprints and compared to the photos I took inside the bank and the ones I have from outside on the street. Did a bunch of measurements—"

Ben smiled. "Of course you did."

"—and there's something between those two buildings, between the bank and Gary's place."

"Maybe the bank's safe." Jocelyn shifted as if she planned to step away.

With his hands on her hips, Ben pulled her back against him.

Joel shook his head. "No, this is on the second floor, above the safe."

The beeping returned. Only this wasn't one long squeal to signal the lock being disengaged. This was a motion detector.

She stiffened. "What is that?"

This time Ben let her pull away. The shot of adrenaline killed off the last of the sexual desire brewing inside him. It sputtered right out as he unlocked the cabinet behind him and grabbed the silencers and vests.

"We've got company," he said as he turned her around and put the Kevlar on her. Then he opened her palm and put a small gun in it. "Good thing you're a quick learner."

She stared at the weapon where it lay in her hand. "All this because someone's at the door of the house? Maybe just ratchet down the testosterone and tell whoever it is to go away."

Ben hadn't put up the garage windows. Metal shutters covered every entrance but the door. From the outside, they looked like part of the wall. Nothing out of the ordinary. From the inside, complete armored protection.

Joel reached under the cabinet at the far side of the four-berth garage and a monitor flashed on. Darkness had begun to fall but the security system found the heat signatures. The images adjusted, moving in click by click. The closest camera pinned them at the house's back porch.

"No cookie-selling there." Joel pointed at the man near the kitchen door. "This one? He's not visiting. That's a gun he's holding."

Jocelyn leaned in close and squinted at the screen. "More attackers. You've got to be kidding. Here?"

"Looks like we scared dear ol' Gary," Ben said and Joel nodded.

"What?" She seemed to be having some trouble taking it all in. She turned around in the open space as the familiar look of fear crossed her mouth and her eyes glazed. "You think he sent commandos."

"We meet him and suddenly we have people with guns stalking this place. Nobody followed us back here, so yeah, I blame Gary." Joel clipped on a shoulder holster and put his usual gun in it while he held the one with the silencer.

She shot him a "you've lost your mind" glare. "How do you know no one was behind us?"

"I know."

Ben decided to spare her the car speech from Joel. The man knew his vehicles and could maneuver through the streets with ease. He also had a sense when he was being followed and didn't think twice of circling around for hours to lose someone. "It's one of Joel's specialty areas. It would be hard for someone to tie this property to the team, but if you have skills and access to the right databases, it's not impossible."

"Connor might want to work on that." She pulled her cell out of her front jeans pocket. "On that topic, shouldn't we warn him there are two guys on his back porch?"

"Oh, he knows." No sooner had Ben made the comment than a light in the house's kitchen went on.

"He's walking right into a trap." Jocelyn stepped forward.

Ben grabbed her by the back of the shirt. "You stay here."

"But Connor needs—"

Feeling her body tremble under his hands, Ben leaned down and whispered in her ear, "He's only opening that back door when he wants it open. He's got this. I promise."

As if they'd conjured him up, Connor's voice broke through the garage. Jocelyn jumped and let out a little squeal. Ben held a hand against her but joined Joel in watching that back door across the yard.

The intercom speaker was in the ceiling and Connor gave a play-by-play on the whole scene as it unfolded outside. That was what happened when you had a state-of-the-art security system.

"Two heat signatures. I'm coming around the side in five." Connor's steady voice echoed as he started the countdown. "Five…four…"

Jocelyn's eyes widened. "Is Connor crazy?"

"Popular question." Ben pointed at the far wall. "You stand there and don't move."

"I have a gun."

Now was not the time for this. Joel inched toward the

door to the backyard and sent Ben the "move it" signal, so he went for the hard truth. "And I don't want to worry about you being shot."

"Okay."

That was almost too easy. "Like that?"

"This time, yes. Go." She went on tiptoes and gave him a quick kiss on the lips.

"Two…one…"

Forcing his head back in the game, Ben took his position on the opposite side of the doorway. He nodded at Joel as he slammed the garage door open and the humid night air rushed in. The two in the yard spun around at the sound. The one on the right didn't even get his gun aimed before Joel peeked around the doorway and nailed him in the shoulder. When he tried to get off an off-balance second shot, Ben's shot took him down.

The steady pings of gunfire rang out. The silencers filtered most of the noise, and the property's setback in a group of trees and up on a hill hid the rest. The one remaining attacker took a hit to the thigh and doubled over. His leg seemed to go to sleep. He dragged it behind him as he tried to take cover on the back porch. The railing didn't help and Connor didn't keep furniture there. It was an open space and gave the team an unrestricted shot.

Another shot and the guy went down. On his elbow and still shooting, he dragged his body to the back door. His shots went wide as the barrel bounced around from all the shifting. Nerves seemed to be settling in and his movements turned jerky.

Got him.

Ben gave Joel the signal to move outside. "Let's go."

They could disarm the guy and grab him for questioning. Crouched and going in, they ran across the backyard. The attacker did a double take at the wall of men coming at him. Going faster now, he groaned and half crawled toward the side of the house. His hand slapped against the wooden slats as his gun clanked at his side.

He made it a few feet, but only thanks to the lack of firepower coming at him because of the stated goal to take the guy alive. Joel and Ben were up on him, just a few feet behind, when Connor moved out of the shadows and stepped on his hand hard with a work boot.

"That's far enough."

The guy screamed as the crunching sound filled the night air.

"That had to—"

Joel's words were cut off as the attacker made a lunging move. A gun appeared in his other hand and a roar of rage escaped him as he aimed for Connor's stomach.

Ben slammed a bullet in the back of the attacker's head before he could fire the shot. He fell in a boneless, dead fall, thudding against the wood.

Connor dropped down on the balls of his feet and felt for a pulse. He picked up the weapons as he shook his head. "He's done."

Ben refused to feel sorry about that. He went off plan, but Connor's death wasn't on the menu, either.

Connor stood up and glanced over at Ben. "Thanks for that."

"You guys made that sort of gunfire run-around thing look easy." Jocelyn offered the comment as she started across the yard. She still held the gun. Instead of shaking on her feet, she walked tall and the tremble in her voice stayed at a minimum.

In that moment, Ben knew she'd ignored his order.

She'd been outside and watched it all. She wasn't the type to hide. Not anymore.

That she walked into danger frustrated him, but he admired her spirit. Other people in her position, including many of the tough guys he worked with at NCIS, would be asking for protective custody and riding the danger out in a hotel somewhere. Not her.

Still, the urge to pack her off did kick strong. "You okay?"

She looked at all three Corcoran men but not at the guys on the ground. "I had the safe part of the job. Just stood over there with my fingers ready to dial 9-1-1."

Connor put his hands on his hips. "I hate when people come to the house. You're just begging to be shot when you step on my property without an invitation."

"Obviously," she said. "So, now what?"

"We clear these two out." Velcro ripped as Connor grabbed his phone out of a pocket in his vest.

"How exactly?" Her question sounded more confused than anything.

Ben couldn't blame her. Until he threw in with Corcoran, he'd never known a private group who could "handle" this sort of thing. People broke in, you called the police.

Not Connor. He had government and police contacts, and depended on those to clean up a lot of messes. To preserve Corcoran's anonymity and ability to do the job, Connor kept the name out of reports and the paper. In exchange for letting other law-enforcement agencies get the credit, Corcoran stayed undercover.

"We know people," he said.

Jocelyn smiled at that. "You mean Detective Willoughby?"

His smile slipped at the mention of the new guy Connor didn't have under control. "Not if I can help it."

"I guess that means it's time for me to finally throw up as I've been promising, then go to sleep with a gun under my pillow." She shot Ben a side-glance as she mentioned that last part.

He hated to postpone whatever she had in mind, but he knew Connor would want to move. You did not crash his house and expect him to wait to respond. "Connor plans for us to leave in the next ten minutes."

"Exactly," Connor said. "We call Kent and demand a meeting. I want us back in that bank right now. No more waiting, because the bad guys sure aren't."

"But they aren't winning," Ben pointed out because he wanted to put a lid on the anxiety welling inside him. "You know, to the extent that means anything."

"If I have to break through that wall on the bank's second story, we're seeing what's behind there. I'm tired of the lying and games."

Joel pocketed two more weapons from those scattered on the ground. "I can stay here with Jocelyn. Guard her or maybe take her over to Davis and Pax for safekeeping, then circle around to give you backup."

"We all go." Connor glanced around. "And we need these bodies moved before a nosy neighbor decides to go for a walk and calls in the cavalry."

The words sent a shock of denial through Ben. Connor was the boss, but still… "All of us are going to the bank?"

Jocelyn nodded. "Except for the part where I've lost all feeling in my legs, I agree with that plan."

"You do?" Connor must have found it funny because her response eased some of the strain over his eyes.

"If the bad guys are storming the house, I'm not going

to be here to welcome them. I would much rather be wherever you guys are." She frowned at Joel. "And what are you thinking? I am not leading attackers to a pregnant woman's front door, so forget about the Davis angle."

On one level—the professional, commonsense one—Ben knew that was the right answer. That didn't mean he liked it. His brain and body were definitely not working together on this plan "We'll see."

Joel joined Connor in smiling. "I'm thinking we're growing on Jocelyn here. She's started to get used to having us around."

"I think you're basically comparing us to mold," Connor pointed out.

She stepped over the first attacker and headed for the back porch. Her footing faltered when she looked down, but she quickly recovered. "Call yourselves whatever you want, but I'm coming along."

Ben knew she'd made up her mind. That meant he was stuck now.

Chapter Fourteen

They got to the bank across town in record time. Jocelyn stood in Kent's private office with a wall of male protection around her. Safe and cocooned by Corcoran Team members with Ben at her back and Connor and Joel on either side. But she couldn't shake the feeling that something was off. Really off.

Kent sat in his big leather chair and twirled his cell phone around in his fingers. Between the fidgeting and the sweat staining the armpits of his dark blue shirt, she almost felt sorry for him. Or she would if it weren't so obvious he was hiding something. Even Ed stood guard at his side, frowning down at him.

"Anything you want to say, Kent?" Connor asked for the second time, this version in a lower, huskier "I'm done with you" tone.

Jocelyn realized if he used that voice with her she might crawl under a desk. He sounded two seconds away from whipping that gun out and taking aim. Clearly the man did not like people storming his house.

Plastic thudded against the wooden desk as Kent dropped the phone, then slapped it flat against the top. "It is after hours. Why did you call me here?"

"Wrong question." Ben shifted his weight until his

legs were hip-width apart and he crossed his arms over his chest. "We should be asking why you were already at the bank at this hour and not home with your wife."

"It is almost midnight," Joel added.

"My life is not your business." Kent slid the phone toward him under his palm.

Before the cell traveled one more inch, Ed reached over and snatched it. Jocelyn had been about to do the same thing and sent Ed a half smile in appreciation for stopping all the unnecessary banging.

Connor didn't move. "Oh, I think it is."

"Not to cause trouble, but what is going on here?" Ed asked. "It's late and the bank's business is done. Why not meet at Kent's house or at the police station? I don't understand."

"Because they're not police." Kent reached for the phone. "Maybe we should call and double-check their authority."

Connor shrugged. "Go ahead."

When Kent hesitated and the phone stayed in the cradle, Jocelyn zeroed in on the subject that mattered most to her. "Call your wife while you're at it. I'd love to meet her."

"What?" Kent's gaze flew to Jocelyn's. "I barely know who you are."

Maybe it was the tone or the way his gaze met hers then quickly skidded away. A bunch of tiny little clues that led to one very obvious conclusion—he knew exactly who she was and not just because she used this branch for her banking.

No, guilt vibrated off him. He had put her in danger or he had stood back and let it happen. She'd bet her life on it, and that was exactly what she'd been doing for days, whether she knew it or not.

"I think you do." Jocelyn gained confidence the more the thought spun around in her mind. "You know who I am and why I'm in danger."

Ben put a hand against the small of her back. "She's the one your employee dragged into this mess. The one people keep trying to kidnap or kill."

After a swallow big enough to see his throat move, Kent folded his hands together on the desk in front of him. Then unfolded them. Then they disappeared on his lap. "I understand the bank robbery was upsetting, but—"

"Enough." Connor barked out the warning, and all motion and the small noises in the room stopped. Even the desk chair ceased creaking as Kent rocked.

"What?" he asked as he wiped away a new sheen of sweat on his forehead.

"Stop with whatever you're hiding." The words exploded out of Jocelyn. The frustration that had been building finally burst loose and she refused to hold off one more second from breaking into the interrogation. "Enough women are dead."

Kent's head wobbled as if he was about to go down. "What are you talking about?"

Ed stepped in closer, glancing from Kent to the rest of the room. "Wait, uh, who's dead?"

"Okay, this isn't getting us anywhere." Connor pointed at the ceiling. "Where does the staircase up to the balcony eventually lead?"

"Emergency exit." Ed gave the answer.

Connor ignored him. "Where else?"

Jocelyn liked his style. All of them, actually. She started thinking of them as her men. They came in, they took charge, they refused to back down and they were willing to die for women they didn't even know.

Even now Ben touched her back, giving her a lifeline and reassuring her of his presence.

"We checked." Ed nodded in Joel's direction. "Right? There's nothing else up there."

Connor exhaled, letting his displeasure flow over the room. "That's not true, is it, Kent?"

"Keep in mind this is your last chance to come clean," Ben said from behind her.

Kent started shaking his head and didn't stop. "You can't do anything worse to me."

Joel took a step closer. "Worse than what?"

"Me."

At the sound of the familiar male voice, Jocelyn felt a hand push her forward and heard Ben yell at her to move. She stumbled into the desk and looked around in time to see Gary press a gun to the back of Ben's head.

Another man pointed one right at Connor's face. The surprise visitors had them all shifting and all weapons up and aimed.

She still hadn't processed all she was seeing when Kent stood up and his chair shot back. The men crowded closer to Ben's side of the desk until the guy with Gary pulled a second weapon and aimed that one, too.

Everyone had moved but Ben. He had picked pushing her out of the way and getting her out of the direct attack line over getting a jump on his attacker. He'd traded his body for hers.

Seeing him now, hands raised and anger straining in every muscle of his face, had her fighting off a gasp. She would not give this Gary person the satisfaction of knowing he scared her, that terror stormed through every cell.

"Gary Taub." The harsh tone ripped out of Connor.

"What are you doing here?" Ed asked as he took a step forward.

"Nuh-uh." Gary made a tsk-tsking sound. "Everyone stays where they are. Guns on the floor or the NCIS hero gets a bullet through his brain."

"No." She jumped forward and only Connor and Ben putting out their arms to stop her kept her from running into the madman's hands.

Gary laughed as he talked over her, acting as if her anguish bored him. "Although, I'm not sure how devastating Ben's murder would be to anyone. His own father is disgusted and embarrassed by him, isn't he, Ben?"

"Ask him." Ben said the words through a locked jaw as his intense gaze drilled into Jocelyn.

She knew he wanted her to stand still. To not antagonize the lunatic with the gun. Despite the fear pumping through her, she had no intention of starting a battle that ended with bodies scattered all over the floor. But if Gary went for Ben, her control would never hold.

Connor stiffened his stance but his gun's barrel never left the direct line to Gary's head. "That's enough."

"Touching." Gary spoke right into Ben's ear. "Looks like I'm wrong. A woman who barely knows you thinks you're worth saving. Maybe if she'd spent more time with you she'd know you're not worth it."

What was that…? Jocelyn blinked. She swore Connor and Joel closed in on Gary but she hadn't seen them move and they hadn't made a noise. She chalked it up to an optical illusion, maybe wishful thinking. With a second glance at the floor, she knew the sensation of shrinking space wasn't in her head. Connor's foot had inched in.

She glanced up for verification. Connor didn't look at her but his head dipped in what she took for a nod.

"Let's show her how wrong she is about you." Gary pushed on Ben's shoulder. "Get on your knees."

"Not happening."

"I said no moving." Gary's voice kicked up as he scanned the room. "You have one second to get those guns on the ground or Mr. NCIS will have a nasty accident."

"We're listening." The anger left Connor's voice. He sounded reasonable and calm, as if he wanted to have a nice chat over coffee. "You clearly want to tell us something. Do it."

"I'm afraid I don't have time."

"He's transferring money." Kent said the words so fast they ran into one long word.

Gary barked right back. "Shut up."

"He's running out of time." Kent swallowed and shifted his weight until he balanced his palms against his desk. "He has less than an hour."

"Now is not the time to play the hero, Kent. You know what will happen if you do. I believe I've made that clear over the last few days."

The pieces clicked right into place. Jocelyn saw the total picture. Kent being blackmailed. His wife in danger. "You have his wife hidden somewhere. You're threatening her to get Kent to help you."

Gary's grin bordered on feral. "Aren't you the smart one?"

"Is she even still alive?" It hurt Jocelyn to ask the question.

The idea of this woman, and Pamela, being dead at this man's hands made Jocelyn's stomach heave. An overwhelming wave of sadness crashed over her as the very real possibility that the men she'd come to believe in so much might be too late this time.

The horrible thought floated through her mind and she used all of her concentration to push it away. The worry and the guilt. Later, in the quiet with no one around, she'd analyze everything and let her emotions bubble over. Right now she needed Gary's attention on her while Connor and Joel, and possibly Ben, followed through with whatever plan had them shrinking the room by barely moving their feet.

"Sharon is dead?" Ed asked.

Kent lost all restraint. He came around the side of the desk with his arms waving and eyes wide with fear. "No!"

Jocelyn shifted along the front of the desk or else Kent would have run right into her. He seemed blind to anything but getting to the man holding his wife.

"So, all this really comes down to a burglary." Ben almost shouted the comment. The force of his voice stopped Kent's drive to Gary. "Just greed."

He rolled his eyes. "Don't be stupid. I have plenty of money."

It had been so long since Jocelyn hated someone. When she'd changed her life and her name, she'd promised not to wallow in negative emotions. She had too many other issues to handle.

But with Gary it didn't fester. It imploded, fueling the white-hot heat rolling over her. "Then what? You like kidnapping women and faking bank robberies?"

"Some men might find your feistiness refreshing, Ms. Raine. I am not one of them." Gary's dark eyes squinted at her. "You may wish to keep that in mind."

"What's the plan here?" Connor asked, dragging the attention back to him.

"You're going to spend some time in the bank vault while Kent unlocks the door to his other office upstairs.

The one filled with computers and servers and, not too long from now, the information I seek." Gary nodded to his sidekick. "Colin here will watch over all of you while Kent and I take care of our pressing business."

"What does that mean?" But she knew. There was no way this Gary guy would leave witnesses. He ran a legitimate business. Had clients. He couldn't afford to have anyone out there knowing the kind of man he really was.

"Kent looks like a loser, doesn't he?" Gary laughed while he said it, as if he was telling some sort of private joke. "You'd never know the government trusts him and this small know-nothing bank to transfer huge sums of money to undercover field operatives. The money comes in and Kent's other division, the one he can't discuss without risking the government's wrath, holds the money, then transfers it into the appropriate accounts."

Connor's gaze narrowed even further. "So, this *is* about money."

So much death because one stupid man had to collect more and own more. She hated men like him. Had spent the last year outrunning the memory of one. "You're a petty thief. No better than the guys who rob gas stations."

"Jocelyn." Ben gave the warning. One word, her name, and a look of boiling fury.

Gary gave the clock behind Kent a quick glance. "You may want to listen to your boyfriend and stop talking."

"But she has a point," Connor said.

The sound coming from Gary sounded like a growl. "Money is the least of my concerns. This is about information."

Joel switched his gun to aim at Colin. "Enlighten us."

"Why not? You won't be able to use what you learn to

your benefit anyway." Gary smirked, clearly pleased to share his brilliance. "For that moment when the money goes in, identifying account information for those top secret accounts is not as well protected as it normally is. Parts are decoded and, with the right equipment, which I have, can be caught in that fraction of a second before shutting off again."

Any way she added it up, the answer was money. The man who professed to have enough wanted more. "And you take all the cash."

"No, I'm grabbing the account information. The whereabouts of the people in the program. There are people who would pay for it. Or I can make the necessary arrangements to have an undercover operative found. My choice. Their lives will be in my hands."

"This is about your brother," Joel said.

"Murdered." Gary uttered the horrible word but didn't say anything else.

"You're saying this is about revenge for you?" Ed asked.

Tension choked the room. Jocelyn wanted the team to move. They were waiting and talking, and it didn't make sense.

Gary's eyes turned wild as he spoke. "My brother's team failed to protect him and he got killed. I got a bogus story about his death. Facts I knew were wrong."

Connor nodded. "But he worked undercover and no one could talk."

"But they could pay, and they're going to. They let him die. Hell, they may have killed him to shut him up. Doesn't matter. I'll burn it all down."

"Which means we all need to die, as well." Her terror cut off her breath and threatened to suffocate her.

Greed was simple and straightforward. A ridiculous excuse for so much pain, but an emotion she saw at the hospital in the way heirs fought over dying parents and insurance companies battled about paying out claims. But vengeance came from a twisted place. It consumed, burning everything in its path. Worse, it meant Gary wouldn't care how many people he took with him so long as he went out in his brother's name.

"How do you expect to take us all on?" Connor asked.

"I have the gun and your man." Gary pressed the gun against Ben's head again. "And I'm not alone."

Joel laughed. "Colin here? I'm pretty sure when the bullets start flying he'll run away like the scared animal he is."

"I think I could take him," Jocelyn said, because at this point she might be able to strangle them all with her bare hands.

"You are welcome to try, Ms. Raine."

Kent leaned harder against the desk, and the legs groaned under the impact of his full weight. "He has a partner."

"Oh, yes." Gary shot her one of those smiles that promised pain. "Did I fail to mention that?"

"I think we've heard enough." Ben looked to Connor.

He nodded. "Yep."

The last thing she saw was Ben diving for her. His arms wrapped around her, and his big body slammed into hers. The momentum sent them flying into the desk, then crashing to the hard floor. The room blurred around them as she struggled to bring it all into focus.

Ed reached for Kent, and Connor took Gary out with one bullet to the forehead. While she rolled over the floor tucked against Ben's chest, shots rang out and men yelled. A loud thud echoed in her ears as Gary fell in a boneless whoosh.

Then silence.

Struggling to sit up and settling for balancing on her elbows with Ben still covering her, she glanced over his arm and into the chaos. Connor and Joel grabbed Colin's guns and shoved him hard against the wall.

"You okay?" Desperation pounded off Ben.

She looked up at him while her hands roamed over his arms and she scanned his chest for blood. "You?"

"Answer me. Are you—"

"Fine." She cupped a hand over his cheek. "Thanks to you."

Ben exhaled. "We wanted him to talk. Tell us as much of his scheme as we could before mobilizing the takedown."

Her head jerked back. "The big stall and all that talk was some tactic?"

"Yeah. We run it in a drill a thousand times per month. We know the signals and can do them without a word or movement. It's all in the eyes." Ben winked as he separated from her and reached out to Gary's body. Took out the other man's phone and pocketed his weapons.

Death had overtaken him during the fall. The man's eyes were open and his arms spread out wide as blood ran from the wound in his head.

She doubted Connor missed shots much but he sure didn't miss from that distance.

"No!" Kent pushed out of Ed's grip and scrambled around the desk. "What did you do? My wife. I need to find Sharon."

Joel caught the other man before he ran right up Connor's back. "Colin here is going to help us with that."

"I don't know anything." Colin looked around. His

body shook and his dark eyes were alive with fear. "Please."

Joel shook his head. "Oh, Colin. Begging?"

Between the frantic headshaking and grabbing at Connor's hand where it shoved against Colin's chest and held him to the wall, Jocelyn worried Colin might lose it right there. Worse, he'd shut down before they could get to Kent's wife.

Colin struggled and his body rocked. "Gary's partner kidnapped her, not me."

"Who's his partner?" Ed had moved up and joined in the semicircle penning Colin in.

"I don't know. Gary wouldn't tell me. Said the partner insisted on anonymity but had set the whole thing up."

With a hand extended down to her, Ben got to his feet, then pulled her up beside him. Then he was off. He broke right into the middle of the group of men and put his face close to Colin's. "Not believable."

"I swear. I don't know anything."

Joel whistled. "I hope for your sake that's not true."

Jocelyn joined in because despite all the rage whipping around and the poor woman hidden somewhere, she could not let these men kill an unarmed man. Honest and decent men, she couldn't imagine it happening, but the nerves in the room hovered at the breaking point. "The only reason to let you live is to find Sharon."

Colin's head thrashed against the wall. "I followed orders and hired the men who…" He broke off when he focused on her.

Maybe she could let them hurt Colin after all. "Tried to grab me."

"Did you, Colin? Was that your bright idea?" Ben's voice went deadly soft.

"Gary was obsessed with that note and the conversa-

tion Pamela overheard after hours." Those beady eyes
focused on Jocelyn. "And you were right there behind
him in the cashier line when Pamela recognized him."

"I'm thinking we're missing pieces here," Joel said.

At first Jocelyn couldn't figure out what the comment
meant. She tried to remember every minute of that day.
The actions mirrored every other time she went to the
bank. Picking the right door, walking up. The deposit
slip. Waiting in line...behind Gary.

The memory blindsided her. She opened her mouth,
gasping for breath. She would have grabbed on to Ben
but Kent started screaming.

"Where is Sharon?" With a strength that didn't match
his size, Kent elbowed in between Connor and Ben.

"I don't know."

Joel sighed. "I wouldn't say that again."

"Enough." Ben put the gun to Colin's temple as he
crowded in close with his arm pressed against Colin's
throat.

Dizziness gripped her. "Ben, are you sure you—"

"You've heard about my reputation. You know I
won't think twice about taking down another man, and
today is your day. I'm going to pull this trigger. If a bullet doesn't come out, I will pull again." Ben followed
through and aimed the weapon. "And no one here is
going to stop me."

"You don't understand." Panic threaded through
Colin's voice as he coughed and gagged against the force
of Ben's heavy arm.

"In five...four..." Ben's monotone voice sounded like
a clock.

"Stop him." Colin punched at Ben's arm and the death
grip crumpling his windpipe and holding him still.

Ben didn't flinch. Didn't move.

"I'm fine with this," Connor said.

"Me, too." Joel glanced over his shoulder. "Ed?"

"Three...two..."

Ed nodded. "I'm good."

"A warehouse three..." Colin's words raced together as his body shook from a coughing fit. "Three exits down. Gary said one of his guys would take care of her."

Ben eased back. "There."

"See, was that so hard?" Joel asked.

Kent blew out long breaths as he teetered on the edge of hyperventilating. "We need to call the police."

Connor raised an eyebrow as he looked at Ben. "Which raises the Willoughby issue."

Something silent and profound passed between Ben and Connor. She guessed it had something to do with Colin's "take care of her" comment and the worry Sharon was already gone.

It took a few seconds, but Ben finally spoke up. "Let's get to Sharon first. Then we can figure out the partner situation."

Jocelyn knew then they suspected Willoughby. A plant right in the police department. Again. She wanted her experience to be the aberration. Now she feared it was the rule.

Kent's hands shook as he scooped his keys off the edge of his desk. "I can drive—"

Ben was already talking before the man got the sentence out. "You stay here. Jocelyn can wait with you. One of our teammates, Davis, is on the way to help out and see if there is any other information to retrieve here."

She had no idea when the call went out to the rest of the Corcoran team, but she wasn't surprised. Those watches they wore did everything. Could be Davis and Pax overheard the whole thing.

But one thing she did know. She wasn't staying behind. She was about to make that clear but Kent beat her to it.

"I'm coming with you." Kent stood up straight and his teeth had stopped chattering.

Jocelyn almost didn't recognize the strong man now compared to the sweating mess from a few minutes before. Nervous energy wafted around him. He still shifted and looked half-ready to leap across the room and take his chances running out the door, but there was a new determination coursing through him.

"No."

Jocelyn thought she knew what caused the change in Kent. "Ben, it's his wife."

She expected a fight. Maybe even a question about why that fact mattered. After all, he was single and used to going it alone.

Instead, he nodded. "Let's go."

Chapter Fifteen

They all raced to the warehouse. A nondescript, one-story building the length of a football field. From the outside it looked like something you might find on a farm. Breaking the lock on the entry door proved easy. Ben slammed the butt of his gun into it twice before Connor stepped in and shot the lock the rest of the way off.

Now they roamed through a series of slim hallways and tiny rooms. Ben had no idea what the space was used for, storage maybe, since boxes were piled every-where, but the setup made them vulnerable as they ma-neuvered through the space two by two.

He walked next to Jocelyn gun up and eyes scanning, with Joel in front of her and Ed at her back. Ben didn't like the setup but no way was he leaving her outside to get nabbed by Gary's partner, whoever that might be.

In unison, they cleared section by section with Con-nor and Joel sneaking around each corner and checking the rooms first. Wires hung exposed from the cracked and missing ceiling tiles above them and papers scat-tered all over the floor.

They walked carefully and deliberately, making as little sound as possible. Even Kent, who was all but whimpering at this point, reduced most of his anxiety to shaking shoulders and chewing on his thumb.

Not that Ben could blame the guy. The idea of Jocelyn getting grabbed sliced right through him, splitting him in half. He'd seen Gary reaching for her back at the bank and had thrown a body block. He'd sacrificed his own body and he'd do it again if necessary. Anything to get her out of there safe and fast.

They came to a T in the hallways. Connor looked both ways, then grabbed Colin by the shirt collar. With his hands zip-tied behind his back, the guy couldn't do anything but struggle and spit. Connor shook him hard enough to stop even that. "Give us an idea."

Colin stuttered, "I've never been here."

Connor pushed his gun into Colin's back to let him know his patience had expired. "Wrong answer."

Kent shifted and sighed. "Please, we have to hurry."

"He's right." With a hand on Ben's forearm, Jocelyn lowered her voice to a bare whisper. "Sharon could be running out of air."

Ben nodded. "Colin, I won't think twice about shooting you in the leg, then dragging you through the rest of the building."

"And I won't help you until we find her," Jocelyn said.

Ben knew it was an empty boast. She saved. It was pure instinct for her. He got it because the same drive to fix things beat wildly within him.

But he did love this fierce side of her. He'd watched her race here and there at the hospital, taking care and handling the blood and guts that spilled around her. This, the survival instinct, the way she fought off her doubts and fears and rose to every challenge, filled him with admiration and had his attraction to her zipping off the charts.

He was falling for this woman, and if they somehow survived the next few minutes, he'd tell her.

"Furnace room." Colin blew out a few long breaths, as if trying not to pass out. "He mentioned something about the furnace room."

Connor glanced past Colin. "Joel, do your thing."

"What are you doing?" Kent clawed at Joel's hands as he flipped out a phone and his fingers danced across the screen. "We can't stop."

Joel didn't look up. "Construction blueprints filed with the city."

"What?" Ed asked as he pulled Kent back and pushed him against the nearest wall.

Joel started walking. "This way."

They moved, faster now, rounding two corners and ducking. Watching each step as they hit a wider hallway where the ceiling had been ripped out and wires snaked the walls and floor. They got to a door without markings and Ben stepped up. He tested the knob and found it unlocked. The whole thing smelled like a trap.

"Careful," Connor said as he nodded.

Ben flipped the knob and the door slammed open. He went in high and Connor took low, with Joel watching their backs.

Nothing.

The room was empty. There wasn't so much as a crate or a box inside. Ben didn't know what it meant. This room was clean for some reason, the only one in the place without stuff strewn all over the floor, and that was enough to convince Ben not to go one step farther. "Back out, following the same steps."

Connor nodded. "Got it."

A minute later they all crowded at what looked like

a hallway to nowhere. Jocelyn had Joel's phone and was
staring at something.

"It's back here." She made the announcement and
grabbed for the shelves at the end of the hall. "This has
to be fake."

Ed shook his head. "There's nothing there."

Wide-eyed and half-desperate, she shot Ben a pleading look. "Help me."

Joel looked at his phone, then nodded. "Nice job."

Holstering their weapons, the two joined her while
Connor kept watch. They slid their hands over the dusty
shelves and kicked away the piles of wood and electrical
supplies on the floor that blocked a better grip.

It took less than a minute for them to tug and strain
before the wood near Joel gave. The shelves moved out
to reveal stacks of boxes behind. They all reached at
the same time. Grunting and shuffling, they set up a
line and unloaded.

Connor shoved Colin toward the front of the work
area and took Ed's gun. "You don't need to guard him.
There's nowhere for him to go."

Ben wiped the sweat off his forehead. The stagnant
air of the windowless space had them all wheezing.
Jocelyn's body shook from the force of her coughs, but
she waved him off when he tried to get her to sit down.

Truth was Ben wanted all their help. There was a
woman in there who could be dying. He'd had enough
dying on his watch. This needed to be a win. For Kent,
for Jocelyn, for all of them.

They got to the metal door and Joel went to work
on the lock.

"Please hurry," Kent said from right over Joel's shoulder.

The pick didn't work and the bullets ricocheted,

promising more damage. Connor stepped in. He ripped the top pocket of his vest open and took out a small packet.

Explosives. Ben pushed the crowd back into the hallway as Connor dropped to one knee and put the putty on the door. "We need to take cover."

"No, you can't." Kent tried to go up and over Ben. "She could be right on the other side."

Ben caught the older man around the chest and shoved him back. "It's the only way in."

The comment was a lie. There were other ways. Longer ways. Plans that would guarantee his wife ran out of air. This was the best choice.

Ben didn't say any of that. He was too busy rushing Jocelyn around the corner. They hunkered down and he dropped his body over hers, trying to cover every inch. She protected her head and he protected the rest of her. He glanced up only to see Joel running over to join them.

"Heads down and stick to the wall," Joel said before nodding to Connor. "You're good."

The words were out and the deafening bang had sparks flying and chunks of metal and plaster falling around them. Pebbles of whatever was left rained down on them and littered the ground.

Ben glanced up and saw the door hanging on its hinges with half of it blown away. The hole led to the dark room beyond. When he started to stand up, Jocelyn tugged on his arm.

"I am not staying out here, so don't ask." Her eyes flashed with fire and her stern expression suggested no one mess with her.

Not that he intended to. This wasn't an argument he intended to have. "Since there's a partner hanging around somewhere, as soon as we break in and secure the place, I want you right next to me."

They stood up and she brushed the thin film of dust off her face. "Romantic."

They made a rush to the door, with Kent itching to go in first. Connor's voice stopped him. "We don't know what we're going to see in here."

"I'm a nurse." Jocelyn pushed to the front and waited for Joel to clear the electrical wires and chunks of metal in their way.

"No offense but there are things that can happen and—"

Jocelyn sighed at Connor. "She might need medical attention and I plan on giving it to her no matter what you say."

Fighting was the wrong tact. This needed to happen. "She's going," Ben said.

Joel shoved the last of the debris out of the way and nodded toward the inside. "We're in."

"Hold Kent," Connor ordered.

"But I want—"

Ed slapped a hand on Kent before he could run. "Got him."

Ben and Connor slipped in, checking each corner and the cabinet on the far side.

Connor opened the door and felt around. "Clear."

Ben nodded. "Clear."

Jocelyn rushed in, then came to a hard stop. "That's a—"

"Box on a table." Looked like a coffin. Ben tried to keep his voice steady but rage made it vibrate.

Someone on Gary's payroll put a living, breathing woman in a box. Cut off her air and waited for her to die. What kind of sick bastard did that?

"Get it open. Now," Ben ordered.

"No, no, no." Kent's wail bounced off every wall. It was a high, keening cry like something a wounded animal might make.

The sound was so desperate and raw, Ben wanted to cover his ears. At least grab Jocelyn and run her out of there. Anything not to watch that level of intense human pain.

Kent tripped over something in his walk across the room and would have fallen if Connor didn't catch him. "Okay, settle down. I need you to stand here."

Ed stepped up and let Kent lean on him. "I got him."

He shook his head as the tears ran down his face. The pain was so obvious, so palpable, Ben couldn't even watch him. His gaze went to Jocelyn's pale face, and the terror mirrored Kent's.

Ben was ready to do the one thing he could do. Rip the damn box apart with his hands if necessary. "I have to get to her."

Joel joined him and they grunted and shoved. They tore the top of the box off, ignoring the nails and the bites of wood and stabs against their hands. The wood creaked and snapped. After a few yanks they had the top completely off.

The scene inside didn't give Ben one ounce of comfort. A woman, blonde and still, wearing a shirt and pants lay there unmoving. Ben guessed the shirt had once been white. Now blood stained it a dull red.

Joel shook his head as he stepped back, as if he couldn't look one more minute.

"Is she breathing?" Jocelyn shoved her way to the front and put a hand to the still woman's throat. "I've got a weak pulse and blood."

Kent had his fingers wrapped around the side of the box as he stared down at his wife. "Take her out."

"No, leave her there. There could be broken bones." Jocelyn pushed all the hands away and went to work. She listened to her heart and shifted her clothing. "Let me check her."

Connor tried to move Kent away from the box. "Why don't we—"

"You are not going to stop me from checking on my wife." Kent turned on him, throwing out his arms and ready for battle until Connor nodded.

"Is she alive?" Ed asked as he peeked around Joel.

A beeping started somewhere near Jocelyn. She spun around with her arms up and Ben aimed his gun. He just didn't know what was attacking this time.

"Ease up. She has my phone." Joel reached over and slid it out of Jocelyn's back pocket. A couple of clicks and he looked up, his mouth even more grim than before. "We've got company."

"What?" Jocelyn's eyes narrowed. "Who?"

"Willoughby, I bet." That man showed up at the wrong places at the exact wrong times. Ben didn't trust him and certainly didn't want him sneaking in from behind.

"Being here will get you in trouble," Ed said. "That detective might fire first. Go meet him and I'll stay with Kent and Sharon."

No way was Ben agreeing to that. "We're not afraid of Willoughby."

"But she can identify her attacker, which means it might not be safe for her to see the detective." Ed glanced at Kent, then back to the team. "If she wakes up."

"You think the police detective is the partner?" Kent

shook his head. "That doesn't make sense with what Gary said about his partner."

"Meaning?" Connor asked.

"He talked about resources in the police department but made them sound low on the food chain. Not his partner."

A loud intake of breath cut off whatever came next. Ben heard whimpering and saw Jocelyn lean over the box. She whispered something as she tried to hold down the arms flailing around her. The woman kicked and slapped as the high-pitched screams, shrill and terrified, filled the room.

Ben looked to Connor and Joel. They both frowned as the horrifying sound wound up and got louder.

"It's okay. You're safe." Jocelyn kept up the soothing words as she held the men back with a stiff shake of her head. "Take deep breaths."

Kent stood still as if frozen in place as soon as the pained screams started. "Sharon."

The yelling subsided, decreasing to sobbing. She hiccuped and sniffed. "Kent?"

"You can move your hands and feet." Jocelyn nodded to Ben and he came in closer. "He's going to help you up. Kent's here, too."

Under Jocelyn's direction, Ben put a hand under Sharon's shoulders as Kent held her hand and Jocelyn checked her back. "Let's get you—"

The frail woman's body heaved and another scream tore out of her. She was crying and pointing. She grabbed on to Jocelyn and hid behind her.

Ben glanced over, thinking he'd see Willoughby standing there. "What the—"

Colin and Ed both stood blocking the door. Ben remembered Connor taking Ed's gun but he held a weapon. Colin's restraints were gone. On closer look, they'd both found guns, which meant they had more than the ones they showed they were carrying before.

"She wasn't supposed to wake up," Ed said.

Joel shifted position, coming out from behind Connor and slipping his phone back into his pocket. "Guess we know the identity of Gary's partner."

"To be fair, Colin didn't know until now, but he's loyal." Ed shrugged. "Which is smart because I plan to be the winning side here. I've been working on this for too long. There's too much money at stake."

"And Sharon can identify you," Connor said.

Ed smiled. "Sorry, boys."

He swung his arm around in an arc as he fired. Bullets pinged and chunks of plaster exploded from the wall. While firing, they all ducked and dived for what little cover the room provided. In the small space, something was bound to hit someone. Ben planned for it to be the bad guys.

Ed ran for the doorway but Ben's bullet caught him in the back. Another from either Joel or Connor brought him down in a dead sprawl. Colin had a longer job getting to safety. With Ed gone, Colin's shield disappeared but he kept firing even as he yelled.

The booming sounds came from every direction. Ben tried to pivot around the box as he shot. He had to get Jocelyn to safety. She'd thrown her upper body over Sharon and for a second Ben thought she'd been hit.

He reached her right as he felt a burning across his neck. That fast his vision blurred. His grip failed him right as his legs gave out. With one last lunge, he snagged Jocelyn's arm and brought her to the floor. She fought him but he rolled her under the table, giving her the best protection in the room.

He scrambled away, trying to draw attention to himself. Shifting, he put his knees under him, thinking to get up and catch Colin before he snuck away, but the room flipped on him. The last image he had was of a shadow looming in the doorway.

Then his head hit the floor.

JOCELYN DUCKED UNDER the table. She wasn't quite sure how she got there. Pieces of memories ran through her mind. Ben grabbed her. Sharon…poor Sharon. Even now Jocelyn could hear her shouting and begging to get out of the box.

Jocelyn peeked up through her arms and saw Colin make a final desperate run for the doorway as a bullet hit his thigh and Connor yelled at him to stop. Blood ran and a burning smell filled the room. Jocelyn blinked and saw boots. Her gaze traveled up until she reached Willoughby's face. He stood there in full riot gear. When Colin made a final lunge, Willoughby cracked him in the head with the end of his gun.

He glanced around at the wreckage. Blood and broken supplies everywhere. "Someone going to tell me what's going on?"

Connor stepped up carefully. One foot at a time, gun still raised. "How did you get here in time?"

"Was watching at the bank and followed you here." Willoughby nodded in Joel's direction. "Then I got a call from him and all I could hear was someone talking about money and the shooting started. We were a few hallways away and I followed the noises to here."

"This is the one time it's good someone else drove, since being followed helped," Joel said as his shoulders eased and he abandoned battle mode.

"Okay." Connor blew out a long breath. "Good thinking, Joel."

Willoughby motioned behind him. "Got my men with me."

Jocelyn watched the police officers file in behind Willoughby in the doorway. He'd brought everyone. He rushed in to help and she didn't know what to make of that. At some point she'd have to apologize for assuming he was with Gary. It was an old reflex tied to the uniform.

"He's the one?" Willoughby used the toe of his boot to nudge Ed's unmoving arm.

Connor nodded. "Him and Gary Taub, who's back at the bank. Dead."

"A few of my men are there." Willoughby waved his men in. "Secure this scene, too. Everyone you see moving in here is clear."

Jocelyn struggled to her feet, still unable to believe Willoughby, the jerk who threw his weight around, had ridden in at the last minute to contain the situation. She looked at Sharon, who nodded and mouthed that she was okay.

Jocelyn didn't agree. "Sharon needs an ambulance."

"Please help her," Kent said.

Jocelyn noticed the blood on Connor's face from what looked like a nick across his cheek and the shot to Kent's wrist. He held it but didn't complain. In the end the desk jockey had turned out to be quite the savior for his wife.

She turned around to smile at her own savior. "Ben, are you—"

Connor was already moving. He dropped to his knees at the far end of the box, right in the corner. "Ben's down. We need an ambulance."

It was as if someone flicked a switch. Police officers

came into the room. Willoughby got on his radio as sirens rang out in the distance.

Her mind went blank. Sounds were muffled and everyone seemed to move in slow motion. She saw Joel's mouth as he cried out and slid in next to Ben. But the walls closed in on her. She stared at Ben's still body and the blood covering Connor's hand as he pressed it against Ben's neck.

"No, no…no…" She didn't know she'd said the words until she pushed Joel out of the way and shoved in next to Ben. He was so still, his skin almost gray.

The room whirled to life again.

She was not losing him. Not now that she'd found him and had fallen so hard and so deeply that she couldn't figure out how to separate herself from him.

Without thinking, she whipped her shirt off, leaving only a thin tank top on. She rolled the material into a ball and pressed it against Ben's neck. Blood soaked the material and covered her hand. Still, she pushed and ground, using all her strength to stanch the flow of blood.

Dipping down, she listened for breathing, tried to watch his chest rise. Nothing happened and her frantic search for a pulse turned up only the weakest flicker. "You will not die on me."

She wanted everything with this man. She would not watch the life seep out of him.

One of his eyes opened. A haze covered it and she doubted he could even see her. She grabbed for his hand with her free one. "I'm here, Ben."

"I'm sorry."

"Don't talk."

"It meant everything that you trusted me." His head lulled to the side. "I'm sorry it ended like this."

His eyes rolled back into his head and panic tore at her insides.

"I hate your job. I refuse to deal with the danger and fear." The words flowed out of her. She barely knew what she was saying. She just knew the fear infected her like a poison and she wanted it out. "No more, Ben. Do you hear me?"

But he couldn't. He was unconscious and deathly still. Seeing him like that filled her with a fury that kicked around her insides and had her doubling over in pain. Her muscles shook as she fought to hold him steady. She couldn't tip his head back for CPR, so she put her fingers against his jaw and lowered it.

The position wasn't perfect but she didn't have a choice. "Joel, hold this tight against his throat and do not let go for any reason."

Joel nodded as they shifted positions.

Connor shouted in the background to the people slipping in and out of the room. "We need an ambulance now. Get it here."

Willoughby helped Kent sit down and lifted Sharon out of the box. The chaos raged on but Jocelyn's focus stayed on the CPR count and watching Ben's chest for any signs of life. Her arms ached and her heart hammered hard enough for her to feel it in every limb.

"Jocelyn, he's not—"

She didn't even spare Joel a glance. "He will live. I will not walk away until I know he's okay."

And he had to be okay.

Chapter Sixteen

Ben heard shouting in his head. Male voices, then Jocelyn's. They screamed at him as a rush of what sounded like water beat against the inside of his brain. He wanted to fight against it. Find quiet. But Jocelyn… He ran toward her.

His eyes popped open and confusion settled in. Lights came into focus above him and he could make out the tiny dots in the ceiling tiles. He heard the beep of machines and smelled the antiseptic. He tried to move his head but something held his neck still, and even that small twitch had pain thundering against his skull.

He took it all in. Every piece, including the pale blue walls and the railings on the bed. He was in a hospital.

His eyes finally focused and instead of seeing the woman he wanted, he saw blond hair and scruff. Davis.

"Where's Jocelyn?" Ben ground his back teeth together and lifted a shoulder off the mattress.

"Hold on there." Davis held a hand against Ben's chest. "She's fine."

"She and Joel went to bug your doctors." Connor's head appeared above Ben. "Apparently she's not happy with how long it's taking you to wake up."

"You staying there or do I have to punch you to keep

you down?" When Ben gave a small nod, Davis sat in the chair next to the bed. "You look terrible, by the way."

"I can always count on you for reassuring words." Ben tried to laugh but something in his neck pulled and yanked, sending a headache spinning through his brain. He lifted his hand and felt a thick bandage. He remembered the burning sensation. "Did I get shot in the neck?"

Davis nodded. "Yep. Kind of lame. You're supposed to duck."

"This from the job when you were too busy hiding in your house to help." Seeing Davis's mouth flatten, Ben felt a pang of guilt the second he made the joke.

"Not by choice."

"I wanted Lara safe," Connor said.

Davis shook his head. "For the record, I'm not riding a desk for the next seven months."

"Understood."

Ben wanted to run a hand over his face. That battled with his need to shut his eyes. He'd get to that as soon as he laid eyes on Jocelyn. He just had to see for himself she was fine. The idea of her hunting down doctors eased some of the anxiety knocking around inside him, but a guy had to check these things out for himself.

"Women," he said under his breath, knowing this group would understand the sentiment.

"You got problems with one?" Connor asked with amusement in his voice.

The memories tore into him. He went from blank to having a full-motion picture of the gunfire in his head. She stood in the middle of the shooting, protecting Sharon. Threw her body over Sharon and ignored her own safety.

Jocelyn had begged him not to die, then cursed him

and his job. Every horrible second spooled out in front of him and he felt helpless to calm it all down.

"This was too close." He whispered it more in his head, not realizing he'd said it out loud until Connor agreed.

"But she did great. Kept you alive long enough to get you help. We owe her."

No, they didn't understand. They were praising her. Even now, Connor told Davis stories about all she'd done and how she stood up to him.

Ben listened but the same warning kept flashing in his mind. He broke into the cheering session. "She shouldn't have had to do any of it."

Connor frowned. "Gary was after her. You were the bodyguard."

"And next time I'll bring the danger to her door. And the time after that." The fear. That was what he remembered the most. Her dropped mouth and pale lips. The panic that had her eyes darting as yet another man leveled a gun at her head. "Tell me I'm wrong."

The hollowed-out feeling in his stomach wouldn't go away. Jocelyn in danger qualified as the one thing he could not handle. Gunfire, chases, his blowhard father, the wrath that went along with dismantling the NCIS... those were rough circumstances, but livable. Seeing someone put Jocelyn in a box... He closed his eyes as his mind rebelled and his stomach churned at the idea.

"It doesn't have to be like that," Connor said in a low voice.

"Where's your wife? Jana, why isn't she here?" Ben winced but he had to ask.

Connor's face went blank, as if all the life leached out of it. "Visiting her—"

"We all know that's not true. Something happened.

Likely something about the intense work we do drove you guys apart."

Connor wrapped his hands around the bed railings tight enough for his knuckles to turn white. "Maybe you should stop talking like you know about my personal life."

"That's enough," Davis said.

"Tell me I'm wrong, Connor." When Davis tried to talk again, Ben turned on him, too. "And you're twisted up trying to protect your pregnant wife. You both know what I'm talking about."

Davis put a palm flat against the top of Ben's pillow, and the mattress dipped. "But she is my wife. We worked through the danger stuff and we're together."

"It's so much." Waves of exhaustion pummeled Ben. "The stuff with the NCIS isn't dying down. My father won't even speak to me. How do I bring a woman into that? How do I ask a woman who has known violence and survived it to wade back into it with me?"

"She is not weak." Connor punctuated each word.

She was anything but. Ben had known that from the beginning. Her strength was part of the reason he was falling so hard, so fast. "I know that."

Davis answered, "Then give her a chance to see if she can handle your life. Don't push her away."

Ben couldn't move his head or block the pain out. "Right, do that and have our lives get more entwined and then, what, I pick her broken body up out of an alley?"

"Ben, come on." Davis pushed off from the bed and stood up straight again. "That's not going to happen."

"You can't promise that." Man, Ben wanted him to. He wanted a guarantee that Jocelyn would be okay. He wanted to know he'd never be the one to put her in a position where fear gripped her.

"I wouldn't be married and having a kid if I didn't believe it."

"I care about this woman. Really care." Those weren't words he said easily and they didn't even touch the full load of what he felt for Jocelyn. "Like, I don't even understand how I can be falling for her this hard."

Davis rolled his eyes. "Then let her in."

"How can I ask her to take a chance on me?"

THE MAN WAS LUCKY he was confined to a hospital bed or she might just march right over there and smack him. Jocelyn couldn't believe the nonsense he was spewing. Sweet on one level, but frustrating on every other. Did he actually think after everything they'd gone through, after he stuck by her when she was being hunted, that she would walk away?

Men.

"You should be asking me that question, not them." She walked into the room, keeping her arms wrapped around her stomach.

She was so stupidly happy to see him awake and breathing that she wanted to crawl up there with him and throw her arms around him, but he had to get his head out of his butt first. If he planned to go all martyr on her, she would fight him every step of the way.

"I want you safe," he said, ignoring the friends standing on either side of him and watching only her.

"Which, in your mind, can only mean not being near you." Never mind that she wasn't in danger because of him. "Well, I would remind you that you're the one who did the chasing. You asked me out. I said no, and you kept coming back."

Davis smiled at that.

Between the colorless skin and drawn expression,

Ben looked ten seconds away from passing out. "There are people who think being near me is a death wish. My track record isn't good."

Her heart broke a little for him. She cursed his stubborn father and everyone else who dumped their insecurities on Ben.

She used all her control to stand in that spot rather than go to him. "I don't see you that way. Not me. Not your team. No one in this room."

"What if you're all wrong?"

"So you live a celibate life from now on? How realistic is that." Now that they'd slept together, she knew there was no way. He didn't hold back in the bedroom. No way could he deny himself.

And he better not unleash all that passion on anyone but her.

He gave a quick glance at his friends but they didn't move. "I want you somewhere safe."

"Why don't you let me decide where I go and who I'm with?"

"Jocelyn, I'm—"

She leaned in with a hand behind her ear. "What, are you sorry?"

"Don't do this."

She ignored how his voice grew louder. "You better at least be sorry for the right thing."

Color flooded his cheeks. "Meaning what?"

Anger. Good, she could handle anger. Indifference would kill them.

All those fears of being on the wrong end of violence had held her back. With Ben, something inside her had broken free. That shield she clenched in front of her had crumbled. She needed his to do the same.

"Don't you get it, Ben? You should be sorry for nearly

bleeding out in my arms and wasting your last bit of energy on giving me the 'it's been swell but we're over' speech." The memories zoomed through her, taking her voice louder with every word. "Who does that? What kind of man puts his girlfriend through that?"

Davis shook his head. "Oh, dude."

She pointed at him. "Exactly. Davis gets it."

"Girlfriend?" Ben tried to sit up straighter but the bandage limited his movements and the wound had him wincing.

Knowing he was in pain took the edge off her anger. Her frustration came both from seeing him rushed away in an ambulance and hearing him talk about walking away from her for good. She didn't want to deal with either ever again.

"Yes, Ben. I don't sleep around. I barely date."

"I know that."

She could only assume his stubbornness made him blind. "Then you know I risked everything on you."

His intense gaze didn't leave her face. "Because you were in danger."

"No, because I want to be with you, talk to you, sleep with you." Careful not to hit the bed, she stepped in when Connor moved back. She slid her thigh on the mattress next to his legs and stopped there even though she ached to get closer. "All of it and all the time."

He picked up her hand and played with her fingers. "All the violence."

"Goes with your job. I won't lie. That's not easy for me. It scares me to death." When he gave her a pained frown, she rushed to finish her point. "But I also get that you have friends and people who watch out for you and that you're careful. You don't take stupid risks."

Davis cleared his throat. "He's usually on his game, though he's not doing so well here."

"You begged for a date." She ignored Connor's laugh and Ben's scowl. "You were relentless and now you want out? No. I'm not giving you a choice. You wanted me? Well, now I want you back."

"You do?"

"I might even love you a little, which we're not going to talk about now, certainly not with company listening in, but the one thing I am not doing is leaving you." The truth sat out there now and she couldn't call it back. She didn't even want to. After everything they'd been through, he deserved to know the truth.

"I like her," Davis said.

Connor nodded. "She fits in with the other women in the group."

Davis made a sound like a hum. "And it wouldn't be bad to have a nurse on staff."

Ben didn't even spare them a glance. He kept his attention on her as he slipped his fingers through hers and held on tight. "Both of you get out."

"Maybe we're watching out for her," Connor said.

She didn't break eye contact either. Couldn't. "I can handle Ben on my own."

"Yeah, I think you can." Connor patted Ben on the shoulder. "We'll find Joel and Pax and come back later."

Davis laughed. "Much later."

Ben barely waited until the door closed behind his friends. "Love?"

She knew he'd grab on to that one word. Other men, no. They'd ignore it and try to work around it. Not Ben. She said *love,* and excitement flared in his eyes. "A little and it's just at the beginning stages, so don't kill it by being a moron."

He tugged her closer. "Come here."

"Oh, now you get bossy." She put her hands on either side of his shoulders. "I'll tolerate that, since you've been shot and stabbed and who knows what else. But as your nurse, I would suggest you be careful."

"I'm taking my bossiness cues from you." He tried to lift his head and hissed instead.

She took pity on him and leaned in closer, letting her lips skim over his. "Honestly, you could use a clue or two."

"I'm sorry," he said when they broke apart again.

"For?" And this was a test. If he didn't get it right... well, she wasn't going anywhere. But she didn't want to fight with him, either. "And do not say putting me in danger or anything like that."

"How about for trying to push you away?"

She kissed him again. Short and sweet but enough for the desired connection. "Better."

"I want you safe and am willing to do whatever that takes." His hand brushed up and down her thigh. "But I'm also not stupid. When a woman like you throws around the *L* word, a man listens."

The words knocked down the rest of her protective wall. This man, this amazing man who carried a gun and could probably scale buildings if he wanted to, meant everything. "Are you sure?"

"That falling thing." He toyed with the end of her hair. "The love—"

She put her thumb and forefinger an inch apart. "Little bit and at the beginning."

He pushed those fingers farther apart. "Me, too."

Her heart jumped. "Really?"

"Why do you think I'm so desperate to lock you away where my job and this life can't touch you?"

"I lived for months and months being afraid." Talking about her life back then stole something from her, but she needed him to understand. "I'm not afraid of you."

"After what happened to you and how you had to fight…all the attacks over the last week…how is that possible?"

Hearing him rendered almost speechless was just about the most flattering, attractive thing ever. The idea she could knock this controlled man off his game made her smile. "I think it had something to do with seeing a policeman step up and do the right thing."

"Willoughby?"

She still had to figure out a way to apologize to the guy. He had even come to the hospital to check on Ben, Sharon and Kent and never once threatened or suggested the crimes rolled out any way other than the way they actually did. No blame. "He came through, but that wasn't all."

"Meaning?"

"Your team thrives on the challenge of the job without enjoying the violence. That makes a difference. You view danger as a necessary evil but don't seek it out, and that matters to me." The words spilled out of her. She needed him to know she didn't lump him in with the law-enforcement types she'd known before. "With you guys, danger and gunfire are normal, and I don't fully understand that, but I've seen you all handle it without turning into the scary people you hunt."

He lifted their joined hands and placed a kiss against her skin. "Thank you."

"Your dad is wrong, you know." Now, there was a man she wanted to shake.

Ben's eyes closed. When they opened again, they were heavy and a bit sad. "He's set in his ways."

"No, Ben. He's wrong. You're a hero." She balanced a hand against his pillow and leaned in real close. "My hero."

He skimmed his hand over her stiff arm. "Does that mean you'll come home with me?"

The question sent that tiny spark of hope inside her roaring to a flaring flame. He was talking about them. No more doom and gloom and mentions of leaving her behind.

She loved it. "You think you're leaving the hospital so soon?"

"I thought you'd sign me out and take care of me in our bed at home." His hand found her waist. "If that's okay with you."

Her heart danced with excitement. "Our?"

"You really want to go back to your apartment?"

He meant the attack in her family room, but the lifeline he offered went beyond that one terrible night. Whether he knew it or not, he was talking about building a future. "I need to be wherever you are."

"Then close that door and we'll start practicing in private." He tapped the mattress. "I bet the bed moves."

She laughed as her head fell forward and her cheek brushed his. "I think we're actually pretty good at 'it' already."

"True, but that's not what I meant." She felt his warm breath across her ear right before he nuzzled her there. The kisses on her neck came next. "I'm thinking we need to work on turning a little into a lot."

Which was exactly what she wanted. "That's what I want."

"Then let's get started."

* * * * *

A sneaky peek at next month...

INTRIGUE...

BREATHTAKING ROMANTIC SUSPENSE

My wish list for next month's titles...

In stores from 18th April 2014:

☐ Sawyer – Delores Fossen

& The District – Carol Ericson

☐ Scene of the Crime: Return to Mystic Lake
   – Carla Cassidy

& Navy SEAL Surrender – Angi Morgan

☐ Lawless – HelenKay Dimon

& The Bodyguard – Lena Diaz

Romantic Suspense

☐ Cavanaugh Undercover – Marie Ferrarella

Available at WHSmith, Tesco, Asda, Eason, Amazon and Apple

Just can't wait?

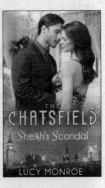

When five o'clock hits, what happens after hours...?

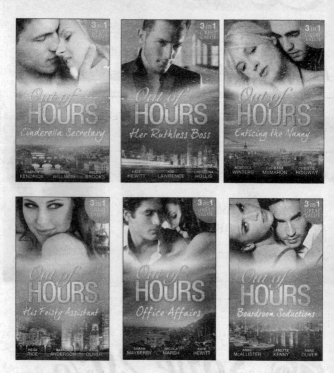

Feel the sizzle and anticipation of falling in love across the boardroom table with these seductive workplace romances!

Now available at
www.millsandboon.co.uk

0514/MB469

MILLS & BOON® Book Club

Join the Mills & Boon Book Club

Want to read more **Intrigue** books?
We're offering you **2 more** absolutely **FREE!**

We'll also treat you to these fabulous extras:

- **Exclusive offers and much more!**
- **FREE home delivery**
- **FREE books and gifts with our special rewards scheme**

Get your free books now!

visit www.millsandboon.co.uk/bookclub
or call Customer Relations on 020 8288 2888

The World of Mills & Boon®

There's a Mills & Boon® series that's perfect for you. We publish ten series and, with new titles every month, you never have to wait long for your favourite to come along.

By Request
Relive the romance with the best of the best
12 stories every month

Cherish™
Experience the ultimate rush of falling in love
12 new stories every month

Desire™
Passionate and dramatic love stories
6 new stories every month

nocturne™
An exhilarating underworld of dark desires
Up to 3 new stories every mon

M&B/WORLD4a